LOVE SPIKE

Brian's hands and feet are wheels, and they're all in flames as he tears over the tracks. The ties rattle off like xylophone slats and the rails flap behind him like spaghetti. He's just a hot wad of streaking power.

Then comes a short instant of stillness, his last breath before hitting the final lap. He's running silent but carrying the loudest message: I got the power, I got my mojo working. I wanna wanna wanna be your man. Yeah, Brian is full of love, ready to deliver a hot load directly from his heart to hers . . .

SHOCK TOTEM

SHOCK
TOTEM

THOM METZGER

AN ONYX BOOK

ONYX
Published by the Penguin Group
Penguin Books USA Inc., 375 Hudson Street,
New York, New York 10014, U.S.A.
Penguin Books Ltd, 27 Wrights Lane,
London W8 5TZ, England
Penguin Books Australia Ltd, Ringwood,
Victoria, Australia
Penguin Books Canada Ltd, 2801 John Street,
Markham, Ontario, Canada L3R 1B4
Penguin Books (N.Z.) Ltd, 182-190 Wairau Road,
Auckland 10, New Zealand

Penguin Books Ltd, Registered Offices:
Harmandsworth, Middlesex, England

First published by Onyx, an imprint of New American Library, a division of Penguin
Books USA Inc.

First Printing, January, 1991
10 9 8 7 6 5 4 3 2 1

 REGISTERED TRADEMARK—MARCA REGISTRADA

Printed in the United States of America

PUBLISHER'S NOTE
This is a work of fiction. Names, characters, places, and incidents either are the
product of the author's imagination or are used fictitiously, and any resemblance
to actual persons, living or dead, events, or locales is entirely coincidental.

*BOOKS ARE AVAILABLE AT QUANTITY DISCOUNTS WHEN USED TO
PROMOTE PRODUCTS OR SERVICES. FOR INFORMATION PLEASE WRITE TO
PREMIUM MARKETING DIVISION, PENGUIN BOOKS USA INC.,
375 HUDSON STREET, NEW YORK, NEW YORK 10014.*

1

The corridor was brightly lit, though empty. It was clean and completely uncluttered. The walls were painted that foul greenish hue that only large institutions use. The overhead bulbs were enclosed in spherical wire cages, slicing the light into gridlike patterns. The floor was black-and-white checkerboard tile, swept and mopped countless times to a dull, porous finish. The walls were thick, allowing no sound—dreamer's moans or insomniac's mutterings—to be heard beyond the confines of the cells.

Ollie sat at one end of the hall in an old wooden school chair tilted so that the front legs were off the floor and his head was resting on the wall. Bristly reddish hair stuck out in tufts above his ears. His nose was large, almost bulbous, and shone like hard rubber. On the top of his head was a pinkish spot of bare scalp that grew a tiny bit larger every day. He wore a baggy institutional uniform, little different than those worn by the patients locked on the other side of the heavy iron doors. Where a badge would have been on a policeman's uniform, he wore a yellow smile button. And where a gun would have hung was what he called his "pac-

ifier,'' a device made of nylon straps and steel loops. He
was good at using the pacifier, able to immobilize a patient
with one hand and fit on a restraining harness before other
staff could arrive. He enjoyed using it. In the privacy of his
own room, he sometimes fastened the coils to his wrists and
tightened the ratchet with his teeth, as if to remind himself
what it felt like to be helpless.

It was well after midnight, and he was officially off duty,
free to spend his time as he wished. He had no reason to
be sitting in the empty hall, watching the regular patterns
of light and darkness as if to make sure they didn't shift or
disappear. But he also had no reason to be anywhere else.
He slept only a few hours a night, and spent the rest of his
off-duty time roaming the corridors or sitting as if at a vigil
in some bright midnight hall.

Like most of the other staff, he had been provided with a
room. It was almost as barren as those of the patients. He
had no car to drive into town, nor did he go on the occasional times when one of the other orderlies invited him.
He didn't like to spend time in the staff lounge, with the
buzzing refrigerator and the television that only got one
channel. And though the hospital was surrounded by acres
of well-tended gardens and groves, Ollie didn't like to go
for walks outside. He felt safe only when he was inside the
building. He felt truly comfortable only when he was at
work, making certain that no rules or restrictions were being broken.

So most nights, after having supper alone in his room,
eating the same meal as the patients, obeying the same rules
about cleaning his plate and returning his plastic spork to
the right receptacle, he'd wander the halls, find a quiet spot
that seemed in need of watching, and settle in.

Of late he'd been drawn to the locked ward on the third
floor. It seemed that his presence was needed there.

One of the bulbs in the ceiling fixtures buzzed slightly,
as if an insect inside was trying frantically to escape, then
threw off a brighter throb of light, and died. Ollie got off
his chair, carefully placing the front legs on the floor first,
and went down the hall to the janitor's closet to find a re-
placement bulb.

Passing the room where the night nurse usually spent her

time, crocheting brightly colored clowns to sell at craft fairs, he heard a faint noise from one of the monitors.

The nurse wasn't in the room. A half-eaten plate of divinity fudge lay on the table, next to a few balls of yarn and a small clown who was unfinished from the waist down. He hadn't been stuffed yet and lay flat, limp, though smiling fiercely up at the ceiling.

Ollie went to the control panel and saw a green light glowing there. He turned up the knob marked 21C. "Burning! Uhnnn! Burn-ing!" he heard a thin voice say. He smelled smoke, but it was probably from one of the dozens of butts heaped in an aluminum plate nearby.

Checking the clipboard roster hanging by the control panel, he found that it was the Cerniac boy causing the disturbance. He wasn't surprised. "The way you look when you cook, has got me hanging on a hook, and I love it," he sang, then made drum sounds with his mouth, leading back to the chorus again. "Burning! Uhnnn!"

Though it wasn't officially against the rules to be singing in the dark, grunting like a bass guitar, and making snare drum sounds with his lips, the Cerniac boy was definitely not behaving himself the way the staff would like him to. Ollie stood by the monitor, listening carefully. "The way you slam and jam gets me where I am, oh baybay!"

The smell was stronger now. Ollie turned and saw the night nurse taking her place again on the big vinyl-covered couch full of cigarette burns and tears mended with electrician's tape. She nodded her greeting to Ollie, and as if somehow aware that a second person had joined the audience, the patient became silent.

Ollie waited, like a hunter waiting for his mark to lower his guard and come out in the open, but no more music came from the monitor. All he could hear was a soft, relaxed breathing, as though the patient had fallen instantly asleep.

"Brian's been awfully good lately," the nurse said. "I guess they finally got his meds right." Ollie was surprised that the nurse didn't know Brian had been on a program of placebos for months. It made Ollie feel important to think that Dr. Haak had let him in on the secret. That the night nurse wasn't aware of the placebos seemed odd to Ollie, but not odd enough for him to think about it very long. Ollie didn't think very long about anything, except his stack of magazines with the almost naked women draped over huge, shiny motorcycles, and about Dr. Haak, whom he feared and revered as a Stone Age man would revere an oak tree struck by lightning.

"He's not supposed to be doing that."

"Doing what?" The nurse cut herself another chunk of divinity and popped it into her mouth.

"Singing like that. And dancing. I think sometimes he dances when nobody can see him."

"Brian? Don't worry about it. He's a nice boy. I never have a speck of trouble with him."

"But he's not supposed to do that. It's against the rules."

The nurse shrugged and began working again on her doll. Having already produced a few dozen of them, she was able to work at them without paying any attention to what her hands were doing. The little face lay in her lap, surrounded by coils of yarn and half-finished limbs, grinning at Ollie.

He waited awhile longer, turning the knob marked 21C up to maximum volume, but only heard one more fragment of a song, a faint, dreamy voice singing, "Get down tonight, get down, get down." Five minutes of quiet passed, the nurse's metal needles clicking like crab's feet scuttling over loose gravel. Her eyes were half open. The only movement in her body was the steady rhythm of her fingers and an occasional yank, pulling more yarn off her skein.

Ollie went back to his post in the hallway. Another bulb had died while he'd been gone. A cordon of shadow lay across the corridor, obscuring a few of the doorways. Ollie went to the cell marked 21C and pressed his ear against the door. A soft thumping—one, two, three and four and—came from inside. He listened for a while longer. The pattern didn't change. After a while he gave up his vigil and went back to the staff wing to get a few hours of sleep before the start of his next shift.

There were chambers and hallways in the hospital that Ollie had never seen. There were wards he'd never been allowed to work in. On occasion he'd stray from his assigned work area and end up in a strange wing of the building with no idea of how to get back. Most of these places were empty, unheated and unused. Some had old tools and discarded therapeutic equipment stacked in heaps: circulating chairs, dipping stools, calipers for measuring skulls, and cagelike devices that it seemed no human body could fit inside of.

When the hospital had first gone into operation, around the turn of the century, it had been called St. Dymphna's Asylum for the Mentally Afflicted. Years later, when prayers to saints and the use of novenas had fallen from favor in psychiatric circles, the state of New York had taken over and rechristened the place Mt. Kinnsvort Developmental Center, though everyone but the administrators refered to it as the Red House. Most of the statues and icons had been removed, though some, those that were too hard to get at, remained. Staff and patients alike went about their business, barely noticing them.

Ollie's window was shaped as a narrow arch, but instead of stained glass, he had four iron bars that had been pitted and coated with rust long before he was born. Standing close to the window and peering to one side, he could just see a niche where a saint still stood. It was level with the fourth-floor windows, and apparently the workers who'd converted the asylum to more modern uses hadn't had the nerve to go up a fifty-foot ladder to haul down the marble statue.

Pigeons nested at the feet of the saint, collecting food and twigs there. Ollie heard them, sunrise to sunset, cooing just outside his window. Looking beyond the ground, past the neatly trimmed hedges and crushed stone paths, beyond the high iron gate and far down the valley, he could just see Haeger's Knob and, when the haze was burnt off the hills, the peak of Mt. Litchfield.

Ollie stood at the window in his pajamas, watching the sun rise on the Catskills. He waited until the shadow of a certain birch tree was distinct and pointing with a certain branch toward the front door of the hospital, then shivered and seemed to wake. He cranked the glass louvers on his window shut and put on his uniform. He usually had the first shift of the new day, loading the breakfast wagons and distributing the trays. He needed to be up and on the ward before any of the patients' doors were unlocked.

The other orderlies were lounging in the kitchen, drinking coffee out of styrofoam cups and waiting for the head cook to dish up the gray-brown heaps of oatmeal and pour the exact same amount of orange juice for every patient.

Ollie loaded his wagon and followed the others to the elevator.

Reaching the ward he'd been patrolling the night before, Ollie saw that a third bulb had blown, though by then the daylight made the three dead bulbs hardly noticeable. A few bits of broken glass were on the floor, and a trace of the gritty white dust.

He wheeled his cart down the hall, unlocking doors and carrying a tray into each room. His first patient was waiting eagerly for his breakfast, sitting fully dressed on the edge of his bed. "Good morning, Ollie," the little man said, and was digging into the oatmeal almost before it was set down in front of him.

Ollie watched him for a moment, to make sure he was really swallowing and not just moving the food from one side of his mouth to the other, then went down the hall to the next room.

Shortly, he came to 21C and brought in the tray. Brian Cerniac was curled up at the end of his bed, a corner of his pillow clamped between his teeth. "Let's go. I don't have all day." Ollie kicked the iron leg of the bed and Brian pulled farther away. He was a teenager, but having spent over a decade in the Red House, he'd never had a chance to learn the expressions and postures that were right for his age. In front, his hair was cut short, almost to the scalp. But it hung long in back, reaching the base of his neck. His skin was pale, a fine shade of milky white.

"If you don't eat now, you won't get anything until supper." This wasn't true, but Ollie enjoyed saying it. He held out the tray, but Brian refused to take it.

By then the rest of the patients on the ward were awake. The old man at the end of the hall started in with his wailing, then Ollie heard a plastic tray clatter to the floor and one of the orderlies shouting. The old man started arguing and whining when he was told to clean up the mess. Ollie put down Brian's tray and went to help.

The patient was far down the road to senility. No nursing home would take him. He refused periodically to eat, had violent spells, and had to be sent to the correction ward now and then to make him more cooperative.

By the time Ollie got back to his normal rounds, handing out the now cold breakfasts, Brian had gotten dressed and was sitting in his chair. A plate, cup, and monkey dish were lined up before him, all empty.

"It was really good today, Ollie," he said. "Thanks a lot. I really appreciate it." Ollie inspected the room, to see if Brian had just tossed the food under the bed or crammed it into the cracks around the windowsill. There was no sign that he hadn't actually eaten everything on his tray.

Ollie got onto his hands and knees and looked under the little desk in the corner of the room. He opened the drawers, but found no lumps of oatmeal or peach slices.

"Stand up," Ollie said. Brian did as he was told. He'd seen the other patients refuse to obey Ollie's commands. He was the one they brought in when someone was being uncooperative. He was the one who gave shots to people who were afraid of needles. He was the one who had given Vincent on the 27 ward an overdose of Hexamil and then convinced Dr. Brule that it had been an accident.

Brian stood up quickly and held his hands over his head. Ollie gave him a quick frisking and scowled at him. "If you're diddling me, Brian, I'll make sure you get nothing but oatmeal to eat for a whole month."

Brian didn't say a thing.

"Dr. Haak wants to see you again today. You're going to get therapy four times a week now." He collected the dishes and left. After telling another orderly which patients hadn't been fed yet, he went to the monitor room. Through the speaker, he heard somebody whimpering like a sick cat, and Arnie, the one who didn't speak much English, singing what sounded like a lullaby. He shut off all the circuits except the one marked 21C. The springs on Brian's bed creaked, and a soft voice came through the system: "Calling Dr. Bri-nor, calling Dr. Bri-nor." Ollie flicked a few switches on the intercom panel, then realized that it was Brian's voice that

he heard. "Oww! Get down tonight. Dr. Bri-nor dead on
the heavy funk. Low-down dysfunction in ward triple-X.
Arrhythmic discharge mechanism. You should be dancing.
Stat! Stat!" Then a low, buzzing sound welled up and just
as quickly disappeared. Ollie set the dials back at the levels
he'd found them and went to the storeroom to look for light
bulbs.

He was back at Brian's room shortly before lunchtime.
"Ictus, say it, say it. Ictus." The boy was at it again,
stuck on some word he'd heard one of the doctors say. When
Ollie was feeling up to it, he wouldn't give in to Brian. He
refused to give him the satisfaction. But unless he was ready
for a long fight, hearing the same word repeated hundreds
of times, it was easier to give the boy what he wanted.
"Ictus, Ictus. Say it."
Ollie said it. "Ictus." He had no idea what it meant, or
if it was really a word. As soon as Ollie had given up and
said it, Brian relaxed and became silent.
"Okay, come on. Time for your session." He'd lost that
little skirmish, but he was still in control. He made his voice
louder. He gave Brian a long, hard scowl.
The boy made sure his bed was neatly made, the way
Ollie liked it, and followed him out of the room.
They went through the locked double doors at the end of
the corridor, but instead of turning right toward the stairway, Ollie led him to the left, through another set of doors,
and into a part of the hospital where Brian had never been
before.
Ollie turned back and grinned at him, saying, "It's okay,
from now on you don't have to go with the rest of them.
You get special treatment now." Like the other residents at
the Red House, he'd gone a few times a week to the main
therapy center for his treatments. Everybody at the Red
House was assigned to at least one of the psychiatric staff.
The suicides usually saw Dr. Bigler for counseling and
maintainance of their antidepressants. The more manage-
able schizophrenics had Dr. Nguyn and his reality-
reintegration program. Those who were at the Red House
simply because no nursing facility would take them got shuffled back and forth between the doctors who hadn't staked

out their territory yet. A few of the patients were forced to sit in a circle and participate in Dr. Jones-Hutchin's sharing sessions. A Pakistani doctor whose name Ollie couldn't remember or pronounce did work with behavioristic therapies, hooking people up to blinking lights and buzzers. And a grandmotherly old woman—the only holdover from the St. Dymphna days—had a small room in the northwest wing full of theatrical props to help her "dear ones," as she called them, act out their feelings.

Soon after Brian had arrived at the Red House, he'd been assigned to the neuro-electrical people and had eventually ended up with Dr. Haak. As far as Ollie could tell, the neurology and bioelectrical doctors were at the top of the heap at the Red House, having their pick of the most interesting patients. Brian was the only one who went to see Dr. Haak more than once a week.

In this new part of the hospital, the floors were as clean and barren as in the other, more familiar, corridors. The air smelled of the same disinfectant and detergent. The light coming in through the narrow windows was just as cold and colorless, but here the original decorations and furnishings hadn't been removed when the state took over the hospital. White plaster petals capped the window frames. Holy water sconces were placed at every doorway, though they hadn't held anything but dust for years. The saints remained, now without names or purpose but saints all the same. Some of the windows had cleverly colored panes instead of the Plexiglas that was used in the locked wards.

They went left and right and left again, Ollie thinking carefully to remember all the turns, then came to a large oak door with a knob made in the shape of a star. Ollie knocked.

They waited a moment, then Ollie knocked again and went in. This room was more dimly lit. It had been a small chapel years before. All the pews had been removed, but the long rectangles of discolored floor showed where they'd been, facing the altar. That was gone too, but not the stained glass windows or the carved ornamentation on the walls. A pair of bone-white angels looked down at them. Crosses and crowns, lamps and loaves, scrolls and open books and symbols that Ollie couldn't decipher surrounded them.

The room was crammed with electrical equipment. Banks of relays and coiled cables were heaped by the door. A high pile of as yet uncrated gear blocked one of the windows. In the middle of the room was a large bedlike apparatus. Once an operating table, it had been modified by the addition of various restraining devices, padded panels around the sides, and a series of transformers built into the base.

A woman was sitting at a desk, writing. She had her back to them. From where they stood, all that could be seen of her was her upper body, in a white lab coat, with one thick, ice-blond braid hanging to the middle of her back. Ollie hesitated, unsure if he was to stay or leave, but Dr. Haak turned from her desk and pointed to a chair by the door. Ollie felt the same wrench that he felt every morning upon seeing Dr. Haak's face: as though she'd stuck her hand into his chest and given his heart a sharp squeeze. He sat meekly and folded his hands in his lap.

"So how is Brian today?" she said.

He didn't say anything. He looked from her smiling face to the cradlelike machine that lay before him.

"You'll be coming down here from now on, Brian. We ran out of room in the therapy center, and I volunteered to move my setup down here. It'll be just the same as before, don't worry. We'll be spending lots of time together."

Ollie started to speak, to tell her that there had been a disturbance on Brian's floor and that he'd taken care of it. But she hushed him, holding a finger to her lips. Ollie was still, his hands clamped between his knees. He noticed that she was wearing lipstick, and lowered his eyes, as though he'd seen something very private and special.

"Come here, Brian, we need to get your baseline data." She had him sit down in the chair next to her desk and took his blood pressure, temperature, and pulse rate. With the cuff around his arm and thumb on the soft spot of his wrist, Brian began to relax. But then she got up and pointed to the criblike machine.

"Things have been going so well for you that the director decided we can move on to bigger and better things. You've done so well with the ECT. Better than we hoped." She touched the side of his face, smoothing back a few stray hairs. "Do you remember how depressed you were before?

How you used to lie in your bed all day and not want to take part in any of the activities?''

Brian said yes and nodded gravely, as if ashamed.

''Well, some day you're going to be completely better. Wouldn't that be nice?'' Her tone of voice was that of a pet lover speaking to her favorite dog.

They stared at each other for a while, unmoving, then she went to a steel cabinet, took out a hypodermic setup, and said quietly, ''You'll be coming to see me four or five times a week from now on. We've decided that that would be the best for you.''

When she had the needle prepared, she said, ''You'll need to take off your clothes.''

Ollie looked up, but kept his eyes on Dr. Haak as Brian began unbuttoning his shirt. ''Oh bay-bay,'' Brian said. His foot started tapping. His pants fell around his feet and he repeated himself. ''Oh bay-bay. Say it. Say it.'' He stepped out of his briefs and stood before the doctor, naked now, shrugging his shoulders and repeating the words.

''Brian,'' the doctor said. ''Stop it, Brian.''

But he kept going, squinting and screwing up his face as if surges of pain were passing through him. ''Oh bay-bay, say it, say it.''

''Brian, listen to me. Didn't we agree this kind of behavior was bad for you?'' He didn't stop. ''Brian, we talked about this, didn't we? You know it's not what we want for you.'' His voice had gotten quieter. He was listening. ''Every time you do this, it makes me feel bad. You don't want to disappoint me, do you?''

He slowed down, then was quiet. Dr. Haak was the only one who could make him stop once he was on a jag. Brian wanted to please her just as much as Ollie.

She gestured for the orderly to help her, and moved the boy toward the cradlelike apparatus. While Ollie held Brian's arm still, the doctor slid the needle in and squeezed the whole load of clear fluid into his vein.

Soon Brian was placid again, standing with his arm around Ollie's shoulder.

''Let's get him in the cradle,'' the doctor said. Ollie cranked down one of the padded panels and helped Brian to climb in. They laid him flat on his back, and then Dr.

Haak fastened the restraining straps on his legs and arms. She checked her watch, smeared a gray paste on his forehead, and taped a pair of electrodes to his skin. Ollie adjusted the slack in the straps while Dr. Haak went through a checklist, making sure that all the equipment was in working order. A faint sigh escaped from Brian's lips. A smile flashed across his face and then he lay motionless.

Ollie waited for the doctor to double-check the electrodes, then cranked the sides up to their highest position. As she brushed against him, fussing with set of rheostats connected to the cradle by a thick black cable, Ollie took a deep breath, holding her scent in his lungs. She smelled faintly of perfume, but mixed with that was a different scent: the savor of her hair and skin and clothes as personal and unmistakable as a fingerprint.

The doctor positioned herself so that she could read the Brozmann gauges and keep her eyes on the boy at the same time. She gestured for Ollie to back away and pressed a small red switch.

Current ran into Brian, making him buck up against the straps. His head was thrust back and the veins in his neck stood out red and swollen. The doctor checked the EEG readings after the first shock, then adjusted the voltage slightly and ran another jolt into him. Ollie thought she was most beautiful when she had her hand on the switch. Her doctorly expressions were gone then. Her eyes were bright. Her nostrils were flared and her lips parted, breathing almost as heavily as Brian.

In the therapy center, Ollie had assisted her a few dozen times as she'd performed ECT on Brian. And on more than one occasion he'd stood in the corner of the electroconvulsive lab while Dr. Haak had argued with the others. Then, as now, Brian had been lying naked, milky white, while the doctors fiddled with the dials and fine-tuned the blasts of current that were run into his brain.

More than once, Dr. Haak had used the phrase "push him through the wall," and this had made Dr. Simonsen—who shared the lab with her—argue even louder, making threats that Ollie didn't understand.

"Damn it, Martin, did I go squealing to the director when you insisted on using that pyretic on the Karstein woman?

Nobody's tried infective agents on schizophrenics for a hundred years. It's been discredited by every study ever made. But did I tattle on you? The old biddy was dead in a week. Did I make trouble for you?''

They both had known that Ollie was in the room while they'd argued, but went on as though he was no more important than the chairs they were sitting on.

"He's the one I want," Dr. Haak had said. "Just this one. You can have the Korean, the Osterberg boy, Walter, any of them that you want. I won't put up a fuss. But I want this one." She'd pointed at Brian, still strapped into the ECT chair. "He's the only one who's gone through the wall and come back again. The only one. And I want him, Martin.''

Dr. Simonsen had agreed finally, and a few weeks later her whole lab was being hauled to the eastern end of the building. And new equipment, little gun-metal boxes buried in styrofoam packing like Easter eggs in baskets of cellophane grass, started accumulating in her new room.

And now, with the equipment finally in place and operating properly, with Brian hooked in and sedated, with free rein to do whatever she wanted with him, she seemed on the verge of tears. Ollie had seen her smile only a few times. He'd never heard her laugh. It was impossible that she'd cry in front of her underling, but Ollie felt that it was coming, and was sure that it would be a sight he could not stand to see.

She ran a last jolt into Brian, then without even looking at the EEG readouts, started unfastening the belts and straps. The electrodes were the last to come off, leaving two shiny spots on his bare scalp.

She told Ollie to get out and come back in an hour. He hesitated, but she gave him another of those awful looks, as though she was about to melt in front of him, and he fled, hiking back through the cold stone corridors to the kitchen.

2

Coming down the Thruway from Albany and then heading west on Route 84, Saul Marx had a few uninterrupted hours to spend with the latest installment of what had become an almost perpetual headache. The course of the pain—moving upward along his spine and turning at a right angle to bore into the back of his left eye—made an inverse image of his trip to Mt. Kinnsvort. He preferred not to think of the headaches as migraines. By calling them that, it seemed he gave them more power, more control over him. As they almost always did, this headache started in his shoulders, an involuntary tensing of the muscles, and slowly coalesced, focusing its strength as it rose along his spinal column until it rested in the same place, just behind his left eye, a black, swollen spot that sent out tendrils of pain until it grew tired and decided to return to wherever it was that it hid.

By the time he was in the Catskills and off the state highway, the headache had taken its final form, pressing hard and insistently on the tender tissue of his brain. At times he dealt with the pain by half convincing himself that it was a good thing. He tried to think of the pain as his friend, a companion who was never far away. But usually that lasted only a short while, and then he was into the big bottle of aspirin in his glove compartment, swallowing three and pulling over to take a long swig of milk from his thermos.

He shut off the engine and sat awhile with his eyes closed, enjoying as best he could the warm summer air, the smell of freshly cut grass, the absence of human voices. Though it made traveling more tiresome, he'd broken the volume knob off his radio a few months before. Any irritation—static between stations, the yammering of announcers, ads for products he didn't even understand the use of—served to accelerate the course of the headaches.

So he enjoyed the quiet for a while, broken only a few times by a car speeding past, and eventually felt the knots and coils loosening inside his head. He looked down at the map, folded and refolded into a fragile sheaf of tattered squares, and found the town of Osric circled in red ink. If the road signs were reasonably accurate and if he had caught all the turns, he'd be there in under an hour.

He finished off his milk, positioned the map on the seat so that he could see it as he drove, and set off again.

The blossoms on the fruit trees had bloomed and fallen away. Everywhere he looked, the hills were green and lush with the summer's new growth.

As the presence of the headache receded, his thoughts began to untangle themselves. He wasn't exactly angry that he'd been reassigned again, but in the past his superiors had at least given him the illusion that he had some choice in the matter. He hadn't been fired from his old job, and it wasn't exactly a transfer either. No one had suggested that his opinion was needed in the matter. A rerouting slip had appeared on his desk, the same kind of slip used to transfer a truck or a pallet of typing paper from one branch of the state bureaucracy to another. He'd read it over and immediately begun clearing out his desk.

He assumed he'd be working out of the same agency. His paycheck would certainly still have the emblem of the state of New York on it: two women in togas and that strange little scale with the word *Excelsior,* which he read every time and never bothered to look up. His position in the hierarchy had shifted so many times that he'd given up trying to locate his place on the big bureaucratic tree diagram: this agency is a subset of this office, which is a branch of this department.

For a while he'd traveled around the state as an inspector of municipal jails, making sure they were up to state specifications: so many square foot per prisoner and so many prisoners per jailer. Then he'd worked on the security detail at the Empire State Games, and of late he'd been acting as a liaison between the state tax people and the IRS.

So when he got the slip telling him to pack his things and head for a little town in the Catskills, he wasn't surprised. He'd never worked directly with mental health facilities, but the job seemed fairly straightforward. They wanted certain people kept in and certain people kept out. He was sure it wouldn't be as irritating as working with the federal people. With them, he spent more time trying to figure out what they really wanted from him than actually carrying out the assigned tasks.

Outside of Osric, he stopped at a corner store to fill his gas tank and milk bottle. The old woman behind the counter took his money without saying a word. She watched him get back into his car. He rolled up the windows, locked the doors, and turned on the air conditioning. The blast of cold air against his forehead felt good. The pint of cold milk that he finished in one long draft hit his stomach hard, but warmed quickly. He imagined it soaking in all the acid and bile that seemed to collect in a bitter pool just below his heart.

Another car pulled up at the pumps, and a man dressed in brand-new vacationing clothes got out to stretch. On the roof were two lemon-yellow golf bags, and lashed to the back end of the car was a small bicycle, plastic streamers hanging limply from the handgrips.

The man went inside the store to ask directions, and Marx rolled down his window to listen. The store owner spoke at great length to the tourist explaining various ways of getting to the main resort area along Route 17. She smiled a big horse-toothed smile at him, and he thanked her, carrying a plastic bag full of candy back to the car.

Marx was still dressed as an Albany functionary. The

clerk in the store had seen instantly what he was, and had taken an instant dislike to him. After the vacationers had moved on, she turned her stare back toward Marx, waiting for him to get off her property. Though he hadn't worn a uniform in years, he still had the smell. State troopers were bad, local sheriffs were worse, but rent-a-cops were at the bottom of the pile. People could tell very quickly that his only purpose for being anywhere was to enforce laws that he cared nothing about. He popped two more aspirin and headed toward Osric.

It was an actual town, not just a name on the map where two county roads crossed. It was shabby, and he didn't see any houses that had been built in the last few decades, but it was a real town. It had a Catholic and a Methodist church, a small fire house, a grange, a block and a half of shops, and a few Victorian mansions, indicating that at least some time during the town's history someone had been prosperous.

In front of the post office—a converted mobile home— stood a piece of World War I vintage field artillery. Its muzzle was pointed down the main street, as if to give some protection from the hundreds of inmates locked behind the doors of the psychiatric hospital at the edge of town.

He followed the cannon's trajectory and a few minutes later was parked in a large, freshly paved lot. Leaving his bags in the trunk, Marx went to the high iron gate and pressed the buzzer. An orderly appeared on the other side of the wall, pushed a few buttons on the electronic locking mechanism, and pulled the gate open. "Up the path, through the big doors, and to your right. The director is waiting for you."

Marx went where he was told. As he approached the huge building, he heard doves cooing. The wind was moving in the tops of the pines that stood on either side of the path. He liked the sound. He went through the front door and noticed quickly that the air inside was much cooler. He paused briefly, straightening his tie, and realized that his headache had vanished completely. A pair of nurses came out of the elevator, crossed his path without looking his way, and turned down a side hall. He liked the sound of their crepe-soled shoes and their nylons swishing as they walked.

After a few wrong turns—finding himself in a room with wooden pews stacked on their ends—he eventually came to the director's office.

Dr. Brule was a fat man in an expensive suit. His hair looked like dried rubber cement. He shook Marx's hand and balanced his left buttock on the edge of the desk.

"Bob Leslie tells me good things about you." Marx had seen the name Robert Leslie a few times on interoffice memos. He was fairly high in the organization, and as far as Marx knew, he'd never spoken with him.

"He said you're just the man we need in this situation." Dr. Brule didn't explain what he meant by that.

"So once you're settled in and know your way around the place, we can get right to work. Have you found a place to stay yet?"

"No," Marx said. "I just got into town this afternoon. I thought you might have a few suggestions."

"Well, there are some widows hereabouts that rent rooms, but I don't expect you want to put up with cats and doilies and that kind of thing." He laughed, one hard, sharp bark. "I tell you what: why don't you stay at my place for a while, just until you get your sea legs, so to speak? Lorraine and I would be glad to have you for a while."

There didn't seem to be much point in disagreeing with the director. "All of our young ones have flown the nest. We'd love to have a guest for a while." He rattled on about his wife and her wonderful meatloaf, then began telling Marx how glad he was that the "big boys" had seen fit to send along such a capable man.

He then got on the subject of Marx's predecessor. "Dixon was a good man, don't get me wrong. But I have a feeling that he just doesn't have the touch for sensitive work. He'll probably be fine heading up security at another kind of institution, but this isn't a prison here. This is a developmental center. You can't charge around accusing highly skilled psychiatric specialists of leaving doors unlocked and giving the residents too much freedom. I told Bob Leslie that we needed somebody with a deft touch. That's just what I said, 'a deft touch.' We need to keep security shipshape around

here, but we need subtlety. I hope Dixon is happy in his
new position. I'm quite sure he'll do a top-notch job somewhere else, but we need somebody who knows how to get
the job done without ruffling feathers. And that's just what
Bob Leslie said: 'Saul Marx knows how to not ruffle feathers.' Those are his exact words.''

Dr. Brule shifted his weight. "Dixon wanted to hire
guards and have them patrol the halls as though this was a
prison. That's exactly the wrong approach. We have the rep-
utation of being one of the best, the most forward-looking
mental health facilities in the system. We can't very well
have armed toughs barging in on the staff, checking their
every move, making all sorts of foolish accusations. You
can catch more flies with sugar than with vinegar, don't you
agree?''

Marx wasn't sure what flies and vinegar had to do with
mental patients.

Dr. Brule smiled broadly, showing an expanse of pink
gum above and below his teeth. "There are rules and regulations here. There is definitely a wrong and a right way
of doing things. But we don't need somebody nosing around
in matters that they don't and can't understand. There's a
time and a place for everything. Bob Leslie said, 'Saul
knows his place. He knows how to get the job done without
making a nuisance of himself.' Those were his exact words.
Let me tell you something, Saul, I look forward to you
having a long and happy stay here at Mt. Kinnsvort.''

He handed Marx a thick manila envelope and told him he
could go over the papers in the next room. Marx found the
folder to be full of drawings, mostly wiring diagrams of
the in-house security system. He spread the schematics out on
a desk and tried to orient himself, turning the papers this
way and that until he had north aligned properly. Improvements and changes had been made in the wiring. In places
the plans had been scratched over and redrawn so many
times that it was impossible to tell which lines served which
rooms. The network of intercoms, automatic door locks,
alarms, heat sensors, and basic wiring was too tangled for
Marx to make much sense of. He felt the headache coming
back. It was just a trace of pain, like a small reconnaissance
party scouting for the main body of an army.

* * *

He was assigned a young orderly named Winston to give
him a tour of the hospital. Winston worked mostly on the
locked wards. "We got the real goners up there. You know
what I'm talking about? They long gone and never coming
back. You hear the docs all talking about these fancy words
and hooking them up to big machines, but they just crazy
people. The best thing you can do for them is to strap 'em
in and keep 'em that way. You know what I'm talking about?
We don't do that and we mopping brains and blood off the
floor all day." He laughed, though it sounded more like
someone trying to clear his nose, and waited to see if Marx
found the joke funny. When he got no response, he shrugged
and led Marx to the staff dining area, introducing him to
some of those who were getting ready to go onto the wards.
They were a sullen, uncommunicative lot, few of them
meeting Marx's eyes as his guide pointed to each and said
their names. At a large table a game of poker was in progress, half a dozen men and women hunched over their cards.
Coins and well-worn chips were stacked like little towers
and turrets. None of the players looked up as they were
introduced.

A bell rang in the next room, and a few of the staff got
up from their chairs and headed toward their assignments.

"They all so nasty 'cause they don't think we need no
security man around here," Winston explained as he led
Marx down the hall. "We getting along fine here. They
probably just thinking you one more pencil pusher from the
state nosing around and telling us how many regulations we
been breaking. A couple of years ago they even had a spy
here, somebody pretending to be a nurse who found out all
sorts of stuff and really raised hell. Just stupid stuff, like
why we calling the ones on the fourth floor vegetables right
to their faces, as if they knew the difference. Or why we not
letting anybody have coffee or cigs when they been bad.
Well, how the hell we gonna keep 'em in line? Shit, they
don't mind getting put in the cool-down room or getting
extra behavior therapy, but you should hear the ruckus they
making when you take away their smoking privileges."

Marx nodded and asked Winston to take him outside. He
tried to pay attention as they took stairways and back cor-

ridors and came out a low door on the side of the building.
But he was sure he wouldn't have been able to find his way
back to the staff lounge without some help.

The grounds were well kept, and except for the removal
of a few statues and brass plaques, hadn't been changed
since the St. Dymphna days. They walked along a crushed
stone path, and Marx smelled boxwood mingled with the
sickly sweet odor of a linden tree in bloom.

They came to a pathway that led down to a small grotto
in the side of a knoll. Marx pointed and Winston took him
that way. Coming around a corner, now surrounded on all
sides by dense foliage, he saw a niche dug into the steep
rock slope. It was empty. But two little wooden benches
still faced the hole in the hill, and flowers still thrived above
it: a sprinkling of violets and may apples. Marx tried to
imagine the statue still in the niche, and patients sitting
there before it, praying for mental healing.

He wanted to stay there awhile and enjoy the quiet, but
Winston was clearly uncomfortable there, even with the
overt traces of religion removed.

"Are the patients allowed to come down here?"

Winston shook his head. "Not many. Hardly any. Those
that get sent here already been shuffled around through other
places. This kind of the end of the line for a lot of them.
Anybody good enough to wander around and sniff the flowers wouldn't get sent here."

Winston was getting bored with the tour, and Marx told
him he could find his way back.

From anywhere that Marx went on the grounds, he could
see—or at least feel the presence of—the hospital. By a small
man-made pond, he looked back and saw the roofs and turrets of the building poking above the trees. More like a
fortress than a hospital, Mt. Kinnsvort was a huge red brick
structure built during the full flowering of Victorian behe-
moth architecture. With dozens of dormers—like ax heads
driven into the roofs—gables, and minaret-like towers, from
a distance the hospital resembled a Mideastern castle, a
place where a minor satrap would hole up with his assas-
sins, houris, eunuchs, and vizers. There were actual Arabic
touches to the design: ornate fretwork, complex scrolling

above the windows, and everywhere the repeated motif of the triple-peaked arch.

He made it to the perimeter and inspected the high iron fence that apparently went all the way around the grounds. It was certainly too high to be scaled without great effort, and seemed to be in good repair. He found no loose sections, no places where animals had dug underneath, no cement work that needed attention.

From that angle he got a good view of the building. Dozens of narrow, barred windows were visible, but he saw not a single face looking out. It was very quiet there, peaceful. Birds swooped and sighed above the shrubbery. Somewhere in the cool shadows beneath the trees, small animals were moving. A bee buzzed by, but paid him no attention. It flew out of the shadows, heading for the bright yellow and red flowers that grew along the path's embankment.

A few hours later he was back in the director's office, sitting in a large leather chair. Dr. Brule had called in all the psychiatric staff who were not too busy to meet the new head of security. They were just as suspicious and uncooperative as the caretaking staff, but less obvious in showing their displeasure. They all shook his hand, told him how glad they were that someone of his caliber had been brought in, and then sat stiffly, waiting to be excused by Dr. Brule.

Marx thought of his aspirin bottle waiting for him in the car. He thought of a tall, cold glass of milk as the director went through the staff's accomplishments.

"Dr. Simonsen has made some very important strides in our understanding of how the body's immune system can be tapped to effect mental healing. There are some who even believe that he's started a new revolution in the treatment of bipolar depression. But Martin is too modest to put it in those terms." Dr. Simonsen was a tall, bland man whose face Marx forgot almost as soon as he turned to look at the physician next to him.

"Dr. Yanconelli has just received a Felderman Grant from the National Science Foundation to study neurotransmitter imbalance, wasn't that it, George?"

"Close enough," Dr. Yanconelli said. "We don't want to bore Saul with technical talk. I certainly don't like it when plumbers and car mechanics throw their jargon around.''

''Exactly, exactly.'' Dr. Brule next introduced the resident sleep-deprivation expert and the thyroid man, and then pointed to a woman who'd said nothing thus far.

''And this is Caroline Haak. Don't let her looks fool you, Saul. She's second to none in her field.'' Marx noticed Dr. Simonsen rolling his eyes and another man scuffing his feet irritably on the carpet. ''She's our ECT expert. None better in the state, perhaps the country. And that's counting Bialofsky at Johns Hopkins and what's-his-name at Walter Reed. Caroline is a real pearl.''

She was somewhat younger than the other doctors. She was blond, fair and fine. And if she hadn't been wearing the same bored, hostile expression as the others, it would have been hard to keep his eyes off her.

Soon she, and all the other staff, had made excuses and gone back to their work, and Marx was stuck again with Dr. Brule.

3

Brian was on his bed, doing the Prong and listening to the invisible Negroes inside his head. Usually the music came loud and hard, big slabs of greasy funk from the Other Side. Inside, deep inside, he gave a powerful grunt and let loose another blast of heavy funk. He was singing and listening, in the audience and on the stage, cooked down to a black vinyl disc and stretched to a slender metal arm with a needle at the end, all at the same time. "Oh bay-bay, oh Cherry Jelly bay-bay!" The bass was slapping against his hypothalamus. The snare drum was snapping in his forebrain. "You got the power! Oh bay-bay, you can do the Prong all night long." He was shaking his booty but not moving a muscle.

He looked up at the end of the song and saw Ollie standing in the doorway, afraid to cross the invisible line. He'd been there off and on all day, angrier and uglier every time he came back.

"Supper looks really bad today, Brian. Beets. And cherry pop. And spaghetti. And you're going to have to clean your plate right down to the shine."

28

Luckily, Ollie was too stupid to know that today wasn't a red day. Brian could eat all the beets in the world today. Yesterday had been a red day. Then he would have bitten his tongue out and done just like Billy in 21F did—monkey crouch on the end of his bed, ticking like a time bomb about to go off—and not let one drop of red beets or red jello or red spaghetti get past his lips. Ollie just liked to talk ugly and look ugly and make everyone on the ward hate his guts.

Brian smiled and nodded. That made Ollie even madder. But he didn't cross the line. He just stood there in the hallway sniffing like a dog for some hidden food or maybe a piece of evidence. They found evidence in Victor 21P's room, wound up in a napkin behind the dresser. And it had already started to stink. Brian didn't see Victor for a while after that. He hadn't been in the TV room or the gym or crafts class. Then he came back and wouldn't say a thing about where he'd been and what they'd done to him.

Brian started wiggling a little bit and doing his good foot dance, but not enough to give Ollie an excuse to call in the rest of the orderlies. Brian always knew how far he could go. And then he stopped, just like Ollie knew to stop at the line across the doorway that Dr. Haak had drawn with her finger. She'd told Ollie not to take one step over it unless he wanted to go back to wherever it was that he came from.

As long as Brian could remember, Ollie had been in the Red House, just as ugly in the old days but with a little more hair. He'd been there longer than anybody else, even Dr. Haak. Even old Herb the Chinese man with the fingernails and the red eyes in 21R. Ollie had always been there, but it hadn't been so long before that he'd started in on Brian. Maybe a year or two. He wasn't exactly sure when it had begun. And every day it was getting worse. Putting his fingers in Brian's food when he handed the tray to him, making comments and laughing when Brian was in the shower, grabbing him by the nose and flinging those pills down his throat and making him open wide to make sure they were really gone. Ollie was always there, but since Dr. Haak had drawn that line on the floor and started having Brian come see her almost every day of the week, Ollie was getting really ugly.

Another orderly showed up and walked right past Ollie,

into Brian's room. He said, "Okay, let's go. The doctor wants to see you. Time for treatment." Ollie waited, sniffing now loudly like a bull and as soon as Brian was past the line, he grabbed him and told the other orderly that he'd take care of Brian. The first one didn't care. It was a long walk, anyway, down to the new treatment center. So he let go and then Ollie and Brian were alone. "Looks like you're getting to be the star attraction around here. You think maybe Dr. Haak has got the hots for you? What would you think about that, spaz? Wouldn't you like the doctor to be hot for your body? Or maybe you don't even know what to do with her when you've got your clothes off and you're all alone with her."

He held Brian tightly, squeezing his upper arm hard enough to hurt but not hard enough to leave bruises. He knew better than to do that. Ollie was good, really good, at going just far enough but not too far. He'd made that mistake only once before, using his pacifier on Brian when he wouldn't eat his macaroni and cheese on a yellow day. Rumor said that Ollie almost got kicked out of the Red House for that. Somebody, probably Dr. Haak, had come down really hard on him for treating Brian that way. He didn't see Ollie for a couple of weeks after that incident, and it wasn't until three months later that he'd been reassigned to Brian's floor. He'd learned his lesson. Dr. Haak had probably put him in the cradle and hot-wired his cortex. Ollie wouldn't like that. It would be too much for Ollie, so he learned to behave himself and squeeze tight but not too tight.

Brian was awfully white, veins and cords and tendons showing through like he was covered with tissue paper and not real skin. Bumps made bruises. Scratches made wounds that bled too long. And brush burns hurt for a week. Ollie knew all about that and made sure that he didn't go too far.

They walked for a long time in the dim, cold halls. It was taking them longer than the last time they'd gone to the new place. Ollie wanted to be alone with him, Brian could tell that. He didn't let go. He steered him left and right and left. He was talking, but Brian could hardly hear him.

"You're her little lamb now, aren't you? Her little white lamby, just like on Easter morning. How does it feel to be her lamb, huh, spaz-boy? How does it feel? Don't you want to be her little lost lamby?'' He was snorting the way he always did when he thought he was being funny or clever. Brian laughed. Sometimes that made him be quiet. But Ollie didn't pay any attention. He just went on about sheeps and rams and things that didn't make any sense.

They went up a flight of stairs, then another one, winding around and around until the light had gone almost all away and all of a sudden it was back, bright and hot on his face and they were standing inside a little round room. Nobody had been there for a long time. It smelled of dust and dead flies. It was about the size of Brian's room, but there were no corners. They were high up, very high, inside one of the towers. Ollie pulled him over to the window and pointed. Brian could see a long way, miles maybe. He hadn't seen that far in a long time, too long to remember very well. From his room on the ward all he could see was the side of the building and a few pine trees. But up there in that tower it felt like he could see forever. It made him feel good, big and airy and bright as the scene Ollie was laying out in front of him.

Brian felt one of his words bubbling up, filling him. ''Discharge, owww! Say it, say it.'' But Ollie wouldn't say it. He didn't care if Brian was hooked on the word. Maybe he was going to lock Brian in that room, looping around and around with the word dragging him like a fish on a hook. Maybe there'd be nobody to say the word and Brian would be stuck there forever. ''Discharge, discharge. Say it!''

Ollie had a bad look on his face. He was still holding on, tighter now, tight enough to leave bruises and then Dr. Haak would know everything. Ollie didn't seem to care anymore. He hated Brian's words. He hated to hear them and he hated to have to say them to get Brian to be quiet.

Ollie pushed Brian up against the window, and he felt the scummy dust against his nose and forehead. He was looking down on tall trees. He could see workers on the lawn, but they were tiny and their machines sounded like little toys.

''Do you know what, lamby-boy? Nobody ever comes up here. The janitors don't even have the keys. Nobody bothers with this place. How about I just leave you here for a few days and you can be all alone? You can say-it-say-it until

you're blue in the face, but nobody's going to find you here.
I could tell the doctor that you got lost. How about that?
Wouldn't you like to spend some time here? The doctor
might even forget all about you being her little pet.'' He
was holding Brian with both hands, hard against the glass
as if trying to push him through. "Did you know I used to
be her pet? Is that news to you? Or does she talk about it
behind my back? When she tells me to get out and the two
of you have your little time together, does she talk about the
old days?'' The sun was directly ahead, hanging over a green
mountain. Brian was looking straight into it. He didn't blink.
He wanted all the light to go inside him. The sun was getting an aura, and the mountain too, a halo of hot light just
like before his seizures. Ollie's voice was getting far away.
His hands were tight like the pacifier, tighter than the clamps
in the cradle, but Brian could hardly feel them. Ollie was
shouting and he could feel the spit on the back of his neck,
and it was burning through his hair, through his skin,
through the bone, and right into his cortex. Ollie was shouting, but Brian could hardly hear a thing. He was hanging
on the edge there, as if Ollie had pushed him through the
glass. He was dangling there, hundreds of feet off the
ground, and even outside the sounds were muted. The lawn
mowers and the hedge trimmer were still like little hissing
whispers. The cars on the road and the delivery van honking
its horn at the gate were far, far away. Their sound was
blocked out, smothered by the sound the sun made.

Then Ollie had shut up and let go. Then they were face
to face, but Ollie wouldn't meet his eyes because he always
lost in a stare-down. Ollie was quiet all of a sudden, as
though he'd looked at his hands and seen what he'd done
and there was no way to hide it now. His fingerprints were
on Brian's skin now, invisible but still there. Coming up to
the surface slowly like a picture developing. And Dr. Haak
would know what he'd done and it would be all over.

The room was round again. It smelled like dust and an
attic full of dead people's clothes again. Brian wasn't looking at the sun anymore, but the glow was still there. Not
burning like Ollie's acid spit on the back of his neck, but a
broader heat. It was smoother, making the little black scorch

marks fade away, healing them up. He was looking straight at Ollie and now he had the aura.

Sometimes the aura made people look like twins, or triplets, all trying to fit into the same spot. Sometimes it made them shiny and hard like a mirror full of fire. Sometimes it made them go away completely and only have a shadow left behind. Sometimes it was invisible, but an aura all the same, making everything else around it shaking as if seen through water.

Now Ollie had it and he looked like the sun. It hurt to see him. But Brian looked anyway because sometimes everything hurt—to touch, or look, or smell, or remember—and the hurting was okay. Ollie's lips were moving. Sound was going into the air and into Brian's ears, and they were the same old words Ollie always said, about the good old days and how beautiful Dr. Haak looked and how much she loved Ollie but couldn't show anybody because it was a big secret. The words were going into his ears, but he didn't hear a thing.

Ollie reached out, grabbing, and then they were going back down and around the spiral stairs, first through the place where there was no light, then back where everything could be seen. Ollie was hurrying, pulling him faster and faster down the long halls where the echoes didn't seem to go away but bounced in the dust and piled up by the walls.

They passed a saint standing with her face into a corner like she'd done something wrong, and she had the aura too, a real halo. It was carved out of wood like her face and body and clothes, but there was another part to it: spiky light and hissing like the gas fire rings on the stove in the kitchen. The saint said something that made Ollie even more afraid. And then they were running, Ollie sniffing for air and Brian pulled along behind like a kite, not even touching the ground. Ollie's arm and Brian's were knotted together as the string, and he was flying behind, getting lighter and lighter until he was just a cross of skinny sticks with a diamond shape of tissue stretched across it.

The saint was yelling that Ollie was in big trouble and Ollie was snorting for air and they went around a corner and found that big wooden door with the knob like an iron star.

Ollie stopped to catch his breath. He straightened out his white jacket and licked his hand to smooth down his horns of red hair and whispered, "It's just our secret, right, Brian? That room up in the tower, that's just for the two of us. Let's not say a thing to the doctor or she might get mad at us both."

The fire had gone off Ollie's face. The aura was somewhere else, hiding or resting up like it did sometimes. "It's just our secret, right? We don't want to make the doctor upset." Brian nodded, and his head was a bell, a big black iron bell like at the top of steeples in the big churches. It rang loud and long, and then the door swung open.

She knew something was wrong the second she turned around from her desk and looked at them. "You're late," she said.

Ollie was good at lying, but she knew it was a lie anyway. "We had a little problem up on the 17 ward. I had to help Otto get it straightened out." She could have called right then and found out he was lying, but she didn't bother. She knew everything about Ollie. He didn't have to open his mouth and she still knew what was in his mind.

"We'll talk about it later." She got up and led Brian to his chair, strapping on the blood-pressure cuff. Ollie stood unhappily to one side, waiting. The doctor ripped the cuff off and led him directly to the EEG setup. "Come on, we need to get him ready." Ollie helped her paste on the electrodes and ran a quick scan over the control panel. The needles started to tremble and the graph paper started to crawl forward. She pushed Ollie out of the way and took her place at the board, adjusting the levels. "He's peaking," she said excitedly. The paper moved forward, with Brian's brain rhythms printed there in red ink. "He's only produced this pattern a few times before." She wet her lips. One hand was clamped between her knees, as if to keep it from doing something wrong. She fiddled with the dials with her free hand, then got up suddenly and started to yank the wires off Brian's head.

"Get him in the cradle. I don't think we have much time." Ollie helped Brian to stand and unbutton his shirt for him. Ollie wasn't just afraid of being punished for taking Brian to the round room. He was afraid of what Brian could do once he was strapped in and discharging. He yanked down Brian's pants, then picked him off the floor to get them clear of his legs.

Soon they had him in the cradle, and the needle went into his arm, pumping in muscle relaxant so that he wouldn't break any bones once the seizure started. There were times when they knocked him out and all he remembered afterward was the taste of gas and a prickling sensation on the skin of his neck. But this time he was going in wide awake.

A new set of electrodes was glued to his scalp, a clip placed on his earlobe and a monitoring patch attached to his chest. Dr. Haak shone a light into his eyes, and he saw the reflection of his blood vessels on the walls, on the ceiling above him, and on the doctor's face. The light vanished and then he heard her say, "He's slipping. I think he's pulling out."

Brian knew what she wanted from him. He knew that look on her face just like the look people get peeking in the shower room or flipping through a dirty magazine. Once one of the orderlies had left a magazine full of naked women in the TV lounge and they'd divvied it up, everybody on the ward getting a picture or two. Brian had one that showed a woman—or a girl, he wasn't very good at guessing ages—in a steamy bathtub. Her body was just visible below the surface. She was very pale too, or the light made her look that way. Brian had hidden the girl as long as he could, sneaking her out to look when none of the staff were around. But Herb 21R squealed about the magazine, and the orderlies made a sweep through the ward and confiscated all the pictures.

Now Dr. Haak was looking at him the way he had looked at the girl in the bathtub. And Ollie was looking at the doctor the same way. She had the aura now. Softer, more like liquid than fire, and truer too. It seemed to really belong to her, as if it had been traveling, hunting, and finally had found its way back to its true place. It hummed like a light bulb. It sang him a lullaby to make him relax.

She told Ollie to go to his place by the other control panel, and when he was stationed there, checking over his gauges, she pressed her fingertip to her lips and transferred that touch to Brian's. As she pulled her hand away, he saw a blob of light throbbing at the end of her finger. She smiled at him, just as the girl in the picture had smiled at him from her smoky bath.

From where she stood, she could just see the EEG read-out. She took a final look, then closed her eyes as if praying and flicked a small red rubber-coated switch.

The blast hit Brian like a spear of fire, the barbs tearing their way into his flesh. The hot juice cut his body like hundreds of razors. He thrashed and writhed, but the juice didn't get wrung out of him. It went deeper in, curling and boring like a worm in a piece of poisoned fruit, trying to find its way out.

Dr. Haak took her finger off the switch and the current was cut. Brian flopped back down onto the plastic sheet, now sticky and damp. The doctor took her place again above him, and from the look on her face it seemed it was she and not Brian who'd been run through by the spike of electricity. She was sweating. Her eyes were bright. She yelled instructions to Ollie, then went to the console again and readied herself to drive in the spike again. Over the hum of the transformers and the hum building steadily inside of Brian, Ollie shouted back some readings from his monitor. Dr. Haak pressed her finger again on the switch, routing the voltage into Brian's brain. He convulsed as before, and when that blast had passed, she was nearby again, shining her little flashlight in his eyes. She turned his head onto the side and pushed a hard rubber probe into his ear, as if trying to look directly into the areas of his brain that she'd just seared.

"One more time and he's done," she said, checking the other ear and then returning to her place. She flicked the switch a third time and the last blast tore through him, as if sent directly from her hand, through the wire, and into his flesh. It came and it went, but still the crackling fire remained in his head.

Above the noise he heard her shout at Ollie, "Get out! Now!" He must have argued, because she disappeared for a moment, yelling threats at him. Then Brian heard the door slam and the dead bolt slide into place. Dr. Haak returned, tore the monitor pads off him, but left the electrodes pasted on his scalp.

"You're ready, Brian. We've got you right where we want

you.'' She unfastened his leg and chest restraints, and, working her hands flat under his back, flipped him over. Though lying on his stomach, his face pressed against the clammy plastic sheeting, he could still see her hovering above him.

Using a pair of needle-nosed pliers, she plucked the two small rubber rivets out of the back of his neck. Then she squeezed a glistening drop of conductive jelly into each of the open holes and slid the silver-tipped ends of the cable into the shunt. Instantly he felt protected again, though the route to his brain was actually more open now.

It was raining inside his skull. Light-filled clouds were passing in the inner sky. A moon, two moons, opened like his eyes and he saw through them: Dr. Haak with the looped length of cable in her hands, two sharp prongs on the loose end. She was happy. Or as close to happy as she could get. Brian liked it when she was happy. He liked to give her what she wanted.

Pulling the long, thick braid on the top of her head and fastening it there with a carved bone comb, she let Brian see her shunt. The two black dots on her neck, identical to his. She pulled out the little stopper and dipped the free ends of the wire into the jar of jelly. She was working blind, using her fingertips to find the holes. Wincing, taking a little gasp of air, she slid the ends of the cable into her shunt.

"This is it, Brian. Are you ready for the big time?" The storm was still inside him. Clouds moved across the moons and he went blind for a moment. But he knew what she was doing. He'd seen her do it before: place a flat rubber plate between her teeth, position herself in the big padded chair by the control board, and reach for the switch. Her finger was gentle. She didn't want to hurt him. It lingered on the small red button, stroking. Then slowly, carefully, it pushed forward and the blast surged into him again.

First came the cold fire. She'd explained it to him as extreme high-frequency power, but for Brian it seemed more like a net or second skin, thousands of thousands of needles penetrating him as the one great needle, Dr. Haak's hot spike of love, went in and out and through him. He was giving her back what she'd given him so many times before.

"Chorea, say it, say it." She didn't get mad this time.

She didn't mind that he had another one of his words. She said it, and her voice sounded like a snake's hiss, the tongue red-gold and full of special venom.

The cold fire passed and then he was stretched on her invisible rack. His limbs out of their joints. His veins and arteries split and squirting redstreams. His brain tissue coming apart neuron by neuron. And then he hit the wall.

He hit it and went through, like the dogs at the circus who jump through the flaming hoops. His skin burned off his back. His flesh burned off his bones. His bones turned to shafts of light.

And he's through.

He goes through the wall, converted to light, and lands on all fours. And he's moving, crawling like a baby with a four thousand horsepower diesel where his heart should be. He's racing on the filaments, crawling at light speed: the rail worm, baby sixteen drive-wheel Soultrain. He's got glowing bones for crankshafts, a stream of greasy black smoke coming out the two holes in the top of his head, and a baby's hungry scream instead of a whistle. He gobbles the rails as he flies above them, starving mouth-breather sucking hot iron into his stomach and spewing it out behind as coils of black funk.

He goes into a tunnel, boring into the rock, the glistening ore lode Mother Earth and sees a light at the end. But it's his own eyeball, four stories high and oozing hot matter, glassy, molten muck and spikes out the top like halo rays. And he's out again.

Back on the surface. His steam blast shrieks loud and long, like the Godfather of Souls getting up for the down stroke. He takes it to the bridge, screaming, "Got a brand new bag!" and he feels the thrust. His whole steel tonnage rocketing off the rails. Into the sky. Leaving them behind like twin trails of baby's milk, hot and rank.

His hands and feet are wheels, and they're all in flame as he tears over the tracks. The ties rattle off like xylophone slats and the rails flap behind him like spaghetti. The caboose falls away, then the freight cars and the tender, all consumed to feed the fire, feed his hunger. He's just a hot wad of power streaking through the Ictus. Dendrites, neu-

rons, synapses, every circuit in the system his domain for
speed and thrust.

Then comes a short instant of stillness, his last breath
before hitting the final lap. He's running silent but carrying
the loudest message: I got the power, I got my mojo working, I wanna wanna wanna be your man. He sees the end
of the wire, the spot where the rest of the world begins. He
sees the two holes where she begins and he slams on
through. Into her main line, delivering the hot load directly
from his heart to hers.

Soon enough, too soon, it was over. Brian was limp, cold,
and hungry. Dr Haak was in her chair, unconscious. Her
hands were knotted in the cable. She'd been clinging to it
the way a priest hangs onto his rosary. Her hair was a mess.
Her lips were bright red, redder than lipstick. Her skin was
flushed. Brian could see the tip of her tongue, small and
pink. She was beautiful that way, all the stress and worry
cooked out of her.

Brian lay in the cradle until she woke. He didn't try to
untangle himself from the straps and electrodes. He just
waited, watching the sunlight move on the stained glass,
tracking through the pictures of miracles and saints.

4

They'd been told that a visitor smells Niagara Falls before he sees it. And on certain days, before seeing the city or the falls themselves, one sees a huge column of steam, like a mushroom cloud hanging in the sky. It's always there, year after year, carrying into the atmosphere millions of gallons of water vapor, but depending on the humidity and the angle of sunlight, sometimes it's invisible. As are the more dubious substances that it carries: leached, belched, and retched into the river upstream.

Price and Whitehead did smell it first, a perfume concocted of chemical by-products and waste. They caught a whiff of the solvent cloud that covers the area day and night. But it was nowhere near as vile as they'd imagined. It wasn't like decay, or smoke, or disease, or putrefaction. It was something they'd never smelled before.

"It's sort of sweet," Chip Whitehead said.

"I suppose. But there's also a tang to it. Something rather piquant." Chuck Price breathed more deeply at the vapor, then realized that the two of them must have looked foolish sniffing the air. He faked a cough, then wiped an imaginary fleck of dust off his jacket sleeve.

They were dressed in similar—except for the labels, identical—dark business suits. They both had hand-tooled leather briefcases. Their hair was neatly styled, every strand in place. Whitehead looked at his watch, grunted softly his approval, and nodded toward the building they were waiting in front of.

It was the Niagara County Psychiatric Facility, somber and slightly shabby like dozens of other mental institutions within their territory. Whitehead checked his watch again and told his partner it was time. They didn't have an appointment. In fact, they could have gone in and gotten what they wanted at any time of day or night. But they'd found that arriving places exactly at noon, as the church bells were tolling, gave their appearances a weightier feel. They strode in side by side, with their dead, slick smiles and their matching fraternity rings. At a quick glance they might have been Jehovah's Witnesses coming to preach among the schizophrenics and suicides.

They went directly to the information desk, asked for the office of records, and arrived there shortly, requesting to see Miss Janet Barrgeld, the clerk in charge.

"My name is Inspector Whitehead, and this is Inspector Price. We're with the State Provost Board." He reeled off a set of acronyms that she'd clearly never heard of. "We'd like to see the records of a young man who was a patient here approximately ten years ago." Whitehead opened a small leather wallet and showed her his badge. It was a plain laminated square with an official seal and a photo of him, showing his widow's peak slightly farther forward on his head. He'd smiled broadly for the picture, displaying his perfectly even teeth.

"Have you spoken with the director? We don't normally allow the files to be seen without prior arrangement."

Price showed her his badge, pointing to the inscription across the top. "State Provost Board," he said slowly. "We need to access to your files. We wouldn't be making this request if it weren't important."

"I'll have to speak with Dr. Hellman." He reached for

the phone, but didn't pick it up. "What did you say this was about?"

"We need to see the records of a former patient. It's very important and we'd very much appreciate it, Miss Barrgeld, if you'd take care of this matter quickly."

She looked from Price to Whitehead, as if expecting some further explanation. They both stared back at her smiling, but as hard and unyielding as carved marble busts.

"Miss Barrgeld, we are representatives of the state government. I can assure you that we have authorization to review documents that are far more classified than anything you have here."

She agreed finally, after inspecting their badges again, trying to read the signature at the bottom of each and double-checking to make certain their faces and photos matched.

She called one of her junior clerks to take over the desk, and led the two to a large record room, stacked nearly to the ceiling with banks of filing cabinets. "What did you say the patient's name was?"

"Cerniac, Brian. We don't have a middle initial. He's approximately eighteen years old. That would put him here eleven years ago."

She tracked up and down the aisles, running her finger along the identifying labels, clicking her nail on the edge of each clear plastic shield. She pulled open a drawer, went through it, and found no one named Cerniac.

"Try with an S," Price said. She hunted through the appropriate drawer, came up with nothing, and tried a few more permutations on the name.

Growing weary of the search, she slid the last drawer shut and asked, "What is this query in relation to?"

Neither Whitehead nor Price answered her.

"This room contains all the records of patients who spent time in this institution?"

"All the long-term referrals and placements. You did say he was here for ten years, didn't you?"

"No, it was ten years ago. It's possible he only passed through." Whitehead showed her a copy of a routing document, indicating that Cerniac, Brian had been diagnosed—pending further observation and testing—paranoid schizophrenic and was recommended for long-term treatment.

"This is a 40/a/117. Why didn't you say he was just a temporary assignment? When we automated the new filing system, we put the temporary—"

Whitehead cut her off. "Miss Barrgeld, just show us where the records in question are."

She took them to another file room, and with little effort found a manila envelope marked "CERNIAC, BRIAN." It contained a few dozen smudged and faded carbons, a report typed on pink paper, some photographs, and a document entitled "PEDIATRIC EXAMINATION, B. CERNIAC."

They thanked her and quickly found a desk where they could spread the papers out. Most of it was of no use to them: ten daily maintainance reports listing medications and treatments Brian had received, blood pressure and electroencephalographic charts, and a fading copy of a CAT scan of his brain. But some of the documents had information that cast new light on the subject.

One of these was a Niagara Falls Police Department report spelling out the circumstances which had brought Brian to the hospital.

"Responded to call 3:12 P.M. White Caucasian minor causing disturbance in area of 99th Street School. On arrival, found boy—later identified by school records as Brian Cerniac—having fit of some sort. Dressed only in old pair of blue jeans and T-shirt. No shoes. Seemed very disoriented. Appeared to be violent, but had yet to cause any bodily harm to other children. Had not attended school there in approx. 4 years, but some of the students recognized him and called him by the names "Spazzer" and "Brain-boy." When approached, produced loud noises, spat at officers, and attempted to flee. Officer DeCampo attempted to coax subject into patrol car, but subject made threatening gestures and appeared to be convulsing. In questioning other children, was ascertained that subject was known to frequent the dumps near 114th and Glide streets near east extension of Love Canal. Subject subdued at 3:23 using restraining harness and delivered to N.C.P.F. at 4:03."

The word *schizotype?* was written in a different hand in the margin of the report.

A memo stapled to the admittance papers stated: "The patient appears to have no memory of the circumstances prior to the incident at the 99th Street School and refuses to acknowledge the existence of family or parents."

Upon entering the hospital, Brian had exhibited signs of severe depression, bordering on catatonia, and another memo mentioned the possibility of using electroconvulsive therapy if medication proved to be ineffectual. In places, there were references to "seizures," and though terms such as "abnormal brain-stem discharge" and "neural arrhythmia" recurred, nowhere was a clear and final diagnosis of epilepsy made.

Price made notes on a pad of legal paper, checked the spellings of doctors' names, date, and locations, and then stacked the papers neatly back in the file. The two men spoke little because they knew exactly how the other operated and usually what was on his mind. They'd worked together since their time at Cornell. As the years passed, most of the knowledge, principles, and ideals they'd acquired in college had fallen away. Now, for both of them, the perfect execution of assigned tasks was the main—if not only—source of pleasure and satisfaction in their lives.

Finding Miss Barrgeld again at her desk, Price went over his notes and asked if the consulting doctors were still working there.

"Dr. Manne? No, I think he passed away. Or retired. I don't believe I ever met him, and I've been here for six years now. And Dr. Haak, no, that was before my time too." Price asked her to think hard on this second name. "Charles Haak. No, I'm sure he was gone by the time I started here. But you could ask upstairs in personnel. They could tell you where he is now. He's probably moved two or three times since he worked here."

The last name on the list was one that the clerk knew. "Dr. Rourke? Yes, she's still here. She's head of the pediatric department now."

Price and Whitehead thanked her, and after getting directions to the pediatric wards, they went in search of Dr. Rourke. They found her and had little trouble in getting her to tell them what she knew. "That was quite awhile ago, wasn't it? '77 or '78?" Margaret Rourke was a tall, bony woman with a harsh, bleatlike voice. "Is he still in the system? I'm not surprised. Our success rate with cases like that is still quite poor.''

Price said, ''Yes, he's still institutionalized. He was transferred from here directly to Mt. Kinnsvort, downstate. They're doing excellent work there.'' They made small talk for a while longer, trading insincerities about the state mental health system, then Price asked her, ''And there's nothing more you can tell us about the Cerniac boy?''

''I was only brought in briefly because the subject was so young. I wasn't of much help, I'm afraid. Bill Manne did most of the work with him. At first he was quite fascinated by the boy. He started doing a little research into feral children. I don't think he'd ever seen such a severe case. The boy wouldn't speak, wouldn't respond to any kind of human comfort. Our best guess was that he'd been living by himself in some kind of 'fort' or clubhouse in one of the dumps. I think he'd dug himself a hole, covered it with scraps of wood and tar paper, and stayed there like an animal. How he survived the winters, I can't guess.

''But Bill's interest flagged when it became clear how bad off the boy was. You know, we only have so much time and energy, and we have to put it where it'll do the most good. Charlie Haak took over for a short while. He'd done a lot of work in schizotaxia. I think he was the one who made the decision to send him on to a long-term facility.''

After she'd made a few more useless comments, telling them things they'd already learned by reading the file, and then lamenting the fact that Dr. Haak's career had been cut short, she said, ''I'm surprised that your agency would send the two of you all this way to find out what you could have learned with a phone call.''

Price shook her hand and thanked her for all the invaluable information she'd given them. Whitehead flashed another of his pearly shark smiles and accompanied his partner out.

They said nothing as they walked together through the wide, brightly lit corridors and out into the sunny June air. The smell was fainter than before. The wind had shifted and was pushing the vapor toward Canada. Price and Whitehead looked, in unison, both ways before crossing the street, and went to a phone booth at the corner. The book was missing, ripped off its silver chain. They decided to head toward the falls, keeping the nebulous column of steam directly ahead of them.

Earlier that day, making their first stop after arriving in Niagara Falls, they'd gone to the Love Canal area. In places the neighborhood had returned to semi-normalcy. The state had instituted a Reclaim Love Canal program and even tried to change the name of the area to the Sunrise City, but only a few young couples were willing to take the risk of moving in, even with the incentives of low-interest mortgages and a job-placement program at the nearby chemical plants. Most of the area was still abandoned. The streets where the toxicity levels were highest had been surrounded by chain-link fences topped with razor wire. Warning signs—in English, Spanish, and universal symbol code—were spaced every hundred yards or so. The houses inside these enclaves were all boarded up. Weeds were enveloping the lawns. The streets and sidewalks had begun to crumble. On everything there, natural or manmade, there hung a grayish funereal pall.

Price and Whitehead went to one of the gates and found the locks to be sealed with Department of Environmental Conservation tags. After a few phone calls and a brief wait, a security guard drove up in a Jeep. He was a sallow young man, barely out of his teens. He seemed far more afraid of Price and Whitehead than the stew of solvents and carcinogens cooking under the neighborhoods he patrolled. He was eager to please them, quickly breaking the seals and unlocking the gate.

After sweeping a clutter of magazines and used Kleenex onto the floor, he gestured for them to get into his Jeep. Price shook his head. ''I think we'd prefer to walk. You get a much better picture that way.''

The guard was slightly put off by this, but accompanied them through the gate and carefully locked it behind them.

Like three friends out for an after-dinner stroll, they made their way into the dead neighborhood.

Price read the guard's identification badge and said, ''So tell us, Tom—you don't mind me calling you Tom, do you?— what's it like working here?''

The guard assumed there was something behind the question other than friendliness, but he wasn't sure what. "It's okay, I guess. We don't get much action, that's for sure. I just check in once an hour—you know, punch my code in at the sentry boxes. Once in a while we get some kids trying to go over the wall, but most of them know how stupid that would be. There's other ways to have some fun. Lots easier ways. That concertina wire is wicked stuff. I sure as hell never tried it when I was a kid."

"So you grew up here?"

"A couple of blocks east. It wasn't so bad on my street. My parents still live there. They figure they've been there for twenty-five years. If anything's going to happen to them, moving out now sure won't change it. Things were never this bad over there." He waved his hands, indicating the abandoned houses, the sickly trees and yellowish weeds. "Back when the shit hit the fan, so to speak, we had some of the sludge in our basement, and when the county started fining people for pumping it into the sewers with their sump pumps, that got a little hairy, but soon enough it stopped and we didn't have any more trouble."

They asked him the name of the street he had lived on, and which grammar school he'd gone to. Then Price stopped and took the guard by the hand. He tried to pull away, but Price hung on tightly, looking him in the eye. "We'd really appreciate it if you could help us out, Tom. You don't by any chance remember a boy about your age, maybe a year or two younger, by the name of Brian Cerniac? He ran into trouble with the police back when all the ruckus was going on."

The guard succeeded in freeing his hand, but then Whitehead put his arm around his shoulder, like a coach reassuring an athlete, or a preacher praying with one of his flock. "No, I don't think so. No. I never heard of him."

"It wasn't in the newspapers, but we thought you might have known him. He ended up in the psychiatric hospital. He was a very disturbed boy. He must have had a terrible home life. His parents never even came in to sign the papers. Officially he's still a ward of the state." Whitehead squeezed the guard, then let him go. "That doesn't ring a bell?"

"No, I never heard of him." The guard backed a few steps away. "I tried to keep my nose clean. That's the only way you can get a job these days. Nobody will hire a trouble-maker." He touched the ring of keys hanging from his belt and seemed reassured by their weight and jingle.

"Well, we were just wondering." They walked on, saying no more until they'd looped back to the gate they'd come in through. In places the ground had the appearance of cracked mud, as if a great heat had cooked all the moisture out. They passed a few deep sink holes with black, gummy crusts at the bottom. And elsewhere were broad scabs of concrete, poured there when the first residents had fled in order to seal the poisons in.

After watching the guard relock the gate, Whitehead and Price thanked him for his time and wished him well with his career.

He drove off quickly, glad to have gotten through the ordeal without making any obvious blunders. Whitehead and Price turned to look back through the fence. Birds swooped above the abandoned areas, crying hoarsely. But even they seemed to feel the toxic curse and didn't land.

After eating supper at the Bridal Veil Diner, they went to the Falls Park, taking a long, relaxed walk along the neatly trimmed paths. The tourist season was near its peak. And with young couples still finding June the best month for weddings, the parks were full. As they strolled, they listened to the newlyweds conversing in low tones, children shouting excitedly to one another, and packs of visitors speaking in tongues that neither Whitehead nor Price recognized.

The sun was near the horizon, but the summer air was still warm. The vapor from the falls moved continually upward, like a small white mountain rising from the gorge. It climbed steadily, becoming less solid as it moved away from its source.

A trio of nuns went by, walking arm in arm. A teenage boy on a skateboard shot past, heading down the sidewalk toward the falls. A clan of Japanese tourists all wearing clear plastic raincoats stood smiling at the edge of the precipice as one of their party directed his video camera at them.

He swept it along the stone fence, then up into the air to catch a shot of the unraveling cloud, then went down again, to his family all waving self-consciously for the camera.

Whitehead and Price didn't go to the edge. Without discussing the matter, they'd decided not to look—at least that first night—directly at the falls. Instead they walked through the gardens and small groves to the pedestrian bridge that led to Goat Island. A helicopter rose from the far end of the island and clattered overhead. The two stopped to watch it fly out over the falls and then dip out of sight.

Following the signs and currents of visitors, they found themselves walking near the river's edge. The Niagara gathered speed there, heading through the last rapids above the falls, as if this extra momentum was needed to push the mountain of water over the edge and into the huge pits below. The water was glassy green. Waves of cool air came off the river as the wind shifted. Price inhaled deeply, but could barely detect the chemical stink above the river's heavy breath.

They stayed at the shore awhile, watching the thousands of tons of water pass before them, then walked back up to the trails. Heading toward the bridge, they saw a small sign that read "TESLA MONUMENT, THIS WAY." Instead of an arrow, a small lightning bolt pointed out the path.

Without speaking, they turned and went that way. Near the entrance to Cave of the Winds, they found the statue, a bronze cast perhaps five times life-size. It showed the great inventor sitting, staring intently at a blueprint of a plan. A plaque fastened to the base read, "In tribute to Nikola Tesla, creator of the Alternating Current generator and founder of the hydroelectric industry in Niagara Falls." He was wearing a gown and had a somber, almost mournful, expression on his face.

Whitehead and Price paused there, much longer than it took to read the plaque. Finally the helicopter returned from its little tour, buzzing low over the treetops, and the two were woken from their dreamlike state.

They took a look at the stone arch nearby, the remains of the original powerhouse. At the top of the arch was a bas-relief showing an Iroquois maiden going over the falls in a canoe. She wore the same expression as Tesla.

* * *

They ended their evening at the Niagara Falls Historical Museum and Wax Gallery. By then the sun had set and the crowds were starting to thin out. Price paid for both their tickets and they went inside, walking past the displays that showed the various inventions used to go over the falls. Barrels, a contraption made of truck tires and fifty-five-gallon drums, and a vessel that looked like a cross between a hang-glider and an inflatable skiff were all labeled carefully and surrounded by photos of those who'd used them to navigate the falls.

Farther inside the museum were a few rooms with wax dummy displays, showing various events in local history. One tableau showed the assassination of McKinley and Teddy Roosevelt's assumption of power in nearby Buffalo. Another showed the legendary Sam Patch—in a red, white, and blue suit with a bear on a chain—jumping directly into the falls. A third, dimly lit and in need of repair, depicted three men in capes and cowls throwing a bound body into the gorge. The label explained that it was an artist's recreation of what had happened to William Morgan, the Freemason who'd broken with that brotherhood to expose their practices. He'd disappeared, and more than one source had him transported from Rochester in the back of a wagon and dumped into the Niagara at Devil's Hole. His body was never found.

Whitehead heard a young boy complaining that the museum wasn't as good as the ones across the bridge in Canada. "Where's Jack the Ripper?" he said. "I thought they were all supposed to have Jack the Ripper." His brother called him into the next room, and the two men followed them.

There, taking up a good portion of the room, was a display showing the first execution by electricity. The older boy read to his brother: "William Kemmler, a convicted murderer, was selected by the state of New York to be the first person in history to die by this new invention, called at first the Electrolethe."

A red button with an arrow pointing to it caught the younger boy's attention. He pressed it and the display came to life, a few sparks flying off from the dummy's hands and feet and the tape-recorded sounds of lightning coming from a speaker hidden in the shadows of the ceiling. The older boy continued reading: "The developer of the electric chair was none other than Thomas Edison. When asked by the governor to prove the effectiveness of the device, the great inventor placed an orangutan in the chair and introduced current into its body. Though the animal caught fire, the electric chair was deemed effective and safe, because a human being is not covered with fur. William Kemmler's hands and feet were then wet with a potash solution and 1,300 volts were run into his body over seventy seconds. Contrary to popular belief, the cause of death is not incineration, though the smell of charred flesh and hair is sometimes noticeable. Instead, the current introduced to the body causes the muscles to spasm and the victim is in effect beaten to death by his or her own body.

The younger boy pressed the button again and made electrical noises with his mouth. The dummy was in an awkward position, as though in a state of perpetual agony. One hand was grabbing the side of the electric chair and the other was clenched in a fist. Sections of the fake hair had fallen out, leaving patches of bare, translucent scalp. His mouth was open in a silent scream, and from a certain angle the viewer could look down the red wax gullet.

When the boys had grown tired with that exhibit, Whitehead and Price had it all to themselves. They took turns pressing the red button, while the other stood watch at the door.

5

On his third day at work, Marx was met at the door by Dr. Brule. He was almost hysterical, grabbing Marx by the sleeve and dragging him toward the elevator. His face was redder than before. His eyes seemed even smaller and more deeply imbedded in the soft flesh of his face. His voice rose and fell like a siren. "We haven't had anything like this happen in years. Only once since I've been here. It's awful, just awful. We had the second best record in the whole system. In less than a year we would have gone a whole decade without a major incident. I can't believe this is happening to me."

Marx didn't bother to ask what had happened. He was clearly being taken to the scene of the as yet undisclosed calamity. Dr. Brule jabbed his finger frantically at the elevator buttons, trying to get the doors open. Finally they slid back and Dr. Brule strode down the hall, jabbering about his retirement and the Chancellor's Award he was in line for. They passed through one of the staff lounges and a few of the orderlies stood, saying good morning to the director. He became quiet, calmer, in the presence of these underlings. He nodded his greeting to them, but the doors slammed shut behind him and he started up again, whining over and over, "I can't believe this is happening to me."

A pair of nurses stood outside one of the therapy rooms. They looked down at the floor as Dr. Brule passed, embarrassed to see him in such a state.

An orderly who'd been introduced to Marx as Ollie lay on the floor. His limbs were folded in like those of a dead insect. Soot and black scorch marks covered the back of his neck. Marx knelt quickly, pressing his fingertips to the orderly's throat.

"He's alive," someone said. Marx looked up and saw Dr. Simonsen holding his stethoscope in both hands, wadded like a ball of yarn. Another doctor came in, looked down at the orderly, and cursed.

"We're not exactly sure what happened. Marge was the first one on this morning. She found him like this. It looks like burns, but there's some bruising along his chest and upper arms. Somebody said he liked to mess with the ECT equipment and might have done it to himself. But that doesn't make much sense, even if he was on the flaky side."

Dr. Brule had folded his arms across his chest, squeezing tightly, as if to prevent himself from exploding. "And all the residents are accounted for?"

One of the nurses shook her head.

"God damn it, it wasn't that Italian woman, was it? I knew as soon as I laid eyes on her she was going to be trouble."

"No, she's all right. It's one of Caroline's shake-and-bakes on the 21 ward. Brian Cerniac. About eighteen years old. Hebephrenic. Schizo-effective epilepsy. No real trouble to speak of."

The director looked around at the doctors and nurses gathered there. "Caroline? Then where the hell is she?"

Two nurses stepped aside to allow Dr. Haak to come forward. She looked like she'd slept in her clothes. Her hair was wild, the long braid twisted and uneven. Marx could barely hear her when she spoke. "There's been no trouble with him until now. He's been responding quite well to the treatments. This is completely unexpected."

They were all silent for a while, looking down at Ollie. Then Dr. Brule said, "Well, is anyone looking for him?"

"We thought we should wait for Saul. It's more a security matter, isn't it?"

"How long has he been gone?" Dr. Brule's voice was growing weaker and thinner as he saw his Chancellor's Award floating away from him.

"It's hard to tell. We don't have anyone here who's done much forensic work." The director was withdrawing, hardly hearing what they said. "Maybe a few hours. Ollie came on at midnight. And Ruth Ann said she saw him in the monitor room about two or so. He was all right then."

They were all looking at Marx as though somehow he'd caused the incident to occur. "So nobody's gone looking for the boy yet?" he asked.

"We thought that would be your job."

Dr. Brule came out of his trance long enough to say, "I don't want the local people brought into this. That fat moron sheriff, what's-his-name—Coombs, Coons—already has it in for me. Since the picnic last year when Siegfried had to be sedated. He'd just love to call in the state police and the bloodhounds and have a big dragnet or whatever the hell it is they do." He told the nurses to get Ollie out of there and then pointed to Marx. "Take whoever you need and find him. All the wards are locked down until further notice. All privileges are suspended until you hear otherwise." He left, muttering and shaking his head.

"Is this the way he was found?" Marx asked. No one answered. "Who found him?"

Dr. Simonsen went to the door, saying he needed to get back to his patients. A few of the nurses followed him out. Others waited uncomfortably, trying to think of excuses to leave.

Dr. Haak crouched by the orderly. She opened her bag, wet some gauze with alcohol, and swabbed the back of Ollie's neck. The flesh was reddish and blistered. She turned him onto his side, told one of the nurses to hold him in that position, and pulled back his eyelids. "He's in shock. We need to get him to the infirmary." A few of those left in the room took this as their cue to leave.

Winston stood by the door, waiting. "We better start

looking, don't you think? Brian's not a bad kid, but you let him run around too long and we gonna have more than just fried brains to worry about.'' He pointed to an older man, an orderly who worked mostly in the vegetative wards. ''Pauly and me will start upstairs in the attics. Guess we don't be supervising no ping-pong and checkers today.'' He pulled the other man's sleeve.

Marx and Dr. Haak were left alone in the room.

''Has the kid done this kind of thing before?''

''No, not exactly. Mostly he manifests withdrawal and depression. Some delusional behavior. Nothing to warrant serious concern.''

''Then why was he in a locked ward?''

''The director overreacts sometimes. I think Brian would have done just as well in an open ward. He isn't violent.''

Marx looked down at the comatose orderly. There were sear marks on his chest. ''He practically killed this man. I think that qualifies as violent, don't you?''

''Ollie was rather harsh sometimes.''

''What are you saying? That it's okay for a schizophrenic to go out of control, administer shock treatment to one of your staff, and then disappear?''

Dr. Haak gave him another of her contemptuous looks. ''Not at all, Saul. Brian is here at Mt. Kinnsvort for a reason. I doubt very much that he will ever be able to return to life outside the system. He needs to be found immediately.'' She left it at that, implying that it was his problem and not hers.

The nurses came in with a gurney, and after sliding a blanket under Ollie, the four of them lifted him up and secured him with web belts.

''Dr. Lorenzo came in. He's waiting down in the infirmary,'' one of the nurses said. Dr. Haak nodded and they wheeled Ollie out of the room.

Marx organized three teams of orderlies to begin the search. One went around the entire perimeter, finding no sign that the fence or gates had been breached. Winston and Paul worked their way down from the attics, looking in all the rooms that hadn't been used since the St. Dymphna days. Beside a stack of magazines with titles such as *Chop-*

per Babes and *Hog-Ridin' Mamas,* they found no evidence
that anyone had been in the upper floors in months. Two
other staff members went ward by ward, checking all the
patients' rooms. Everyone and everything was just as they
should be.

And Marx spent a few hours in the therapy rooms, watching the doctors go about their business. He stayed in Dr.
Simonsen's room the longest, observing him go through a
fever-induction with one of his catatonics. The subject was
a thin, gristly woman with a few wisps of gray hair still on
her head. She sat hunched in a wheelchair, oblivious to all
that went on around her. Dr. Simonsen first injected her
with a sedative, then with Marx's help lifted her to the bed.
Slowly her limbs loosened enough that they could stretch
her out and get the restraining straps around her legs and
chest. The doctor attached an IV unit and began dripping a
murky, yellowish solution into her veins. "I've gotten this
down to about a half an hour. She'll be achieving pyrexia
in no time."

Marx had assumed that the therapy rooms would be like
the classical psychoanalyst's office: paneled walls, muted
lighting, a large couch for the patient to lie down on. Instead, at Mt. Kinnsvort they were more like institutional
kitchens, large and cold and full of activity. Earlier, Marx
had mentioned his surprise at seeing the banks of computers
and monitoring equipment. Dr. Simonsen had snorted dis-
dainfully and said, "We have a few Freudians left here, but
we're slowly getting rid of them. It's rather an embarrass-
ment to have them around. Everyone knows their claptrap
has been completely discredited. Abreactions, ids, super-
egos, dream work. We might as well try to solve these problems by rubbing lucky stones and figuring out horoscopes."

He strapped a flat plastic band across the patient's forehead and hooked the wire leads to a readout panel. Her
temperature, blood pressure, and pulse rates all appeared
on a small screen.

"The body has simple, natural processes for healing itself: fever, sleep, and immune reactions. All we need to do
is help the body, and it will help itself."

The woman's skin was the color and texture of ash. Her
breath whistled in and out of her as if through a broken

accordion. One eyelid pulled itself open. She looked at Marx with all the hatred she could muster. The doctor came between them, fussing with one of the leather cuffs. Marx asked a few more questions, got noncommittal replies, and headed for the door.

"So this is where Dr. Haak has been doing all her work?" He pointed into the room where Ollie had been found.

"Until a week ago. Things have been getting a little crowded here. Jackson's added a few more stalls to his setup, and there's talk of getting a second CAT scanner." Dr. Simonsen looked up from his work, keeping his thumb pressed hard against the woman's throat. "Caroline finally got Brule to okay her request for more space. She moved to the east wing. God knows there's enough room down there. I never did figure out what they used all that space for, back when the Catholics were in charge here."

It took Marx almost an hour, asking all the staff he came upon, where exactly Dr. Haak's new rooms were. Finally Winston and Paul finished their search of the upper rooms and caught up with him near the director's office. They'd helped move some of her equipment and volunteered to show him the way.

After a few wrong turns they found the long corridor that led to Dr. Haak's suite. The saints stood like sentinels along the hallway. Some stared heavenward, transfixed. Others seemed to be deeply withdrawn, trapped in some inner spiritual world.

Marx stopped briefly to look at the statue of Saint Teresa of Avila. Her face was rapturous. The sculptor had done a good job of making her look both beautiful and fierce, almost inhuman. She held her hands to her breast as if in extreme pain. If Marx hadn't had a vague notion of her story—how she had been pierced by spears of divine light—he would have imagined her to be the patron saint of heart attacks.

Winston snickered. "Great thing to have around all these nut cases, huh? Sets a real good example."

Marx allowed him to lead on, and shortly they came to a door with a star-shaped handle. They went in without knocking and found Dr. Haak at her desk, writing. She looked up from her work, and the two orderlies backed into the hall. Winston said something about going to help the others search the grounds and they left quickly.

The doctor had recombed her hair, fixed her makeup, and regained most of her composure since Marx had last seen her. She seemed far more secure back in her own domain. She nodded a greeting and cleared a stack of files off a chair for Marx to sit on. He remained standing.

Early afternoon light streamed in through the stained glass windows, painting the room with muted blues and reds. The heaped boxes, the half-packed crates, and styrofoam chests made the room look more like a warehouse than a laboratory.

"It's been almost twelve hours. And no one's seen a trace of him yet. The door of his room was unlocked. No sign of a struggle either." Marx tried to sound capable, efficient.

The doctor's voice was neither harsh nor loud, but brought his headache up from its hiding place. "I don't think we have anything to worry about. Richard—Dr. Lorenzo—says that Ollie will be fine. Perhaps some memory loss, not that Ollie has that much to remember. Second-degree burns. But he's been a cooperative employee. I don't think we'll have any trouble with the boards. This may not even have to be reported." She smiled. "Dr. Brule may get his award yet."

"But the boy is still loose."

"He'll turn up."

The snake in his head was nibbling at the back of his eyes. He felt a trickle of venom. He wanted to hit Dr. Haak, or at least shake her by the neck and shout at her, "In the real world this is assault with a deadly weapon. Maybe attempted murder. And you talk about it as if it's just a minor annoyance." Instead he took a shallow breath and closed his eyes for a moment. The pain was spreading quickly. It wasn't following its normal path.

"The situation is simple," the doctor said. "Ollie broke a few rules. He shouldn't have let Brian out of his room in the middle of the night. That was totally unacceptable. But Ollie's suffered enough already. You don't think he should be punished further, do you?"

"What about the boy?"

"It looks to me that Brian was just trying to be helpful. He's been responding very well to the ECT of late. He's made progress with me. Perhaps he thought Ollie could benefit from a little time on the line. Of course, Brian doesn't understand a thing about proper voltages and levels. I'm not trying to say that what Brian did wasn't wrong. Of course it was. It's just that he can't be held accountable. This is, you must remember, a psychiatric hospital. Certain rules don't apply here. And, after all, if Brian's adjustment to social rules and conventions was normal, he wouldn't be here."

"As far as we know, doctor, he isn't here anymore."

She crossed her legs and her skirt rode up higher. Marx forced himself to keep his eyes on her face, not that that was much less disturbing. Her lips were parted slightly. He could see her tongue moving in the shadows a glistening red-gold.

He asked the first question that came to mind, about Brian's daily schedule. She seemed to find something funny in the situation and didn't bother to answer. It was the first time Marx had seen her smile. The snake bit him hard at the base of his skull.

He tried another tack, saying, "Winston tells me you've worked quite a bit with the boy. Apparently he has some pretty severe symptoms—seizures, attacks, I don't know what the technical term is. Winston said the boy hears voices and music. And he talks a lot about 'going through the wall.' You wouldn't know what that means, would you?"

Dr. Haak was still smiling, but it was more a shield now than a sword.

"And something about an 'ictus.' Do you know what he means by that?"

The doctor nodded, putting back on her cold professional look. "Brian suffers from severe delusions, hallucinations, and at times exhibits an almost total break with what we would call reality. At times he imagines—he 'sees' and 'feels'—that he is going to a place he calls the Ictus. Strictly speaking, the word just means stroke or attack. He must have heard one of the staff use the word and it stuck with him. He has a mania about certain words. They inbed themselves in his thinking, and the only way he feels he can get free of them is by hearing someone else say them.

"In short, Saul, Brian is schizophrenic."

She put stress on his name. She pointed to his chest. Her fingernails were long and red. "Soon enough Brian will get hungry, or find that he misses his room and will come back to us. The more excited we get about this, the harder it will be for him. Soon enough this will all blow over, and if Ollie hasn't suffered any permanent damage—which I doubt very much he has—in a few weeks everything will be back to business as usual." Marx took this to mean that she didn't want to discuss it any further.

He went back the way he'd come, walking through the hallway of saints. He stopped again to look at Saint Teresa, reached out to touch her bare arm, then drew his hand away sharply, and hurried back toward the wards.

6

It had taken only a few private smiles and feeble female appeals to get Dixon—the previous security man—under her control. Dr. Haak could tell right off that he'd respond well to her bright-but-fundamentally-helpless routine. He'd imagined himself quite a prize, and when the doctor began singling him out for favors and bits of in-house gossip, he was soon completely in her camp. They'd had coffee together a few times; she'd shared with him some totally fictitious secrets; and not long afterward he'd begun bringing her the items she'd hinted that she wanted. He was like a male cat, bringing dead mice to the female, showing off what a fit mate he'd be.

Most of these gifts were useless: a spray can of Mace, a purse-size revolver, disposable plastic strapping that could be used in lieu of handcuffs, an antique billy club, and ear plugs to be use in conjunction with crowd-control noise generators.

But he did bring her one item that made her whole strategy worthwhile. It was a shock baton, a sophisticated version of the electric cattle prod. The baton had been manufactured, along with the other high-tech implements of control, by a small firm outside of Buffalo which did most of its business with South American states.

With a few small adjustments—adding a transformer circuit and replacing the on/off switch—this shock baton could be used to replace her whole electroconvulsive rig. She didn't need the monitoring devices with Brian. She knew when he was ready. She knew exactly how much current he needed to go through the wall. She recalibrated the baton's output, made a simple adapter out of parts bought at the radio repair shop in Osric and could use the baton anytime she wanted on Brian, going directly into him through his shunt.

On the day of his disappearance, she'd returned home early to find him playing with the electric carving knife. He was sitting at her kitchen table holding the knife to his ear. At first she thought he was going to slice into himself, but then realized that he was just listening to the hum of the motor and the hiss of the two blades moving against each other.

"You'd better put that down, Brian," she said, remaining in the doorway.

He looked up, smiling, then pressed the handle of the knife against his ear so that the vibrations could be transmitted directly through the bones of his skull. His voice came out a quaking whisper: "Dr. Bri-nor, Dr. Bri-nor. You're wanted on the 21 ward. Low-down afferent discharge module." He flicked off the switch and spoke in his normal voice, "Good afternoon, Dr. Haak. You're looking very nice today."

"Put down the knife, Brian. You know we've got rules here, just like at the hospital." She opened her purse and took out the two halves of the converted shock rod, quickly snapping them together. The handle was made of black rubber. The electrode end was shiny silver steel, drooping slightly. "You don't want me to get angry, do you?"

"Get in touch with your feelings," he said, but put the knife down and slid it across the table.

"Now get up and come over here." He stood and went to her, putting his arm around her waist. He looked sheepishly down at the floor. She lay the shock rod on the back of the stove and stroked his head, murmuring, "Brian's had a hard day, hasn't he?" She wanted to take him into the spare room right then, lie him down on the bed, hook up the shunts, and take another hit off his brain. But there was a limit to how many times a day Brian could fire the hot blast into her. She knew she shouldn't be greedy. He was all hers then, hers for as long as she wanted to keep him. There was no need to rush things.

She tried to make small talk with him, but always her mind came back to the thought of the two of them linked by the cable, firing the voltage back and forth. She picked up the shock rod and rubbed her thumb over the rubber-coated on/off switch. Her other hand ran back through his hair, touching lightly the two plugs over his spinal column. She drew back suddenly, by force of will, and said, "I brought you some presents today." She went outside to her car and shortly returned with a few shopping bags.

That afternoon she'd driven all the way to New Paltz to buy Brian some new clothes. She assumed that it being a college town, she'd be able to find clothes there that would be appropriate for someone his age. She handed him the shopping bag and told him to go into the bathroom to change. He stood stiffly, unsure what she really wanted from him. "Go ahead. You'll look great in them. I picked them out just for you." He opened the bags and looked inside. Having worn institutional clothes for the last ten years, he was scared by the idea of being even moderately in fashion. "It's okay. Trust me. You don't need to wear those old things anymore. From now on you're going to be just like everybody else." She faked a frown. "Or maybe I shouldn't have bought you such nice clothes. If I don't watch out, soon enough you'll have to beat the girls off with a stick."

He looked at the shock rod hanging limply from her hand.

She tried to embrace him, but he pulled away, all the muscle in his body tense and rigid.

"So," she said, trying to sound cheerful, "what do you want to do tonight?" As soon as she'd said this, the thought of what he'd done every night for the last ten years made the situation seem ridiculous. As far as she could determine, he spent his evenings listening to his mind replay the songs that had been popular on the radio just before he'd been institutionalized.

His overriding need was to hear these "churning urns of burning funk," as he called them. Like most of the other schizophrenics she'd dealt with, he had his own private system, and he clung to it, working it, the same way day after day. But it was no more significant than the fact that certain psychotics imagine themselves controlled by satanic forces, or that a strangely high percentage of mental patients find rerun situation comedies and cigarettes to have great importance in their lives.

So what she was actually going to do with him, day and night, seemed a rather grim question. He did sleep a lot. He could be pacified with certain common objects and electric appliances. But there would still be hours and hours when she would be alone with him and have almost nothing to do.

"Well, you can put the clothes on later," she said at last. "It's not that important." She led him into the living room and sat him down on the sofa.

She'd lived alone for years and spent a great deal of her time in the lab or at the therapy rooms. Consequently, her house looked more like a bachelor's hovel than the home of a prominent psychiatric physician. The sofa had stains on it that had been old back when her husband was still alive. She'd had to turn on her floor lamp by screwing in the bulb for as long as she could remember. Stacks of journals and research manuscripts were piled waist-deep by the walls. But she didn't see any of that. She saw only Brian, sitting uncomfortably with his hands clasping his knees. She didn't know what to do with him, but there was absolutely no chance that he was going back to Mt. Kinnsvort.

The night before, she'd stayed in her suite long after the rest of the daytime staff had gone. She sat at her desk, huddled in a pool of yellowish light, tinkering with one of the EEG leads. She'd taken it apart and reinsulated one of the connections, trying to cut down on the interference caused by the overhead fluorescent lights.

When the sun had set and the lab was swathed in shadows, she looked up from her work, as if coming out of a trance, and put away her tools. She found her brown paper bag and fished out the remains of the sandwich she'd brought for lunch. She finished it in a few bites, then wiped her hands on her lab coat, getting smears of mustard on the stiff white fabric. Then she checked her watch and went down the long hall of saints to Brian's ward.

She'd had Ollie's schedule changed so that he'd be on duty from midnight to eight, and found him in the monitor room, listening in on the patients. There'd been some trouble that day on the 14 ward, and Dr. Haak had suggested that the night nurse station herself down there. Ollie was alone. He was startled to see Dr. Haak there at that hour, but nodded and went quickly to fetch Brian when the doctor had told him, "Go get our friend."

A few minutes later, Brian was standing with Ollie in Dr. Simonsen's suite. He was half asleep, still in his baggy flannel pajamas.

"Make sure the doors are all locked," the doctor said. Ollie obeyed, and when he returned, he found the doctor holding Brian's hand and murmuring to him. Ollie waited, unsure whether he should look.

"Come here," she said. He did as he was told and saw that the doctor had brought along the shock rod. It seemed bigger in her hands, as if it was drawing strength from her. It was a deep black with shiny skin. The tip looked like a silver eyeball.

"You lied to me yesterday," she said, gesturing to Ollie with the rod. "You said the reason you were late was because of some disturbance on the 17 ward. I talked with Marge and Otto. You made the whole thing up, didn't you?"

Ollie didn't bother to deny it.

"We can't have you lying. That's totally unacceptable, Ollie. And Winston tells me that you've been sneaking up to the turret rooms with those awful magazines. You didn't take Brian up there, did you?"

Still he didn't answer.

"Ollie, this is very important. I've got to know if you took him to the attics before you brought him to my suite."

His head was bowed. He was afraid to meet her eyes. She pressed a switch on the shock rod and stabbed the device at him, like a duelist stabbing forward with a rapier. The silver knob just touched his chest. A loud crack came from the rod as it discharged, and Ollie was thrown backward against the wall. Dr. Haak smelled a whiff of ozone. It was the only stimulant that she allowed herself, abstaining even from coffee. The ozone was a special treat. It made its way quickly into her, and she felt her thoughts becoming clearer.

Ollie tried to protect himself, but she gave him another jolt, on the hand this time, and he curled into a ball, his head in the corner. "Ollie, listen to me. Did you or did you not take Brian up to the attic?"

He whimpered yes and curled more tightly in on himself, expecting another shock.

"What were you doing up there?"

He muttered something that she couldn't hear and got another shock for not speaking up. "I was going to hide him there," he said at last. "Then maybe if you forgot about him we could go back to the way things used to be."

"Things are never going to be the way they used to be. They're going to get better and better." She gave Brian's hand a reassuring squeeze. He was awake by then, watching, taking the situation in as best he could.

"But he's a loser," Ollie said. "He's not the right one for you."

She jolted him again and hissed, "I'm a well-respected psychiatric physician, Ollie. Don't you think I know what's best for myself?"

Ollie nodded agreement, trying to avoid another shock, but a moment later he made another comment about Brian. Her anger was rising with every word he said. The sound of his whining was beginning to grate.

"Get off the floor," she said. He stood, looked up briefly, as if afraid of being blinded by light streaming from her face. "I want you to apologize to Brian for what you did to him."

He said he was sorry, but Brian didn't seem to understand.

"And I want you to promise you won't ever listen in on him again. Unless you have permission from me or the night nurse."

"But he's doing things against the rules. Singing some times. I hear him all the time. Just a couple of hours ago, I heard him. 'Shake your groove thing all the way.' I heard

it. Really. And sometimes he dances. You don't want somebody like that.''

She flicked the switch on the rod and discharged into the
air, spitting a blue-white gout of light and cracking like a
whip. She held the tip close to her mouth, breathing in the
ozone. "I'm afraid, Ollie, that you're the one I don't need
anymore. You failed. You don't make the grade. Just like
the rest of them. I'm afraid that Brian is the only one who
really has what it takes.''

The boy's head swayed from side to side, as though his
neck was growing weak.

"One more chance," Ollie said. "One more time on the
wire and I can prove myself. I can go through the wall just
like him.''

"You had your chance. I hooked you up and ran you at
least five times, Ollie. You just weren't up to snuff.''

"I'm better than him. All he does all day is sing those
stupid songs and wiggle around like he thinks he's the king
of the dance floor.''

Ollie was whining again. She hated that tone of voice,
the hurt-little-boy expressions. She grabbed him by the wrist
suddenly, yanking it up behind in a hammerlock. She
pressed the end of the shock rod against his neck, firing in
another blast. But this time she didn't let up, sending a
steady barrage into him. He was writhing and gasping like
a fish on dry sand. She was murmuring into his ear as she
seared into his flesh: "I don't like it when you make fun of
Brian. It's not very nice, now is it? I think it's rather cruel
to make fun of someone like Brian.'' She smelled his cooked
flesh and pulled the rod away.

Ollie fell to the floor. She knelt, made sure he was still
alive, and then turned to Brian. "You see? Ollie disobeyed
and we had to use the rod of correction.'' She smiled. "But
if you do what you're told, you'll get the joy stick.''

She considered taking Brian down to her lab right then,
hooking up the cables and running him, but she knew she
needed to be careful. The effect of the ozone would wear
off soon. The old deadness inside her would return. The
numbness would surround her heart again. Her husband had
talked about a hardness in her soul, as if it was a quantity
that could be measured, an actual physical attribute. But she

didn't believe she had a soul, or a heart other than a fist-sized mass of muscle that pumped blood. Ozone had a simple, chemically understandable effect on her. The electrical discharge from Brian's brain, routed from the rod through him and into her, was not yet completely understandable. But it wasn't a mystical event. It was just electrons firing across microscopic gaps. It was just body chemistry.

She fired a last blast to get a last whiff of the gas. The small bluish explosion went off inches from the boy's face, but he didn't wince or back away. She wanted to smell the gas again, just as she wanted to go running through the hall of dead saints, dragging Brian behind, and throw him into the cradle for one more jolt. But she denied herself, as she'd been denying herself for years.

She'd seen other members of the staff give in to their lower wants. One doctor had built up a heavy morphine addiction, allowing himself a tiny bit more of the drug every day. Another had indulged his instinct for prepubescent girls. She wasn't going to end up like them, out of control, disgraced and shunned by the medical community. She knew when to stop and when it was safe to start again.

"Okay, Brian, we're going to go on a little trip now. Would you like to visit the place where I live?" He probably didn't know that anyone lived beyond the confines of the Red House. "Wouldn't you like to see the place where I live?" He nodded his agreement, but it was obvious he had no idea what she meant. Probably he assumed he was going for some new kind of treatment. That's all life had been for him until Dr. Haak had freed him: one useless therapy after another, like dozens of coats of paint that can't hide what's underneath.

She checked Ollie again, moved him onto his back, then went to the room next door. The old ECT apparatus was still there under a plastic sheet. She undid the wheel locks and pushed the ungainly cart into the room where Ollie lay.

"Here," she said, handing Brian the electrode paddles. "Now you try it." She guided his hands, pressing them against Ollie's temples. "All right, hold it right there." Brian did as he was told. The doctor adjusted a few dials and shot a final blast into Ollie. He thrashed on the floor, emitting mewling sounds. When the current was cut, he lay

with his mouth wide open. His tongue still twitched as if
the aftershocks were still moving through his nervous system. Brian remained where she'd positioned him, still holding the paddles to Ollie's head.

"Okay, you can let go." She had him touch a few more
smooth metal surfaces, leaving clear fingerprints.

"Ollie's getting funky," Brian said. He watched closely
as the last tremors passed through the orderly. After the
spasms had passed, a foul odor became noticeable. Some
subjects lose bodily control during their treatment. It didn't
surprise the doctor that Ollie was one of those subjects.

"Nasty, nasty, Ollie's getting down," Brian said.

The doctor wanted to get him out of there before he started
in again with his good-foot dance. She took him by the hand
and led him through a service corridor cluttered with janitor's tools and crates of canned goods. They went down a
stairway, groping blindly along the wall, then through a
caretaking staff lounge. A radio was on in the room, a faraway voice muttering like a dreamer. Brian slowed as he
heard the voice, but Dr. Haak tugged on him and soon they'd
found their way to one of the building's back entrances.

They headed for the parking lot, following a path through
the trees.

Brian walked with his head tilted back, looking up at the
stars. They were bright and very clear. It seemed that he
was trying to get all their light inside him, drinking it in
through his eyes. Though Brian could look out his window
at night and see the stars, and though he was allowed to go
out on the exercise yard at times, it occurred to Dr. Haak
that Brian might not have actually been under the stars,
unprotected by roof or walls, in over a decade. For a moment they paused, and even she was taken with their brilliance. The air was cool, almost as bracing as a whiff of
ozone.

They stood together near the fence, both with their heads
tilted back, both taking in the night air and the silver-blue
light. If Dr. Haak hadn't been there with him, Brian might
have stood there until daybreak and been found, cold and
hungry and still in his pajamas, by the incoming day staff.
She snapped out of her daze and led him through a side gate
in the high iron fence.

She opened the car door for him and helped him in. They said nothing during the drive to her house. They went down the hill, past the cannon, and through Osric. The area where she lived was only a few miles from town, but it was sparsely inhabited. All of the farms there had failed years before. And it was sufficiently far from the tourist camps and resorts that she seldom saw any vacationers on the road. Not a single car passed them on the way to her house.

She'd gone back to work the next morning as though nothing had changed. She'd met with the new security man and even helped organize the search parties. She'd bought Brian new clothes and then driven home that evening to find him just where she'd left him, sitting at the kitchen table.

And now as she worked at the counter, opening a few cans of chow mein and mixing up a rudimentary salad, Brian was waiting for his food as he'd waited every day for ten years. But already she noticed a slight change in him. She'd assumed that morning that she could leave him there with the doors unlocked and her tools and kitchen implements out in the open. It hadn't occurred to her that he might want to experiment with these new objects.

At Mt. Kinnsvort he'd never been interested in TV. Now he had it on and was paying close attention, though she was sure he had no idea what the news announcers were talking about.

He sat with his eyes only a few inches from the screen, and she realized that he wasn't watching the overall picture on the set but the individual pixels. In certain of the tests she'd performed on him, he'd again and again failed to discern large patterns. He could perceive the individual dots of light or bits of sound, but frequently had failed to make a larger whole out of them.

She went back to the stove, stirred the chow mein, and began laying out the plates and silverware. It was a big table, easily large enough for eight. At one end was a stack of reports and manila folders. Three of the chairs were heaped with groceries she'd bought that week: canned goods, boxes of cereal, and six-packs of soft drinks. She laid two places next to each other and gave Brian one of the smiles that would have reduced Dixon or Dr. Brule to fawning puppies. She knew exactly which shading of which expression she

needed to make them agreeable. But with Brian it was much
more difficult. He seemed to be able to see right through
her sham smiles and come-on glances. He knew what she
was really feeling, what she wanted, at every moment.

Turning away and giving the simmering chow mein a last
stir, she filled two cereal bowls with salad and placed them
on the table.

Brian clamped his lips tightly together and shook his head.
"It's just lettuce," she said. "You like lettuce. It's good for
you."

He opened his lips just enough to whisper, "It's green,"
then squeezed his eyes tightly together and turned his head
away, as if in the presence of something nauseating.

"Brian, I've seen you eat lettuce." She didn't want to
argue with him. It didn't make any difference to her whether
he ate his lettuce, but still she went to the refrigerator, got
out a bottle of salad dressing, and doused the lettuce under
a stream of bright red liquid. "Okay. It's gone. It's not
green anymore."

Brian opened his eyes, but shook his head again. "It's
still green underneath. You can't just cover it up."

She shrugged, scraped the salad into her bowl, and started
eating. Brian relaxed, turning his attention back to the TV.
He ate the chow mein with no protest, the vegetables in it
apparently sufficiently overcooked to pass as gray-brown.
At first his "color days," as he called them, seemed just
one more delusional system, not much different than those
of many other patients at Mt. Kinnsvort. But it didn't follow
the same rules as most manias. Every day Brian had a color
which he was forbidden to eat. The most common was red.
Green and brown followed closely. There was no pattern to
how the color days were determined. It seemed that he just
woke up every morning knowing which color was taboo.
She'd never been able to predict the next day's forbidden
color. Tomorrow he might eat peas and beans and cabbage
and any other green food, but that night trying to get lettuce
down his throat would be a fierce struggle. And she certainly didn't want to start off their time together on such an
unpleasant note.

After dinner, they went out onto the porch and watched
the stars come out. Dr. Haak lived in a two-story frame

house that she rented from her nearest neighbor, an old man who lived two miles down the road to Osric. In the other direction, she'd have to go all the way to Rennsbrook before seeing another inhabited house. Woods crowded in on her place from behind. The front yard had long ago been allowed to go wild, high now with thistles and Queen Anne's lace. She put her hand on Brian's as they sat together on the big porch swing.

Another star came into view, and Brian fixed his eyes on it, as though in some way trying to connect himself with it. "I want to go home," he said at last.

"You know that's not possible now, after what you did to Ollie. Dr. Brule is awfully angry with you."

It was apparent that he knew what he'd done, but also what she'd done. He repeated himself: "I want to go home." She realized then that he didn't mean back to Mt. Kinnsvort.

"We'll be going on a nice trip soon. We'll be going a long way from here. Won't that be nice?" Her bags were packed. Her finances were in order. She only needed to get the rest of her equipment from the laboratory and she'd be ready to leave Mt. Kinnsvort for good.

Brian was looking at the North Star, as though trying to orient himself, trying to find himself on an imaginary map. He didn't answer her question.

7

Price and Whitehead went directly to Mt. Kinnsvort's office of finance and budget. They flashed their teeth and their credentials, made references to bureaucrats high up the chain of command, and got down quickly to inspecting the records. Word went quickly through the hospital that two Albany trouble-shooters were on the premises, and Dr. Brule hurried down to deal with them.

He was clearly afraid of them, and they did nothing to allay that fear. "Dr. Brule," Price said, shaking his hand, holding on long and squeezing tightly. "We've heard so much about you." He didn't say what or from whom. "You'll forgive us for getting to work here without actually checking in with you."

"Not at all, no problem. I'm just surprised that you're here at this time of year. Usually the auditing process doesn't take place until September."

"We're not really here to audit the books, Dr. Brule. Although that might be an upshot of what we find. But so far we certainly have no reason to think Mt. Kinnsvort warrants extra attention in that area."

They went on for a while, playing with Dr. Brule, talking about payroll and supply outlays and capital improvements, all the while skirting the issue that had really brought them there. Dr. Brule's expression went from discomfort to barely controlled panic as they worked through his request for budgetary increases in the next fiscal year.

At last they gave signs that they were satisfied by his explanations and he seemed to relax. "Well, it was a pleasure talking with you gentlemen. If there's anything else I can be of assistance with, please let me know."

Price flicked a bit of lint off his partner's shoulder. "Actually there was one other little matter that we need to look into, if you don't mind. You have a patient here named Brian Cerniac, isn't that right?"

Dr. Brule didn't respond for a moment. He breathed shallowly, trying not to hyperventilate. "Yes," he said at last, his voice a strained squeak. "Brian Cerniac. Yes, he's a resident here."

"We'd like to take a look at his records." Price and Whitehead smiled together, like undertakers giving their condolences to a dead man's family. "There seem to be some irregularities. We just need to straighten out a few facts."

Dr. Brule agreed, of course, and took them to the suite where most of Brian's treatments had been administered. Dr. Haak was there, packing up some surgical tools.

The director introduced her, and she gave Price and Whitehead a cloying, too-feminine smile. They were instantly repelled by both the tone of her voice and the mock flirtatious way she appraised them both.

"These gentlemen are here to check up on your Brian. Could you get out his records?" He already felt his head on the chopping block. He knew there was no way for him to avoid the worst-case scenario. And he was beginning to suspect that they were dragging it out on purpose.

They dawdled, poking through the records, making small talk, and asking for explanations of certain charts and graphs. Finally, when it seemed that Dr. Brule was about to break down and confess that the boy was missing and that all their attempts to find him had been failures, Whitehead slipped the records back into Brian's file and said,

"We want to commend you, Dr. Brule, for the way you've handled this case."

The doctor had been sitting with his head in his hands. He looked up, unsure what Whitehead meant.

"You made the right decision not to bring in the local police. That certainly would have made the situation worse. I'm afraid they don't quite have the touch for such sensitive matters."

Dr. Haak nodded her agreement. "Yes, you're exactly right. The director has handled this the best way possible. When Brian is brought back, he'll be in a much better condition than if we sent out search parties with dogs and that kind of thing. The credit really should go to Dr. Brule."

He stood, bracing himself on the arm of a chair, and acknowledged their praise without saying a word. Price and Whitehead had broached the topic, let Dr. Brule know they were fully aware of the situation without once mentioning that the boy was missing.

Price told him that he'd like to speak with the man in charge of security, and Dr. Brule perked up, seeing an opportunity for getting away from the two. "Yes, Saul Marx. A good man. He's doing all he can to see that the situation is brought under control as soon as possible. A bit of bad luck, falling into something like this just a few days after starting in a new position, but he's a capable man. I'm sure he'll see this whole matter through."

After giving them directions to Marx's office, Dr. Brule started rattling on about the high quality of the staff at Mt. Kinnsvort. Price cut him off, saying he'd like to speak to the security man as soon as possible.

Once alone again, away from the fat, nattering director and the woman with the flushed, overheated look on her face, Price and Whitehead relaxed. They strolled down the hall, peeking in doorways. They stopped for a while to watch a team of doctors huddled around a patient who was strapped into a high-backed chair. Brilliant lights were flashing around the patient in rhythmic patterns. The purpose—they found out later—was to break up the neural organization of the patient's psychosis. The theory was based on research conducted on veterans of the Vietnam and Korean wars. It was believed in some quarters that mental illness was in fact not much more than a bad habit, though a particularly deeply ingrained habit. More than one research team came to the conclusion that by enforcing new patterns, breaking up the actual habit on a cellular level, certain schizophrenic behaviors could be extinguished.

Along with the pulsing lights came loud, cracking sounds, like Morse code tranmitted by gunfire. Price and Whitehead stood behind the Plexiglas wall that separated the control room from the experimentation chamber. Even muffled by the glass, the sound was painful to the ear.

They eventually found Saul Marx, sitting in his office with a bottle of aspirin in one hand and a tall glass of milk in the other. His office was tiny. He had only room for a small desk and a battered love seat that he'd salvaged from one of the lounges.

He seemed to know what they were there for before they spoke, pushing a sheaf of papers across the desk toward them. They were blueprints of the hospital and diagrams of the grounds. "As you can see, the boy could be hiding in any of a hundred places."

"What makes you think he's still here?" Price said, flicking through the pile of papers. "It's been forty-eight hours since he vanished. He could be halfway to Binghamton by now."

"We have no evidence that the perimeter has been breached, and no report of anyone in Osric or beyond sighting him. It's possible that he's somewhere else, but Dr. Brule doesn't want the local people in on this. So we keep looking here and hope for the best."

"He needs to be found quickly," Price said. "We can't let him wander for days."

"I'm doing all that I can."

"It looks like you're sitting in your office doing nothing."

They stared across the desk at Marx. They were both smiling, hard, intent, unwavering smiles. "You've only been here a week, and you've already got a major problem on your hands. This is going to look bad on your record. We were told by Bob Leslie that you've had a few mishaps in the past. You wouldn't want something like this to threaten our pension, now would you?"

Marx didn't argue. He was in no position to.

"Now, why don't you tell us what you've done so far to deal with this problem?"

Marx described how he'd searched the hospital with the help of the staff, how he'd gone all the way around the perimeter looking for some sign of disturbance, how he'd tried to question the orderly involved but gotten nowhere. "He's still unconscious. The boy must have really given it to him."

"Given what to him?"

"The juice. Electricity. He had burn marks all over his neck. He still has aftershocks, attacks of twitching and shaking. The boy must have trumped him from behind and then gone at it with the ECT machinery."

They went on awhile in this way, grilling Marx as though he was the one who'd attacked the orderly. Eventually they asked to see Ollie's records and looked through them quickly. "This is all you have on him?"

"That's all that's in the personnel files," Marx said, twisting his head from side to side, trying to relax the muscles in his neck. "He's been on the staff here longer than just about anyone else. They have a pretty high turnover here."

They asked to see Ollie's room, and Marx squeezed out from behind his desk, moving a chair so that he could open the door. He led them to the wing where the live-in staff had their rooms. It was almost identical to the wards, with the same dull green paint on the walls, the same harsh lighting. Marx unlocked Ollie's door and led them inside. On one wall was a large poster of a huge motorcycle, bright chrome and glossy black. The bed was neatly made. The little desk in the corner was empty. Price opened the chest of drawers and poked through the clothes, finding nothing of importance.

Whitehead went to the closet. Sliding back a nylon windbreaker and a heavy parka, he found a black leather jacket. He took it off its hanger and held it up for his partner to see. Around the shoulders were intricate patterns of steel studs. Black fringe hung from the pockets and cuffs. Various insignia were attached; skulls, swastikas, daggers, pyramids, and Maltese crosses. From the zipper slide hung a tiger's tooth.

On the floor at the back of the closet was a stack of motorcycle magazines. He pulled them out and dumped them on the bed.

"Were you aware that Ollie had these things?" Price asked.

Marx shook his head. "I was more concerned about the boy. It didn't occur to me to go rooting around in here. There didn't seem to be any reason."

Price leafed through the magazines. They consisted mostly of photos of women draped around huge motorcycles. None of the women were wearing much. They were all posed as though trying to seduce the huge bikes. A few of the pages had the corners bent down, marking the shots that Ollie was most interested in. One showed a woman perched on the broad leather seat. Her feet were propped up on the handlebars. She had a long blond braid. Price looked closely. Ollie had drawn two black dots on the back of the woman's neck.

"Ollie had some problems," Marx said, "but he did a good job. Dr. Brule gave him the highest marks on his last evaluation."

Price turned his attention back to the jacket. The leather was in perfect condition, the metal ornaments bright and apparently brand-new. It seemed that Ollie had never worn the jacket outside.

Price and Whitehead went to the door. Without actually using the words *failure* or *demotion* or *unsatisfactory,* they made it plain that they were not at all pleased with the progress Marx had made. Price dismissed him with a wave of his hand. Like the director, Marx took the first opportunity to get away from the two.

They came in on Dr. Haak as she was packing cables and tools into a leather valise. She went on working as they spoke, making no attempt to hide what she was doing.

"We want the boy," Whitehead said. "He's here somewhere. We want him back."

Dr. Haak fastened a pair of cords together, making sure that the male and female ends meshed properly, then coiled them and fit them in with the other equipment. "Saul's been working hard. He'll find him soon."

"Don't be so flip, Caroline. You know he's going to have to call in the state police eventually. And then things are going to get a lot more difficult. We want him back now, before this gets out of hand."

She looked up from her work, giving them her little-girl-lost look. "I don't know what you're talking about."

Price sighed heavily, disappointed in her. "The work you've been doing here has been very valuable. There's no question that you've helped us a great deal with this project. But I'm afraid it's out of your hands now. We want the boy back. We can shut the whole facility down and search it floor to floor with dogs, but that would be rather sloppy. And you know we don't like to be sloppy. We'd much rather you cooperate with us. Just as you have all along."

He came closer, jabbing her with his finger. "We can have this building taken apart brick by brick. But that's not the way we like to work. And then we could have all your side projects brought to light. You'd never work in this state again. You'd lose your license, your accreditation, and any chance of being funded ever again. But what would be the point of that?

"You've had your fun, Caroline. And you can continue to have your fun. But you're going to have to find yourself a new lover boy. We can't abide your being so selfish. This isn't just your pet project. There's a great deal of state money involved in this. And you know money spent this way makes the Board awfully anxious. You don't want them to think you're ungrateful, do you? Not after all they've done for you."

Dr. Haak remained silent. She'd dropped her mock-innocent smiles.

"Without agency funding, you couldn't afford even to go back to your rat-splicing experiments and monkey wiring. You'd be absolutely nowhere, Caroline. No friends in high places, no money, no protection. So why don't we just go back to the way it used to be? Ten years of work. You don't want to see it all go down the tubes because of a selfish whim. That doesn't make any sense, does it?"

He picked up a piece of wire and idly wound it around his finger, as if giving her time to think. "Teamwork," he said after a while. "Cooperation. One for all and all for one, that's the way to get things done."

"We won't embarrass you," his partner said, "by asking you to take us to your little love nest. There's no need for your colleagues to see that. Why don't you just fetch him for us, or drop a hint where Saul could look for him? And then we can go back to business as usual. Doesn't that seem like the smart thing to do?"

Turning at the door before leaving, they both bowed slightly, as if acknowledging applause, tacitly admitting that the whole episode had been more theatrical than perhaps it needed to be. Of the two men, Price had more of the actor in him; he'd even taken part in some collegiate theatrical productions. But that side of him had withered away, just as Whitehead's interest in music had faded as they'd worked their way up the bureaucratic ladder. It became clear to both of them that side interests would only drag them down, slow their progress in the hierarchy.

8

As soon as Dr. Haak had gone that morning, Brian got right to work in the kitchen. She'd shown him the sandwich and glass of orange juice he was supposed to have for his lunch that day. She'd told him not to go outside under any circumstances. She'd kissed him on the forehead and locked the door behind her. And as soon as he heard her car engine start, he propped her refrigerator door open. He liked the sound of the compressor, a steady midrange hum. Next he turned on the oven and left the door open so that he could see clearly the big glowing orange coil. After he'd gotten the mixer going, the two metal blades clattering away nicely, and jammed the toaster dial on "HI," he started hunting for the electric carving knife. Dr. Haak had hidden it the night before, telling him that she didn't want him playing with such dangerous things.

He couldn't find it, but he did discover the motorized can opener and started in immediately on the job of taking the lids off all the cans he could find. Soon the kitchen counter was piled high with open containers of condensed milk, fruit juice, peas and beans, luncheon meat, soup, and one big Virginia ham. The noise from the can opener blended with the rattle of the mixer, making a nice wail hovering above the freezer's drone.

After he'd taken care of that, he dug through her pantry and found the electric iron tangled up in its brittle rubber cord. But as soon as he plugged it in, his whole system shut down. A fuse blew and all the appliances creaked and whined and moaned to a full stop.

The kitchen fell totally silent. The heat from the stove and the invisible waves from the freezer and the vibrations from the mixer all went away, rising up through the ceiling and into the open air. It made him sad but not too sad, because he knew all about fuses and circuit breakers. They were usually in the basement, in the darkest corner in a rusty metal box on the wall. He rooted through the drawers until he found a flashlight, and shone the beam into his eyes until he could only see white spots. But he still had work to do, so he pulled the light away and went down to the cellar to get his system going again.

He spent awhile searching in the basement. When Dr. Haak had moved in there, she'd piled boxes and heaps of old clothing, magazines, bicycles and toys, old cookware, mason jars and firewood and even a few appliances in the cellar, making room on the first floor for her things.

He did find the fuse box and it was just as he had known it would be: the door hanging on a rusty hinge, gum wrappers and dead flies piled on top. A few of the holes where fuses were supposed to go had been bridged with tin foil, now blackened and scorched. He went through the little heap of fuses on the concrete shelf nearby, but they all had been blown. He held up each to the beam of his flashlight, inspecting the burnt cores, like kernels of carbon inside diamonds.

He'd gone through them all twice when he heard the door upstairs open. Two pairs of footsteps crossed the kitchen floor. Someone closed the refrigerator door, then the footsteps separated, one set heading down the hallway to the bedrooms and the other going upstairs. A moment later they met again, directly above his head, and he heard two men whispering together.

Brian started shaking. He felt the heat along the base of his skull just as he did before having one of his spells. His

heart became weak and something cold started spreading
out from his stomach. The basement door creaked open and
one of the men flicked the light switch. But besides the faint
yellowish glow from Brian's flashlight, the basement remained in darkness. One of the men left and came back
shortly. A bright beam shone down the stairs. Brian wanted
to go toward the light, step into it like he was on stage and
everyone was clapping for him. But he knew better.

Muffling the sound against his leg, he shut off his flashlight. As the men came down the steps, he quickly bur-
rowed into a heap of old clothes. By the time they'd reached
the bottom, he was hidden and safe, buried in the mildew-
stinking pile. An old woman had lived in the house before
Dr. Haak, and all of her clothes, stockings and slips and
moth-eaten dresses and tattered things made out of satin
with ribs and straps on them, had been dumped on the floor
there. But it wasn't just old lady smells that filled him. There
was also wet-packed dirt and ancient hair and air trapped
for years in the cellar.

The men spent only a few minutes there, kicking through
the junk, overturning the old wringer washer and shining
their light in the corners. They were getting angry. Brian
could tell by the way they breathed and the way they were
smashing things that were already broken.

Soon they were upstairs again. Brian heard plates breaking and furniture being tipped over, food swept off the
shelves and curtains being ripped off the walls. The two
intruders went down the hall to the bedroom, breaking the
glass on the picture frames and kicking holes in the old
plaster walls. Soon enough, though, they were through with
their job and left.

Brian lay awhile in the stinking silence, curled up like a
baby bird in a nest of old clothes. When he couldn't feel
the heat from the angry red faces in the rooms overhead, he
untangled himself and went up the stairs.

The men had smeared something on the walls. It looked
like chocolate pudding or cake frosting. Brian stood in the
kitchen for quite a while, unsure what to do. The aura he'd
seen briefly had gone away too, as if sucked out through the
broken window over the sink.

He knew he couldn't stay there any longer. Dr. Haak

would think he'd made the mess. Or the men would come back when he wasn't on the lookout. And in either case, he would end up getting a double dose of the rod of correction.

He knew it was for his own good. Dr Haak always told him that when she plugged him in, and usually it wasn't too bad. Usually it pushed him through the wall and then he'd be able to bring her back his gift from the Other Side. But he didn't want to see the look on her face when she saw the mess. He didn't want to hear her yell and call him names.

He dug through the wreckage on the countertop, found the toaster, and tucking it under his arm, went outside. He looked right into the sun. He stood on her gravel driveway facing east and let the sun fill him to the brim with fire and light.

The sun was hissing, all the tiny particles of light making their sound as they went through the air and into his eyes and stored themselves up—like bright coins in a piggy bank—somewhere deep inside him.

He felt himself tipping over. He knew he didn't want to fall down and lie there in the dirt all day until the doctor came home. So he shut his eyes, like shutting off a switch. But the sunlight was still inside him, stored up like a battery, enough for him to run on for quite a while.

He needed to head west, toward the place where the sun went down every night. He turned away from the sun and climbed into the pine woods. Soon the trees blocked out all the direct light. But at least for the time being, he had his direction.

Still with the toaster under his arm, like a football player running through enemy lines, he picked his way up the slope. Very soon Dr. Haak's house and her road were hidden from view. Very soon he was all alone in the woods.

He hiked most of the morning. The pines gave way to trees with smooth white bark and then oaks heavy with acorns. They were more widely spaced. The underbrush thinned out to low weeds and patches of green creepers. The terrain got steeper for a while, then leveled off and he walked along a ridge top for a long distance, a deep ravine to one side. He tried to head due west, but the way the streams ran made this impossible.

When the sun was directly overhead, he came upon a packed dirt road and followed it.

But seeing a house in the distance and hearing the sound of a lawn mower, he pushed off again into the woods.

He was getting hungry. He knew there were things he could eat in the woods, but he also knew there were things which were poisonous. And he had no idea how to tell one from the other.

Taking a brief rest, he tipped his toaster upside down and shook a few burnt crumbs into his hand. They were barely enough to taste. He knew if he sat down right there and gave up, no one would ever find him. He'd end up a skeleton, picked clean by little animals. A nice white skeleton sitting against a tall tree with a toaster under his arm. But that would mean he'd never see Dr. Haak again.

He looked for the sun. The clouds had been building in the sky all day and he wasn't sure where it was. A breeze had picked up as he stood there, and somewhere nearby two huge old trees rubbed their trunks together, creaking and moaning like animals. He knew that if he stood in one place absolutely still for a long enough time, then squirrels and rabbits would come out of their hiding places. He thought of making a trap out of the toaster, maybe hooking it up so some little creature would get his foot stuck inside and then get cooked because Brian didn't want to eat red, raw meat. That came to him as he was lying in the heap of old clothes: he couldn't eat blood or uncooked meat.

"Red equals west," he said as the sun tried a little harder and showed itself to him. "The west is the best." He set out again, traveling down a steep slope and then following the path of a dry streambed.

Soon he came on another road, this one paved, and walked along the shoulder, keeping his eyes fixed on the point where it disappeared around a curve. After Brian had gone around the bend and found a new spot to focus his attention on, a pickup truck roared past. It was hours later when the next car went by.

Near supper time, when all the others at the Red House would be getting their plastic trays, the road widened to two lanes and cars began to pass him in either direction. Still he'd seen no buildings since noon. But he knew that they were near. Groups of people, maybe even hundreds of them, were gathered somewhere at the end of the road. He wanted to cut off into the woods again, but the road headed due west and that was his direction.

He passed a sign that said something about a resort and a campground, then saw a little building made out of logs. A plaster Indian chief stood out in front, holding up his hand as if to stop traffic. A few cars were parked near the store, all of them with travel trailers hooked on the back.

Brian kept going, walking steadily until he saw the sun close to the horizon. Soon it would be the longest day of the year. He'd heard Vinnie, back at the Red House, talking about that. Vinnie said that soon the sun would be turning and heading away from the earth. This made Brian uneasy, but he knew it happened every year and nothing bad came of it.

By the time that shadows were thick and strong, Brian had come to a place where squat clapboard houses were built in groups. He smelled a body of water, a river or a lake. He felt cool air rising from it and moving through the trees.

A carload of teenagers went past shouting and laughing. One of them threw a beer bottle at Brian. It shattered on the ground in front of him, and he bent to inspect the shards. A big light on the cabin across the street made the glass sparkle. He looked down at the glass until the pattern was clear and then did as it told him to do.

He went down a gravel driveway, cut through a few yards, and came to the edge of the lake. On the far shore lights were on, a string of yellow pinpricks. A motorboat was out there in the darkness, buzzing like an angry hornet. Loud music came from a building right at the water's edge. People were inside, eating and drinking. He looked in the first parked car he came to and saw a package of cough drops in the backseat. The window was rolled down. He stuck his arm in and grabbed the cough drops. They were all in his mouth in a moment, a gummy mass of lemon-flavored sugar. From inside the bar came the sound of drums and a steady, thumping bass. Brian started to do the jerk, but he stopped himself. This was no time to be getting down. There was work to be done still.

In the far corner of the lot, a van was parked. Words were painted in fancy script along the side. On the top was a clear plastic dome. Coming closer, he saw that there also was a painting airbrushed on the van. It showed a group of vans all pulled up to a moonlit lake, like animals come to a midnight watering hole. Brian was getting the feeling. His cough drops were all gone by then, a pool of syrup at the pit of his stomach. There might be food inside the van. Sometimes people traveled on vacation in the vans and slept in them. Sometimes they were people's homes.

He peeked in the driver's side and saw a bag of cheese curls. Quickly, Brian was inside, sitting behind the wheel, stuffing the salty snacks into his mouth.

When he was full and had washed the gritty orange paste out of his mouth with a can of lukewarm cream soda he found on the dashboard, he relaxed and looked into the back. The van was a conversion job, outfitted with shiny black vinyl trim and iridescent greenish fur on the floor. A mirror ball hung from the ceiling. On the left side of the compartment was a bar crammed with bottles and glasses. And on the right was a small closet locker, also covered with leatherette, which contained a sound system and racks of audiocassettes.

In the rear were two huge loudspeakers. They too were encased in the smooth vinyl, but their faces were open, the insides exposed. The woofers were big enough to beat his heart into submission. The tweeters were strong enough to pierce his eardrums, if that was necessary.

He got out of the driver's seat and looked through the cassettes. It was mostly dance music, names and titles that were unfamiliar to Brian. He pulled a cassette out of its plastic box and stroked his fingertip over the inch or two of exposed tape, as if reading the message encoded there. The cover showed a high-platform shoe with flames erupting around the sole. Brian ran his finger under the title. "Disco Inferno," he said, as if reading from scripture.

He turned on the amplifier and slid the tape into place. He heard the music before the tape started moving. The bass was thumping in his spinal zone. Chicken scratch guitars worked their way out of a dark corner. Then the music slammed out of the speakers, knocking Brian against the wall. He crawled over the thick fake-fur carpet and turned the volume up a notch. It hurt. It went right through him, like a shock wave. Luckily he had the windows rolled up.

Luckily the owner had the walls well insulated when it was converted. That way Brian had the music all for himself, punching and yanking at him, making him do the Do.

He felt around the base of the engine cowl, a rounded lump between the two seats. Unfastening the two latches, he lifted the cowl away, revealing the engine. Though little light came into the van from outside he could see the battery half hidden under a jumble of wires and vacuum hoses. With the voices now hitting hard on his brain stem, Brian licked one fingertip and touched it to the negative terminal. The singer said, "Burn, baby, burn." Brian licked another finger and laid that on the positive post.

He felt the jolt rip through his arm, across his chest, and out the opposite hand. It was good but not good enough. "Minding my business, doing my jerk, come on now, bay-bay, everybody get to work." Brian was doing it, but he wasn't satisfied. He looked around for his toaster, tore out the cord, and quickly cleaned the wire ends to two small spikes. Then he tore the plug end off and wound the bare metal leads around the battery posts. He brought the free ends together and a blue spark jumped the gap.

Brian pulled the black rubber rivets out of the back of his neck, and as the congas and claves and agong-gongs meshed together into a network of pure rhythm, he jabbed the two spikes into his shunt.

"Big business, owww! Say it, say it!" This time there was no Ollie or Dr. Haak to say it, and he was stuck in the loop, cold fire erupting as he went toward the wall.

It's there, a red rash on his skin, a red flush like Dr. Haak just before taking a hit off Brian's main line. It's surrounding him, tight and hot, cooking him down to his essence.

He's cutting, boring like a drill bit in soft white wood. Curls come out the back, smoke goes up, scorch marks and hot torque pushing on the pressure point one more time, he goes through. To the Other Side.

He's the Funky Worm in the land of Ictus. Everything's hot and bothered on this side of the wall. Lights flash off the dance floor to give him the latest steps. He's slamming in the groove, Mr. Sex Worm with a bad attitude. Somebody's singing, "Give it to me, give it to me," and he goes for the vein, drilling into the flesh.

In the Ictus he can touch everybody from the inside, boring like a worm in an apple. They all love him and he loves them. "Welcome, welcome, Funky Worm." Everybody wants to be his host. They all want him and he wants them.

"Ride on home through your baby's mainline." That's his message now coming fresh from the floor. They all take their places for the conga line, and they're not disappointed. Sex Worm is at the head, leading them in and out and in and out until they're tangled in a huge knot.

All of the saints from the long, cold hallway are on his side now, getting down and dirty like they did one thousand years before. In the dark dark ages, the dark dark disco days when the sun never came up and people danced until they died and went directly into the Ictus. They marched from town to town with skulls on sticks and skulls painted on their clothes and beating bones of martyrs on drums made of human skin. They danced their funky doom from town to town, spreading the news. Dance-o-mania for the final days. Black plague was cooking in the ground, turning babies into monsters and the air into stinking smoke. The bubbling germ was in the ground and coming out. Saint Brinor's dancers were dead on the downbeat, making his kingdom come and working the skull-funk magic.

And now Brian's leading the new new new St. Vitus troupe inside the Ictus. Where the music never stops and everybody's a fine and shiny sex machine. He's got his wild saints heading from town to town with the message that you just can't say no to: Get in line, get on down, get it together, get off that hot squat, get your cool unit working and do the Bri-nor jerk.

He's coast to coast in this land of endless funk. Live from inside his skull transmitting on the frequency that anybody can receive. Door to door, trick or treat, dance or die. He's sending out the beam: one hundred thousand watts of clear channel power, but still there's one station who won't carry his signal. It's H.A.A.K. He can't find her anywhere on the dial. She won't open her head and let him in.

His saints are flying six feet off the ground along the dead, broken streets looking in every window, peeking through the crack under every door, and still they got no sign of her. No silhouette behind a window shade. No whiff of that perfume she generates every time she's hooked up body and soul to Mr. Funky Sex Worm. No scorched footprints on the pavement where she walked or glistening trails in the dark air where she passed. He starts screaming her name, like a siren rising from the top of his spinal tower, a shriek with her name mixed into its rising and falling.

He screams like a baby, hungry and wet and tired. He screams for her and no one else, but still she won't answer.

When he woke, he was behind the steering wheel of the van, somewhere in a dense pine forest. The sun was just on the horizon, milky light streaming past the black tree trunks.

There were no buildings anywhere in sight. He knew he'd traveled a long distance from the lake and the bar. The air inside the van was stale, as though he'd been breathing out fever exhaust all night, burning the air itself, as he'd burned the air in the Ictus.

He rolled down the window and heard birds singing.

Where his hands had been, clamped tightly on the steering wheel, were two sodden, matted spots, the green fur soaking in his sweat.

Somewhere, somebody was very upset, wondering where his van had gone off to. Dr. Haak was worried too, maybe even crying. And even Ollie was thinking about Brian, not awake yet from his shocks and burns but still alive, resting up like a seed under the ground.

The engine cowl was still lifted back. Brian ran his fingers over the curves and shafts of steel, over the wires and hoses and belts. He wondered how the van had known where to take him. It seemed so dead then, just cold, greasy metal. But last night it had been alive, responding to him just like Dr. Haak responded to him, linked by the cable.

The slot where the key went was broken off, and a small loop of wire hung from the hole. Brian poked with the wire, trying all of the flat silver contacts, and after a few tries he got the engine to turn over.

He fastened his seat belt, put the van in gear, and backed onto the road.

9

Dr. Haak had come to Marx and spilled what she claimed to be the whole story. "They might have all the right credentials and work for people at the top of the hierarchy, but they're still animals. I know what they'll do with Brian if they get their hands on him. I've had dealings with them before." She was talking nonstop about Price and Whitehead, ranting as Marx drove with her through Osric and out to her house.

At times during her harangue, it seemed that she just hated them, simple intense dislike. But at other times her reaction to them was far more complicated. She was clearly afraid of the two, going on at great length about some other doctor, Janes or Jones, who had refused to turn over some of the experimental data he'd collected while working with a twelve-year-old synesthetic. "It was worse than a smear campaign," she said. "They had photos of him in bed with the patient. Tapes recordings. They had so-called witnesses to his so-called crimes. It was like a witch hunt. I'm surprised they didn't burn him at the stake for heresy."

Dr. Haak had apparently gone home that day, found her

place ransacked and the boy gone, and sped back to the Red House. She'd gone right to Marx's office and laid out the whole situation. Now as they drove through the thickening pine forests, she shed her professional cool like a stripper shedding her clothes, giving him glimpses of her real self.

"I had a run-in with them a few years ago," she went on. "Someone high up in the chain of command had decided to infiltrate a spy into the staff. We assumed that they were just looking for minor infractions and abuses. But soon enough Price and Whitehead showed up and started putting the screws on us, demanding all our data and wanting private interviews with the subjects. I refused and they went over my head. As far as I know, they never actually got to Brian that time. God knows what they would have done with him if they had. I hid him down in the isolation wards and moved all his files so they couldn't get a hold of them."

She spoke as if a martyr, the forces of evil conspiring to persecute her and her alone.

She took one hand off the steering wheel and grasped his knee. For a moment she looked him in the eye, not paying any attention to the road. "So you see why I need your help." Actually, he didn't see anything except a large delivery truck barreling down the road at them. He tried to grab the wheel to pull the car back into the right lane, but she deftly maneuvered around the truck without looking directly ahead. "I can't go to Dr. Brule. As far as I know, he's on their side too. All he cares about is his pension and that idiotic award. And I can't really trust the others. They're all too weak." Her hand rose up his thigh, fingernails raking the coarse weave of his pant leg.

She spoke of the rest of the staff with disdain: "Swenson had to be transferred. Did you see her file in with the disciplinary cases? She was working with suicides. She had the idea that they could better come to terms with their desire for death if they reenacted some of the events in their miserable lives. Sexual trauma, beatings, drug abuse, the whole sordid mess. But it wasn't just play-acting. Dixon, the last security man, found her and two of her girls down in one of the sub-basements doing some kind of baptism with the blood of a stray dog. Rumor had it that they'd been mixed up with a cult before being referred to the Red House. I don't think Dr. Brule ever found out about the incident. Dixon agreed not to report it if Swenson just got out of his jurisdiction. A few months later, he was transferred out too.''

She pulled her hand away from his leg to take the next curve. She didn't bother with the brake, squealing around the bend in a cloud of dust and gravel. "So you've just got to help me. That's all there is to it.''

It didn't seem that he had much of a choice, at least until he got out of her car.

She tore up the driveway to her house and swung the car around next to the front porch.

She'd left the place just as she'd found it. She hadn't exaggerated how bad the mess was. He tried to imagine what it had looked like before it was sacked. He tried to picture Dr. Haak living out there in the woods, but the different versions of herself that she'd presented to him didn't jibe. The Dr. Haak he'd first met at the Red House—cold, haughty, emotionless—seemed to be a different person than the woman who'd erupted into his office, demanding vengeance. She poked at the piles of spilled food. She righted one of the kitchen chairs and sat down. Her tone of voice changed; she seemed close to tears.

"I worked so long on this project. And as soon as things were going smoothly, they had to show up." She dipped her finger into a pool of applesauce on the table. "He'll starve to death in the woods. He can't get along by himself.''

Marx allowed himself to get a good look at her, now that her wildness had subsided for a moment. Vulnerable that way, almost helpless, she had a charm that was beginning to wear Marx down. Crazy women, always crazy women he found himself involved with.

"So what is it that you need from me?''

"We've got to find him," she said. "Every minute we spend here, he gets farther away.''

"Where do we start looking?''

She shrugged and sat limply, staring at a little lake of liquified ice cream.

He tried again: "What can you tell me about the boy?

Maybe that'll give us a place to start. Where would he go if he was running away?''

"Nowhere. He has absolutely nowhere to go." Her eyes were closed. Her hands were like lifeless stone in her lap.

"But maybe he thinks—"

"I said 'nowhere'!" she shouted at him. "Didn't you hear me? He's helpless. He doesn't have the first idea of where he is. Until two days ago, he hadn't been outside the walls of the hospital for a whole decade." As quickly as her hysteria erupted, it faded. She sank back into the chair, burying her head in her hands.

They sat silently together for a while, then Marx got up and made a brief inspection of the house. The mattress in one of the bedrooms had been slit open and the stuffing pulled out. Food had been thrown about in the hallway. It was already starting to go bad, a faint sickly odor noticeable in the air.

By then the sky's light had mostly drained away into darkness. Marx looked down the cellar stairs and tried the light switch. The basement remained black. Next he tried the lights in the kitchen and they too failed to come on.

"The fuses are blown," Dr. Haak said, lifting her head from her hands. "Everything was turned on when I got here: stove, mixer, refrigerator. It's a wonder he didn't kill himself or burn the house down."

He told her he'd go down and replace the fuses, but she shook her head. "I used the last one. We'll have to do without."

She got up and searched under the kitchen sink. After pulling out cleaning supplies, paper bags, and a shoe box full of plumbing parts, she found a small metal can. She pried the lid off and quickly had the Sterno burning. The fumes went directly to his head. Oil-based paint, gasoline, any petrochemical product affected him the same way. He'd read in a magazine about neuro-toxins and assumed that anything that gave him such a woozy, poisoned feeling must be eating away at his brain tissue.

The small reddish flame held the shadows back for a while, but eventually night came in all around them, like the tide rising, filling the house.

They sat on kitchen chairs with the canned heat on the

floor between them like a tiny campfire. The light softened the lines of her face. She relaxed as the darkness grew, and the frantic edge disappeared from her voice.

She started telling him about herself. At first there was some hesitancy, but soon she found the thread she wanted to follow. ''I wasn't in ECT research at first. That was my husband's field. He'd worked with Goldfarb and Russell. Mostly limbic system work. There's even a small node of nerve tissue in the amygdala named after him.'' She laughed softly. ''The Haak body, it's called. As far as we know, it has the function of regulating nerve impulses out of one of the pleasure centers. Sort of a limiter, like those things they put on rental cars to keep drivers from going too fast. Some people have Haak body dysfunction. Their experience of pleasure is off the scale, so to speak.'' She laughed again, a soft, self-mocking laugh. Once again it struck him how beautiful she was. And once again he found himself reconciled to his situation: drawn to a woman whose semblance of sanity was rapidly disappearing.

''How much of what you told me about the boy is true?''

She ignored the question for the moment, telling him a few more facts about her work that were too technical for him to understand. But she did wind her way back to his question. ''My husband was working at a psychiatric hospital upstate, in Niagara County. I was still in school, at the U. of R. med center. At first I wanted to work in one of the softer branches, nothing so technical as ECT. Can you believe that at one time I was actually a believer in Jungian analysis? Of course, med school cured me of that. And then I met Charley and my interests veered toward his. A lot of research that I used for my post-graduate work was really his. It made it easier to get into a good program.''

Marx could tell she was coming around to Brian eventually. He waited for her to find the right place to bring the boy into the story.

''Do you know what schizotaxia is?'' Of course he didn't. ''The idea has become outmoded, but there are still a few people interested in it. Back when Charley was at Niagara County, he was working with it, trying to get some hard evidence rather than just conjecture.'' She paused, got up, and looked in the refrigerator. At the back was a half-empty bottle of vodka, by then room temperature. She took a swig and handed Marx the bottle across the fire. He too drank, enjoying the acidlike trail that moved downward from his mouth to his stomach. It made a perfect combination: neurotoxins, a witch doctor, and alcohol.

"Schizotaxia," she started again, as if reading from a dictionary, "is a basic neurological impairment of the ability to integrate thoughts and emotions. It's often characterized by thought disorders and anhedonia." She took another drink. "Anhedonia is the inability to feel pleasure. Charley was working with a a few rather modest cases of what he thought was schizotaxia. Then we met and his work took a slightly different direction.

"Not long after that, Brian arrived at the hospital. The police had found him living near a chemical waste dump in Niagara Falls. Various people worked with him, labeling him everything from paranoid schizophrenic to mentally retarded to just plain old-fashioned demon possessed. He didn't respond very well to anyone's pet theories, and after a while Charley ended up with him."

A breeze had picked up as she'd spoken. Marx heard newspapers rattling. A cold draft came in under the door and went out through a broken window. Dr. Haak stood up; her voice was louder then.

"Charley was a little too bold, a little too reckless and sure of himself. I was a widow a month after we were married."

Marx moved closer to the fire. He concentrated on the little pool of liquid flame.

"It took me another year to finish up my degree. Then I did a fellowship with Willhorn in Boston. But I didn't forget about Brian. he'd been transferred to Mt. Kinnsvort by then. I didn't have any trouble finding a position there. The director was thrilled to have someone as well regarded as the wonderful Dr. Caroline Haak on his staff."

She made a sound that might have been a laugh.

"And then Brian and I were together again. Only this time I knew considerably more than I had as a graduate student. I knew what I wanted and I knew how to get it. I didn't make the same mistake as Charley. I took my time. I worked with other subjects, saving Brian for the time when all the bugs would be ironed out. But somehow Price and Whitehead found out. Somebody relayed that information back to them and now Brian is gone.''

She paused, looking intently at the fire, as if trying to read a message in the flickering light. When she began again, her voice had the matter-of-fact tone to it again. She started explaining Brian's color taboos and the behaviors that went along with them. ''Red is the most common. Probably twice a week. Then green and white. Then clear, black, and orange. Sometimes one will go on for a few days, but usually they change every morning. It's just delusional behavior, like all his talk of going through the wall and zooming around in the Ictus.''

Marx was listening, trying to follow her words, but his attention kept flagging. The air was too heavy, the light too low, her presence was too much to allow for clarity of thought. She had him hooked, and he wasn't sure if she was even trying.

''He has humors to go with the colors also. Red is blood, of course. White is milk. Green is phlegm. Purple I haven't figured out yet. Yellow is bile. Clear is water. And black is funk. I don't know where he got the system from, but it's definitely based on the medieval idea of the four humors. They were supposed to determine an individual's personality. But Brian's change almost every day.''

Her voice dwindled to nothing and she stood with her hands cupped over the fire. He half expected her to dip them in and hold out a handful of flame for him. If he'd never seen her back at the hospital in her white coat and with her hair neatly bound, he might have thought her to be one of the inmates. She could easily have been a woman escaped from the Red House, haunting the house where she'd lived years before.

They rose together. Marx nudged the can of flame with his foot and the fire almost died. Dr. Haak began to unfasten the buttons on her dress, working downward from her neck. Marx waited as she stripped off another layer of defense. The buttons down her front came away. The dress hung loose from her shoulders, a *V* of bareness—painted red by the fire—reaching to her navel.

She began murmuring, a low chantlike sound. As her

dress fell away, as she stepped out of the pile of clothing and came at him, the chant grew louder, but still he understood none of the words. She was singing to him, and the voice went directly through him, knocking loose cobwebs and setting up reverberations that did not die away.

Marx was naked quickly. She led him away from the fire, down the hall to one of the bedrooms. Together they cleared the books and jumbled clothing off the mattress. The bed creaked as she sat down.

The room had only one window. A sickle moon was just visible through the trees. It acted more as a beacon than a source of light.

She was humming in the darkness, murmuring the words that she'd learned from the boy. But Marx wasn't paying attention to her voice. His hand found her leg. He slid it upward, then felt her hair brushing against his face. She drew closer and soon they were knotted like greased cables, shifting slowly against each other in the watery, almost imperceptible moonlight.

10

The next morning she went directly to Dr. Simonsen's suite and made small talk with him as he set up one of his subjects for another bout with his new fever-inducing agent. They traded gossip about Dr. Brule, and she mentioned that she'd seen hardly anything of the director since Price and Whitehead had arrived there. "I suppose they must have connections higher up than they've been letting on. Brule seems terrified of them."

Dr. Simonsen grunted a noncommittal reply and went on hooking his subject in. She was an old woman, thin and gray and barely conscious. Dr. Simonsen fastened her into a high-backed chair. Her head was held upright by a web belt that fastened across her face.

"So, you haven't had much contact with them?" she asked.

"Who?"

"Price and Whitehead. I thought maybe they'd been poking around here too."

"No, not really. I guess they looked in once. They weren't very interested." He jabbed a needle into the woman's arm and squeezed in a dose of milky-white fluid. He went to the monitor board and read through her vital signs. "I thought they were just here to keep an eye on Saul. He could certainly use some help with the kid still missing." Dr. Simonsen was staring raptly at the computer screen, watching the progress of the woman's fever. Hunched over that way, the back of his neck was exposed from the top joint of his spine to the base of his skull.

Dr. Haak stepped forward and pulled her hand out of her pocket. She slammed a plastic ampule against the side of Dr. Simonsen's neck, the dozens of tiny needles pushing the contents into his bloodstream. He turned away from the console, clutching at her, trying to speak, but already the drug was taking effect. His voice came out a thin squeak. His hands were numb and useless. Quick paralysis spread throughout his body. After a few moments he crumpled to the floor, his limbs twisted at awkward angles.

"I don't like it when people lie to me, Martin," she said. "Especially about such important matters. It didn't take very much work to find out you were the one who called in my friends Price and Whitehead." Dr. Simonsen was trying to speak, to deny the accusations. "I had a little talk with Saul last night. He mentioned a few things that made it all come clear. Were you afraid of having your funding cut? Or did you want a bigger piece of the pie? Maybe a few dozen subjects to work on, or the directorship here once Brule retires? So you gave my friends the news that Brian and I had finally succeeded in going through the wall. Isn't that right?" He tried to shake his head, but could only manage to open his mouth slightly and emit a faint mewl.

She kicked him in the stomach, then knelt so that he could see her more clearly. "You knew this was my life's work, Martin. And you went squealing to them anyway. You decided to threaten the most important thing in my life just so that you could get a few steps higher up the ladder."

She kicked him again, aiming for his groin. His breath came in stifled gasps. She liked the sound.

The woman in the chair was looking down at him. She didn't seem alarmed, not even surprised, as though it was perfectly normal for the staff there to be poisoning and kicking each other and making strange accusations.

Dr. Haak read quickly through the notes on the monitor table, then went to the refrigerated cabinet where Dr. Simonsen's serums were kept. She found a hypodermic and filled it with three times the dosage he'd been using on his subjects. Holding the needle in front of his face, she said, "What do you think, Martin? Will this do the trick?"

He knew what was happening, but couldn't move, not even to shake his head.

She rolled back his sleeve, pumped the serum into him, then reloaded the needle with an equal amount, and injected that into the opposite arm.

She didn't need sophisticated monitors to see the result. Very quickly his face became flushed, then dark red, glowing with fever. Sweat coated his skin and his eyes rapidly took on a filmy appearance, like partially cooked eggs.

"You should have known better, Martin. It's always a bad idea to go behind somebody's back, especially someone who thought they were your friend. I'm very, very disappointed in you." She kicked him a few more times, but then drew back. She didn't want to leave any sign of a struggle.

She went to his computer and typed in a few notes. They were cryptic but not so cryptic that someone looking over them wouldn't take them to mean that Dr. Simonsen had finally decided that the serum was safe enough to use on himself.

When she turned back, he looked like a piece of pottery that had been left too long in the kiln. Under the scarlet glow his skin had taken on an ashen hue. His tongue poked out between his lips. It was already becoming dry and brittle.

She got up from the terminal and said, "You know, Martin, I never told you this, but I always thought this whole train of thought would come to a bad end. It seemed like a mistake from the first time I heard about it." She touched his forehead and then his hand. The fever was still burning, but would soon run its course. Once his basic functions had begun to break down, his body wouldn't be able to keep the fires going.

"And you weren't very good in bed either," she said. "Actually, I hardly felt a thing. It was nothing, absolutely nothing."

She wanted to kneel by him and lay a wet kiss on his seared lips. She wanted to feel the scorched breath hissing in and out of his mouth, but she restrained herself. It would have been ten times, a hundred times less than one little spark from Brian's shunt.

"And by the way, Jean has been having an affair with one of the men in town for about a year now. I think it's the one who drives the pickup with the bullhorns on the roof. Do you know who I mean?" Mrs. Simonsen was a small, frail, bloodless woman. The idea of her having an affair with a hard-drinking yokel seemed a bit ridiculous. But if Dr. Simonsen heard and it made his death a little more miserable, it was fine. Dr. Haak nodded to the old woman in the chair, told her that an orderly would be along in an hour or two to undo the straps, and headed toward the infirmary.

She liked to think that she hadn't lost her looks in the years since med school. And the fact that she could still bring men to their knees with a minimum of effort seemed to confirm this. She was sure that at first Charley Haak had thought of her as just one more fringe benefit of having a position at a large teaching hospital. He came in twice a week, driving from Rochester to Niagara Falls on the Thruway, and had his pick of the young hopefuls there. Their first time in bed had probably been no different for him than any of a dozen other such encounters.

Except that she hadn't given up. She had her hooks in him, if only by the very tips, and she wasn't going to let him go. She claimed what was hers, and soon enough not only had he given up the pursuit of other young women, but he had taken her on as his research assistant.

They'd met during a seminar he had given. She'd heard of his work in the field of anhedonia and limbic system dysfunction, and sought him out. She sat in the front row of the little lecture hall, skirt high on her thighs, lips painted scarlet, eyes following him without blinking. Shortly he was aware of the new prospect waiting for him and had hurried through the lecture to get at her.

In bed with him, she was fierce, almost maniacal, as though trying to break through some unseen barrier. She had him body and soul, but she managed the whole episode so that he could hang onto his belief that he was the aggressor and not she.

At first she thought of him as just another tool to work with, a way of getting closer to what she wanted. But over time something like affection grew in her. He gave her privileged information, opportunities, a long head start into the world of real neurological research. And she was his willing subject, a worst-case scenario to test his theories on. But there was something else that bound them. Even after the first excited experiments and the disappointment that followed, they remained together. It became clear to her that they were not going to solve her problems in one simple step, like yanking out a tooth or lancing a boil. It would be a long, difficult process. She allowed him to keep trying, working at her like a miner searching for a vein of gold deep in the earth.

It made things easier for them that she could feel no pleasure. Her anhedonia colored their entire life together. Beyond the lab, beyond the research and scientific exploration, she was still fundamentally a woman who could feel nothing. It gave a melancholic flavor to their times in bed, as though she were blind and being forced to look directly into the sun.

He implanted the shunt in the back of her neck a few months after they met. It sealed their relationship, like giving her his class ring to wear. Up until that time his primary work had been with rats and rhesus monkeys. He'd found a way to easily stimulate their pleasure centers, but with humans the situation was far more complicated. He could have wired her up and run current directly into her septum pelucidum. He could have fitted her with IVs and catheters and kept up a stream of intense pleasure, like a sleeping beauty laid out in a steady, endless orgasm. But what she had in mind was a more organic, more natural solution to the problem.

And beyond that there was the question of safety. He'd devised an apparatus whereby rats could press a lever in order to give themselves a shot to their pleasure centers. Over half the subjects had remained in a state of pleasure shock, refusing—or forgetting—to eat or drink until they died of dehydration.

So first came her shunt. And then he instructed her how to implant one in his nervous system. She'd had enough basic surgical training to do the actual cuts and splices, and with his tutoring, going over diagrams and X rays and working through test runs on monkeys, she was ready.

Except for one other researcher at the med center, a Dr. Fine, whom she'd never met, Charley had never discussed specifics of his work with anyone else. This Dr. Fine had been a kind of mentor for Charley, but as his work and his life seemed to revolve more and more around her, he'd slowly severed his ties with his old partner.

After the last trial run on a cadaver, hooking into its pleasure center and firing current to test the connections, they decided that she was ready. It was late in May, during a week of unusually hot weather. They knew the time was fast approaching when she'd have to open him up unassisted and bury the shunt in the tissue of his spine. They decided on a date, when they were sure few people would be in the hospital wing where he had his lab. All of the details had been worked out. They just needed to wait a few more days until the appointed time.

They were sitting in his apartment in front of a fan. He was naked. All she had on was one of his T-shirts. The fan stirred the heavy air, but did little to cool them. They sat there in silence for a while, then she mentioned what she'd been thinking about for weeks.

"You might die," she said.

He shook his head.

"What am I going to do if I make a mistake? I can't just call up emergency and tell them I botched an operation."

"You'll be fine. Everything will go perfectly." His hand was on her leg, glued there with sweat.

"It could happen, Charley. And then all your work, everything will be lost. If you die, I'll just be a research assistant. I've got no claim to your papers. Everything, the hard-wiring, the schematics, will be property of the hospital, or even the state."

"I don't want Jerry Fine getting his hands on it," he said at last. "If anything goes wrong, I want you to continue my work. You deserve it, not him."

And so they decided to get married. They had the blood

test done that night, took care of the marriage license the next day, and had a justice of the peace officiate.

They went the next night to the lab as husband and wife. That part of the wing was dark and empty. Somewhere down the hall monkeys were screaming, but as they shut the heavy door on his lab, the last traces of the sound were sealed out. The table and tools had all been prepared ahead of time. He'd shaved a spot on the back of his head and run the preliminary tests already. She opened him up just as she had the monkeys and cadavers. She traced out the pattern of nerves and veins. She followed his instructions exactly and fitted the shunt just where it was designed to fit. She ran a few quick tests and then sewed him up, leaving only a slight bulge under the skin and two raw red holes.

She performed the operation flawlessly, and except for a few hours of low-level fever afterward, he had no adverse effects. It had taken her a few weeks to heal after he'd implanted her shunt. His took awhile longer, but by the end of June he was ready for her.

The scabs had fallen away, leaving two small holes about the size of those left by a snake bite.

She'd been bringing equipment—piece by piece—back to the apartment during the weeks after the operation. By the time he was healed, she had the entire apparatus operational. It was crude and ungainly, transformers and circuit boards jury-rigged in gunmetal boxes, controls and dials connected to the cables with black electrical tape. It was midsummer's night when everything was finally in place. They came to the bed, took off their clothes, hooked themselves into the system, and ten minutes later, Charley Haak was dead.

They'd succeeded in finally getting her to break through the barrier. They sent a hot shot into her pleasure center, and for the first time in her life she'd felt pure, unmitigated sexual pleasure. But she was either too strong for him, or the equipment was not calibrated correctly, or it was just the inevitable last act of their life together. When she finally felt the fireball exploding inside her, she let loose an equal discharge through the cable, past his shunt, and into his brain. He died hot, sweaty, and charred in the arms of his wife.

She thought of it as an overload, though the exact nature of his death was never determined. She was in no state to analyze the evidence. Because she had finally made it through the wall, wrenching her outside herself, it was quite awhile before her mind returned to more ordinary matters. By then Charley was starting to cool off. He'd thrashed beneath her, gasping, but she'd barely noticed. When she was finally back in the real world, he was starting to stiffen. His eyes were wide open, blank and lifeless. The muscles in his face were already beginning to go rigid, pulling his mouth into a lopsided smile.

She untangled herself from the wires, unplugged her shunt, and went to call Dr. Fine. She was numb, unthinking. She went about the job at hand as if cleaning up after a party. She pulled the wires out of the back of her husband's head, wrestled a pair of shorts and a T-shirt on him, and dragged him out of the bedroom.

A half an hour later there came a knock on the door, and she realized that she was still naked. She threw on a bathrobe and went to open the door. It was Dr. Fine. He was a middleaged man, bland in all respects. He might have been a family dentist or accountant. They didn't bother with small talk or explanations.

Supporting Charley under the shoulders, they carried him down to his car, as if helping a drunken friend home. Dr. Fine drove off with the body and she was left alone again, feeling still the echoes of the eruptions in her pleasure center. Taking off the bathrobe, she went back to bed. She lay there for hours, replaying in her mind Charley's death and her rebirth.

The next day she was informed that her husband had been found shot in the back of the head in his lab. The story that the police chose to believe was that a junky had broken into the lab looking for drugs, found Dr. Haak there, and killed him in his panic. The matter was taken care of quickly. The funeral was brief and poorly attended. She moved out of the apartment and took a long sabbatical. She didn't know where her husband was buried. She'd never seen Dr. Fine since the night Charley had died. Later, she heard through a colleague that the lab had been very thoroughly ransacked by the intruder.

Ollie was in a private room in the infirmary, and though still unable to get out of bed, he was making progress. He'd had a small amount of memory loss after the accident, but

his burns were healing nicely and Dr. Lorenzo thought he'd
be able to start in the physical therapy room soon.

Dr. Haak greeted the nurse in charge and closed the door
behind herself, going into Ollie's room. She went to the bed
and took Ollie's hand, patting it as she spoke:

"How are you feeling today? Betty says you're really
coming along."

He recognized her and tried to pull his hand away.

"Come on, Ollie, I thought we were friends."

His voice came out a croak: "I didn't tell anyone."

She lay her bag on the side table and rooted around inside. He'd seen her carry the rod of correction disassembled
in the bag. He tried to reposition himself to get a better
view of what she was doing. His eyes were bright, as though
he'd been crying. He tried to speak again, but no sound
would come out of his mouth.

"You didn't tell anybody what?"

She leaned over him, pressing her stethoscope against his
chest. A tiny wisp of sound was transmitted through the
rubber hose to her ears.

"I won't tell. I promise." He sounded as though he was
begging. She continued to keep the other items in the bag
out of his view. "Don't worry."

"I'm not worrying, Ollie. I'm as happy as can be." She
kissed him on the forehead, then touched the tip of his nose
with her finger. "You just concentrate on getting better.
Don't worry about me."

She packed her equipment, and after giving his hand another squeeze, she left. The nurse at the desk smiled as she
went past. Winston was coming down the hall, perhaps to
visit Ollie. She nodded a greeting to him, and he seemed
pleased that she'd acknowledged his existence.

Upstairs, Dr. Simonsen was dead. His patient was probably still staring down at him, as if expecting him to get up,
brush himself off, and go back to the business of pumping
her full of poison.

By the time his body would be found, Dr. Haak would
be long gone, taking the last of her necessary gear with her.
By the time anyone remembered that she'd been the last one
to visit him in his lab, she'd be on the road, with all her ties
to the Red House completely severed.

11

It took Brian most of the next morning o get the car under control. He stalled it. He ran it into an embankment of plowed-up gravel. He made the engine cry and whine like a dirty baby. He laid patches of greasy black rubber on the road. He cooked up a cloud of bluish smoke and blew it out the tailpipe. But by lunchtime the van was his and doing what it was told.

He decided not to go very fast. With the orange speedometer needle pointing straight up, ugly noises came from the back of the van.

It was another red day. He needed to head west. For a while the road was cooperative, but then it started snaking and looping, and soon enough he'd lost most of the headway he'd made earlier.

He had the sound system turned way up, pumping out a solid wall of hot mix. "Skin tight, feels so right, at the break of day and the dead of night," he sang back at the speakers. And though his voice was as loud as he could make it, he still could hardly hear himself over the grunt and throb of the music. His head was in the groove. He was getting a maximum dose. "Ooh-ee!" he sang, "Say it proud, I'm back and I'm loud."

He'd look through the stack of cassettes that morning and found one called "Free Your Booty and Your Mind Will Follow." The cover was a little too much to start off the day with. It showed men with black skin and red lips and blond wigs and silver suits like astronauts. They were clearly and unmistakably getting down. Brian thought he'd save that one for later, when he needed it most. But he kept thinking about the title. He wasn't sure what his booty was, but he knew he wanted it to be free.

Before he'd gotten going that morning, he'd made a better inspection of the van. In the refrigerator he found a quart of orange juice, a six-pack of beer, and a pound of hamburger wound up in clear plastic. He'd known right at that moment that today would be a red day. The sight of the ground meat made him sick. He threw it out immediately and then went through the food cupboard. Finding a half loaf of bread, he began making dough balls for his journey. First he tore off the crusts, then he wadded the slices of bread into compact spheres about the size of marbles.

He'd gone through most of his supply when he saw a man up ahead on the road. His thumb was out and Brian knew that meant he had to stop for him. Or he was doing the hustle and trying out a new move. Either way Brian didn't have any choice but to pick him up.

His hair was thinning, and he combed it straight back over the bare spot. He had a small suitcase covered with the same checked pattern as his jacket. As soon as he was in the van, Brian pushed in the cigarette lighter and then waved the glowing red coil near his face. "Red-hot, say it, say it."

The man looked behind and saw the mirrored ball.

"Say it, say it! Red-hot."

He shrugged. "All right, I'll bite. Red-hot."

Brian relaxed. He liked the man already. The music was quiet for a second, to let them talk. But as soon as the man told him what direction he was going, it came back on, the bass drum thumping them both hard in the back of the head.

"Nice car you have here. Did you do it all yourself?"

"Do what?"

They were quiet for a while, listening to the low-down on the devil's gun. Brian pushed the lighter into its socket again, but the man shook his head. He didn't want anymore. "How about some dough balls?" Brian said. The man was hungry, he could tell. He popped one of them into his mouth. It must have tasted good. He ate another one. "There's orange juice in the back," Brian told him.

The man got out of his seat and went to the refrigerator. He came back with two cans of beer. "Do you mind?" he asked, and Brian told him to go ahead. The song ended and Brian asked him if he wanted to hear some more.

"No, that's okay. How about we take a little break?" He finished the first beer and was playing with the pop tab on the second, snapping it against the top of the can. He started drinking, and as his face got pinker, he talked more loudly.

"My name's Eddie Heck. You've probably heard of me. I was on Carson a couple of years back. And I did Merv Griffin right before he went off the air."

Brian didn't know who Carson or Merv Griffin were, or what somebody would do with them.

"My name's Brian. I was with Dr. Haak for a while, but now I'm on my own."

Eddie waited a moment, as if for further explanation, and getting none, he started in again: "No, really, I'm a comic. I was playing Gsellmeier's Resort, over on Lake Lysander. What a royal piss-hole. I hardly made enough to pay for my bus fare down here. That's why I'm traveling with Mr. Thumbo now." He made the same hitchhiking move as before. "Three shows a day for a bunch of old farts and shrivs. They wouldn't know a funny line if it took a bite out of their asses. And the moron in charge told me I had to play clean. Nothing too raunchy. How the hell am I supposed to make people laugh if I can't work dirty? That doesn't make sense." He stopped talking and looked down the road. "So where are you headed?"

"Home."

"Where's home?"

Brian pointed straight ahead. The road disappeared about a half a mile down. The hills weren't quite so high there. But the woods were still thick and green, pressing in on both sides.

"I've got to get home. How about you?"

Eddie seemed a little embarrassed. "Well, I was living for a while in Poughkeepsie. In a hotel there. That's my professional address. You know, centrally located. That's where the bookers can get me if they have some work. But I got the feeling that this may have been my last gig. Shit, I could make a lot more panhandling." He pulled out a little wad of bills. "I'd offer you some money for gas, but I really don't have it."

"That's okay," Brian said, reaching over to open the glove compartment. He pulled out a plastic wallet. Inside were ten traveler's checks still attached to their spine. "I've got plenty. It came with the van."

Eddie whistled like men do when they see women they want to kiss. He thumbed through the checks. "You mean this isn't your van?"

"Sure, it's mine. This is the traveling funk-mobile, right? It's got the mirror disco ball and speakers so big they could break the windows, and when I'm not paying attention, it knows where to go all by itself." He pointed to the engine cowl. The wire he'd taken off the toaster came out from under the cowl like a snake out of its hole. The two copper ends were like a tongue. "I've got everything I need. Why wouldn't it be mine?"

Shortly they came to a gas station. Brian pulled in and told Eddie to get some food, handing him a few of the checks. "But nothing red, all right? No cherry pop, no red suckers, no raw meat. Okay?"

Eddie came back with a large paper bag full of groceries. He tore open a bag of pretzels and handed a few to Brian. "So where exactly are you coming from? I mean, where have you been?"

Eddie seemed nice. He hadn't told Brian to do a single thing he didn't want to do. But still Brian knew that he had to keep some secrets. He didn't want anyone to know about the mess back at Dr. Haak's house. "I've been on vacation," he said. He wasn't sure what a vacation was, but it seemed that people had fun when they were on them and got to drive a long way to get there. "Red-hot funk-van dream vacation for one."

Eddie opened another can of beer, and they started off

again. "You know, when I started out in this business, it was easy for a fellow to make a decent living and not have to take these crappy jobs. I was almost on Ed Sullivan. One of his scouts caught my act at the Steel Pier, and he thought I was a real winner. But things didn't work out. Things never work out the way you think they're going to. I might have been in Vegas by now, headlining, with one hand in the till and the other up some broad's dress. And instead, look where I am, working the circuit in dog-shit heaven.

"I made some mistakes. I'll admit that. But it hasn't been all my fault. I was dealt a hand and I played it, but there's not much chance of taking the pot if all you've got are deuces and treys." Brian had no idea what he was talking about. "And my ex sure didn't make it any easier for me. God damn, she's a pain. Still chasing me for alimony, as if I've got anything to spare. Hounding me, whining and complaining all the time. Every time I get a new job, I'm afraid she's going to turn up there out in the audience, screaming about what a loser I am. Shit, I told her right up front that we might have a hard life together. It's not easy traveling all over the country, scraping up a buck here and a buck there by making people laugh."

Brian wanted to turn on the stereo again, but he knew it wouldn't be polite. He kept listening, trying to figure out what Eddie was talking about.

"You know why they fired me over at Gsellmeier's? Do you know why? Because I was working dirty. They said, 'This is supposed to be a family resort. No more dirty jokes.' Well, what other kind of joke is there? That's what I want to know. Shit, they kicked me out without even paying for the work I did there. 'You got your room and board,' they said. 'We'll call it even.' They claimed I was scaring folks away. But everybody knows people go to the clubs to hear dirty jokes, right? If they want to hear clean ones, they can stay at home."

They drove a while longer, and Brian finally found a road that headed due west, though it was only one lane and at times it dwindled down to gravel and loose sand. Eddie wasn't paying much attention anymore to where they were going. He just kept on with his stories and playing with the empty beer cans. He had his suitcase in his lap and was moving the cans around on it like they were pieces of a game.

"Did you ever hear the one about the long line at the Pearly Gates?" Brian shook his head. He was trying hard to keep the van from going over the edge of the road.

"Well, it seems these two fellows died and went to the gates of Heaven. But it must have been a busy day for the angel of death, because there was a long line at St. Peter's office. So the two fellows got to talking. One asked the other what he did back on earth, and he told him, 'I screwed every woman I could ever get my hands on: married or single, jail bait or golden-ager. How about you?' The other one looked embarrassed and said, 'I was the pastor of a large Baptist church, and never once in my life did I look at a woman with lust in my heart.' So obviously they didn't have much else to say to each other and spent the rest of the time in line looking down at the clouds.

"So the first one goes in the little office where St. Peter is checking out the newcomers, and then the other one is called. He goes in and sees that there's only two doors out of the office, one to Heaven and one to Hell. Before St. Peter could say a word, the pastor said 'Did you just have a man in here who led a life of total and abject debauchery?' St. Peter said yes. 'And did you let him go to heaven?' Again St. Peter said yes, wincing like he'd been caught doing something wrong. 'Well, why in the world would you let such a sinner go on to Heaven?'

"So St. Peter stands up, pulls back his robe, and flops his big unit on the desk. Then he points to a yardstick over in the corner. 'You see,' he says, 'we had a little wager. And I'm afraid I lost by a good three inches.' "

Eddie started laughing and slapping his hands on the dashboard. "Three inches! Don't you get it? Three inches. He lost by three inches. I guess that's why they call him St. Peter!"

His face was getting redder and redder. And his laughing wouldn't stop. Brian wanted to laugh too. It seemed that the joke was funny, but he wasn't exactly sure why. He tried to imitate Eddie, rocking and shaking, but it seemed fake. He didn't want to hurt his feelings, but laughing wasn't something Brian was very good at.

He wanted Eddie to be his friend and he knew how important it was to laugh at your friends' jokes. But the best he could come up with was a hoarse bark like a dog choking on a bone. He tried again and gave up, concentrating on keeping the van on the road.

Eddie handed Brian the last beer from the six-pack. "Hey, you're making me feel like a pig. I drank up all your brews."

Brian opened the last can and went at it, slurping like a baby with a bottle. He felt the heat and the dizzy cloud forming inside. Eddie had a slight glow, the aura coming to him slowly. The van was getting lighter too, bouncing over the potholes and washouts.

"I want to be straight with you, pal. I lied a little while back. And I don't think we should be lying to each other, not if we're going to be traveling partners. I never was on Carson. But one of his scouts did tell me that my stuff was great. And it was a friend of mine, not me, who got on the Griffin show. You probably saw him. Teddy Gozzo. Funniest damn comic in the whole world. He could work a graveyard and get a standing ovation. You know what I'm talking about? You go to see him, you'd better wear old clothes because it's a sure thing you'll be pissing in your pants by the time he's through. Of course, they didn't let him do his best material on TV and he bombed. Last I heard he was tending bar in Erie, PA. But his stuff was great, absolutely dynamite.

"He told me I could use this one anytime I wanted." Eddie cleared his throat and sat up a little straighter in his chair. "A guy with a really deep, husky voice goes to the doctor and asks him to castrate him so his voice will be higher. The doctor doesn't think it's a good idea, but he does it anyway. Later on the guy comes back and complains that his voice is too high now and wants the doctor to sew one of the family jewels back on. So the doctor starts searching around in his cabinets for them. 'Oh, nurse,' he says, 'have you see that little bottle I put on the shelf the other day?'" Eddie started cackling, but stopped long enough to say the punch line in a extra-deep bass voice: 'You mean the one with the olives in it?'"

Eddie looked like he was going to have a seizure, laughing and squeezing himself and jerking around in the seat.

"They just loved that one at Gsellmeier's. All the old shrews sat up bolt straight and started drooling. I just know they loved it. But that jackass manager said, 'Nothing dirty. Just stick to the stuff you could say on TV.' "

Brian looked over at Eddie. He tried to form his mouth like his and make the sound of laughter, but still all that would come out was a broken noise like Ollie made when he had his allergies and had to clear his throat all the time.

Eddie calmed down for a minute. "What's the matter? Don't you like jokes?"

"No, no, jokes are good. I'm always telling jokes back at the Red House."

"That's where I've been on vacation," Brian said. "It's like a resort. People come there when they're not feeling good, and by the time they leave they're like brand-new. Day by day, in every way, we're getting better and better."

Eddie wiped the foam out of the corners of his mouth. "Is that part of the Barker Brothers' chain? I think I played there once. Great big place on the lake? Fake German decor? The waitresses all wear lederhosen and they have a polka band?"

"No, I don't think so. It's modern. We have all the latest developments. State-of-the-art." He ate the last of the dough balls and asked Eddie to pour him some orange juice. "I heard a joke there just the other night. They get all the funniest comics there." But then the steering wheel was glowing and the van was barely touching the road.

"There were three patients who all had thyroid disorders. So the first one went to the doctor and said, 'Please help me, my meds don't seem to be working.' The doctor changed the meds and sent the patient to the infirmary for a week. The second one said, 'Help me please, I've got acute psychomotor agitation and chronic rigors.' So the doctor increased his rate of iodine and that seemed to fix him right up. But the third patient didn't go to the doctor. He just stayed in his room all the time, and finally they had to send in the orderlies and take him to the involuntary ward until he was more cooperative."

Eddie didn't laugh. He looked into the little hole in the top of a beer can and waited.

"And then they operated and cut out part of his basal

ganglia.'' Brian shook as Eddie had while laughing. He made the sound old Ernie did when the orderlies were looking for a vein but couldn't find it.

"I don't get it. That's the whole joke?''

Brian was embarrassed. He knew he left something out. But he wasn't sure what or where. "Maybe I mixed it up a little.''

"But I don't get it. Where's the punch line?''

"I guess there isn't one.''

"Well, pal, I think that one needs a little more work. And your delivery leaves something to be desired too. You can't tell a joke with your head tucked down in your armpit and your body all hunched up like that.''

Eddie's speech was getting slurred. He started a few more jokes, but didn't finish them, his voice trailing off each time before he got to the end. Between these broken-up jokes he was humming and drumming his fingers on the dashboard. His breath smelled heavily of beer. His eyes were reddish and unfocused. Brian had seen orderlies drunk or half drunk, and it always made them uglier and meaner than usual.

Every year there'd be a Christmas party in the staff lounge. At the last one, the orderlies had gotten really wild and played Hammerlock on one of the women on the 22 ward. Brian heard later that somebody had gotten suspended and the woman had to be sent to the hospital in Binghamton until she got better. Ollie never went to the parties. He was always the one they counted on to watch the wards until they were done drinking. He'd sit at the end of the hall, staring at nothing while they were all singing Christmas carols and getting drunk on Purple Jesus Punch.

"Hey,'' Eddie said, as if waking up. "What's brown and sounds like a bell?''

Brian didn't know.

"Dung!''

His laughter quickly turned into a fit of coughing. He was bent over, holding onto himself. Brian saw a place ahead where the shoulder was wide enough and pulled over.

He put his arm around Eddie's shoulder and hung on until the fit was over. "Maybe you'd better lie down for a little while,'' Brian said. He helped Eddie out of the seat and into the back of the van.

Eddie sat there awhile, leaning his head against the fur-covered wall. His coughing went away, but he still looked very sick.

"That son of a bitch Gsellmeier," he said quietly. "All he'd give me was money for the bus. Not a penny for the shows I did. I don't even have enough to make it back to Poughkeepsie. He wouldn't even talk to me face to face, so I could run my hard luck routine on him. He just told the bartender to give me my walking papers." Eddie was perking up a little bit, telling another story. "But yesterday I saw the old man down in the kitchen and I went after him. He ducked into the men's room to get away, but I followed him in there too. He went into a stall and I took the one next to his. 'How about another twenty?' I said. 'Just another to get me back home.' He wasn't saying anything in there, just grunting and groaning. I kept at him, seeing I had a captive audience, so to speak, and he finally said, 'All right, all right, I'll give you fifteen and I never want to see you again.' So then I said, 'For God's sake, Mr. Gsellmeier, can't you squeeze out another five?' " Eddie's spell had passed by then. He was holding onto the floor carpet to keep from laughing too hard. "That son of a bitch, I got the last laugh on him."

The only time Eddie seemed happy was right after he told a joke. In the middle of one he seemed nervous, afraid that it wouldn't be funny. And between, he was depressed, thinking how bad things had gotten for him. But before the laughing started, he was really happy.

Brian put on a tape, but Eddie scowled and waved his hand. It was either too loud or too funky. Eddie couldn't dance in the state he was in. The only thing that seemed to make him feel better was laughter. Brian took the tape off and opened up the engine cowl. He made sure the leads were still attached to the battery and held the ends up so that Eddie could see them.

"Sometimes back at the Red House, the orderlies have lots of fun with the ECT setup. One Christmas they got drunk and took a bunch of us down to Dr. Haak's rooms and made us do the funky butt by hooking the wires to our heads." The van's engine was still running. He brought the two bare ends close together and a spark jumped across the gap.

"They took Vince and Billy 23 and Lucius and me down to the lab and hooked us up. First they did Vince. He was shaking his booty all the way down. It was really something. They all thought it was the best act in the world. They couldn't stop laughing. Then they did Billy, but he didn't react so well. They must have had the electrodes mixed up because he just lay there and shivered a little bit. And afterward he couldn't remember his name. Then they heard somebody coming, and they had to get us out of there and back to our rooms so they wouldn't get suspended."

Eddie didn't get it. "Is this another one of your jokes with no punch line?" The beer was still making him groggy. "Is this some kind of magic trick you're talking about? I hate magic tricks. They're nothing compared to a good joke."

"No, it's not a trick. It's funny. It's the real thing."

He gave the gas pedal a push to get the engine running faster and then took his place near Eddie so he could see the whole thing. "It's a joke. Maybe you can do this on Carson next time."

He made sure the ends were smooth and clean, and then slid the first into place. As soon as the second one was in, he started twitching and bumping against the wall. He thought he was doing the good foot dance, but it was hard to tell. The aura was everywhere. Eddie was wearing a crown of fire. The inside of the van was getting bigger, the walls and ceiling pulling away from him. He heard himself laughing—not grunts or barks like before, but real laughs like Eddie made. He shook his groove thing a little while longer, then he came out. Eddie had stood up. He'd pulled the wires out of Brian's shunt.

"Are you crazy? You could kill yourself doing that."

He held the two wires close together, and a blue flash went from tip to tip. He dropped them and they lay in the fur, hissing. A tiny glow was visible there, like a lightning bug in deep grass. Brian picked up the wire. Eddie wasn't laughing. He didn't get it. Maybe it would take a stronger dose. Before Eddie could stop him, Brian had jammed the leads in again and started to really boogie.

The cold fire came quickly this time. He saw the wall coming at him like a tidal wave. He could barely see Eddie. He could just hear him shouting to stop it. But the juice was in his main line and he was on that one-way track again. He was going for a joy ride and there was nothing Eddie could do to stop him.

Music started exploding at his feet. A different song in each bomb. He was on the dance floor and in a mine field. It was smoking, burning, shaking, as he stepped on each mine. The mirror ball was going around, shooting out streams of fire.

The lights were shining inside his skull. The shock waves were riding up and down his spine. The aura was getting bigger and louder, like a sun coming too close to the earth. He was speeding toward the wall, brilliant and unstoppable.

"Ictus, Ichor, Icky, Ictus! Say it, say it!"

Then he was through.

12

She told him he could call her Caroline, or even Lynn. "That's what my husband called me." But anything less formal than Dr. Haak brought her too close to him too quickly. He was already in up to his neck. He wanted—at least for a short time longer—to be able to breathe.

They'd passed Monticello and Liberty on Route 17, and were heading toward Roscoe. But he didn't pay much attention as they drove. It was out of his hands by then.

His two suitcases didn't take up much room. She'd filled the back of the station wagon with her equipment, cardboard boxes of files and books, three pillowcases stuffed with her clothes, and a few kitchen implements. In the backseat was her laptop computer, her black doctor bag, and enough groceries to last them a few days. At a quick glance, they might have been a couple of white trash skipping out on their rent.

She drove much too fast. She steered with one hand and passed tractor trailers on blind upgrades. Marx just closed his eyes and let her drive where—and how—she wanted to. If constant low-level danger was the price he had to pay to be with her, he was willing. It was worth it to be with a woman who wanted him body and soul, and who could make his headaches disappear. That was enough for him. It was more than enough.

Lenny had driven like a madwoman too. She had the same air about her, as though at any moment she might break and go into a fit of weeping or screaming or threats or unstoppable desire, or all at once. Always he found himself involved with women whom other men found twisted or remote or simply frightening.

His wife's name was Helen, but he called her Lenny. She'd been always on the verge too, but he could have lived with that. He could have found a way to get along with her when she was having one of her "spells." He could have spent his whole life tiptoeing around the areas that were likely to set her off. But he never got to. Four years after they were married, a drunk had forced her off the road at sixty-five m.p.h. and her car went head-on into a power pole. Most of her went through the windshield. The drunk had turned back, found her as dead as she could be, and fled. The police never caught him. Marx had considered tracking the drunk down, but never bothered. Even if he had found him and gotten the matter to court, the drunk would only have had his license revoked and been given a year in jail. It just wasn't worth it. Every minute, every bit of energy he spent on the matter, would have just made the pain worse.

After that, life on the base became intolerable. He continued to work hard, enforcing rules and ordinances that were of absolutely no consequence. He was considered quite good at what he did, making sure the security and surveillance systems on the base kept the men in and intruders out. But as soon as his time was up, he got out and stayed out. They tried to get him to reenlist, but he just wanted to get away from that place. During those last months, waiting to be a civilian again, he worked out a complicated system in order to avoid the corner where Lenny had died. He succeeded in not once driving past the embankment and the new power pole and that section of repaved road.

Dr. Haak pounded her fist on the horn as she sped around a slow-moving truck. The sound of the horn, more a hoarse bark than a musical tone, pressed against the tender spot in

Marx's skull. The sensation passed. The little stab of pain didn't remain, stored up to come back later.

She turned off Route 17 after a while and, using the map Marx had brought along, headed toward Lake Kenneshoa. They made slower progress off the main highway. The terrain became hillier and the road narrowed to one lane in each direction. But they did reach their destination before the sun had set.

A state police car was parked on the shoulder of the road. The weeds alongside were beaten down where other vehicles had parked earlier that day. Dr. Haak pulled in behind the cruiser and shut off the engine.

After the long drive, the constant whine of the decaying transmission and her random horn blasts and curses as she fought around slower-moving traffic, the silence was wonderful. Neither of them got out at first. Neither of them were eager to face what was waiting for them in the woods.

A trail had been cleared, away from the road. A state trooper appeared and came toward them to tell them to move along. Marx had found that they often did a credible job of hiding their disdain for civilians. This trooper didn't bother. He wore the same expression of anger and disgust that Marx had seen on dozens of other policemen, as though along with marksmanship and legal procedures, they'd all been trained to look the same and speak with a similar sullen condescension.

Before he could shoo them away, Dr. Haak flashed her credentials and one of her I'll-let-you-in-on-a-secret smiles. The trooper looked over the banged-up station wagon, confused that an important psychiatric doctor would travel in such a undignified vehicle, but she quickly asked a few questions about where and when the body had been found, and they were soon being led into the woods.

"A couple of kids stumbled over it," the trooper said. "Two boys out with BB guns." It was always two boys with BB guns, as though it was their job to wander the woods looking for corpses.

In the woods, the shadows were fuller and heavier. The air was cool and smelled of wet leaves. Marx was surprised that Dr. Haak seemed to enjoy being out in the woods. She stopped twice to look at low-growing plants, as though out on a Girl Scout nature hike. They crossed a stream by jumping from rock to rock, and after descending into a deep gully, they came to where the body lay.

"His name is Edgar Allen Heck," the trooper said. "He was a two-bit comic. Played at some of the resorts hereabouts. Mostly back toward Liberty and Grossingers. There's not much of a Borscht Belt left this far west now."

Around the body the grass had been beaten down. They'd set up a low canvas covering over Heck, a cross between a body bag and a pup tent.

"He's got a record. A few drunk and disorderlies. One assault with intent." The trooper handed Dr. Haak a piece of paper. "He jumped off the stage a few months back, at the Limewood, and practically killed a guy who was giving him a hard time. He'd already been blackballed by most of the better places. Apparently he'd been fired from this last job for making a nuisance of himself."

He unzipped the covering. Eddie Heck lay on his stomach. Most of the hair on the back of his head had been burned off. His clothes were covered with twigs and burdocks and dried mud.

"He's pretty banged up. It looks like the burns on the back of his head were done after the fact. The ground was too messed up to get a quick read of what happened, but it looks like he was dragged through the brush. Do you think your boy had it in him to haul a body around in the woods?"

Dr. Haak didn't bother to answer. She was looking down at the corpse like a mourner at a funeral. For a moment her expression shifted slightly. She wasn't exactly smiling, but it seemed at least for that moment that she was going to laugh.

The trooper looked back at Eddie Heck. "We thought at first it was just some local boys taking it out on an outsider. You know how sometimes these big-city types go after the local girls and their fellows get a little too carried away defending their honor. Usually they just mess them up a little and leave it at that. But the more we looked this one over, the less it seemed like a simple rough-up that got out of hand. Whoever did this was a pretty sick cookie. There's something jammed up under his fingernails. It looks like slivers of a credit card. I don't think the local boys would do something like that.''

Dr. Haak knelt beside the body.

''You can touch him if you want. The forensic people have been here already.''

She put on a pair of membrane-thin gloves and asked for the trooper's flashlight. Turning the head to one side, she looked into Heck's eyes. Then she rubbed the back of his head, knocking off a few flecks of soot. Marx caught a whiff of charred meat and backed away.

''It's a good thing you got here when you did. I was just going to radio in for the stiff-wagon. The captain didn't mind leaving him out here so that you could take a look, but there wouldn't have been much left of him if we'd waited until the morning to pack him up. Too many animals hereabouts. We even have some wild dogs. Pretty nasty customers. Some of them big enough and mean enough to go after deer.''

He seemed to like the idea of killer dogs.

Dr. Haak took one of her probes out of her pocket and inspected the comic's ears. Eddie Heck was a large man, certainly larger and stronger than Brian. It was hard to imagine the boy doing all that damage.

''I guess you had some real sick puppies over at the Red House, huh? I heard that's where all the real head bangers get sent. Was this kid of yours psycho enough to do something like this?''

Dr. Haak had what she wanted. She didn't need to be pleasant with the trooper. She didn't need to speak to him anymore. She stood and with a wave of her hand indicated that she was done with the body.

To fill the uneasy silence, Marx made a few meaningless comments about the angle the body lay at and possible causes of the comic's death. The trooper shrugged and zipped the body bag. He made sure the stakes were secure in the loamy ground, then pointed to the break in the foliage where the trail began.

By the time they got back to the car, twilight had almost drained from the sky. Just a faint reddish haze remained above the treetops to the west. A truck went past, its headlights cutting wide swaths of brightness in the gloom. Dr. Haak signed her initials on one of the papers the trooper had given to her, and handed the whole sheaf back. She thanked him, as if thanking a shoe-shine boy for a job well done, and got in behind the wheel of the station wagon. She had the car running and in gear before Marx could close the door behind himself.

She turned at the next crossroads, heading back toward the main highway. Marx asked her a few questions about the boy, got vague and noncommittal answers, and soon gave up.

Near Route 17, cottages, stores, restaurants, and motels started appearing with greater frequency. They approached a hamburger stand with a huge globe out front as its sign. A red arrow pointed to the spot on the map where New York state was. The words "YOU ARE HERE" were written underneath in pink neon. The name of the stand seemed to be The Best Burgers in the World.

"Are you hungry?" Dr. Haak said.

Marx nodded and she pulled into the gravel parking lot.

Inside were a few truck drivers at the counter and an old couple nursing plastic cups of coffee. Dr. Haak slid into one of the booths and Marx sat across from her. He tried to make small talk, as if they were on a casual date, but the fact that he'd quit his job that morning and driven fifty miles to view a mutilated corpse kept poking into his thoughts.

He was surprised at the way the doctor ate, dousing her pile of french fries with a small mountain of catsup and letting the juice from her hamburger run down her fingers and onto the plate. She made soft grunting sounds with each bite into the soft, greasy meat. When the plastic plate was clean and all the catsup mopped up and licked from her fingers, she sat back and for the first time that day seemed relaxed. The sleepwalker gaze had finally gone from her eyes.

Marx asked her the question he'd been wondering all day. "Do you think it was Brian?"

She shook her head. "He wouldn't have done that. He wouldn't kill somebody."

"What about the orderly? He came close with him."

"Brian didn't do that."

Marx felt the cold snake unwinding in his belly. He thought for a moment that she was going to tell him that she'd attacked Ollie. But then she said, "It was Price and Whitehead. There's no question about it." She started breaking the tines off her fork and imbedding them in the styrofoam plate.

"You're joking, right?" She didn't joke much, and when she did, it was never funny.

"I'm not kidding, Saul. Price and Whitehead. They did it. They were in the hospital that night. I saw them poking around. They went after Ollie and made it look like Brian did it. It's all part of their miserable little plot. They want to take Brian out of my hands. They want to take him away and never let me see him again. If they get a hold of him, they'll claim he's homicidal and drag him off to God-knows-what kind of hellhole."

"Why would they want to do that?" The question seemed foolish.

"They hate me. They hate anybody and anything that doesn't fit neatly into their system. Who doesn't play by their rules."

Marx hadn't eaten his hamburger. It lay on his plate in a hardening pool of greasy blood. "What's the matter, aren't you hungry?" she said, grabbing the hamburger and getting it down in three bites. Marx finished the rest of his milk and realized that he hadn't taken any aspirin all day for the first time in months. He closed his eyes and thought about the inside of his head, savoring the absence of pain.

She paid for the meal, and soon they were driving through an area where motels and bars and restaurants were crowded close together. The neon signs were beginning to bother his eyes. They came up on the Kountry Kourts, and Marx told her that he wanted to stop there for the night. She agreed, pulled the wagon under the dimly lit portico, and went in to get a room.

Even with the windows closed and the air conditioner running, they could still hear traffic passing outside. The road was perhaps a hundred feet from their door.

The doctor went into the bathroom and turned on the shower. Marx lay on the stiff bedspread, watching the momentary washes of striped light appear and disappear on the walls as cars turned at the nearby corner and shone their headlights into the room.

He was roused from his dreamy state as the rattling whine of the shower pipes ceased. The bathroom door opened and a cloud of steam billowed into the room. Marx smelled cheap soap, hard water steam, and the distinct scent of Dr. Haak's hair. A car pulled into the parking lot, shining its lights directly through the louvered blinds. For a moment she stood there motionless, like an animal caught and transfixed by the bright bars of light. But the car engine died and the darkness flooded back into the room.

She came to where he lay. "Give me your hand," she said. "I want to show you something." Sitting down on the edge of the bed, she grasped his hand and brought it to the back of her neck. He thought she wanted him to massage the muscles there, but instead she guided his fingers to the soft hollow at the base of her skull. Two soft dots protruded from the skin there. They were perfectly round and felt like rubber.

"Do you know what a shunt is?" she asked him. The way she said the word made it seem like a very private, intimate thing. He didn't want to know what a shunt was, but it was obvious that she was about to tell him.

"The man my husband did his original research with developed a way of tapping into the central nervous system. My husband perfected the technology. He implanted one in me just before our wedding. And I implanted one in him." She kissed Marx on the forehead. He felt her humid breath against his face. "Do you know what the marriage of souls is?" She'd talked about alchemy earlier that day, using names and terms that made no sense to him. Transmutation, seminal pneuma, fixation of mercury, he assumed that this "chemical wedding" was more of her cryptic jargon.

He tried to make her stop. He didn't want to hear another word out of her. She was there with him naked, steaming, vulnerable, and all she wanted to do was talk about brain shunts and her husband and alchemical nonsense. She held his hand tight against the two little pegs.

"I've never told anyone about this. No one at all. This is the very first time."

His hand went around her waist. Her skin was still damp from the shower. He imagined her skin red, glowing with fever. "Brian has a shunt too. I put it in him. He's very important to me. I need your help in getting him back. If Price and Whitehead get a hold of him first, all my work will be wasted. There's not much point in me going on if I can't have him.'' Her lips brushed across his cheek, searching for his mouth. ''You'll help me find him, won't you? You're the only person I can trust.''

A tractor trailer went by, rattling the windows. A few rooms down, someone was shouting over a radio. The air conditioner started making a high-pitched hum, then shut itself off.

His shirt came apart in her hands. Her hot breath moved down his chest and belly. Her hands were around his waist. He looked down and saw her head hovering in the darkness. Her eyes were two pinpricks of light, her teeth a white crescent.

The remains of his clothing came free from his body and her head descended from sight, into the rich, rank shadows.

13

When Brian came back from the Ictus, the van's door-open buzzer was going, the green and red lights on the tape deck were still glowing, and the mirrored ball was still turning around. But Eddie Heck was gone.

The sun had been up a long time. Already the air was getting hot and sticky. Flies were buzzing around the wet spot on the carpet where one of the beer cans had spilled. Brian closed the passenger door and the electric noise stopped. One of the lights on the dashboard went out too.

Last night, before he had been pushed through the wall to the Outer Side, he had gotten one look at Eddie's reaction to his dance number. He'd never seen anyone do the jerk before. He didn't get it. It hadn't made him laugh. He was just afraid.

But then Brian had gone through the wall and Eddie was out of sight. Almost immediately Brian had seen Dr. Haak. She was with a man, naked. It was dark and they were together, fused as if by the shunt cable but not exactly. Brian had moved around her like a bee trying to find the best way into a flower. He watched her from the outside at first, as she shook and moaned and tangled herself up with the man. He tried to talk to her, but his voice wouldn't go through. Then he went inside on the bright beam, just like when she looked in him with her light. It was chaos inside of her: ugly noises and flashing lights, faces grinning and faces scowling, explosions and voices and the smell of funk so strong he could almost taste it.

Then the currents had shifted and he was far, far away from her. There were no miles or meters or feet in the Ictus. No minutes or seconds or years either. But there was near and far. He'd gotten close to Dr. Haak. And then was swept away to places darker even than that motel room where she lay with her head on the man's chest.

And when he came back, Eddie Heck was gone. He knew that other people in that same situation might have cried because their friend went away. But Brian didn't cry. He wasn't sure he even could. He had wanted Eddie to be his friend, but there were plenty of other people to meet now that he was getting farther and farther from the Red House.

He looked in the little refrigerator. All that was left there was some orange juice and a head of lettuce already turning brown around the edges. Brian felt a little sick looking at the lettuce. The idea of eating it made something greasy and wet and heavy start moving in his stomach. That day was definitely a green day. No wintergreen Lifesavers for him. No broccoli or lime Kool-aid or bananas unless they were really ripe.

It was a green day, so he needed to head north. He fiddled with the wires hanging from the steering column and got the engine going. It took him awhile to back out. Reverse was the hardest for him. It made him dizzy to go backward. But eventually he was on his way and heading as close to due north as the roads would allow.

Waiting at a stop sign, he dug around inside the glove compartment and found a pack of gum. He unwrapped a few pieces, threw the gum out the window, and wadded the foil into a ball. Clamping down hard on the foil, he got a little buzz to run into the fillings of his teeth. They didn't let him do that at the Red House. Dr. Lorenzo had said it was bad for him, and always afterward they had to increase his doze of Thorazine. And though it didn't exactly feel good, it did wake him up. It made his eyes clear and the last shreds of darkness disperse like fog blown away by the wind.

Along one side of the road were high power poles carrying a dozen thick black lines. When Brian concentrated, he could feel the spillover from the wires. A magnetic field leaked out of the lines, making a steady invisible stream that reached for miles. Brian tried to hold the van inside the sway of the current, moving with it rather than fighting against it. He knew that if he just put his mind in the right state, he could let the radiation from the wires carry him. But he kept slipping, trying too hard or letting pictures enter his head. Eddie Heck standing above him, trying to bring him back from the Ictus. Dr. Haak wide awake, lying in the dark bed next to that sleeping man. Ollie back at the Red House getting better day by day, coming slowly out of his coma.

The foil was starting to fall apart in his mouth. He didn't like all the shreds. He rolled down his window and spat. The air rushed into his face. He'd seen how dogs drove with their heads out the window. He knew then why they liked to do that. He closed his eyes for a second, imagining the van like a bullet from a gun, shooting down the road. But a car horn made him look. A farmer in a pickup truck was snarling at him, making his hand into a dirty sign. Brian got back onto the right side of the road, and for the rest of the day he didn't try driving blind again.

As he went on, he began to feel something nibbling at him. Even back at the Red House in the same room he'd lived in for ten years, he needed to know at all moments what his alignment was: north, south, east, or west. And the farther he got from there, the more important it was for him to be in the groove, running in the path that would take him home.

It was still quite hilly in that area, but more often than before he saw farms and pastures. And in places the land flattened out so that he could see a long distance. Far to the west, the sky was a blackish purple, like a nasty bruise. It was coming toward him. The air had that heavy, soggy feel to it, like a bag ready to burst.

The procession of power poles veered away from the road

and crossed a pasture. Cows stood motionlessly there, all facing the same way. Brian pulled over to the side of the road, near the last power pole that stood by the curb. He shut off the engine and crossed the shallow ditch of weeds. A fence kept the cows from leaving the pasture. It was made of two limp strands of wire supported by a variety of posts. Some were gray and old, weathered like stone. Some were made of orange plastic. Some were lengths of two-by-four with rough, broken-off ends. They all had white ceramic cylinders where the wire attached to them. Still the cows had not moved. They were watching the darkness in the west.

Brian licked his fingertip and touched the upper wire. A jolt of electricity surged up his arm, throwing him backward. He tried it again, forcing his hand to remain a second or two longer. After a third and fourth time he got the jolt to reach into the roots of his brain. With his fifth try, a bright flash like a tiny lightning strike poked into a part of him that until then had always been in darkness.

He didn't want to go too far, though. He wasn't quite ready to hang on and feel the hot feed like a second bloodstream rushing inside him. He wanted just one more shot of illumination. He touched the wire again and saw a large stone building, with letters painted across the front. An old man was sitting on the stoop. Most of the windows were boarded up. When the jolt was gone, passed through him and into the ground where it always wanted to go, the picture of the building was gone too. It faded and he was left with only the cows and the grass and the power poles disappearing into the woods.

It wasn't long afterward that he saw the building and the old man again. This time they didn't fade from view. Brian guided the van along a narrow, rutted road, and as he came around a tight bend he saw the building below him in a stand of huge white trees. It was four stories tall and had a dark slate roof. Between the second and third tiers of windows the words "GARMANTOWN" were written. The paint was faded and the plaster falling away, exposing the raw stone beneath. The old man wasn't sitting on the step. He was near the road, doing something with his mailbox.

Brian pulled in the gravel driveway and yanked the wires
out to shut off the engine. The man laid his tools down on
the grass and nodded a greeting to Brian. He was tall and
bony. He was very old, but he still had most of his hair. He
couldn't straighten all the way up. Brian got out of the van
and said, "Do you have any food? I'm awfully hungry."
He held out the change that Eddie had gotten from the traveler's checks. "Nothing green, though. Not today."

The old man led him into the building and pointed to a
counter where a long time before, longer than Brian could
understand, jars full of licorice and jawbreakers and anise
stars had been. Now they were all empty. Lying beside the
jars was a metal bowl full of red candies.

"Five for a quarter," the old man said. Brian gave him
a dollar and took a handful. They burnt his tongue, but he
didn't spit them out. Three or four at a time, they were just
like fire. Quickly, though, the red coloring and the hot flavor went away and they were just sweet. "Atomic fire
balls," the old man said. "You don't see them around much
anymore."

After Brian had eaten his fill, he allowed the old man to
give him a tour of the place. He had visitors on occasion.
The building was listed in a few of the tourist guidebooks.
Canal buffs came there sometimes when they'd run out of
more important sites to visit.

The old man's name was Melton Garman. His grandfather
had built the place back when the Erie Canal was making
New York into the Empire State. Other canals were pro-
posed, planned, and started. None of them made any money.
By the time they were ready for use, the railroads had already made them obsolete. In the field behind Garmantown
was half of a stone arch, where an aqueduct had carried the
canal across a creek bed. Anthony Garman, the builder, had
thought he'd make a fortune operating an all-in-one stopping place for canal traffic. On the second and third floor
were rooms where travelers could spend the night. On the
fourth floor was a ballroom complete with a stage and a
large dance floor. And taking up the first level of the building had been a number of small shops that were to have
served the people who came through on their way upstate.

The canal was never finished. No traffic ever came through and Anthony Garman had gone bankrupt.

The old man led Brian into a room crowded with rough plank shelves which held high-button shoes, slabs of raw leather, and cobbler's tools. "I got these at an estate sale near Cortland," he said. In the next room was a simple blacksmith's shop. "And these were donated by a fellow who knew my Uncle Arthur."

Mr. Garman had grown up on a farm miles from the building, and had heard stories as a boy of his grandfather's folly. "They used it for a while around the turn of the century as a grange, but most of the time it's sat empty." When his parents had died, he'd sold the farm, bought the building, and started refurbishing it, hoping to make it into a tourist attraction. The entire first floor was crowded with antique furnishings and products. He liked to call it the first Ghost-mall.

He'd converted a few of the hotel rooms on the second floor to be his apartment and lived there alone, showing the mall museum to anyone who stumbled across it.

The largest room on the first floor was devoted to archaic scientific equipment. He had a forerunner of the fluoroscope, ball magnets, generators, dowsing equipment, Klein bottles, a steam turbine made all of brass, a mirror that reflected only certain colors, and a complete skeleton of a condor, put together with wire and hanging from the ceiling. Along one wall was a huge casket. Mr. Garman opened the lid and pointed inside.

"Did you ever hear of the Cardiff Giant?" Brian hadn't. "It was a hoax. A good hoax. They carved a man out of stone and charged people to see it, claiming it was a prehistoric man, petrified. They've got it up at Cooperstown, I think." Inside the casket was a huge form of grayish stone-like material. It was shaped like a man, with his hands crossed over his chest. "Well, my boy, this is the Trumansburg Giant. Just like the one they have up at Cooperstown, only bigger and better. But nobody made much money on it. Some fellow heard about the Cardiff Giant and thought they'd go one better. They cooked up beef blood and iron filings and cement, salt and eggs, and formed it like a man and baked it until it was hard. Then they buried it where they knew somebody was going to be digging a drainage ditch. There was some hoohah about it for a few weeks, but then the truth came out and everybody forgot about it. The story was that they busted it up with sledge hammers and threw the pieces into Cayuga Lake. But in fact my grandfather offered to cart it away to get it off their hands, and it's been here ever since.'' He slapped the giant on the head. ''Over one thousand pounds, he weighs. I still remember when they brought him here. I was a little boy, but I remember.''

The old man went on with his tour, as he had many times before, reeling off facts and dates and little bits of information that Brian couldn't keep straight. Eventually they came back to the scientific machines. Mr. Garman took both of Brian's hands and placed them on a large glass globe. Then he went across the room to another globe just like the first and stood facing him. Soon Brian felt a tingling sensation in his palms, and he knew the old man was feeling it too. He was pleased with Brian, excited that the machine was working. ''Just like radio,'' he said. ''No wires, no cables. It goes right through the air.'' Inside the globes were coils of copper wire, making the globes look like huge lightbulbs.

Brian closed his eyes and tried to send a message back to the old man. He concentrated and felt himself linked to Mr. Garman.

''It's called a telemeter. It's one of Tesla's first inventions. I've got the only one left in America. I think there's one in a museum in Belgrade, but those fools don't know how to make it work.'' They played with the device awhile longer, sending messages back and forth. But Brian didn't know the code the old man was using, receiving the transmissions as a series of long and short pulses.

Mr. Garman didn't mention the vision Brian had had at the electric fence, though he acted as if he knew all about it. They both needed each other. Brian wasn't sure what for, but he knew that soon enough Mr. Garman would explain it all to him.

He pointed to a small machine bolted to a tabletop. ''One of the very first Tesla coils.'' It was made of coiled copper wire and a heavy iron armature. Leads went in and came out of the same side. "My father worked for him in Teluride and then in the New York lab for a while. Until that bastard Edison had it burned down. He salvaged what he could and kept it here. I doubt anyone knows about these things, or cares. Tourists mostly like the Van de Graff generator and the Treadway apparatus." He showed Brian a few more of the machines, but didn't turn any of them on. Some were made by this Tesla that he kept mentioning, and some were based on his ideas. They all had to do with electricity or the transmission of power. "You know, they worked together for a while. Edison could be a real sweet-talker, and Tesla fell for it. Who knows what he stole from him? But as far as I can tell, the Edison people don't have most of these devices or even know about them." He opened a little wooden cabinet and showed Brian a bronze statue. It was just a bust, cut off at the neck. The face was long and thin. The man was deep in thought. "There he is, Nikola Telsa. I don't show this to just anybody. I keep it for special occasions." He took a flannel rag out of a drawer below the bust and polished the forehead.

Brian had never heard of this Tesla. The plaque attached to the base read, "1856 (CROATIA)–1943 (N.Y. CITY)" He didn't know what or where Croatia was, but he did know about New York. "He made all these things?"

"No, not all of them. No. Just the best ones. My father did the actual fabrication on some of them. He's even named on a few of the patents. Tesla didn't care very much about patents."

They spent most of the afternoon in that part of the building, looking at the machines, hooking up the leads on a few of them to Brian's hands, just like Dr. Haak had with the ECT setup. But he didn't go through the wall. He stayed right there in the big, high-ceilinged room with the old man and equipment that smelled of grease and rust and ozone when they were turned on.

After a while Brian thought that maybe Mr. Garman was giving him a series of tests like the doctors did back at the Red House. He held instruments close to his eyes and watched the meter needles swing back and forth. He fastened on cuffs and had Brian sit for a while in a metal-lined booth. He shone light into his ears, so bright that Brian could see traces of it on the backs of his eyes. He diddled with dials and taped wires to his forearms and fastened a big spiderlike thing onto his chest with a wad of reddish putty. All the while Mr. Garman talked and Brian tried to understand.

Tesla was an inventor, that much Brian got. He made lots of machines and devices and was friends with pigeons and died in New York City with no money. He'd either been in a place like the Red House, or somebody wanted to put him there so he wouldn't hurt himself. Thomas Edison had been his friend for a while, and then they had a fight and might have tried to kill each other from far away with their electrical machines. Lawyers and clerks and judges had argued for years over who owned which of the inventions. And men in dark raincoats poured gasoline on his lab and set it on fire.

Mr. Garman found Brian's shunt quick enough and asked him a few questions about it. "Dr. Haak gave that to me. She's got one too and sometime we do the Do. That way she gets really excited and happy, and I'm her one and only. Nobody else at the Red House has one, except maybe Ollie, but she doesn't love him anymore because he's not man enough."

Mr. Garman pulled the plugs out of the shunt and peeped inside with his flashlight. All of the old man's poking and probing didn't send Brian through the wall, but it was definitely getting his funk motor turning. He asked where the bathroom was, and when he came back, Mr. Garman was unpacking another machine from a cracked leather case.

Brian liked the smell of the place. It reminded him of Dr. Haak's lab. Only it wasn't clear what he was supposed to be doing there. He didn't want Brian to shake his booty. He didn't want him to strut his stuff. He didn't want to hook into Brian's shunt and take a free ride into the Ictus. Like a teacher maybe, or a doctor trying to figure out a problem, he kept asking questions without coming right out and saying what he was looking for. It was a little like the tests that the doctors at the Red House claimed were just games for fun.

Over and over he said the words Acee and Decee, like they were names of two armies that were at war. He talked about the battle of the currents and how Acee and Decee had fought it out "for the soul of America." And how the whole thing had started in a place called Niagara Falls.

Brian heard the name and almost instantly the invisible Negroes started laying down a river of hot and heavy funk.

He knew about Niagara Falls. Once in a while that name would come out of him while he was talking with Dr. Haak, and she'd get a look on her face like Milly the night nurse got when one of the others were talking dirty. It was a powerful name, that much was for sure. It made Dr. Haak look unhappy, even afraid, so he tried not to let the name come out when he was around her.

"Nikola Tesla was the man responsible for establishing Acee in America. The generators at Niagara Falls were the first successful Acee operation in the world. Without him we'd still be back in the Dark Ages."

The words seemed to be going directly into Brian without him having to use his ears. Mr. Garman had a machine on his head too, wires and straps and red-colored discs attached all over him, and the words were going direct.

"That bastard Thomas Edison was the Lord of Decee. He did everything he could to make sure the whole country was wired with his system. And Tesla was the Lord of Acee. They fought it out for years. Westinghouse was in the battle too, and Oberfurst and even Teddy Roosevelt. Edison had a traveling electrocution show, so that people would think Acee was too dangerous to use in the home. He had a wagonload of dogs and the show would travel around to fairs and scientific meetings and places where the police and city councils would gather. He even helped develop the first electric chair, so that it would be perfectly obvious how dangerous Acee was. It wasn't that far from here, up in Auburn at the state prison there. His people worked for free, so that the state would have a fancy new way of killing murderers."

Brian wasn't actually going through the wall, but he was getting peeks at things on the Other Side. He saw a dog standing on a metal plate. The dog dipped his head to get a drink of water from the bowl they'd put out for him, and all of a sudden the dog was shaking and moaning and smoke started coming up around his paws where they touched the metal plate. And Thomas Edison was there with a big smile on his face, and right next to that was a man strapped into a chair like the ones in the basement of the Red House that they didn't use anymore because somebody said that kind of treatment wasn't safe anymore. This man couldn't get out of the chair and he was shaking and thrashing and his eyes were bulging out like balloons that somebody was stepping on. Edison was giving a speech. Brian couldn't really hear it, but he knew it already: "Acee is a demon which will destroy us, a genie which we never be able to get back in the bottle once we've let him loose."

But even with the dogs burning all over the country like witches burning at stakes, and even with Edison giving speeches and helping the state get rid of murderers, still Acee won the war.

Brian was right at the wall, with his head through but his body still behind. He was looking in and it seemed that Mr. Garman was holding him back. He saw all the men who'd fought the war: business leaders in dark suits, scientists in white lab coats, policemen in blue suits. They were all gathered in a place that was very dark. Dark enough to hide their faces but not what they were doing. Brian felt Mr. Garman's hands around his shoulders, trying to keep him from going too far in. But even without going through, he could see enough and hear enough to know what was happening. These men in the darkness were planning what to do once the battle of the currents was over. They had contracts and patents and writs and trademark certificates. They had lawyers crouching nearby, like dogs waiting for bones thrown from the table. The light there was red, bloody red. The smell was awful. Burnt hair and skin from the man in the chair. Burnt fur from all those dead mongrels Edison had toured the country with. And a different, newer smell too, one that Brian remembered from a very long time ago. It was powerful, rancid, poisonous. It was a smell that never occurred in nature because it took these men in the darkness with their new ideas to make the smell happen. They admitted defeat, accepted Acee as their master, and went about figuring ways to make money off the new situation. They were pouring black ooze into the ground. It was seeping down, spreading out. It came out of tanks and pipes and rubber hoses. It leaked from rusty containers and sloshed over the tops of big barrels. The smell was coming from the black goo. The men were breathing the goo. Their hands were covered with it. And there was no way that they could get it off.

Then Brian was back again in Garmantown. The old man

had his hands around him, as if trying to keep him from floating away, rising up, drifting right through the ceiling and into the sky. They both had the wires and straps and old-fashioned machines still attached to them. It took Mr. Garman a few minutes to unfasten all the connections. Then he sat down, holding his head up with his hands. He was very tired. He looked older and more sickly than just a few hours before. Brian felt sorry for him. He knew that soon enough he would have to die because everyone had to die when they got old. Brian wondered if Mr. Garman was going to die right there, sitting on the wooden bench in the room full of machinery.

Brain waited. He was good at waiting; he had a lot of experience with that back at the Red House. And after a while a little life came back into the old man. He got up, finished taking the equipment off Brian, and then told him he needed to lie down for a while. "I want you to promise me something," he said. Brian had to listen hard to hear what he was saying. "I want you to promise that you won't go anywhere while I'm asleep. There's still things we've got to talk about."

Brian promised. "I can listen to my tapes. I've got a lot of them."

After Mr. Garman had gone upstairs, Brian took another handful of fireballs, popped four in his mouth, and went back to his van.

Mr. Garman didn't say much during supper. He ate like he moved: slow and careful and without any wasted motion. He'd cooked their meal on a big old black stove and served Brian his food on white china dishes.

They had bacon and eggs for supper, which was a little confusing. But it was the first real meal Brian had had since leaving the Red House, and he didn't mind very much that the food was wrong for that time of day. Mr. Garman also gave him a glass of orange juice and a big mug of coffee with lots of sugar. Brian drank it as fast as it came off the stove. Mr. Garman didn't seem to know that Brian wasn't allowed to have coffee, even though he understood all about Dr. Haak and going through the wall and things like that.

It wasn't a sure thing, but a few times the orderlies had

slipped up and given Brian coffee or tea with his breakfast, and Brian had felt queasy and light-headed afterward. And twice after he'd gotten coffee, he went directly into one of his seizures without any help from Dr. Haak.

He ate everything on his plate that night. He watched Mr. Garman and imitated him. He didn't like to put catsup on his eggs, but he didn't want to be impolite.

They sat in Mr. Garman's apartment on the second floor. Through the kitchen window they saw lightning flashing in the hills a few miles away.

At first the coffee didn't have any effect on Brian. But as the storm came closer, Brian started to hear the thunder claps before he saw the bolts of lightning, and started to feel them before he heard them.

"Storm's been itching to blow all day. Surprised it hasn't hit yet," Mr. Garman said. He had a piece of egg stuck on his chin. Brian knew it wouldn't be polite to reach over and brush it off, so he wiped his own chin instead and pretended that the food was gone.

Another bolt struck, and Brian felt the building shake. The gas fire under the coffeepot went out. Mr. Garman got up to light it again. "We need the rain. It's been awfully dry lately."

Brian's shunt itched. "Excuse me," he said, got up from the table, and went down the hall to the bathroom. The only window there was small and round, like a porthole on a ship. He put the seat down on the toilet and stood on it, poking his head out the hole. Rain had started to fall, big, heavy drops. A few hit him on the back of the neck. They were cool on his shunt, lessening the itch. Another lightning bolt hit, only a few hundred yards away. For a moment the grove of huge birches was brightly lit, as if by a bonfire. Brian smelled ozone. It reminded him of Dr. Haak's shock rod. He felt her out there in the darkness, looking for him. He was sure she was following him. And when he got to his final destination, he knew she'd be there. That was the way it had to be, though he wished she was with him then as the lightning and the rain came harder, gathering around and above him.

Another blast hit, on the other side of the building. Brian got down from the toilet. He walked toward the kitchen, but instead of going back to his supper, he turned and went up a staircase leading to the third floor. It was dark in the stairway, making the lights inside him seem stronger. They were synchronized with the lightning bolts, signaling back to the huge explosions like faint echoes. He reached the third floor and kept going, past the fourth and up an even narrower staircase that took him to the roof.

The shingles were wet and slippery. He knew if he wasn't careful, he'd fall and there would be no one below to catch him. The wind had picked up, pushing the rain at him from the side rather than from above.

Lightning struck again, and he saw the van, the old pump well, the heap of tires, the firewood, and the broken stone fence. Instantly they were gone, sucked back into the darkness. And Brian was alone, very alone. His knees were getting weak. The coffee was percolating up through him just like it did in the pot. For a second his head was made of glass and hot brown drink was bubbling inside it.

The wire from the toaster was in his front pocket. He reached for it as he heard the front door, four stories below, slam. Mr. Garman was out by the van, looking for him. Brian smoothed the ends of the wire and slid them into place, deep in their holes. That made him feel a little better, a little less vulnerable. Still he was dizzy, though. Still the lightning was firing inside him before it exploded in the air.

With the wire plugged into his neck, he lifted the other end and held it above his head. He was an antenna. He was picking up the good vibrations. Thunder shook the building. He heard Mr. Garman down below, calling his name.

"Hardest-working man in show business," Brian sang. He did a little good-foot dance, coming close to the edge of the roof. "God Father of Souls. Mr. Please, Please, Please. The New Minister of the Super Heavy Funk." Brian's voice was getting louder.

Another flash lit the front yard and Mr. Garman looked up. He saw him teetering on the edge. He waved his hands, trying to make him back away. "Get down," he shouted.

"Get down!" Brian shouted back. "You got to get up to get down." His wire was up. He was ready.

"Hit me one time!" He shouted up at the sky. Lightning

fired back an answer. Brian staggered backward, but he didn't lose his footing. "Hit me two times!"

"Brian, listen to me. Don't move." The old man's voice cracked. He was too old to be shouting and standing in a rainstorm. "I'll be right up. Stay there." He was afraid to go inside. He thought Brian was going to go over the edge.

The thunder exploded again, like two flat hands slamming onto his ears. "Hit me three times!" A triple blast came in reply. The thunder was his drum. The cracks of lightning were his rim shots. The rumbling of the ground was his bass line. A huge burst filled the entire woods, making every tree, every weed and patch of bare dirt as bright and as visible as if hit by a monstrous searchlight. It wasn't like the light of the sun, though. It was wilder, hard and hot and greasy. Then everything went black again, inside and outside his head. "Out of sight!" he sang. His wire was still up. He was still waiting for the big bang. "Hit me four times!"

Mr. Garman was below, shouting. But by then the storm was too loud. He was miles away. His voice was just a tiny speck of sound.

Something was out there, waiting for him. It wanted him as much as he wanted it. "Hit me five times," he sang, and his voice was caught up by the thunder, amplified and routed down into the ground like a huge spike, a red-hot nail of purified power.

The hand that held the wire seemed to be far away. The arm was stretching until it was a long cable and his hand was a kite flying high in the storm, singing, "Hit me, hit me, hit me." A blue sphere of light surrounded his hand. The brilliance didn't go away between the lightning flashes. It was like a lantern sending out light for him to travel by. It was pointing west. It was telling him to go in that direction. "Hit me six times. Hit me seven times!" he shouted, and then everything became too much. Too loud. Too bright. Too wet. Too high. Too funky. The blue lantern in his hand went away and everything was dark. He was alone. The darkness was absolute and no matter how much he called out to it, the light wouldn't come back.

14

Oberfurst House was on the Cornell campus, perched at the edge of Cascadilla gorge. From the outside, it looked like any of a score of other buildings there. And on the inside too, there was little difference between it and its neighbors: alumni gathering places, havens for obscure bureaucracies, fraternity houses, and headquarters for this council and that board.

As freshmen, both Price and Whitehead had passed by Oberfurst House hundreds of times and given it almost no thought.

But in their senior year, they were invited into the arcana, and from that point forward, their lives would always be bound up in the workings of those who came and went through the intricately carved doorway smothered in rich green ivy.

They attended Cornell at the very end of the 1960s student upheavals. Neither of them were interested in wearing faddish clothing, taking drugs with strange acronyms for names, or breaking into the university offices. They wanted to make a few connections, establish themselves as young men of promise and ambition, get their degrees, and then go out into the world linked by their invisible ties back to Cornell, just as their fathers had done.

Neither the senior Whitehead nor Price were aware of Oberfurst House. It had been there since the turn of the century, but at the time they were attending Cornell, no new blood was needed. Whitehead and Price junior were simply at the right place at the right time. They had skills that were needed, and they had the proper hard, angry look in their eyes.

It wasn't a fraternity. They didn't live in the house or take part in the usual sex-and-liquor-related activities. It wasn't a professional organization, for there were too many fields represented: chemical engineers, law students, some premeds, MBAs, electrical engineers, and even a few linguists. It wasn't a social club either, though they did spend many of their holidays and vacations together. And it wasn't a religious brotherhood, despite the fact that in the long run, years down the line when each member was called to task for what he'd done with his life, faith and belief were the matters which had the most importance.

More than one senior member described Oberfurst house as an island of sanity in an ocean of chaos. Men of all faiths, all areas of interest and expertise gathered there to help one another attain their goals. They were men dedicated to order, decency, and to the higher good. And they were men who once initiated into the brotherhood, could go through their lives with the absolute certainty that they would die very wealthy.

Price and Whitehead had traveled by night, directly from Mt. Kinnsvort to Cornell. They were sitting in the Oberfurst House dining room, drinking coffee and enjoying the view. Looking out the huge bay window, they could see into the gorge. And as on countless other occasions when the fog was rising, it seemed that the gorge went down forever. It was an abyss that morning, a crack in the earth, a glimpse into the deep, hidden places below.

Other brothers were eating breakfast too: a doctor whose practice on Long Island was making money for him faster than he could spend it, a retired air force general, a recent graduate from the school of economics, and an Episcopalian priest whose congregation, on the upper East Side of Manhattan, was one of the wealthiest in the world. And though it was good to meet with these brothers, to share a meal and small talk, this wasn't the reason they'd returned to Cornell.

They had a nine o'clock meeting with Dr. Robert Valentine. And just as the bells in the nearby clock tower were tolling nine—the deep and sonorous clangs barely penetrating the walls of Oberfurst House—the door opened and in came Dr. Valentine. He was in his early sixties, slightly overweight and slightly deaf. The others in the room showed him a deference that mere brotherhood would not have required.

"Chipper, Chucky, it's good to see you," he said, shaking their hands.

After greeting the others there and making small talk for a while, Dr. Valentine showed them to the window, and the three of them looked down into the gorge together. Wisps of steam rose from the pit, purling and tangling in the air like wraiths damned to be buffeted forever. Far below, as the mist parted for a moment, they saw the roof of one of the power stations long ago abandoned. Cornell still used the power generated by the Cascadilla and Fall creeks, but the system had fallen into disrepair. It was cheaper to buy the current directly from one of the big utilities.

The face of the gorge was dotted here and there with vegetation, and in places water spilled from a crack or outcrop in the rock. It was a beautiful sight, and it never failed to put Price and Whitehead in a pleasantly melancholic mood.

"Everything is going well, I assume," Dr. Valentine said.

Price gave a brief report. "The boy's not far from here. We think he's found the old man. He should be heading west again this morning. Dr. Haak and Marx are still unaccounted for, though. They showed up at the scene of the comedian's death. Since then they haven't been seen. But I don't think we need to worry that they'll be where we need them when the time comes."

Price didn't lower his voice as he spoke. The other men in the room didn't know exactly what he was talking about.

As far as he knew, they played no direct role in the situation, but there was no reason to doubt their trustworthiness. They went on with their meal, enjoying the cool, sure, secure atmosphere. They continued eating as though Price and Whitehead were discussing a recent vacation or a minor business matter.

"We only have a week," Dr. Valentine said. "You think everything will have fallen into place by then?"

"There've been no hang-ups yet, except the minor problem with the Haak woman. And even that wasn't totally unexpected. She's always been a bit of a loose cannon. Good at what she does, very good, but not predictable. If she'd handed the boy over to us directly, that would have been perhaps one fewer variable to deal with, but I don't think we have anything to worry about."

From where they stood, they could see no bridges or buildings or pathways. They might have been high in the Adirondacks, miles from the nearest house or road. A few rays of sunshine broke through the cloud cover, but were quickly swallowed up by the fog, and the rich, beautiful grayness rose again.

The other men there admired Price and Whitehead. They were still quite young. They had many years ahead of them. They might find themselves—at age sixty or seventy—in the inner councils. If in fact the inner councils existed. There were two theories among the peripheral members. Some thought that the brotherhood was in fact like an extended family, a chain of interlocking cells. And others believed that it was made up of circles, and circles within those circles. It was considered unseemly to discuss such matters, though. The men were encouraged to find their places and accept them. No one was ever looked down on for doing what they did as long as they did it well and wholeheartedly.

"And the orderly? Did you find out who attacked him?"

Price, for the first time that morning, was uncomfortable. "No, not yet. But either way, If it was the boy or the Haak woman, it makes no difference."

"I wouldn't have brought it up if I thought it made no difference, Chuck." Dr. Valentine's expression remained flat and placid. "If the boy did it, that indicates something, don't you think?"

"Everything else has gone completely as we expected," Whitehead said, "He can go into the state now with complete regularity. His responses to the treatments have been quite consistent."

"If you accept Dr. Haak's data at face value." Dr. Valentine had his eyes fixed on a spot far out over the gorge. He was looking, it seemed, at something hanging above the void. "She might have been feeding you altered, or completely fictitious, data. Did that ever occur to you?"

"We doubled-checked. We had Dr. Simonsen going over all her findings. He ran his own tests on the boy. Everything clicks."

"And where is Martin Simonsen now?"

Neither Price nor Whitehead spoke.

"I asked you a question."

"He's dead, and all the evidence points to the Haak woman."

"You're quite sure of that?"

They both nodded.

"That's very unfortunate, boys. Martin was a useful player at that location. But I'm sure the state police will take care of the details. I believe the commander for that division is Oscar Brandt. A good man. He graduated here the same year as my younger brother Louis. He'll do what he can, I'm sure. But if ordinary channels don't give us what we need, we'll certainly have to take special steps. We can't have a madwoman roaming around the countryside, killing off our brothers at whim."

The three of them sat there in silence awhile longer, watching the gray coils of fog. Then Dr. Valentine pulled himself out of his reverie and stood. "I want to show you boys something. It'll make things clearer for you."

They followed him out of the dining room, down a long corridor, and into a section of the house they'd been in only a few times before. A small elevator, of turn-of-the-century vintage, was revealed as Dr. Valentine pulled back a pair of carved wooden doors. They got into the car, Dr. Valentine moved the control knob to the Down position, and they began to descend.

Once they were moving, heading downward through a shaft carved in the rock of the cliff side, Dr. Valentine said,

"I'm sorry if I was a little hard on you upstairs. This whole project has been a great strain on all of us." He was speaking more loudly than before to be heard above the elevator's whine. "You both know how important this is for us. Every detail has to be checked and rechecked. Every bit of our data is being scrutinized. This is the big one, boys. We can't afford to let our egos get in the way. Every detail needs to be ironed out."

They traveled downward for quite a while. The elevator was old and moved slowly, but it seemed they were going deeper than they'd ever gone before.

When they'd been initiated as undergraduates, they'd ridden that same elevator down into the earth, but then they'd been blindfolded and their wrists tied behind their backs. It had happened late at night. They were taken, naked and bound like prisoners, to the bottom and led out onto a narrow shelf of rock. They could feel the spray from the falls. They knew they were at the bottom of the gorge. Their hands were unfastened and they were told not to remove their blindfolds until they'd counted to one hundred. But even with them off, they could see almost nothing. The fog was too dense. Far above them was Oberfurst House, like a fragment of sky seen from the bottom of a well. They were left there: cold and helpless.

Dr. Valentine stopped the elevator at a level marked with a red circle and a pair of hatch marks. He pushed open the doors and the two partners followed him out. They were in one of the old generating stations somewhere near the base of the gorge. The corridor was made of rough stone dripping with condensation and white trails of niter. They passed a pile of broken clay conduit pipe and, farther along, a heap of parts from one of the turbines that sat at the heart of the station. Bare electric bulbs were spaced far apart along the ceiling.

They came around a corner and the sound of the falls—a dull rumbling—became audible. Dr. Valentine stopped before a wide iron door and began unfastening the three locks.

When Price and Whitehead had been initiated, there'd been no secret handshakes, no passwords or pseudo-mystical rituals. There were no oaths or swearing allegiance on huge black books. There were no ridiculous costumes or sophomoric rites. They'd just been left on the cold, miserable, fog-choked shelf of rock until they were both almost comatose. Then they'd been brought inside, wrapped in blankets, shot full of sedatives, and placed in one of the plush, regal bedrooms in the house far above them. They both remained unconscious for close to fortyeight hours. And when they finally awoke, they were brothers. It was that simple. They were in and they'd never be out.

Dr. Valentine pushed open the door. "You boys were never shown this before because there was no reason. Not many of the brothers are aware of what we really have down here. There are plenty of projects that I'm sure I'll never even hear about. If there's no way I can contribute to a project's success, there's no reason for me to know about it, is there?"

Price and Whitehead both nodded. The room that the doctor led them into was even more dimly lit than the corridor. There were, however, more signs that activity had taken place there recently. Beside a Plexiglas shower stall and a few large metal tanks, there was a metal rack where three vacuum suits hung.

Dr. Valentine began unfastening the clasps and seals, and told the two to do likewise. Shortly they were all suited up, breathing pressurized air. The doctor worked a few controls and a second door opened. This one was of far more recent vintage, forming an air-tight seal. Neither Price nor Whitehead were scientists. They had earned their degrees in business administration. They knew that Dr. Valentine wasn't showing them this merely to impress them. There was a concrete, practical reason for them to be taken there.

As they went forward into that foul, dripping subbasement of a sub-basement, into the nethermost end of the bottom-most pit, a reddish light arose. It throbbed, a harsh, painful shade, the visual equivalent of a fever headache. Beyond mounds of broken plaster, piles of rotting and long obsolete equipment, empty oil drums, heaped black cables, and puddles of dried, blackish muck, was the glowing object.

The size of a small car, it was shaped roughly like an egg. It was flattened on the top, as though it was dead and slowly collapsing. And though the surface of this egglike thing was black, it emitted a light of its own.

"The first bolus," a tiny voice said in their ears. They turned and looked at Dr. Valentine. He was speaking into a small microphone inside his mask. "It's been close to a hundred years. It was the prototype of the others to come."

The bolus, as Dr. Valentine called it, threw off a throbbing light that was too painful to look at for more than a moment or two. Price and Whitehead knew just enough about physics to realize that the thing was emitting frequencies far above and below the range of visible light.

"It's not radioactive," Dr. Valentine said. "Not in the common sense of the word. We were never interested in working with fission or fusion per se. Too many unknowns, too many variables. We determined early on that atomic energy was a dead end and left it to others to make their fortunes there. There were bigger things in store for us."

Still he hadn't said why they needed to see the bolus. They stood in front of the glowing red-black lump like tourists looking at a peculiar natural formation.

"This was the first of many. And for reasons that aren't quite clear to us, it seems to be the most stable. There's never been any trace of a leak up on ground level. And though a few years back there was some seepage that made it out to the lake, no one has thought it necessary to actually remove the bolus. You could say we've grown quite attached to it, or it to us." He went on in that vein for a while, explaining in nontechnical terms how huge amounts of electrical power could be generated by harnessing the bolus and others like it. But he was skirting the obvious question: what did it have to do with the Cerniac boy?

The doctor stepped back behind Price and Whitehead as he spoke. He was telling them about Stefan Oberfurst, the man responsible for the brotherhood's existence. It was nothing they hadn't heard before.

Suddenly he grabbed them both by the spigotlike valve on the back of their necks and gave them a sharp yank. The suits lost pressure quickly, the air from the cavernous room rushing in to fill their headgear. The smell was overpowering, like a mixture of charred flesh and burning chemical waste. They staggered backward, trying to get out of the chamber. But they heard Dr. Valentine's voice again in their earpieces. "There's no rush, boys, you've already been exposed."

They could have grabbed the doctor, pulled off his headgear, and forced him to breathe the same foul miasma, but they knew it would be useless. "Your initiation back when you were in school was a bit of a red herring, though not completely. That was when you got your first taste of the bolus, even if you didn't know it then. However, now you're really one of us. Not only has the bolus left its mark on you, entered and filled you, but now you can see it for what it really is. You have nothing more to fear once you've seen the bolus face to face."

He pointed. "Go ahead. Get a close look. One more breath won't make any difference. You've already gotten the maximum dosage. The bolus has had its hand on you for years. You've been taking it in by osmosis. A little bit at a time so as not to give you a shock. But now you're full, you've reached your peak. Your cups runneth over, so to speak."

They walked uneasily toward the throbbing mass. Up closer, they saw that the surface was mottled with tiny glistening spots. The smell was awful, as sickening as anything they could imagine. Without being told to do so, first Price and then Whitehead knelt and placed his hands on the surface of the bolus. They closed their eyes and felt the emanation running through them, like a ghostly presence passing through their flesh. They'd felt the same sensation before on a number of occasions, but never known the cause. Now face to face with the bolus, they didn't fight the feeling anymore. They opened themselves and allowed it to take possession of them.

"This will give you boys a little more impetus to get the job done right. We'll be counting on you."

15

It didn't take long to find Garmantown. Whitehead and Price stood at the edge of the pine woods, looking down at the building. The old man was out front, straightening the things that had been knocked about by the previous day's storm. Water lay calm and shining on the rutted driveway. A piece of lawn furniture was hanging from the lower limbs of a birch tree near the road. Scraps of charred wood lay strewn on the yard, blown off a tree that had been hit by lightning.

Without speaking, the partners decided that the time had come to leave their hiding place. They came out of the woods like two traveling salesmen coming to sell the old man something he didn't want.

"Melton Garman," Price said. "You're under arrest for sheltering and abetting a fugitive." Price showed him his badge. Whitehead took the rake out of his hands. "You are accused of giving refuge here yesterday to Brian Cerniac. You knowingly abetted him in his escape from justice."

The old man didn't bother to argue. He knew they could kill him right there, dispose of the body, and not even receive a reprimand from the authorities, let alone be brought to trial for murder.

"You're too late, sonny," Garman said. "Brian's beyond you now."

"We'll find him."

"It won't matter. There's nothing you can do to him."

Price punched the old man in the stomach. It felt good. He punched him again. Dr. Valentine had been right. Once the initial effects of the bolus had worn off, once they were back on the surface breathing clean air and seeing real sunlight, they actually felt stronger, more quick-witted, perhaps even a touch more virile. He grabbed Garman by what little hair he had left and pulled him upright so that they were looking eye to eye.

"We don't need the boy just yet. It isn't quite time. It doesn't matter to us what he does or where he goes as long as he ends up in the right place. We're not really chasing him, Grandpa. We're just making sure he makes all the right turns".

He jerked his arm, pulling out a handful of hair. The old man fell to the ground. "Get up, Grandpa. We want to take a little tour of your place."

Grabbing him by the arms, they lifted him and walked him into the building. Inside, they dropped him into a chair and began poking through his collections. Price opened a glass jar and took out a few peppermint sticks. Unwrapping the cellophane, he stuck them all into his mouth. In a display of local artifacts, Whitehead found a carved war club labeled "Seneca, 17th Century." He hefted it. The end was shaped as a ball with one metal spike sticking out, like the claw of an animal breaking out of an egg. The club was made of dark, smoothly finished wood. The balance was fine. The grip fit his hand perfectly. He swung it over his head and brought it down on a shelf full of ceramic bowls. The shelf itself broke, sending shards of pottery and wood into the air.

He began smashing all the glass and clay objects at hand, and the sound of the breaking was beautiful to his ears. It was as though he'd never heard such music before. But soon all the breakables in that room had been used up and he was forced to stop.

Price was opening and dumping out drawers, kicking through the neatly wrapped artifacts. The old man didn't seem upset. His face was placid. At times a faint smile even showed itself.

When Price and Whitehead had grown bored with wrecking the room, they turned their attention back to the old man. "You missed one," he said calmly, pointing to a ceramic umbrella stand. Whitehead smirked at his partner, cocked back his arm, and let the war club fly. The tall vase exploded, spitting red and blue and yellow shards.

"Direct hit," Price said, grinning like a schoolboy.

Whitehead retrieved his club and swung the barbed end at Garman. But he aimed high and the spiked end streaked over his head, just grazing him. A fine red line appeared on his scalp, seeping blood. Garman hadn't flinched. It was as though he hardly noticed the two men and all the destruction they'd made.

"You know, Grandpa, we can kill you right here and now. There's nothing to stop us."

"And it wouldn't do you a bit of good."

Whitehead giggled, then swung the club, smashing a hole in the wall. He liked the smell of plaster dust. He did it again. Since he'd been exposed to the bolus, odors had taken on a new status for him. It seemed that the scent of the bolus was still in him, flavoring everything else he came in contact with. "This would crack your head like an eggshell."

The old man didn't answer. He sat stiffly, with his back straight and his knees together.

"Did you hear what I said?"

"I heard you."

Price climbed up on a countertop and took a grotesque Iroquois mask off the wall. He fit it over his face and tied the leather thong behind his head. It was carved out of heavy wood, and the features—twisted lips, bulging eyes, and piglike nostrils—were painted in garish scarlets and blues. He adjusted the mask so that he could see, and came at the old man making low, animallike sounds. He dug in his pocket and pulled out a sheaf of papers. Thumbing through them, he came to one with the seal of the state of New York on it.

"This is a warrant." His voice was muffled by the mask. "We can tear this place from top to bottom."

"And you wouldn't find what you're looking for. Brian left here early this morning. He's miles away by now. I gave him directions. He's staying off the main roads. He can go for hours without passing through a town."

"We don't want the boy!" Price shouted. "He's going right where we want him. We don't need to grab him and drag him along if he's willing to go there by his own free will."

"Then why did you come here?"

Price was light-headed. The sound of the voices seemed to come from far away. He'd seen junkies going through withdrawal. He wondered whether it felt like what he was going through. But there was no drug that could take away his shakes, his fever, or his queasy feeling.

He pressed the mask against the old man's face. "You can kill me right now," Garman said. "I know where I'm going. I don't have much to worry about. The pain will last a few seconds and then I'll be through. But you boys, you've got something serious to worry about."

"Shut your mouth!" Price screamed. He could barely breathe inside the mask. But he didn't want to take it off.

The old man went on: "I made the right decision. I don't have anything to worry about. I got out while there was still time. My soul is safe."

"What are you talking about?"

"You boys are going to die long and painful deaths."

Whitehead hit the old man, knocking him to the floor. A trickle of blood ran from the corner of his mouth. But he didn't stop talking. "It's obvious you boys have been exposed. I could tell that as soon as you showed up. I knew you were out there in the woods. I could feel it. You've been exposed, there's no denying it. It's in you now and there's no way to get it out."

Price kicked the old man, landing the tip of his well-shined shoe in Garman's belly.

"You don't know what you're talking about," Price said. "They take care of their own. They're not going to let us down."

Whitehead grabbed his partner and told him to be quiet.

When the old man had recovered from the kick, he got up and sat again in the chair.

"Believe what you want to believe. It doesn't matter to me. You've got a lot of time. Years. Decades. You won't be seeing any symptoms until you're as old as me. Maybe older."

"What do you mean, symptoms?"

Whitehead put his hand on Price's shoulder. "Chuck, come on. Calm down."

"No, I'm not going to calm down. I want to hear what he has to say."

"He's just an old man. He doesn't know anything."

"That's right," Garman said. "I'm just an old man and I don't know a thing."

"What do you mean by symptoms?" Price was shaking him by the shoulders. "How do you know about the bolus?"

"Chuck, shut up."

"No, you shut up and let him talk."

For a moment the color of the light in the room shifted to a deep greenish blue, as if seen below the surface of the ocean. Just as suddenly the light returned to normal. Price thought he saw a nimbus around the old man's head, just barely visible. It glowed like a fluorescent tube.

"How do you know about the bolus?"

"Don't you wonder how I know about Oberfurst House too?"

Price struck him again. Hearing that name on his lips was like hearing the secret name of God spoken by a heathen. It was sacrilege, blasphemy.

Garman wiped the blood off his mouth. He remained on the floor. His voice was weak now. He paused frequently to take breaths. "Don't you recognize one of your brothers?" He had a sick smile on his face. "High above Cayuga's waters," he sang. "I'm a Cornell man too, boys. As was my father. He was there early on, at Oberfurst House. Not from the very beginning, but nearly. Before they even knew what the bolus could do. They were a little more open about it in those days. If you look thoroughly in the literature, I believe you'll even find a few articles about the phenomenon. *Electrical Insights* did a cover article about it. But of course this was long before you boys were born."

"I don't believe it," Whitehead snarled. "He's making it all up."

"Go Big Red!" Garman said, and moved his arm as if waving a pennant. "Four and a half years I spent on the Cornell campus. And I was an exchange student to the Telluride Institute too. You boys know about Telluride, don't you? Tesla's outpost in the west."

"I don't believe it. It's all a lie."

"I can prove it if you want. I have photos. I could probably dig up my diploma if you really want to see it. In the next room."

They grabbed him by the arms and dragged him through the doorway. Electrical equipment took up most of the space there. The old man pointed to a small shadow-box frame on the wall. "My senior ring. My Gallsworthy Cup. And pictures." The first showed a group of men wearing long leather aprons and goggles. They were grouped proudly around a huge transformer. "That's me, the third from the left. In with the in-crowd, so to speak. My father being friends with the Big Man certainly helped. They were all hoping that I'd follow in his footsteps."

"When was this taken?"

Garman thought for a moment, but didn't answer.

"How old are you?"

Still there was no response. The old man seemed to be calculating in his head.

"We're wasting our time here. He might have gone to Cornell. That doesn't mean that he knows anything."

"I knew enough not to get involved. I saw my father get sucked in. In over his head. He was wary at first, he knew the whole enterprise was a risk. But Stefan Oberfurst was a powerful man. He had a way of making even the most skeptical into believers. My father came under his spell. He contributed his part to the effort. He even had a son, me, to carry on his work. But I knew enough to get out before it was too late."

He pointed to another photo. This one seemed to be a long exposure of a lightning strike. It consisted mostly of a series of jagged white lines. But looking more closely, Price saw that behind the glare, like specters, were two men in long protective overcoats. "Nikola Tesla and Stefan Oberfurst," he said. "They worked for a while together. This was after the big war with Edison. Oberfurst was an apt pupil. He learned quickly. He knew he would never be the kind of engineer that Tesla was, working in a dozen different fields. So he concentrated his efforts. He devoted himself to a narrower area. He stole designs, ideas, applications, even a few patents from Tesla. But by then Tesla was already slipping into the darkness. His insanity was starting to overpower him. He'd given up millions of dollars to Westinghouse over the Niagara Falls generators by just tearing up a few pieces of paper. I imagine a few months after doing the initial work on the bolus, he'd completely forgotten about it." Garman paused to take a breath. Price and Whitehead were listening closely.

"His mind was already racing to the next idea, and the next after that. By the end he claimed he'd developed a death ray, a way of communicating with other planets, and a method of transmitting electricity right through the earth's crust. But Stefan Oberfurst was a much more practical man. He saw applications, an entire industry built around a few basic ideas. He saw the first bolus cooking like a monstrous egg, putting out millions of watts of power. But unfortunately he didn't foresee the effects of being exposed. He didn't recognize the symptoms until he was too far gone."

The word *symptom* woke Price and Whitehead from their stupor. As one they grabbed the old man and slammed him against the wall. "What kind of symptoms?"

Garman smiled at them. "It starts out as a rash, usually. A very nasty rash. Then you get fevers, sores in the mouth, night sweats, jaundice, loss of memory. Usually it's diagnosed as cancer. But it doesn't respond to treatment. I watched my father rot for years. By the end he was so full of morphine he didn't know his own name. All because he listened to Stefan Oberfurst and believed."

Price brought his knee up suddenly, jamming it into the old man's groin. He bent over, groaning, and Whitehead chopped down with his arm, cracking the back of Garman's head.

"You're lying," Whitehead hissed. "This is all a story.

You're just trying to be clever. But you're not going to con us with this crap.''

They picked him up and sat him in a wooden chair. Price tore a length of wire off a nearby electrical display and bound the old man's hands behind him. All Price's loops and knots weren't necessary, though. A few twists of sisal twine would have held him.

Price still had the warrant. He clutched it in his hand like a toddler with his security blanket. "This is legal," he said. "Everything we do is legal." His fist caught the side of the old man's head and jerked him sideways. The chair tipped, but stayed on the floor. He asked Garman a few more questions, hardly expecting a coherent answer. The old man muttered something further about Tesla and Oberfurst and the Cerniac boy, and at the sound of that name Price and Whitehead went into a frenzy, breaking windows and smashing furniture. Price found a large pipe wrench and ran around the room, bashing out the glass on all the meters and dials, as if trying to poke out the eyes of the machinery, to keep it from seeing what they were doing.

Soon they'd piled a heap of broken wood, torn papers, and other inflammables around the old man's feet. Looting through the next room, Whitehead found a can of kerosene. He dumped the contents around Garman and shook the last few drops onto his body.

They just needed a spark then or a tiny flame. Price found a large lens in with the broken tools and positioned it so that the beam of concentrated light fell on a stack of newspapers.

He looked down at the warrant and cursed. As a black spot formed on the stack of newspaper, he stepped toward the old man and said, "You have the right to remain silent. You have the right to the services of an attorney." A fine trail of smoke appeared, and then a little flicker of flame. "You have the right to . . . the right to . . ." He shrugged and kicked the heap of papers toward the old man, and the kerosene caught. In seconds Garman was sitting on a throne of fire.

The two ran for the door. On the way out, Price found his war club imbedded in the crumbled plaster of the wall.

He wrenched it loose, and hurried to catch up with his partner.

It wasn't long before the first floor was burning nicely. They thought they heard the old man's voice. He wasn't crying or begging them to save him. It sounded more like prayer, a low, hoarse muttering. Soon, though, it was drowned out by the sound of the flames.

They watched for the better part of an hour, until the fire reached the upper story and then broke through the roof. They stood a safe distance away, watching, waiting, enjoying the smell of wood and shingles and flesh burning. Then, still not having said a word to each other since starting the old man's pyre, they turned and headed back into the woods.

16

Marx had thrown all his staid, bureaucratic clothing in the incinerator at the last hotel where they'd stayed. He was dressed now in plain jeans and a Hawaiian print shirt. And Dr. Haak too had gotten rid of her professional clothes. She'd filled a plastic garbage bag with them and stuffed it into a metal can at one of the scenic overlooks they stopped at frequently. She wore now a long dress cinched at the waist with a silver chain, which made her seem far more feminine than the drab skirts and lab coat she wore back at Mt. Kinnsvort. The dress was loose around her chest and shoulders, and she wore it with the top few buttons undone. The sleeves were full, billowy, making her look like a woman who'd just walked out of a medieval tapestry. She'd even gotten rid of her flat, sensible shoes and had on now a pair of sandals that laced high up her calves. Her toenails were painted the same flame-red as her fingernails.

Though they were supposedly looking for Brian, it seemed she was following no rational plan. They'd stayed two days in a little motel outside of Cortland, watching TV and going out at night to wander the streets when all the shops were closed. Then they went south on Route 81 and stopped just over the Pennsylvania border. She made a halfhearted attempt to explain their wanderings, but Marx didn't pay much attention. It was obvious that she was just marking time.

Being in Pennsylvania seemed to make her uneasy, and they didn't even spend the night there. After poking around a gift shop and eating packaged sandwiches from a vending machine, they headed back into New York again, driving past Elmira to Watkins Glen.

With all the other tourists, they hiked the gorge at the state park there. They said nothing as they went up and down the winding staircases, in and out of the dripping tunnels. They stayed close together, at times holding hands, but barely a dozen words passed between them in the hours they spent in the park.

The night before, they'd talked well past midnight. She'd finally broached the topic that they'd been avoiding for days. It had taken her awhile to get going, but once the flow started, it seemed to Marx that he might not be able to stop her.

That night they'd gone directly from eating to sex. They both put down their half-eaten double cheeseburgers at the same moment, and went at each other like cannibals. Her breath had tasted of burnt meat. Her skin was rank and musky, as though she'd been sleeping for days in a cave, wound up in animal skins. He'd pulled her to the floor, popping the buttons off the front of her dress, and quickly they were entangled, rolling in the waxed paper from the hamburgers and the little paper boats for the french fries. As before, sex for them was fierce, frantic, bordering on desperate. And as before, when it was all over, they pulled away from each other silent and sullen.

They drew apart, exhausted and slick with sweat, but still she was unsatisfied. "It isn't you," she said in the darkness. "Really, it has nothing to do with you. It's me. It's all inside of me. I've always been this way."

"It still bothers me." He felt sick. He felt empty and worthless.

"It's something wrong with me, not you."

Their first time together, he'd gotten a hint of things to come. She'd made sounds like he'd never heard before, desperate noises like someone trying to crawl out of a very deep pit. They'd gone back at it that first time, again and again. It surprised Marx just how much he had in him. But then, as in that catsup-and-grease-stinking motel room in Watkins Glen, she'd finally given up and turned away from him, shaking, on the verge of tears.

"And there's nothing we can do about it? We're just stuck with things this way?"

She didn't answer at first.

He felt a twinge of dread, a hint that things were finally going to be explained to him. She pressed her face into the hollow of his shoulder, breathing her hot breath against his skin. He held onto her tightly, as though she was the one who needed comforting, the one who needed to be protected from something thus far unsaid.

"There is a chance, a small chance."

He waited, a cold coil unwinding in his belly.

"You remember what I told you about my shunt?" He remembered. It was all nonsense to him, idiotic and dangerous games medical people played with each other. He still wasn't completely convinced it was true.

She took hold of his hand and guided it to her neck. The two little rubber pegs protruded slightly, like moles. Since the night she'd told him about the shunt, he'd succeeded in not thinking about it, pushing away images of her husband, of the Cerniac boy hooked in with the wires, like an animal in a lab.

"It was my idea, not his. I mean, it was my idea that I be the first one to receive the shunt." She talked about it as though it were a gift, given and received. "He didn't want to do it at first. He said it was too dangerous. He was right about that. I survived and he didn't."

Marx was getting the strange, heady feeling again that she was holding him over an abyss. The more she said, the more the entire situation seemed impossible. That he was there naked and spent, that he'd thrown away his job to go chasing halfway across the state for an escaped mental patient, that he was listening to a beautiful but barely sane woman whose clothes he'd just torn off, all seemed completely impossible.

"So what are you trying to say?" His own voice seemed very far away. "That you want to implant one of these shunts in me?"

"No."

He relaxed. He imagined she'd go into a confession that was a little more rational. Perhaps she'd start weeping and tell him that she couldn't find satisfaction except through some perversion.

"No, I don't want to implant a shunt." Her voice was almost too quiet to be heard. "You already have one."

The drunken feeling rose up inside him again. He wanted to reach back and check his neck. But he didn't move. He was too afraid that she'd somehow performed an operation on him without him knowing it. Given the other things she'd told him, that wouldn't have seemed so strange.

"You've had one for fifteen years. But the actual stomas aren't open. They're just below the surface. It wouldn't take that much to open them up. It wouldn't be much more than cosmetic surgery."

At first he wanted to convince her that she was simply mistaken. Then he began to think her sanity was even more fragile than he'd assumed, that she was obsessed with something awful that had happened to her years before. Then he just wouldn't listen. But she knew too much. She'd been through his records and had apparently seen files on him that he didn't even know existed. She had all the facts. And given that what she was saying was impossible, it made perfect sense.

"This is crazy," he said. "How could I have had an operation without even knowing it?"

"I don't have everything put together yet. Not every last piece. But I don't need the tiny details to see the whole situation.

"The man my husband worked with early on was Dr. Gerald Fine. He's the one who actually developed the technology. But his research went in a different direction than Charley's. Fine was interested in what he called thanatomorphic experiences. In layman's terms that would be post-death or during-death experiences. He needed human subjects and of course there was some difficulty in getting volunteers. Even offering shorter sentences to some of the inmates at Attica wasn't possible, as it had been with the Starns vaccine and Shermerhorn's experiments with trepanation. But Jerry Fine knew how to get what he wanted. There was a U.S. Army base less than an hour from his laboratory. The 128th Air Tactical Battalion. What he couldn't do with felons he could do with soldiers. After all, he used to say, they've sworn to uphold the Constitution and defend it against all enemies.

"You served seventeen months on that base. You were one of his first tries. It's a cruder version that those my husband developed. But it's good enough. And it's waiting for you, Saul. It needs to be opened, liberated, allowed to do what it was designed for."

He argued with her, but at every turn she seemed to know more about his life than he did. As she saw the situation, it was quite simple. He'd come down with what he was told was a bad case of pneumonia. In fact, they—and it wasn't exactly clear who they were—had infected him with rhyprome, which mimics the symptoms of pneumonia. He was in the base hospital for over a month. The cut on the back of his neck, which he was told he'd suffered after falling out of his bed, was the doctor's point of entry. The implant was made, but then sealed over. She explained that later, at Mt. Kinnsvort, some of the worst-case patients had been given live shunts, run through their paces, and disposed of. But the group he was part of was used for a slightly different purpose. "They were thinking very long term, Saul. Years down the line. They wanted to see what would happen to someone with the implant over the course of a decade or two. In your case, it was headaches. Two other men from your base suffered migraines so severe they killed themselves to end the pain. Another found out somehow about the implant and was going to spill the whole story. But he died in a car crash before the story came out. And there are three men still at Mt. Kinnsvort, where we've been observing them for years."

"We?" Marx lay in the darkness with his eyes wide open. Her voice went on and eventually he stopped fighting it.

"My work is government funded. A person in my field can't get clearances and grants and subjects unless he plays by the rules. Until a few days ago I was one of their best. I knew more about the shunts, and what happens to a subject during discharge, than anyone in the program. But we had a parting of the ways. I don't need them anymore. And I won't abide their interference. What I do with my patients should be solely up to me. I think I know better than bureaucrats what's best for them.''

He'd seen articles in supermarket tabloids, usually tucked in the back with the weight-loss testimonials and astrology ads, about people claiming that the government was somehow controlling their minds. They had titles like ''Uncle Sam Made Me a Murderer'' and ''Secret Government Agency Monitors Your Dreams!'' It took Marx some screwing up of his courage, but he asked at last, ''They use the shunt to control me, is that it? I've been doing what they want all these years?''

She shook her head. ''No, that wasn't the purpose. I suppose it would be possible with the right technology, but that wasn't in their plan as far as I know. What Dr. Fine had in mind was wiring his subjects in such a way that they could both take in impulses and store them, like a semiconductor building up a charge. He called it 'pushing them through the wall.' Brian's the only one we've had much luck with. He's consistent, he's easy to work with, and when he discharges, it's like nothing in the whole world.

''I suspect he can do it all by himself now. He can build up a charge and then let it loose, and he gets dragged along with it right through the wall.''

The air conditioner clicked on, and Marx felt the cold draft drying the sweat on his back and along his legs. He shivered and the spasm seemed to go right into her. She held onto him even more tightly.

''Saul, as far I know, you've never been tested. I've seen all the records and it looks like all they did was make the implant. That's probably why you didn't have such negative aftereffects.'' Her lips brushed his. Her whisper was like a voice speaking inside him. ''We can open you up, Saul. I know how to do it. It would be easy. We can make the conversion. You said you wanted to help me. You said you were on my side. That's all I want from you, nothing more. Just a chance.

''I can't guarantee it, but I have a feeling that if we open you up, you'll never have any more headaches. Isn't it worth a try? How long has it been, fifteen years? wouldn't it be worth it if it worked?''

Yes, fifteen years since he'd entered the base hospital with what he'd thought was pneumonia, gone into a coma, and gotten out to find his wife dead, his assignment changed, and even his appearance slightly different.

They'd told him their version of the story, how Lenny had been run off the road and had died instantly. They'd given him a new position and different responsibilities. They gave him a new apartment and even had his belongings moved for him.

And he looked in the mirror that first morning after getting out of the hospital. Someone he didn't quite know looked back at him. The features were the same, the shade and cut of his hair and his expressions hadn't changed. But there was something definitely different.

"They killed Lenny, didn't they?" He believed it with his heart already. It made emotional sense even if the details hadn't all fallen into place yet.

She nodded. "I'm not exactly sure why, but it looks like she was suspicious of the whole thing. And when they didn't let her see you for over a week, it just confirmed her fears. Even someone in intensive care is allowed visits from his wife. She started making inquiries and poking around. She asked questions and tried to find the other men who'd been admitted to the hospital for minor ailments and stayed in a long time. And a week later she was dead in a car crash. That much is for sure. A car did run her off the road, but I doubt very much it was an accident."

He could easily imagine Lenny poking her nose where an army wife shouldn't have. And it was just as easy to imagine them killing her for it. He'd never been directly involved in covert operations, but he'd heard third-and fourth-hand stories about troublemakers—protesters during the war, squatters outside a nuclear power plant, even a lawyer who'd filed one too many freedom of information requests—disappearing or suddenly developing psychotic symptoms and having to be institutionalized for life.

"They really did kill her, didn't they? She's not in an insane asylum?" That would be much worse. He'd rather it was clean and final.

"I think so. All the evidence I've seen indicates that she really did die."

Marx hadn't seen the body. He'd been in the hospital when it happened. They didn't tell him about the accident until the body had been cremated. Marx hoped it was that simple. The thought of her locked up and fed a diet of psychosis-inducing drugs would be too much to bear.

He wanted to be asleep, dead to himself and the world. He pulled away and climbed into the bed. She asked him a few more questions, but he didn't answer. He lay facing away from her, think of nothing, of a black, empty place, of a void that went on forever.

The next morning he felt her get out of bed and heard her go outside, then fell back asleep. It was past noon when he finally awoke. The sun was harsh and hot on his face. The room smelled of air conditioning and stale junk food. He went into the bathroom, but avoided looking in the mirror, afraid that the sight of his face would bring back the events of the previous night. He got into the shower and stayed there until the hot water ran out.

When he went back into the bedroom, she was there, dressed and ready. She bound her hair again in a ponytail, positioning it back over the two black dots on her neck.

"I don't want to talk about it," he said before she could open her mouth. "Okay?"

After eating a silent meal in the Checkered Flag Diner, they drove the short distance to the gorge park and began the ascent. He counted all the stone steps that they went up, saying, "Three hundred, four hundred, five hundred," as they passed those points in the climb. He pictured the actual numbers turning as on a car's odometer. He heard the sound of the numbers in his head, like a chant or even a prayer, keeping away the other thoughts.

The falling water made a pleasant sound. The stream-carved rock was beautiful, but he barely noticed. At the five hundredth step he took her hand, and they walked that way quite a distance, still not speaking. Above them, beyond the stone-walled gorge, the sun was hot and brilliant. But they moved in the shade of the dripping stone walls, protected from the light. It seemed they were traveling along a pathway into the very distant past, as though when they reached the top, years or decades or centuries would have passed. But they finished their long climb and all was the same. Marx saw a young couple licking drips off the same ice cream cone. A bus load of tourists were milling about, getting ready to go down through the gorge. A ratlike dog was yipping at its owner's heels, running in circles as if possessed. For the first time since leaving Mt. Kinnsvort, Marx felt a stab of pain from the base of his skull, working its way upward. He'd had nothing approaching a headache since going over to the doctor's side. Until that moment, whatever spell she was working had kept the pain far away. The sun hurt his eyes. The sound of the dog's noise set off small waves of pain. It occurred to him that his headache might have merely made a tactical withdrawal marshaling its strength for an overpowering attack.

"All right," he said at last. "We'll do it."

She nodded and squeezed his hand. Her skin was damp and hot. He caught a whiff of her scent and breathed deeply, trying to fill his lungs.

"Are you going to need any special equipment?"

"No, I brought everything from the lab."

They hitched a ride with a German couple back to the base of the gorge. The woman talked almost nonstop about "great natural beauty" and "wonderful scenic vistas." Marx nodded politely and thought of scalpels and probes working their way into his head. "You are most fortunate to be living in such a wonderful country," she said, pointing down at the gorge.

"Yes, we're very fortunate," Marx agreed.

Dr. Haak was ready to operate soon after they got back to the motel. As Marx lay on the bed, waiting for the anesthetic to hit, he imagined all the other sordid events that had taken place there: adulteries, petty drug deals, drunken fights. He was reasonably sure that no one had performed surgery there before.

She kissed him long and hard before he became unconscious. Then she waited at his side, one hand holding his as if to reassure him, and the other holding a scalpel.

17

Once Ollie was back at work, he saw how much the Red House had changed. Dr. Brule was gone. Some said he'd taken a long vacation to rest up after all the ruckus. But the gossip in the staff lounge claimed that he'd had a breakdown and had to be sent to another facility for special treatment. Dr. Simonsen and Dr. Haak were gone, but no one said a word about them. There was a new director, whom Ollie had yet to meet. And the two men from the state board, Mr. Price and Mr. Whitehead, kept looking around and asking questions.

They were much nicer to Ollie than the others at the Red House. He had a vague memory of them coming to visit him a few times while he had been in the infirmary, asking about Dr. Haak and Brian, but he'd been no help to them. They always got around to talking about the night he was attacked, and until recently he had no memory of what had happened. He just knew that he hurt all over and wanted to get back at whoever had done it to him.

They said they needed his help. They said it was important to build up his strength again so that he could go back to work. They made the nurses treat him well, and assigned extra help for him in the physical therapy room. They even made sure his food was hot and he had double portions of dessert. And slowly his memory started to come back and the strength returned to his body. Finally one day he pieced it all together and remembered what had happened.

"It was Dr. Haak for sure. She used the rod of correction. She burned me and knocked me around. She was mad at me for messing with her Brian."

They asked him twice if he was sure.

"It was her. She must have worked late that night, and she showed up in the therapy rooms and started in with the rod. She was really mad at me. Because I knew all about her and Brian. She was doing things with him that she shouldn't have. She called him her little lamb."

They seemed to be very happy once he'd figured out the whole story. They promised that as soon as he was ready, they had a very special job for him.

There was a new orderly working his shifts, so he wasn't needed there anymore. But Mr. Whitehead put his arm around Ollie's shoulder like they were good friends and told him that there were bigger and better things waiting for him. In the wing where Dr. Haak had had her new suite, they set him up with his own office. It had a desk and a few bookshelves and a painting of a seascape on the wall. He had his own telephone and electric pencil sharpener. But he didn't use them much. He spent most of his time in the main area of his new lab, behind a thick glass wall, looking in on his subjects. They even gave him a white lab coat just like the doctors wore and a plastic name plate to pin on his breast pocket.

At first Ollie was afraid to start his new job. Until then he'd only done things that orderlies do. But Mr. Whitehead and Mr. Price both told him how much confidence they had in him, and explained that he could start simply and work up from there.

His first assignment was just to learn his way around the control board. They gave him rats to start with, and when they made sure he knew how the system worked, they gave him a monkey with a name he couldn't pronounce. He called it Bobby instead and had him wired up and discharging, as his new bosses called it, in a day. But things didn't work out exactly right, and they had to bury Bobby way out by the fence.

He thought they were going to be mad at him for using the monkey up so quickly, but they didn't say a word about it. And the next day his first real subject was delivered to the lab. It was a bony old woman that he seemed to remember Dr. Simonsen working with. By the time Ollie got her, she was pretty far gone. She didn't respond very well to therapy. Her output was on the low end of the scale, and she seemed to be fighting him the whole way.

She looked pretty bad, wearing just a flimsy gown, most of her hair gone, her skin gray like ash. She seemed to be mad at him all the time, staring at him with her little yellow slit eyes. Ollie spent a lot of time with her, fussing with the cuffs, making sure the electrodes and pads were in the right place. His work with Dr. Haak came in handy then. He was familiar with all the equipment. But this was the first time that he had been in charge.

He asked his new bosses what exactly he was trying to get from his subjects, but their answer was vague. They told him they needed someone with experience and who wasn't afraid to do what needed to be done. He didn't press them. They'd been so nice to him. He didn't want to get on their wrong side.

And the work itself was much better than delivering meals and changing bed sheets. He was completely in charge of this new lab and didn't have to answer to any of the doctors and nurses who used to boss him around.

His second subject was more lively than the first. It was a man whom he'd never seen before. He acted as though he'd never had therapy, being much less cooperative than the old woman. Ollie had to use the restraining harness on him and the Sheffield bit in his mouth so that he wouldn't gag on his tongue. His output was much higher, right into the red zone. It worried him that he might use the subject up too quickly, but Mr. Whitehead and Mr. Price had already given their approval to push the subjects as hard as necessary. This was important work and everyone needed to give their all.

The second subject thrashed and sweated a lot more than

the first. Ollie had to stop a few times to adjust the straps and reposition the electrodes. And after the first session with him, he had to tape his fingers flat so that he wouldn't gouge his palms anymore.

Ollie had a working knowledge of the EEG readouts, and he knew about blood pressures and skin conductivity. But most of his gauges and meters had no labels, and those that did just put out numbers and letters that made no sense to him.

His third subject was the hardest. At first Ollie thought he was going to get absolutely nothing out of him. He had to keep stopping the therapy to make sure the subject was alive. There was always a faint trace left. When Mr. White-head and Mr. Price inspected the data from the third sub-ject, they seemed quite pleased and took the papers with them when they left.

That night, when Ollie got back to his room, there was a stack of brand-new motorcycle magazines and a plate heaped high with fudge brownies waiting for him. He stayed up late, going through the magazines, dog-earing the pages that he liked best and eating most of the brownies. He tore a few of the centerfolds out and taped them carefully on his walls. While he had been in the infirmary, all the other staff who'd been living on his floor had been moved elsewhere. He had the entire floor to himself. He didn't have to worry about noise anymore, or inspections, or any doctors coming around and telling him it was bad for him to have those pictures looking down at him all the time.

His favorite of this new batch showed a woman who looked a lot like Dr. Haak. She had on a tight leather vest and high black boots and nothing else. Her legs were clamped around the body of the cycle. Ollie lay on his bed a long time looking at her, squinting, then letting his eyes relax and making her into Dr. Haak. It wasn't hard. He could easily imagine her on the bike, tearing down the road with flames coming out the tail pipe and her hair streaming behind.

He fell asleep looking at her, and woke an hour or two later from an uneasy sleep. The lights in his room were still on. The biker babe was still there, hovering like a guardian angel above his bed. And though his door was open, he heard no sound from the hallway.

He got off his bed and tied his shoes. Back when other staffers had lived on his floor, there'd always been a low undercurrent of noise, no matter what the hour. When he'd go on his late-night walks, he'd hear the low murmur from a radio, snores, bed springs creaking, an electric fan, or just the soft hum of twenty people all breathing together in their sleep.

But that night the only sound he heard was the buzz of a fluorescent light and the click of his heels on the tile floor.

He went to the end of the hall and down two flights of steps. Instead of turning toward his new work area or to the kitchen and staff lounge, he went in the direction of the main entrance. He'd never once gone there on his night walks. The sight of the offices and reception rooms at that hour was strange, as though they'd been abandoned years before.

He never went outside. He hadn't gone through the big double doors in years. But that night he grasped the big knob without thinking and swung the door back. The night air rushed past him, cool and damp and laden with all sorts of smells that he couldn't recognize.

The main driveway stretched in front of him, leading to the gate. On either side were flower beds and tall trees. The wind was moving gently, making them sigh and whisper. He passed through the doorway and went down the front steps. There was no moon that night. The stars were thick and bright, lighting the gardens and groves he walked past, giving everything the appearance of a place far below the surface of the ocean.

He shivered and stuck his hands in his pockets. He had a little loose change, a set of keys for his new lab, and a few pencil stubs.

The gravel made a low crunching sound as he went away from the building. He didn't turn to look back. But he could feel it behind him, huge and enormously heavy, the hundreds of windows watching him like a wall of eyes. He didn't want to look back because he was afraid of seeing a window lit up, and that would mean that someone knew he was leaving.

The high iron gate was open. Mr. Whitehead and Mr. Price were waiting for him. They both had on long black raincoats. It was too dark to really see their faces, but he was sure in an instant that it was them and that they'd woken him and brought him to that place.

"Ollie," one of them said. He could never tell their voices apart. "We've been very pleased with the work you've been doing. Very, very pleased. But it was just training, a trial run. We thought you were the one we needed for this special job and now we're sure."

They came close to him, both putting their arms around his shoulders. They made a huddle there, all three linked, their heads close together.

"Dr. Haak was working with us, Ollie. But she's gone over to the other side. She's broken her promises to us and done things that are very wrong. We need someone to straighten her out. Do you think you could do that?"

It didn't seem they really wanted him to answer.

"She's made some very serious mistakes, telling things to people who shouldn't hear, doing things she has no right to do. We thought we had a good relationship with her, but it turns out we were wrong. She's betrayed us."

Ollie nodded. She'd betrayed him too. She'd thrown him away for the boy. She'd used the rod of correction on him for no reason. And worse, she'd left him all alone.

"She needs to be taken care of. Do you think you're the one to do that?"

Ollie nodded again, and they went together away from the Red House, heading into the shadows that hung heavily from the trees. Soon they were moving in complete blackness, but Ollie wasn't afraid.

18

He came around a long bend in the road and saw the high-tension wires. They were held up by huge metal towers, like the skeletons of monsters who'd had their flesh burnt off. They were nothing but metal bones, but still in some way alive, compelled to hang onto the endless black cables. He knew that at night, or when no one was watching, they marched forward, carrying the power away from Niagara Falls.

Brian saw them and slowed down. He had all the windows closed tightly so that no music would leak out. All the dials were up to ten. The meter on the cassette player was peaking, the needle pushed all the way to the right, into the red zone. The bass was coming hard and heavy. He felt it inside his body, like a hand massaging his heart, beating on it the way doctors do to bring somebody back to life.

He slowed the van and stared. But it wasn't just the sight of the towers that grabbed him. They emitted an invisible field, electromagnetic waves throbbing out unseen but not unfelt. He was inside the field. He felt the power—just like the funk—touching his head, tugging him. The shunt was a hook inside his brain, and the cables were the fishing line, pulling him toward the west.

The towers were monsters marching out of his memory, out of the Ictus. They wanted to get him, not to hurt him but to carry him home. A thin trickle of memory began to flow inside him, like a spring just breaking to the surface. He didn't fight it this time. He sat still and watched the pictures from a long time ago just as the others at the Red House watched TV. He was passive, accepting. They came and he didn't turn his eyes away.

He saw a street of small houses. A school. A green play-ing field, a swing set and a jungle gym. He saw black, reeking sinkholes opening up in the ground. Kids playing with firerocks, throwing them at the ground and jumping back as they exploded. He saw black ooze coming into his basement, a thick jelly running down the walls, throwing off a greasy light of its own.

"Dead on it!" Brian said, getting the van going again. "Low down and dirty! Cerniac Device coming in for a land-ing." As he picked up speed, he veered into the middle of the road so that the van was straddling the white line. At least on that stretch of road, the visible and the invisible lines lay right on top of each other. "Baby Bri-nor funky homecoming." His right foot started pumping on the ac-celerator, as if it was a drum pedal. His head did the jerk. "Uhnnn! Can you feel? Uhnnnn! Got to feel it!"

He didn't need the music from the stereo anymore. The beat and the heat, the pump and the white-hot thump were coming together inside his head. "Soul power!" he shouted at a herd of sheep grazing by the side of the road. "Raw soul!"

The old man had given him a map with arrows and little notes written on it, but he didn't need it anymore. He was right on the money, cruising the main line. The black ooze in his memory kept dripping, running down the basement wall. The fire rocks kept exploding and the holes in the baseball diamond kept opening up like big, ugly mouths, trying to swallow up the other kids. The smell was every-where. It was bad, bad as it comes, but it was home. And that's where he wanted to be.

He came to an intersection, and without looking at the

map, he made the turn. He felt it, he knew it was right. A few miles farther along was another fork in the road. This time he closed his eyes, saw the streams of yellow and white and pale blue light running to the left, and he allowed himself to be swept along in that current. It was like swimming in a fast river. He just needed to keep his nose pointed forward and he'd go where he needed to go.

Since he'd left Mr. Garman's place, he was seeing the aura almost all the time. During the storm it was so thick and juicy that it leaked out as lightning. He'd learned that up on the roof: lightning happens when there's so much aura in the air that it can't hold any more.

His hands were tingling. He saw a faint aura there, like the afterglow when a light bulb is turned off. He squeezed the wheel and it got stronger.

There was a hum in the air too. It grew louder as he steered the van exactly into the middle of the current, and faded to near silence when he had to go far to the side of the road to let a truck stacked high with hay go by.

The place he was moving through had a curve and swell to it, like huge waves in the ocean. He felt pressure in his ears as he rose, and the sudden pop of release as he went across the crest. And then he was going down again, gliding into a valley. The power lines were still in sight, but they were moving slowly away from the road.

Reaching the bottom of the swell, he started picking up blasts of static. He switched on the radio to see if it was just noise on that band width, but beside a hoarse, angry-sounding man preaching about precious bodily fluids and hair and a station playing easy-listening versions of country-western hits, he couldn't pick up anything with much definition. As the trees became more dense around the road, shading it from the harsh summer light, the static welled up, drowning out the funk. It was beyond interference by then. He knew there was a signal mixed in with the noise, a message for him and him alone. He closed his eyes and tried to pick out the long and short pulses, but they remained hidden.

He must have kept them shut too long. The noise grew and got stronger, and suddenly he jerked awake, pulling hard on the wheel to keep the van from going into the ditch.

By then the noise had filled him completely, like air filling an empty tire. It was overpowering, a steady, rising howl.

He saw a historical marker up ahead and put on the brakes. He pulled up beside the metal sign and tried to read it through the haze of pain and throbbing light. "On this site in 1779, during the Sullivan Campaign against the Six Nations of the Iroquois, a small reconnaissance was brutally massacred."

His eyes couldn't keep going. The noise was huge inside him, pounding in his forebrain. He took a deep breath. He clenched his hands on the wheel. He tried again to finish reading the sign. "Scouting ahead of the main body of General Sullivan's army, searching for the Tuscarora dwelling place known as Bad-Water-Town, the seven Continentals were fallen upon and most horribly butchered."

Groping blindly now, Brian felt through his hair and found his cord. It was still plugged into his shunt, hanging down the back like a Chinaman's pigtail. He flipped back the engine cowl and touched the leads to the battery terminals. The jolt hit him hard and fast, clearing away the brilliant haze. He read again, "horribly butchered," but when he licked the leads and fired the juice again into himself, instead of seeing white men beaten and cut to pieces, it was the Indians he saw, their town burnt, their women and children slaughtered. He was sitting exactly where the massacre had taken place, looking back two hundred years into the Ictus, and instead of brave patriots ambushed and killed, it was the Iroquois who were being hacked to pieces by savage white men.

He made contact again, the juice hitting like a fist against his temple. He got a perfect picture, as though his head was poking back two centuries. White men were stalking about, their faces smeared with blood and ashes. Acre after acre of native corn lay burnt flat. Indians—both warriors and the helpless—were cut down like animals butchered for their meat. He looked ahead just an hour or two and saw the soldiers eating the corpses, gnawing the flesh still warm from the bodies.

The main party of American soldiers was a good distance away. Brian felt safe for the moment. He allowed himself to enter that world just a little more. But then two of the soldiers noticed him and pointed, zooming at him like puppets running on invisible wires. One had a dozen Seneca scalps hanging from his belt. The other held a war club, apparently captured from one of the Indians. The ball end was daubed with blood and brains.

It was clear that these two wanted Brian, only Brian, not the Indians or their villages. They'd come there specifically to get him. The nearer one swung with the war club, and it left an afterglow in the air, a swath of brightness. It seemed to be charged with energy, like the rod of correction. Brian was drawn to the club, he wanted to reach out and touch it. But as the men swooped down on him, howling, he got his first good look at their faces: blood-flecked and contorted with rage.

Before they could touch him, though, he plugged in a final time and started losing altitude fast, plummeting away from that wild, bloody scene. He dropped through the black and into the red. Soon he was far away, safe for the time being.

When he came to the surface again, all the light had fled from the sky. The noise too had changed, dwindled, reshaped itself into a pure, listenable signal. He'd slept for hours, recharging himself. And the sound too had rested, now no longer angry and out of control.

He started the van and pulled ahead, following the sound like an animal chasing the scent of food. Shortly he came to a place where a dirt road branched off from the route he was traveling on. He turned there, but only went a few hundred feet before seeing a tall log arch spanning the road. Electric lights lit it from below. Made out of raw planks was a sign that read "CAMP CHARISM." On either side were crudely carved doves, their heads pointed downward, diving into fire.

The signal was coming from beyond the arch. It was beckoning him to come closer. It throbbed out of the dark woods like chants and drumming coming from deep inside a jungle.

He passed under the arch and quickly came upon a large field surrounded by log buildings. Farther on, he could almost hear with his ears the welcoming song. He rolled down his window and finally it hit him clearly. It was the sound of hundreds of voices singing a hymn. He parked and walked into the woods, following a narrow path. A reddish, quaking light swam out of the darkness. The singing stopped suddenly and a single voice took its place, shouting. Still, Brian couldn't make out any of the actual words.

Up closer, he saw that the light was being thrown by a huge fire, and ranked around it were hundreds of teenagers. They were listening to the loud, metallic-sounding voice. It ceased and they erupted in song again. It was beautiful, the wave of music pushing through the woods to grab him. He started to run. His eyes were snared by the small mountain of fire. His ears were swollen with the roaring hymn.

He ran, heading directly at the fire, but just as he came to the edge of the woods, the song ceased suddenly and the single voice rang out again, loud and insistent. Brian stopped. He leaned against a huge tree with rough bark and a pitchy smell surrounding it. He caught his breath and looked beyond the fire. A raised wooden platform had been built next to the fire altar. Two figures separated themselves from the shadows and approached the platform. They climbed the stairs and took their place at the rail. They lifted their hands above their heads and everything—even the fire—grew quiet.

19

At first Price and Whitehead felt foolish in the long black gowns. But once they arrived at the bonfire, saw the masses of teenagers all waiting for them to speak, felt the expectation in the air thick as the pine wood smells, they relaxed and began to enjoy their new role.

From where they stood, the formations of bodies were like blocks carved out of stone, ranked perfectly, aligned in concentric circles around the fire. As the flames rose and the light spread outward, more and more of the faces could be seen, wide-eyed and expectant.

Again Reverend Fine's voice came out of the darkness. He was using his bullhorn, circling around the gathering, going up and down the narrow aisles like a television talk show host working the crowd. As he emphasized certain words and phrases, his voice rose in pitch and sounded like an old woman's cackle. Already he was hitting his peak. shouts of "Hallelujah" and "Amen" rose up in response to his preaching. Spontaneous outbursts of song erupted and swept across the entire gathering, like waves stirred up by a sudden wind.

"You can't do our Lord's work unless you're filled with his spirit!" Fine bellowed. "You've got to open yourself up. You've got to let him in. You've got to say 'Take me, take me, I'm yours.' " Fine strode toward them and up the three stairs at the side of the platform. He took his place between Price and Whitehead, with his arms around their shoulders.

"We're starting on a great journey here tonight. The most important journey you'll ever take. And I'm so very glad that we have with us tonight two very special friends. They've come a long way to share this special experience with us. I'm so very happy now to introduce to you two very holy men, two men who've given themselves over completely to the service of our Lord, Brother Chip Whitehead and Brother Chuck Price!"

They couldn't outshout or outharangue Fine, so Whitehead and Price went the opposite route, almost whispering into the microphone. They spoke to the crowd in low, confiding terms, as if giving away great secrets. It worked well and allowed Fine to use his hoarse exhortations to punctuate their talk.

"It doesn't matter," Whitehead began, "if you're popular or not. If you're pretty or plain. If you're the captain of the football team or a nobody. Our Lord doesn't care one little bit."

"And that's the beauty of his plan," Price went on. "He can use anybody, as long as you're willing to give yourself up to his power and his ways. That's all it takes. The will to have no will. The desire to have no desire.

"Our Lord has a plan for each and every one of you. You're all part of a greater body. Some of you are the feet to carry us along, some the hands to grasp and hold, some hearts, some bones, some mouths to sing praises, and some ears to hear messages. I'm sure you've all heard this before in your home churches. And you've all taken this message to heart and decided that you want more than anything to follow the true path."

Price and Whitehead had been around people who imagined they were speaking in tongues, but the spontaneous welling up of noise that followed their little speech was unexpected and a little frightening. It started low, almost

inaudible, but soon dozens of teenagers were making the
same nonsense sound, repetitive and rhythmic: "Shicketa,
shicketa, shicketa." They were swaying, masses of bodies
all moving as one. Both Price and Whitehead felt the momentum slipping away from them, as if a power really was
moving among the crowd. Some of the kids were weeping.
Others clapped their hands above their heads and shouted.
Fine sensed that the tide was shifting too and shouted into
his bullhorn, trying to get everyone to sing "Kum by Yah."
A few went along with him, groaning the words, but suddenly a girl jumped up from her bench and headed for the
podium.

They hadn't intended to create this kind of hysteria. There
was more important work to be done. Fine had all summer
to induce seizures and have his way with the subjects. Once
they had the job done, it didn't matter what he did with the
rest of the kids. But right then they couldn't ignore the girl.
She was babbling and shaking. She clambered onto the
stage, raving as though she really was possessed by a demon. Whitehead grabbed her and Price turned her to face
the crowd. The hysteria focused itself on her, coalescing in
her strange noises and spastic movements.

"What's your name, girl?"

She could barely speak. Her tongue was flailing like a
snake's. They didn't need gauges and meters to tell that she
was having a seizure. She was exactly the right age, a year
or two into puberty. She was just at the stage where she was
neither a girl nor a woman yet. But they didn't want to start
the evening out with a grand mal. Weepy confessions and
heartfelt testimonies would have been far better.

Price gestured for the camp nurse to come to the podium,
and supported the girl as his partner spoke to the crowd,
improvising.

"Come out of her, in the name of our Lord, the only true
Lord, the Lord of this world and the next."

She was strong, still thrashing and moaning. She smelled
of adolescent sweat and wild hormones. Her hair was long
and tangled. For a moment her eyes met Price's. It seemed
that more than one person was looking at him. He turned
quickly away.

"Out! Out! In the name of our Lord, loosen your grasp on this child and come out of her."

The nurse had finally gotten a good hold of the girl's arm and slid the needle in. Price shouted a few more times and Fine struck up a song. Soon the whole gathering, hundreds of voices in unison, were singing and clapping their hands.

The sedative took effect at last and the girl relaxed in their arms. Price nodded and the nurse led her off the podium, down to a stretcher where two counselors were waiting to take her to Fine's cabin.

When the song ended, Price took over, jumbling together a little sermon about the New Jerusalem on Earth, a heavenly paradise that would come to pass once the power of their Lord was supreme.

Whitehead signaled to Fine, who started prowling up and down the aisles, pointing here and there and accusing individuals of various vague sins. Fine knew which ones were the best bets to pick on. He'd been through their medical and school records, and had singled them out as soon as they'd arrived at the camp. As he made each teenager stand up and make a halting confession, Price and Whitehead could feel the group mind building, the hive mentality coming again under their control. The confessions were completely unfounded, but served their purpose well: refocusing the crowd's attention.

And with enough songs and prayers, teary testimonials and ardent readings, the group's unity did return. Soon not just the bodies and voices were working in unison, but also the minds.

"Are we one in the spirit?" Fine shouted.

"We are one in the Lord," the crowd chanted back.

"Are we sanctified in this great work?"

"We are sanctified!"

But when the huge wave of sound had receded, a single voice broke through from the back. "Maceo, Maceo, say it!" A heavy lull followed the outburst. Then the thin, immature voice cried out again, "Maceo, Maceo, let me hear you blow!" A few of those nearby took up the chant, as though it was a prayer or magic password. And it spread quickly.

Fine aimed his bullhorn in that direction and shouted for

silence. The crowd obeyed, for the time being. "Who started this nonsense?" he bellowed. The crowd was dead silent.

The tepee of burning logs collapsed, sending up a cloud of sparks, and the boy emerged from the darkness, heading directly toward Fine. He was pale and gangly, and had long, unwashed hair, Hundreds of heads turned. Hundreds of eyes followed him as he approached the podium. It was the first time that Price and Whitehead had seen Brian in the flesh. His head was thrown back and his lips were moving, as though speaking to the sky.

"What's your name, boy?" Fine strode down the aisle and took him by the arm. Standing next to Fine, Brian looked even thinner and weaker.

"I asked you a question. What is your name?"

"Brian."

"Well, Brian, do you want to explain to us all why you made this commotion?"

His lips were still moving, but no sound came from his mouth. Price and Whitehead could feel the waves of dissonance coming off the boy. Even for all his grime and awkwardness, there was something imposing about him. In the spots where his skin wasn't covered with dirt, it had an almost luminous quality.

Fine led him down the aisle to the podium, still spewing his pseudo-religious jargon. "You've got to make a choice, boy. Are you going to marry your immortal soul to the one true Lord or continue wandering hopelessly in the wilderness?"

It would have been easier to dispense with the religious trappings and just grab the boy, put him in a restraining harness, and take him away. But they had to play by Fine's rules. He was in charge of that end of the operation. He knew how and why and when to use force on the boy.

"Are you with us or against us?"

Brian started wriggling in Fine's grasp. At first it seemed he was trying to escape, but it soon became clear he wasn't in complete control of his body. It looked like he was trying to keep time with some unheard music.

"I can feel it!" Fine shouted, still using his bullhorn.

"As sure as I'm standing here, I can feel that this boy is possessed by a devil."

At the far edges of the crowd, back where the bonfire's light barely reached, the hushed "shicketa, shicketa, shicketa" rose again, like a chant to keep away evil. The sound made Price and Whitehead nervous. It meant that the teenagers were getting swept up in the alien spirit again.

"I can feel it! He's most assuredly possessed. He's enslaved body and soul to the Enemy." Fine dragged Brian up the steps and onto the platform. Closer now, in the full light of the fire, Price and Whitehead got a better look at the boy. He was finally in their hands. Everything was back on schedule. They just needed to indulge Fine his sham religion, and soon the operation would be complete.

"Come out of this boy!" Fine shouted. "In the name of our Lord, I command you to leave this boy and never return." The nurse had taken her place nearby, ready with the sedative, but suddenly Fine pulled away, rubbing his hands together and scowling angrily at the boy. "Come out of him! Enemy spirit, I command you to leave this boy in peace."

Brian did a little dance step, twisting with his legs and thrusting his hands out, as if holding invisible globes. Fine hesitated, unsure what the boy was trying to do.

"I got the power!" Brian said. His voice was no longer thin and frail. It was like a talking drum. He pointed at the crowd. "I got the Main Man living in my soul. And he's got a brand-new bag!" He shouted "Owwww!" not in pain, but as though he'd been shot through suddenly with an ecstatic blast. "Soul power! Can I count if off?"

"Do you see what I'm talking about?" Fine said, trying to regain control of the crowd. "Full, filled right up to the gills with the power of the Enemy. He dares pit his God against ours. But we know who will, who must, triumph. Don't we?"

The crowd answered him back, but with some hesitation. A few of the teenagers had already slipped over to Brian's side, shouting amens back at him.

Price and Whitehead went forward to bring the whole ridiculous thing to an end, but Fine came between them and Brian, demanding that they leave the platform. "This boy has openly admitted that he is possessed. He's flaunted his unholy pact with the powers of darkness. He's impugned the righteousness of our Lord's ministers. And for this he must be punished."

They'd been sent there to assist in retrieving the boy. Fine was still offically in charge there. They had no choice but to step down and watch the debacle from below.

"He's going to kill him," Price whispered into his partner's ear. "He's going to go out of control with this religious drivel and kill him."

Whitehead shook his head. "I think he knows what he's doing." He didn't sound very confident.

Fine's voice was rising and falling like a siren, hurling insults and threats at Brian. He blustered and ranted, but still didn't come close enough to lay his hands on the boy.

"Hit me one time!" Brian said. "Go ahead, if your Lord is so much." he spun on one foot, stopped suddenly, and reached out to the crowd. "Lay down your baddest stroke and see what kind of thing my Main Man can do." He kept up with this gibberish, shouting to the crowd about groove things, Brand X, the Mother Lode, Nighttrain, and the Wild Syndrome.

Price and Whitehead weren't listening anymore. They were worrying. Fine wanted to beat the boy at his own game, but it seemed that the rules were changing as he spoke.

Worse, the crowd was getting swept up in Brian's nonsense frenzy. Some of the girls had risen from their seats and were singing back at him. They weren't exactly in love with the strange, gawky boy filling the air with his wild ravings, but he certainly had struck a chord deep inside them.

Brian had the microphone now, and Fine had his bullhorn, so that neither could overpower the other by sheer volume. They fought like duelists, trading salvos of gibberish.

Whitehead and Price could have just turned off the power, grabbed the boy, and left Fine to deal with the crowd. But they were afraid that if they yanked the cord, the teenagers would swarm over them, demanding back their "Funky Brinor." And the boy never let go of the microphone. It had become his unbilical back to whatever it was that drove him.

To one side, the kids were stamping their feet and chanting, "Shake, shake, shake that holy booty." And on the other side, they were making whirring sounds like a swarm of angry insects.

At last Fine couldn't stand it anymore and charge at the boy. He wrenched the microphone out of his hands and, pressing the bell of the bullhorn against Brian's ear, shouted, "Come out of him. Spirit of rebellion and enmity, come out of this boy."

Brian started convulsing. He was losing control. His hands clamped on Fine's throat, and to protect himself, Fine did the same to the boy. Quickly the crowd's singing and chanting and speaking in tongues faded away. For the first time since Brian had appeared, the sound of the bonfire could be heard. The two hung onto each other as though desperate not to let another word escape from their enemy's mouth.

"Oh Christ," Whitehead whispered. "He's going to kill him." His partner didn't respond; he didn't move. He was staring up at Fine's broad face, now red and swollen.

Years of planning, months of watching and plotting and cutting deals had come down to this: a teenage schizophrenic and a research neurologist-turned-camp director trying to strangle each other on a rough plank stage. Later, Whitehead would say to his partner, "We should have known better. When he started in with his religious bit, talking all the time about Lord this and Lord that, we should have known he was going around the bend. We shouldn't have counted on him."

But they'd had no choice. Fine was the first one to see exactly how Brian could be made to serve their purposes, though over the years he'd moved further afield, obsessed with his visions of a gold-lined heaven on earth.

"He's going to kill him. Christ, all of this work for nothing."

They noticed a subtle change occurring. The light from the bonfire dwindled as they fought. The illumination became redder as the actual flames shrunk, leaving behind a throbbing hill of coals.

Even the sound of the fire had diminished. It felt as though the air itself was being sucked away. Fine's grunts and Brian's weird mutterings were broadcast over the P.A. system. Everyone there—hundreds of teenagers, Price and

Whitehead, the nurse and the counselors—waited to see which of them would collapse first.

"You son of a bitch," Fine moaned. The microphone was jammed in the crook of Brian's arm, picking up every sound they made. "You slimy little bastard." He was still hanging onto Brian, but seemed now to be clinging for his life. "You son of a goddamned bitch." His eyes had grown glassy.

Price smelled burning meat and knew it was Fine. The boy was cooking him alive. Fine began to slump. His tongue poked between his lips, the color of ash. Huge, heavy gasps filled the air, booming from the loudspeakers. Underneath was the sound of fat crackling, like bacon in a frying pan. Brian finally pulled his hands free and Fine slumped to the floor, wisps of smoke curling up from his hair. Brian was dazed, tottering. The light around his hands ebbed away, and the bonfire began to rise again. He looked down at Price and Whitehead. He seemed to know who they were and why they'd come there.

The rest was chaos. By the time Price and Whitehead had picked through the wreckage and assessed the damage, Brian was long gone. The crowd had risen up, like the flames, and surged toward the podium. They were aiming for the boy, but the mob quickly became a rout and soon hundreds of bodies were surging in all directions. Brian somehow got back to his van, started it, and headed off again. Fine's body was picked up and carried—half martyr, half criminal—by the teenagers, and ended up the next morning hanging by the feet from the tall arch by the road. The platform was torn to pieces and fed to the fire. Price and Whitehead escaped with minor cuts and bruises, locking themselves in Fine's cabin while the rampage ran its course through the night. The state police were there the next day, finding hundreds of semi-delirious teenagers and very little in the way of explanations.

Price and Whitehead got the most important equipment out of there, carrying it with them as they hiked into woods just before dawn.

20

---

arx woke just as the sun was rising. He slipped out
of bed, careful not to make any noise. It was strange
for him to be up at that hour. As they'd gone west,
it seemed he needed more sleep every night. For the first
time in hist life he was taking naps in the afternoon, going
to bed early, and not getting up until the sun was high in
the sky. But something woke him that morning. Not a sound.
The motel was still and silent as he gathered up his clothes.
Not even the light. It was still too weak to bring him out of
sleep. Something had probed through the air, touched him,
and pulled him suddenly awake.

He put on his pants and slipped on his shoes without tying
them. Easing the door open, he looked back at the bed. She
was still deep in sleep, miles and years away. She had only
a sheet around her and wore nothing underneath. Marx stood
there a moment, enjoying the sight. Her flank and legs were
clearly outlined under the sheet. Her hair was tangled in
damp strands across her face. Her chest rose and fell gently.
He liked her best that way. He felt a trail of cool air snake
around his feet and went outside, not wanting to wake her.

The little upstate towns were all beginning to look the same to him. Usually there was a diner, a gas station, a few stores hanging on along the slowly dying main street. Some of them had a motel or a gift shop or a shantylike building advertising "LIVE BAIT AND TACKLE" for sale. The last town where they'd stayed had had a tiny library that never seemed to be open. This one had a motel—the Keuka Krest—and a place called Margie's Ceramics and Things.

Fog was moving off the lake, Seneca or Canandaigua or Keuka, he'd given up trying to keep them separate. The air was much cooler than when they'd gone to bed. It was damp and heavy in his lungs. The hills surrounding the lake had almost no color yet. The fog and the last remains of night still shrouded them.

He walked down the main street, away from the motel, just to put some distance between him and Dr. Haak.

Even though she'd shed almost everything that connected her to the world of medicine—clothing, vocabulary, even facial expressions and the way she held her body—still he found it impossible to call her by her first name.

She'd examined the shunt at the back of his neck every few hours, not wanting to plug into it until it was properly healed. She was clearly becoming more impatient. It had been days now since she'd had a hit off the boy's shunt, and he could easily imagine her soon losing control and coming at him in bed with the cable.

It wasn't fear of Dr. Haak, though, that had made him get up so early and go out wandering that shabby, empty street. It was as though something had called to him, tugging at him through the little node of wires and transistors and relays imbedded in his flesh. There was still some pain around the shunt. He found it hard to turn his neck and certain positions were very uncomfortable, but he was surprised how little trouble the operation had given him. And now the shunt seemed to be finally functioning, receiving something that he didn't understand.

He stopped at the diner. The door was open, but there was no one inside. He heard nothing from the kitchen in back. He waited a moment, eyeing the large, stainless steel coffee urn, wondering whether he should pour himself a cup. He took a few steps into the room, felt a twinge at the back of his neck, and turned around.

In the next block was a small stone church. He tried the front door, but it didn't budge. He sat down on the cold stone steps and looked out toward the lake. The fog was still coming in, moving between the nearby hills toward town. The sun was a little brighter by then, though not strong enough yet to outline the buildings a block or two away.

He felt a throb in the shunt, a nudge that threatened to spread higher, into the place where his headaches usually dug themselves in. He stood and the throb diminished. He sent a few steps toward the motel, and the throb became a distinct stab of pain. When he turned and headed in the opposite direction, it faded to a soft pulsing. At the end of the street was the town square: dewy, uncut grass, a few benches, and a stone marker commemorating a battle or an early settler's life. At the exact center of the little park was a bone-white gazebo. As he came closer, he saw that two men were sitting together on one of the benches in the gazebo. They were talking quietly, as though being careful not to wake anyone in town.

They greeted him with silent nods, and one patted the seat next to him, indicating that Marx should sit there. It surprised him how natural it seemed, sitting down with Price and Whitehead before dawn in some town he didn't even know the name of. The seat was cold and damp under him. Far off—he assumed on the shore of the lake—a motor turned over, caught, and began humming. Shortly it vanished, heading out into the lake. The park was silent again. Not even the birds were making noise yet.

"It's good to see you, Saul," one of the men said. "We need to have a little chat with you."

They'd changed since he'd seen them back at the Red House. Though they both had on their expensive suits and fancy Italian shoes, they seemed rather ratty-looking. One of them needed a shave, and the other seemed to have trouble focusing his eyes. They both spoke as though trying hard to sound reasonable.

"What's the matter, Saul? Don't you remember your old friends? It's Chip and Chuck. Have you forgotten so soon?"

Marx waited. They didn't want to converse with him. They wanted him to listen.

"Have you been enjoying your little vacation? Has Caroline been showing you a good time? I imagine she'd make a fine tour guide. And the two of you certainly have hit it off well."

Price giggled. When it appeared he couldn't control himself, his partner squeezed his knee and glared at him. "It's so nice to see you enjoying yourself, getting away from all the problems back at the hospital. But I'm afraid your vacation has got to come to an end. We need your help, Saul." He clicked his fingers, as though signaling. Nothing happened.

Price concentrated, looking over at Marx. He started giggling again, then stopped abruptly.

"The wheels turn slowly, Saul. But they do turn. Everything has its time and place. And I'm afraid your time has come up. Caroline was kind enough to spare us the trouble of getting you on the operating table. We needed you to be opened up, and she did it for us. So now we're ready to move on to phase two, as it were. You've always been a team player, Saul. We've been watching you for years, and before that our predecessors had their eyes on you. We never really let you out of our sight. And now it's time to get you back in the saddle again, so to speak."

"I quit. I don't want to go back to work."

"Don't think of it as work, Saul. It's more like fulfilling your destiny. Doesn't that sound better? You were selected a long time ago, back when Chuck and I were still youngsters. And they don't make mistakes, Saul. They're very good judges of character. They knew that when the time came, you'd be there."

"I said I quit. I don't work for you anymore."

"You swore an oath when you joined the service. That's not something you're going to take lightly, is it?"

"That was almost twenty years ago. I was just a kid then." He knew there was little point in arguing with them, but still he persisted. They seemed so dense, as if purposefully trying not to understand him. "I served my time and then I got out. I haven't worn a uniform in years."

"You don't need a uniform to serve. You just have to do as you're told."

Marx got up, but as soon as his back was to them, he felt a knifepoint of pain jabbing into him through the shunt. He clung to the handrail, trying to stay upright.

When he turned and looked back, both Whitehead and Price were smiling at him, like salesmen who've just clinched a deal. "You swore an oath, a sacred oath. You've got responsibilities, Saul. This is an important job we want you to take care of."

"I don't want to. I said I quit."

"It doesn't matter what you want. You've got a job to do."

The pain ebbed, but didn't vanish. "There's still the matter of the boy, Brian Cerniac. It was your job to find him. And you didn't accomplish that, Saul. You failed completely and went off on a joy ride with Caroline. You've shirked your duty. So now we need to try a different tack. She's made that a little easier by opening you up for us. The two of you have a lot in common—Brian and you, that is. It seems that Caroline's fallen, shall we say, for both of you in a big way. It seems she has big plans for you. But I'm afraid those plans may have to wait awhile."

He stood suddenly, taking Marx by the hand. "But enough about Caroline Haak. You're the one we're interested in today. You're our new number one boy."

Neither Price nor Whitehead were big men. One on one, Marx probably could have taken care of them both. But just the thought of resisting made a blade of pain shoot out from his shunt. He murmured, "I quit, I don't work for anybody anymore."

But the two flanked him, grabbed him by the arms, and led him down the steps. They walked into the fog. The closer they got to the lake, the more dense it became. Shortly, Marx could see almost nothing. They walked and walked until it seemed they must have been walking on the water.

He had the sensation of flying, or being dragged bodily through the air. They were manipulating him somehow, poking and probing inside him through the shunt, pulling him like an animal at the end of a very long leash.

The fog off the lake became a different kind of fog, an absence of solidity. He was flying in this mist. And just how long—minutes, hours, days even—it took to arrive, he wasn't sure. Eventually the fog did disperse. He had a hazy memory of traveling along tree-lined streets, past tall red-brick buildings. It seemed he was taken over a narrow bridge and had been held upside down over a bottomless gorge. He remembered—or imagined remembering—hanging head down over this misty void. Whitehead's voice was still there, going on and on about duty and responsibility and doing the right thing. It was almost as though the voice itself had swept Marx up and sent him gliding through the air, and that it was the voice which was the fragile strand holding him over the pit.

Then the fog was gone and a real, solid, pure darkness was around him. He was lying on a bed in a blacked-out room. It was an actual room, not a hallucination. The pillow smelled of laundry soap. The blanket was stiff and prickly. He was lying on his side. Something was in his shunt, something hard and firmly attached. He couldn't move. He could barely think. He lay there waiting, and soon enough the darkness peeled back and a group of faces appeared.

Whitehead and Price were there, in the background. It seemed that they were like little boys trying to behave themselves. A bald man in a white smock poked a bright light into his eyes. Another man, gray-haired and gray-skinned, said something that made no sense to Marx, and vanished.

There came another long wait, then unannounced a huge shock ripped into him through the shunt. After it was gone, through the hissing and humming inside him, he heard the men conferring. He knew what was going to come at the end of the long respite. He lay there helplessly, wanting it to come and end the wait.

Finally it did come, and it was worse than he'd expected: a massive jolt that started deep inside him and thrust its way upward, terminating in an explosion of light. Shreds of images broke off from this brilliant bolt. Most splintered and decayed too quickly for him to remember, but a few hung on longer. He saw his wife. She was older; the tension and worry that used to show in her face was gone. He saw Dr. Haak, naked and squatting like a shaman in front of a low fire. She was snarling, furious, pawing with her bare hands in the coals. And last, he saw the Cerniac boy. Though almost everything about the image was wrong—his skin and hair were black, his body much heavier and more muscular, a calm saneness showed in his eyes—it felt exactly right. It was Brian transformed, an inverse image of him, perhaps a picture of how the boy saw himself.

The gray-faced man leaned in close. Marx could smell his breath, mouthwash failing to cover the faintly rotten odor. He squinted at Marx, peered into him with a probe. "Listen to me carefully, Saul. If you do exactly as you're told, everything will turn out just fine. You have one job to perform for us, then you'll be free. We won't ask another thing from you. That's fair enough, isn't it?" They'd killed his wife, invaded and rewired his brain, shuttled him from one useless job to another. And they were still talking about fairness and duty. "The boy, Cerniac, is very important to a project we've been working on. He's necessary to complete the process. Absolutely necessary. We need him to be on the site in three days. He's the last link in a long chain. Do you understand what I'm saying?"

Marx managed to nod. He had no idea what the doctor was talking about. He and the others had spoken to Marx as though he was one of their inner circle, privy to all their secrets and technical jargon. The whole situation made no sense to him: they jolted and meddled in his brain, then spoke to him as though he was their partner and not a victim.

"It seems our associate, Doctor—or Reverend, as he's been calling himself—Fine has made some rather unfortunate miscalculations. We see now that the boy is reaching his peak faster than we'd assumed. Dr. Fine tried to meet him on unequal ground. But now that you've been opened up, you're in the system too now. It stands to reason that you can find the boy and pacify him on his own terms. Your shunt is somewhat more primitive than his, and the tissue around the stomas hasn't healed quite yet. And to tell the truth, you're too old to be of primary use to us. We've found that the optimum age is seventeen or eighteen, when the subject has attained his full stature and strength, but the hormonal patterns haven't quite settled down yet.'' The doctor went on for a while about neural links, systemics, and transmuting something into something else. But Marx was too tired, too beaten and disoriented, to pay much attention. Other doctors came in and inspected him, ran tests and nattered excitedly about the ''big event'' that was going to occur soon, apparently on Midsummer's eve. Marx said yes to the questions they wanted yes to, and no to the others. He nodded and told them he understood when it seemed that would make them leave him alone, if just for a few minutes. He agreed to hunt the boy down, subdue him, and deliver him to the site, wherever that was.

At last they finished their tests and countertests. He convinced them that he was willing, if not ready and able, to do the job, and they put him back to sleep.

When he woke, he was in a pleasant, well-appointed bedroom. Through the half-opened window he heard bells tolling in a tower clock. With some effort he pushed himself up and sat on the edge of the bed. He was somewhere in the middle of a large university campus. Everywhere he looked were grand, somber buildings. Students went past on the nearby walkway, some on bicycles, some on foot. On a broad expanse of green grass a few students were tossing a football back and forth. Nearer, a young woman was lying on a plaid blanket.

Marx felt like a prisoner awaiting his execution. Was all of this—peace and quiet, normalcy, graciousness even—the equivalent of the condemned man's last meal?

He touched the back of his neck. The bandage was taped securely. Either they'd numbed the tissue around the shunt, or the actual wiring was dormant, waiting. He felt no pain. And his grogginess too had diminished.

In the closet, he found a new suit, his size. It was made of better material than he could ever afford. There were a few hundred dollars in the wallet and a credit card in his name.

When he'd showered and dressed and had his fill of the scene outside his window, he went downstairs. A houseboy was cleaning in one of the rooms he passed. A few old men, alumni he assumed, were sitting in the largest parlor, reading newspapers and smoking cigars. He nodded to the young man sitting at the desk by the door, went outside, and headed down the sidewalk, as though if he let it, his body would take him where he was supposed to go.

By reading signs and the names on various buildings, he learned quickly that he was on the Cornell campus. That was in Ithaca, about midstate. He knew, or something in him knew, that he needed to head west.

It occurred to him that it was the suit and shoes which were actually moving, and he was just being carried along by them. But that thought passed as he strolled down the broad, tree-lined streets. It became obvious quickly that some part of him, deep inside, knew exactly where he was going. There were sections of him, regions of memory and will, that he had no access to. He knew that if he fought his steady, purposeful stride, the pain would erupt again in his head. He didn't even consider rebelling. He just glided along like a passenger, observing and enjoying the trees, the sound of human voices, the balmy summer air.

He passed over a bridge and stopped momentarily to look down. He was high above a gorge. A stream was rushing at the bottom, silvery white. The banks of the ravine were lush with vegetation, trees and plants clinging to the steep rock walls. Farther up the gorge, he saw a squat stone structure built at the base of the cliff. Most of the windows had been bricked up. It appeared to be abandoned.

And though he was sure he'd never stood in that place before, he had a clear, certain feeling that he knew all about that little building. It had been used first as a generating station, converting the power of the falling water into electricity. After it had been closed down, the shafts and tunnels had been used for research that was deemed too questionable to take place in the engineering and physics labs. The words "plutonic bolus" appeared in his mind. He didn't know what the words meant, and he felt uncomfortable with them there, as they somehow were more invasive than everything else the doctors had planted in him.

He turned and began walking again, into the city of Ithaca proper. The words kept ringing in his inner ear, like the

after shocks of an enormously loud noise. He saw—or remembered seeing—a squat, egg-shaped mass. It was dark.
It was foul. It was emitting a field that though invisible to
the naked eye, he could see clearly.

Marx found his hand on the handle of a car door. It
opened and without thinking, he reached under the seat,
finding the keys. The car started with the first try, just like
on a game show. He was the big winner. He had the car,
the suit, the wallet full of money, and the brand-new memories.

It took him awhile to get out of town. Many of the streets
were one-way, and even trusting the wisdom of who- or
whatever it was that directed his path, he still made wrong
turns and ended up in a cul-de-sac. Eventually, though, he
did find his way out and was on the main route headed up
the lake. He knew that when he needed to turn off to head
west, it would be obvious.

21

Ollie found the car just where Mr. Price and Mr. Whitehead had said it would be. She'd parked it front of the first bungalow at Karen's Komfort Kourts. The cabins were arranged in a horseshoe around the gravel drive. Dr. Haak's car was the only one there.

It was spattered with mud, and the side-view mirror was broken, hanging off the door. The car looked as though she'd been hit from behind too. The back bumper was scraped and twisted. In the rear compartment of the wagon was a pile of boxes, bags, and crates: things she'd stolen from the Red House.

Ollie waited, screwing up his courage to face the doctor. He tried to remember what he'd been told, how important he was to the operation. He crossed his arms over his chest, almost hugging himself, enjoying the crinkle and creak of the black leather. He thought of himself on a big chopper roaring down the road with flames shooting out the back. He thought of Dr. Haak on the seat behind him, clinging to his waist.

Going around the side of the cabin, he peeked in the

window. The curtains were drawn, but they were thin enough that he could see through them. She wasn't home. Making sure that nobody was looking, he tried the window, found it swung inward, and climbed through.

Except for the unmade bed and a pile of orange peels on the floor, there was little evidence that she'd been there. He looked in the bathroom and saw that she'd washed out her underwear and hung it on the curtain rod to dry. It was wrong for him to look, but he looked anyway. It was wrong to touch, but he couldn't help himself. He thought of what the fine white fabric had touched and closed his eyes, trying to make the image go away. He tried to remember Mr. Price and Mr. Whitehead, their voices telling him how important he was to the effort. Then he thought of the rod of correction and managed to let go.

He grabbed her toothpaste tube and squeezed the whole thing into the sink, making a shiny green and white pile. As soon as he'd done it, he was sorry and tried to clean up the mess. He didn't want her coming in then, that was for sure, catching him with his hands all slimy.

When he'd straightened up as best he could, he went back to the bedroom. She'd brought only one suitcase in from the car. It was closed, standing by the door. On top was a map of New York state. He picked up the map and unfolded it carefully. A few red lines were drawn on it. One went north and turned left at the Thruway. Another wiggled and wandered, also heading toward the northwest corner of the state. He turned the map over and saw a detailed insert of the city of Niagara Falls. Along the river, on the south side of town, she'd circled a neighborhood and written something next to it. After a while he deciphered her scrawl. It said "LOVE CANAL." That sounded like one of those sex movies that some of the other orderlies watched on their VCRs. And written in her hand, it seemed even more obscene.

He folded the map back the way he thought he'd found it, and laid it on top of the suitcase. He wasn't sure what to do next. He was as ready as he'd ever be, but the exact steps he needed to take were still unclear. Mr. Whitehead and Mr. Price had told him that they wanted the doctor to taste a little of her own medicine. Ollie knew how to run all the equipment now. He knew what all the dials and readouts meant. He could give her just enough dosage, but not too much. They didn't want her dead right away. They said that wouldn't be fair. There needed to be justice. An eye for an eye and a tooth for a tooth. She'd done some very bad things and she needed to pay for them.

And after that Ollie would be free to do with her whatever he wanted. They'd both winked at him when they'd told him that. Ollie wasn't sure what the wink meant, but it made him feel good to be in on the joke.

There was a mirror facing the bed. He checked himself in it, making sure there wasn't any toothpaste on his jacket. It was the first time he'd ever worn it outside, and it had to be just right. There was no point in having a jacket like that if it was messed up or sloppy-looking. He polished the Harley-Davidson medallion with his shirt tail, and straightened the silver chains that hung from the epaulets. He squared his shoulders, took a deep breath, and went outside.

It would have taken him hours to go through all the boxes and bags in her car. He looked in through the driver's side window, wondering if he should just start looting through the piles or go about it in a logical way. But luckily she'd kept the rod of correction in the same bag as before. He had to move aside only a few styrofoam trays smeared with catsup to find it. There it was, on the front seat, a squat black bag like all the doctors carried back at the Red House. Even closed and latched, he could feel the power of the rod radiating toward him. He sat there in her car for a while, one hand on the grip of the bag, the other on his chest, as if a current was running through his arm and into his heart.

But he had a job to do. He had his orders, and important people were depending on him. He picked up the bag and got out of the car. He walked slowly, trying to be inconspicuous, toward the beach he'd seen earlier. As he approached the lake shore, he saw more people, and the level of noise increased. The sun was already past its peak. The air was stagnant, heavy and choked with burnt meat and charcoal smells. The schools had let out a day or two before, and all the teenagers from the area had congregated there to celebrate their freedom. The beach itself wasn't too crowded, but the parking lot, the food concessions, and the surrounding lawns were mobbed.

Ollie headed for the big stone bathhouse. He found the men's side and went into the cool shadows. The bare concrete floor was wet, pools of spilled beer and urine mixed with the overflow from the showers. Voices rang in the high-ceilinged room. A few boys were standing at the sinks, joking and admiring themselves in the mirror.

Ollie went to the end of a long row of stalls and locked himself in the last one. He flipped down the seat and sat down. It took him a long while to steel himself enough to open Dr. Haak's bag. He had time. There was no rush. He listened to the sounds filtering in from outside. A car horn was blaring. A motorcycle revved its engine and sped off. Dogs barked and yipped.

But eventually he was ready. With a swift yank he opened the bag and looked inside. The rod was in two pieces. He touched the male and female threads where the two halves joined. Carefully he lifted the black shafts out of the bag and fit the ends together. His thumb rested on the switch, stroking the smooth, rounded knob. The terminal end was bright silver. He imagined pain, visible streams of pain, shooting out from the tip. Pain and pleasure together, braided like two strands of light.

Someone was walking down the row of stalls, banging on the doors. They stopped in front of Ollie's stall, and he leaned over to look under the door. But then a voice called from the other end and laughter erupted. He heard the slap of rubber thongs running on the wet concrete floor. And then he was alone again.

The walls of the stall were covered with graffiti, crude drawings, and blotches of reddish crust. The bottom of the window came just to his eye level. The frame was bare iron, pitted with rust. He pulled on one of the lower panels and got it to move outward a few inches. Leaning slightly, he could look through one crack and get a good view of the lake shore.

From where Ollie sat, the beach was a scene of almost constant motion. Sun bathers stood to stretch, rubbed themselves with oils, adjusted their blankets. Others walked about talking with friends, throwing sticks for dogs, and fussed with the dials on their radios. Ollie watched intently, sure there was something he should be seeing.

It took him quite awhile, but eventually it came to him. The figure lying on her stomach on a scarlet beach towel was not a teenager. It was Dr. Haak. Ollie sat up straighter, pressing his head against the wall to get a better look. It was Dr. Haak and she was wearing almost nothing, all of that skin laid out bare, exposed to the sun. Unlike the others around her, though, she wasn't lying there almost naked to get a tan. She was storing up the sun's energy, like a battery being recharged.

The shock rod was damp in his hands. His thumb rested on the switch. He heard someone coming into that part of the bathhouse and pulled back from the window. He waited for the person to finish before he looked back through the window again. Dr. Haak had turned over. She was wearing a pair of dark glasses. Her hair was spilled out on the blanket, slightly lighter than when last he'd seen her. It seemed unbelievable that the others went about their business with her in their midst, laid out and exposed like that. They threw their Frisbees, drank their beer, talked and laughed with that stark amber body right there, close enough to touch.

He held the shock rod's tip close to the metal door. Suddenly he pulled his gaze away from the window and pressed the rubber switch. A jolt shot out of the rod, and for a moment Ollie felt himself part of the circuit: hand to rod to door to ground and back up through his feet. He liked it. He fired again, now letting his eyes turn back to the bare torso, the long, smooth lines of her legs, the tiny scarlet triangle below her navel. Another blast ripped loose from the rod. His hands quaked. A quiet but distinct crackling sound came from inside the rod. He fired a last time and she seemed to feel the shock, a shiver running through her.

He didn't know how long he sat in the stall, but by the time she stood and rolled up her blanket, pulled on a T-shirt, and headed up the beach to the parking lot, Ollie's feet were asleep and his legs were cramped and numb. As soon as she was out of sight, he wiped the rod clean with a wad of toilet paper, fumbled to take it apart, and get it back into the bag. He yanked the door open and went outside.

She was at the concession stand, squirting catsup and

mustard on a pair of burnt hot dogs. Ollie hung back in the
doorway until she'd devoured the first and walked up the
sand-covered sidewalk back toward town.

He followed her, a long distance behind, as she strolled
back to the motor court. There was a telephone booth within
sight of her cabin. He got in and sat down on the tiny tri-
angular seat. The air in the booth was even hotter than outside. It smelled worse. The sunlight seemed to concentrate
there, making his eyes hurt and his skin burn where it
touched him.

He was almost asleep, huddled in the booth in a twisted
fetal position, when a truck went by, blaring its horn. His
eyes snapped open. He was very hungry. He hadn't eaten
since Mr. Whitehead and Mr. Price had left him in that
town. His head ached terribly. But he wouldn't have com-
plained even if there was someone there to complain to. He
had a job to do and sometimes that required sacrifice.

Another truck roared past, and when the last echo of its
horn had faded, he saw Dr. Haak come out of her cabin.
She was wearing a sleeveless dress and high-heeled shoes.
The hem of the dress was high above her knees. Again Ollie
felt the pounding in his temples. He breathed deeply, counting downward from ten, trying to relax.

She opened the door to her car and he felt panic rising.
She could drive away and he'd have no way to catch up with
her. She could vanish and he'd be stuck there with no way
to find her.

She backed out and headed into town. Ollie untangled
himself and sprinted along the road in the direction she'd
gone. This time, luck was with him. She'd only gone a few
blocks and parked in front of a bar. When he caught his
breath and made sure there was no one in the car, he peeked
into the building.

Though it was still early in the evening, smoke hung thick
around the ceiling. He saw Dr. Haak sitting with her back
to the door, perched high on a bar stool. He slipped into
the room and found a booth in the corner, far out of sight.

Time passed slowly. As the night came on, men and
women started trickling into the bar. They were all dressed
better than Ollie. Their hair was nicely styled and smelled

of perfume. They all seemed to know each other, but said little after "Hello."

Hunger had filled Ollie. His stomach was growling so loudly, he was afraid Dr. Haak would hear him. Luckily, though, one of the men put some coins in the jukebox and a nasal voice came out of the speakers, singing about a "cruel, cruel fool."

A waitress came on duty and began placing baskets of popcorn on the tables. Ollie went through his quickly. It was stale and very salty, turning his loud hunger into nausea. Awhile later, she came around a second time and asked him if he wanted anything. A sign over the bar showed a cartoon hamburger with hands and legs and big bug eyes. "Can I have one of those?" he said.

"I'll see if the cook is on yet."

She took her time, getting the drink orders, but finally did bring Ollie a big hamburger with a pickle speared onto the bun with a toothpick. Reddish grease leaked down the sides. The bun was wet and warm and fell apart as he picked it up. Ollie didn't mind. It was gone in a few bites and he was digging through the roll of money that Mr. Whitehead had given to him.

When he looked back at the bar, Dr. Haak was gone. A wave of panic rose up from his belly. Then he saw her, coming back from the women's room. She looked right at him, or so it seemed, but there wasn't any sign of recognition. Maybe he was far enough in the shadows. Maybe she had other things on her mind.

In any case, she went back to the bar and started talking to the man next to her. Ollie hated to see her that way, flirting and making eyes at him. She kept drawing a stir stick out of her mouth, as if sucking the last bits of meat off a bone. The man's voice was loud; Ollie got most of what he said. But he couldn't hear Dr. Haak over the jukebox and the others at the bar.

A new song came on, quieter and slower. Dr. Haak got off her stool to dance with the man, clinging close. Her face was against his cheek, as if she was whispering to him. His hand moved down her back and rested on her behind, squeezing her through the tight material of her dress. Ollie watched every slow turn they made around the dance floor, and it seemed that the whole thing was happening just to torment him.

By the time it ended, Dr. Haak had her arms around the man's neck and was dancing with her lips pressed against his. The music stopped and they went toward the door, hand in hand. Ollie got a better look at the man as they passed. His hair was very black and swept back off his forehead. His lips were deep red, some of Dr. Haak's lipstick having brushed off on him.

As soon as they'd gone out the door, Ollie followed. They were standing beside a bright red pickup truck, kissing and hanging onto each other. Ollie touched his Harley Davidson medal and closed his eyes for a moment, as if praying. He imagined the two of them getting into the truck and driving off, leaving him all alone in that gravel parking lot.

"What do you think you're doing?" he said. His voice was hoarse. He cleared his throat and said it again.

The man let go of Dr. Haak. She looked at Ollie and smiled. "Oh, hello there. I was wondering when you were going to show up."

"Get in your car," Ollie said. "We've got a lot of talking to do." He was surprised how strong he could make his voice sound.

"Who the hell are you?" the man asked.

"Her husband."

Dr. Haak smiled and brushed back her hair, trying to make herself look a little neater. She didn't deny what Ollie said. The man opened the door to his truck. Ollie came at him with the angriest face he could make. He'd been the one to take care of the wildest and biggest patients back at the Red House. This one wasn't even his size. But Ollie didn't have his pacifier. Even so, unless the man had a gun or a knife, Ollie could probably take care of him.

"Is he really your husband?"

"You heard him." Dr. Haak moved a few steps away, making room for the two of them to tangle. But before Ollie could reach him, he climbed inside the truck cab and locked the door. Just for show, Ollie pretended to try to get it open. The man quickly had the car moving, heading for the street.

As he disappeared, Ollie felt his momentum slipping

away. Fighting and threatening he was good at, but Dr. Haak didn't look like she was in the mood for either.

"I was hoping you'd get over your shyness sooner than this, Ollie." She led him to her car. They sat in the darkness for a moment, listening to the engine hum. He looked down at his lap, realizing that he'd been carrying the black bag all along. He let go. His hand was cramped and sticky with sweat.

"Did you miss me?"

He nodded.

"Were you getting lonely back at the hospital?"

She touched his neck, stroking with two fingers. "You seem to have healed nicely. I don't feel any scars." She unfastened a few buttons on his shirt, moving closer to him. "No permanent marks. That's nice. I certainly didn't mean to hurt you, Ollie. You just needed to be taught a lesson."

She led his hand to her thigh. He expected sparks to fly off from the point of contact, or a reddish glow to rise up. But the car remained in darkness.

"I imagine my friends Chip and Chuck have been talking with you. Did they bring you up here just to see me?"

"They said you went too far. I'm supposed to take care of you." It sounded ridiculous to him, the idea of punishing her. "They said it was time you stopped fooling around like this."

"Like what?"

"Driving all over the state, messing with men, doing things with that Marx you weren't supposed to do."

She started the car, but didn't remove his hand from her thigh. It lay there as if turned to lead, heavy and useless.

It took only a few minutes to drive back to her cabin. He tried to talk as they drove, to tell her that he was there to rein her in, but she wouldn't listen.

As she unlocked the cabin door, she said, "I knew somebody was here today, looking through my things. I hoped it was you." Her lips brushed his ear. He felt her breath like a jet of steam on his skin. With the door closed, he could see nothing. But he knew what she was doing. He heard the clasps on the black bag being opened, and the two halves of the rod being screwed together.

"Did you say you had a lesson to teach me?" He heard the hum of the rod's power supply. "I'm waiting."

By then his eyes had adjusted somewhat to the gloom. He saw her outline. When she turned slightly, he saw the glint of her eyes and the white flash of her teeth. She pressed the button on the rod and a bolt of light filled the room, stinging his eyes. He smelled ozone and a whiff of singed hair.

"I'm waiting, Ollie. I've been waiting a long time. You always were my favorite."

He knew that was a lie, but it sounded so good to hear her say it. The rod discharged again. White spots floated in front of his eyes. He heard a soft hiss and realized that she'd unzipped her dress and let it fall to the floor. She stepped toward him, whispering. It didn't sound human. It was flat and breathy and low, as though something else was speaking through her. The rod came at him. The tip touched his chest. She didn't press the switch, though, not quite yet.

"Take off your jacket," she said, her voice recognizable again.

He did as he was told. He wanted to hold onto it for safekeeping, but she flicked the rod forward and knocked the coat out of his hands. "You weren't supposed to go off with that Marx," he said, and regretted it as soon as the words were out of his mouth.

She fired again, and in the brilliant light he saw her bone-white and naked except for a shiny black triangle at her groin. The image hung in the air like smoke after the light itself had faded.

"What did they do with Saul?" she said. The tip of the rod touched his chest and he fell backward onto the bed. She pressed in on him, bringing her face close to his. "Where is he?" He scrambled back, crouching in the tangled sheets. "It was bad enough that they took Brian, but then Saul too. That wasn't necessary. He was nothing to them.

"I want him back, Ollie."

She circled around the bed, keeping the rod aimed at his chest. "I want him back and I'm going to get him back. Do you understand me?"

His voice came out weak and mewling, like one of the

patients after he'd finished with their treatment. "I don't know where he is."

The rod fired again and again, hitting him in the face first, then scorching his chest. He rolled to one side and she got him on the back of the neck, sending a knife blade of pain into his brain. He tried to crawl away, but his arms and legs were paralyzed. He could barely draw air into his lungs.

She unfastened his pants and pulled them off. The cold metal tip of the rod ran down his chest and into his groin. "Tell me what you did with Saul. Right now."

Even if he had known, he wouldn't have been able to speak. He expected the worst, her anger converted by the rod and shot into his guts. But the low, inhuman sounds issued again from her mouth and she drew away suddenly. He heard her head for the door, and as she went out, he caught a glimpse of her in a loose robe, holding it closed at her chest.

She was back quickly, dumping a box onto the floor. Still Ollie couldn't move. "I've got nothing to lose anymore," she said. "They've already taken everything that I want." She was digging through a pile of tangled wires and parts. Ollie tried as hard as he could, and succeeded in making his left arm move slightly. His tongue pushed between his lips. Dr. Haak was working quickly, flinging the robe this way and that, firing off bolts from the rod in order to see.

By the time she'd found what she wanted and hooked the pieces together, Ollie could breathe a little easier and wiggle the toes on one foot. He felt her hand at his groin, and then a cold steel probe at the back of his neck, searching for the right place to enter. "Remember, Ollie, this is what you wanted. You said again and again you wanted to be my primary subject. I never thought you'd be good enough. But number one and number two are gone, so I guess I'll have to make do with number three."

Sensation was returning to his limbs. His vision cleared enough to see her pulling her hair away from the back of her neck and sliding the two probe ends into her shunt. She knelt on the bed beside him. "This is going to hurt," she whispered, as if trying to reassure him. She stroked and squeezed the muscles of his neck, then finding the right place, stabbed a probe into him. He blacked out for a mo-

ment. He woke, feeling the needle being withdrawn and
jabbed in again a few millimeters away.

This time it was just pain, a raw saw edge of pain cutting
into him. He could barely feel her flip him onto his back.
He could barely see her standing above him, yanking the
black slip of fabric away from her groin, and then lowering
herself onto him. The pain was enormous, roaring inside
his head. She was on top of him, fused to him, moving and
again making the garbled hissing sounds. She held the wires
in his flesh with one hand, her nails clawlike, imbedded in
the skin of his neck. She was rocking in rhythm, and with
every thrust, she tightened her grasp on him, desperate not
to let the connection come apart.

Then, still lying on top of him, she groped to one side,
found the rod of correction, and placed the tip against his
temple. "This is going to hurt a lot, Ollie." She pressed
herself hard against him, the rhythm getting wilder and faster. Her breath was like exhaust from an engine. The sounds
from her mouth were strained, as though something inside
her was close to cracking. Finally she bucked up, moaning,
and pulled the trigger. White light burst inside his eyes. He
wasn't sure what was going in and what was coming out of
him. But it was all too much, the searing current looping
around and around in the circuit they made with their bodies.

22

Marx saw the ridiculous van ahead and accelerated to catch up. He pulled into the left lane as if to pass, but stayed there, cruising parallel to the van. The boy seemed to be singing, jerking from side to side and shaking his head in rapture. A car was approaching, and Marx dropped back to let it pass. Marx sounded his horn and gestured for the boy to pull over, but he either wasn't paying any attention or didn't know what the signal meant. Marx leaned over to roll down the passenger side window. He finally got the boy to do the same, pantomiming the action. As soon as the boy's was open a crack, a tide of sound erupted from the van. Slamming drums and choked guitars and a voice like a camp-meeting preacher about to hit his peak all boiled out of the van.

"Pull over!" Marx shouted. The boy shouted back the same words, as if they were part of the song he was listening to.

Another car came at them, this one honking its horn, and again Marx was forced to drop back.

Any other driver would have assumed Marx's car to be

an unmarked police cruiser, with its drab style and color. But it took a good five minutes of signaling and gesturing and blowing his horn to finally convince the boy he should pull over.

They came to rest on the gravel shoulder, broad acres of cow pastures on either side of them. An occasional car whizzed past, but during most of the time they spent there on the curb, the only sound from outside was the buzzing of flies. Marx got out of the car and approached the van, as if about to give the boy a speeding ticket. From the way Dr. Haak had spoken of Brian, he'd expected a tall, blond, strapping athlete. Instead, Brian seemed frail, almost delicate. His hands were small, fragile-looking. His hair was long in back, reaching below the shoulders. He had probably never needed to shave. But there was an intensity in his gaze, a wild expression on his face that belied the weakness in his appearance. His eyes were almost black against his pallid skin. He was looking directly at Marx, but seemed to be seeing something beyond, or inside, him.

The music was still loud and obnoxious. Marx felt it in his fillings, in the back of his neck, vibrating through his shunt and into his head. His right hand moved, not quite of its own accord, into his jacket and wrapped around the butt of a pistol. He drew it out of the shoulder holster and pointed it at Brian. "Turn off the music. It's too loud."

The boy was bouncing happily on the seat, keeping time. His eyes were fixed on Marx's, as if trying to stare him down.

"Turn off the music." A tractor trailer roared by and Marx leaned closer, hiding the gun from view. Brian got up finally and disappeared into the back of the van. The music ceased suddenly and Marx felt the muscles in his neck relax. But the boy didn't reappear.

Marx went around to the passenger side and opened the door. He couldn't see the boy from that angle either. Poking ahead of himself with the gun, he climbed into the van.

It was dark and musky inside. The walls and floor were covered with damp brown carpet. It looked like the den of a wild animal. Food and garbage were scattered on the floor. He half expected to see a pile of bones in the corner or a little brood of cubs.

The boy was alone, squatting in front of a pile of cassette tapes. He was shuffling and stacking them as if trying to make a house of cards. The pistol in Marx's hand pointed itself at the boy, as if he was a powerful magnet.

"I want you to get out of this van and into my car. You have to come with me."

The boy understood, but didn't move. He'd gotten three levels of tapes stacked up, then touched them with the tip of his finger and sent them to the floor. "I'm going home," he said.

"That's right. If you get into my car without any fuss, I'll take you home. I promise." The boy could tell he was lying. He shook his head and started another construction with the tapes. "We're not far from your home. Only a few hours."

"They got you," Brian said, meaning the shunt, the meddling with his memories and will. "You wouldn't be telling lies and pointing guns and wearing that suit unless they got you."

He was right, of course. But that didn't make Marx give up. "Brian, I work for the government. I need to take you home. There are important people who are waiting for you. They have something very important for you to do."

The boy clasped his hands as if squeezing something between his palms. When he pulled them apart, it seemed he made a faint bluish light. It was gone quickly, if in fact Marx had really seen it. "You were with Dr. Haak," the boy said. "I saw you. Doing all those things we used to do. The hookup. Running your shunt. Pushing you through the wall with no clothes on."

"What do you mean, you saw us?" He knew the boy hadn't been peeking in windows or hiding in closets.

"From the inside. I saw you in the bed when you were sleeping. When you were with her."

Marx felt sick and giddy. Again, forces he knew nothing about were going around his flanks, maneuvering, manipulating him without his knowledge. "What do you mean?"

"I was watching. But she wanted me to; it was all right. I was seeing it all from the inside."

They weren't just surrounding him. They were burrowing from underneath, mining into him from below.

"Those men in the dark coats and those big bright smiles came and took you away. Dr. Haak was crying, throwing things around the little room. She said she was going to kill them, she misses us both so much." He was quiet for a moment, straightening the edges of his little block house. "Then I saw her taking her clothes off, getting into the shower, putting on that short dress, looking at herself in the mirror. It's all right, though. She doesn't mind me watching now. She wants me to. I think she can see me too now."

The gun was foolish, useless. He certainly wasn't going to shoot the boy, and it didn't seem to scare him at all. His job was to get him into the car and put the restraining rig on him and take him where he was needed. They didn't want him dead. He needed to convince Brian he was on his side.

"There are lots of very important people depending on you. You don't want to let them down, do you? They need your help."

"I know that."

"Then why don't you get in my car and I'll take you to them. They'll be glad to see you."

"I know that. I know all about them. I've been seeing them more and more now. They want me to go right into the funk and never come out. But then how will I see Dr. Haak again? I mean, see her from the outside? How can we plug in again?"

"She's going to be there." He almost said, "I promise."

"They don't like her anymore, do they? They wanted Ollie to kill her. I saw that too. They brought him all the way from the Red House to kill her because she won't do what they want anymore. But instead she plugged him in, and they went together into the Ictus. Didn't they?"

As Marx put the pistol back into the holster, he felt a twinge of pain.

"They got you. They want to get me. They want me to be just like you, doing whatever they say. And when they're done, then what happens?"

Marx had no answer. He gave up. He'd tried and he'd failed. There was nothing more for him to do there.

The pain in his head was growing quickly, shooting out tendrils like a root working to hang onto its place on a cliff

side. Brian seemed to be in pain too. It wasn't clear if it
was the same thing, though: punishment for failure and dis-
obedience. Perhaps it was just sympathetic pain. If the boy
could see through his eyes, there was no reason why he
couldn't feel through his nervous system.

He made a last attempt to convince Brian, but it sounded
even more empty. There was nothing he could offer and
nothing he could threaten with. By then the pain had started
to impinge on his vision. Perhaps they knew already that
he'd failed and had decided to terminate him right there,
make an example of him to the boy. It was certainly possible. If they could slither inside him and give him memories
he knew weren't really his, and a new sense of purpose,
then they could just as easily tell him to die, and he'd have
to oblige.

"You don't have to."

"Don't have to what?"

"Die. I don't have to either. The first time I went into
the Ictus, the doctors said I was dead. But I didn't want to
die then, so I came back. I told Dr. Haak about it, but she
didn't believe me at first. She's more interested in the cradle
and the shunt and hooking me up. She talks about going
through the wall, because that's what I call it, but she doesn't
really believe in it. She just knows about shunts and discharges."

Marx could barely hear him. The pain was swallowing
him up. He could barely feel his hands at the ends of his
arms. He was dying, he knew that much. Somehow they
were telling his body to die and it was obeying.

"You don't have to," Brian said again. "You can just go
through the wall and come back once they're gone. That's
what I do. They can't watch you all the time. They leave
you alone and then you can come back."

"I don't think I can do it," Marx gasped. He was lying
on the damp, foul-smelling carpet. One hand was clenched
in the long nap, as though trying to pull it up. He could see
nothing for a while. Then a globe of light pushed its way
through the darkness. A blast of sound hit him like a ham-
mer, but he was still packed in layers of padding. He knew
the sound was loud enough to shake his internal organs,
though he could hardly hear it. The black creepers had

worked their way down from his brain, along his spine, reaching for his heart. Brian had laid his hands on him. He was singing a nursery rhyme, punctuating it with grunts and choked groans. He'd turned Marx onto his back and was poking around his shunt. He couldn't feel it, but he was sure that a wire had been slid in. The boy was kneeling next to him, singing, it seemed, but even with his mouth pressed on Marx's ear, barely a wisp of sound got through.

Then they were on the same line. For an instant the whole mountain of pain that had been building on top of him seemed to waver. He felt the black current stirring and the bottommost tendrils pull away from his heart. A thumping drum a hundred times deeper than any he'd ever heard with his ears was echoing inside him. It was the boy pounding on his back, as if trying to dislodge something from his windpipe. The tendrils moved back, converting to flame, to brilliant light. It hurt just as much, perhaps more, but it was good pain, burning away the bad. It was a fever that had descended on his body, heating itself to an extreme temperature to drive out whatever it was that had invaded him.

The boy's voice was there too now, from the inside, telling him that he didn't have to die.

For Marx, there was no wall to go through. The transition was more like being grabbed by his deepest viscera and having his entire body yanked inside out. The pain was transformed. The darkness was converted. And the huge throb, his heartbeat and the boy's working together, swelled to engulf him.

23

They followed the big high-tension wires, keeping them always to their left. Marx knew that they converged at a central point, and he knew that point was the generating complex at Niagara Falls. But they were still too far out, perhaps fifty miles, to see the other lines coming in toward them.

Marx drove, unsure if he was being pushed, pulled, or went of his own free will. And he didn't care. He'd been to the Other Side, and he wanted to go back. It was different than he'd imagined it. Brian called it the Ictus or the Funk, but neither of those made much sense to Marx. For him, what lay on the Other Side was much simpler. It was the place where his wife was waiting for him.

Dr. Haak had told him that Brian's whole system, his entire world, was a delusion. According to her, the Ictus was nothing but a knot of nerve tissue. The amygdala, the hypothalamus, the cingulate gyrus. He had no idea what these structures were, or if they even existed outside of Dr. Haak's understanding. But the names had stuck with him. They rang like holy words. Dr. Haak had spoken of them the way a mystic talks of God. For Marx, they were a code, passwords to get him back to the Other Side. Whether a tiny cluster of neurons, a "smoking, choking danceteria," or only a simple room where his wife was waiting for him, he didn't care. He just wanted to go back.

He'd seen Lenny there. Dead or alive. It didn't matter. Real or imagined, he didn't care. He might have died and gone to the next world. He might have hallucinated the whole thing. They might have pumped him full of nameless drugs and groundless memories and set him loose. It might be a way of tormenting him further: dangling the prospect of seeing her again. She'd felt as real as in the flesh. Her voice was no different, her touch, or her smile. Even her hair smelled the way he remembered it. She said she'd wait for him. And would keep waiting.

So Marx drove straight toward Niagara Falls. He was tired of the wandering and the hiding. He wanted it all to be over.

He wasn't surprised how quickly they caught up with him. He just didn't expect that they'd use county sheriffs.

There was a roadblock up ahead, three police cars and a few sawhorses lined up on the pavement. Marx knew it would be a waste of time to fight. He pulled up and opened his window, as if about to pay a bridge toll.

"Holy shit," one of the cops said. He had his pistol out, steadying it with both hands. Marx nodded a greeting. The other deputies came closer.

"It's the Nuts-boy," a young cop with a golden-blond brush cut said.

A heavier man, apparently the ranking officer, came toward the van. He had a shotgun in the crook of his arm. "Nuts-boy and his pal," he said.

Blood had dried on the back of Marx's neck, where the shunt wires had scraped the not-yet-healed tissue. It was probably on his face too, smeared off his hands. Brian certainly was a mess. He slouched unconscious in the other seat, caked with blood and grime and bits of food. The shunt wire was still in his neck. It hung slack between them, the other end still imbedded in Marx.

He half expected them to shoot him dead right there. Instead they circled the van, peering in the windows, poking the air with their guns. Finally the fat cop opened the door and grunted, "Out." Flies buzzed around his face. He didn't seem to notice them. His skin was pink and shiny with sweat. His hair looked as though it had been dyed too many times.

"I said out." Disgust and dread were mixed in equal portions in him.

Marx gently pulled the wire loose from his flesh and handed it to Brian. By then the boy was awake enough to move. Marx climbed out of the van and held his hands out to be cuffed. Brian coiled the wire neatly and stuck it in his pants pocket. He too did as he was told, and quickly they were both in the back of a cruiser, manacled at the wrist.

The fat sheriff was in front, watching them. A thin, sallow deputy was behind the wheel. He said nothing and kept faced straight ahead.

"You two have been an awful lot of trouble. You've got some important people mad at you, really mad." He had fleshy lips that hung open when he wasn't speaking. He held his shotgun with one hand, but wasn't aiming at them any longer.

They drove awhile in silence, off the main route now. After a while the fat cop said. "So you really don't remember me, do you, Stretch? I'm disappointed." He faked a frown, then broke into a fleshy grin again. "Nelson R. Armstrong. 128th Air Tactical. You remember now? How about the base? We're not that far from it. Not even an hour. I liked this area so much, I stuck around."

Marx didn't remember the man, but he did remember the nickname "Stretch" Marx. He'd hated it then, but now it just seemed foolish. That had been fifteen years before. Marx had been in contact with hundreds of men during his time in the service.

"Military police, Stretch. We were in together. We worked out of the same office. You remember Captain Barret? He's still there, only he's a colonel now. And he's in charge of security for the whole base. We're still good buddies."

He poked the driver. "Looks like Stretch has gone right around the bend and won't be coming back. Don't even remember the best times of his life. Serving his country."

"What did you say your name was?" Marx's voice was low and hoarse.

"Well, I guess he's not completely fried. At least he can talk." The fat sheriff gestured with his shotgun as he said, "Nelson R. Armstrong. By the time I got out, I was Spec 4 Armstrong. Had a little more hair then. And I still had my boyish figure." He laughed through his nose. "Is it coming back yet? S. and S. Does that ring a bell? Security and Surveillance. Making sure that everybody kept in line. You weren't half bad, either. You could have gone places, Stretch. I heard people saying good things about you. That was a long time ago, though."

Marx had a hazy memory of sitting in a windowless room with a headset on, listening in on various bugs they'd placed in the enlisted men's quarters. At times there'd been a pudgy Spec 2 with bad breath working in the same room. It might have been Armstrong. If his memory wasn't faulty, and this really was a memory and not an implant, Armstrong had spent most of his time flicking through the bands, trying to find audible evidence of sedition or sex. Then he'd get the tape recorder going.

Armstrong was still talking, but Marx had lost interest. Armstrong had been a lackey then, and he still was a lackey. He referred to Brian again as Nuts-boy, and grinned as if making a very witty comment.

By then the boy was all the way back. He was awake and aware of his surroundings. He'd still said nothing since the roadblock.

They turned onto an even rougher road, and bounced along for a while as Armstrong stared back at them, trying to get them to speak. Marx saw a large billboard-style sign up ahead. The car slowed down to make the driveway. The sign said "1,000 GUNS," and in smaller letters, "THE BIGGEST SELECTION IN WESTERN NEW YORK." They pulled up in front of a low cinder-block building. On the roof, red, white, and blue painted tires were laid out to spell "GUNS," as if passing airplanes were going to stop and stock up.

Armstrong unlocked the back car door and grunted, "Out." The driver still hadn't looked at either the boy or Marx. As soon as they were out of the car and the doors slammed, the driver started up and went back the way they'd come. "I wouldn't advise making any sudden movements," Armstrong said. "An awful lot of perpetrators get killed attempting escape."

The building was divided roughly in two. On the right side was the shop, and the left was Armstrong's home. Parked by the door was a pickup truck with a sticker on the bumper that read, "I HAVE A GUN AND I VOTE."

It was much cooler inside the house. It took Marx a few minutes to get used to the lack of light. "You'll have to forgive the mess," Armstrong said with a mock-gentle smile. "The little lady's been slacking off lately. I guess maybe I need to kick her ass a little more often. Especially with all these bigwigs coming here to pick the Nuts-boy up today."

The television was on, casting a greenish glow. Marx looked around the room and realized that a woman was sitting facing the TV. "Honey," Armstrong said. "Look who's here. One of my old buddies. You remember me talking about Stretch Marx, don't you?"

She might have been attractive, taken out of that room full of hunting trophies and rifle parts, given some decent clothes and someone worth talking to. She looked up and fixed her eyes immediately on the boy. For the first time since he'd plugged in with Marx, Brian seemed interested in something outside his own head. Marx wondered if he'd seen the woman before, or seen through her.

"Darlene doesn't say too much," Armstrong said. "She knows better than to shoot off her mouth. Right, honey?"

The woman didn't respond. She was looking at Brian, her eyes locked with his. Marx felt something in the air; he could almost see the cord of light extending from Brian's eyes to the woman's. Brian might have been going through the wall right then and there. Apparently it was getting easier for him to do. He might have been seeing the whole situation through the woman's eyes, picking through her thoughts and memories and emotions.

Armstrong seemed to feel it too, though filtered through his brutish mind, it was just an undifferentiated threat to him. He spoke up again, trying to come between them:

"Let me explain a little something. Everybody's all hot and bothered about seeing Nuts-boy here, but they don't give a deep-fried shit about you, Stretch. They don't care one little bit what I do with you.

"It didn't seem quite right to hold you two over at the county lockup. This isn't something that concerns the local people. So we thought it would be better if you just stayed here for a little while. Protective custody, so to speak. We sure don't want the Nuts-boy to get hurt. Not with all these important people so worked up about him." He snorted, wiped at his face, then unlocked the cuff around Marx's wrist. Leading Brian into the kitchen, he looped the chain around a bend of sweating pipe and fastened him in place. "You make yourself comfortable. Me and my buddy Stretch have got a lot of catching up to do." He patted Brian on the head, as though he was a dog, then wiped his hand on his pant leg.

He ushered Marx through a curtained doorway and into the shop. Marx wasn't sure there were really one thousand guns there, but there were certainly too many to count.

"Really something, huh? Pretty impressive, I'd say. Best selection in ten counties. Semi-automatics, assault rifles, domestic, foreign models. You name it, I've got it."

He pulled a chair out from behind the counter and told Marx to sit down. "You know, Stretch, you and me have a lot in common. You might say we're kind of like blood brothers. Same branch, same unit. But it seems as though you sort of went bad. People had a lot of investment in you. And what happened? You go off with that shrink bitch, refuse to do the job that was assigned to you, and it would appear even assist a fugitive from the law. I would say you went kind of bad. You should have been more like me, Stretch. Obey orders, keep my nose clean, not ask too many questions. That's what they want, and that's what they reward. You should have known all this would get you in trouble. And I'm afraid that this time you're really in over your head."

The atmosphere there was more like an arsenal than a store. He had enough weapons there to arm a battalion. There were a few hunting rifles, but mostly it seemed that Armstrong had collected guns that could be used for actual combat.

"I kept my nose clean and look what it got me. County

Sheriff, my own store, a nice piece of property, and a chance every once in a while to use some mighty impressive ordnance. You know Attica's only a few miles down the road. That's why they set me up here. Every once in a while they've got to call in the heavy artillery, so to speak. After the uprising in '71, they thought it would be a good idea to have a little extra help on hand, just in case. There's an escape every once in a while, and it turns out it's a lot easier to use free-lance help to take care of them.''

He was proud of himself, enjoying the opportunity to tell all about his extracurricular activities. But Marx knew there was only one reason why he was spouting off that way: because soon enough Marx would be dead. It was a perfect situation for Armstrong, having a listener who actually understood and believed and who he had the authority to kill when the time seemed right.

He was taking his time with the story. It seemed that he had hours before Brian needed to be handed over.

''You know, it really used to bug me that I didn't get to go to 'Nam. I thought it would be my only chance to really do my stuff. It bugged me that I had to stay here in the states, keeping track of protesters and troublemakers, taking pictures and listening in on people. It took me a long time to figure it out, but that's the real important battle. We could have dumped napalm and Agent Orange over the whole goddamned country. We could have killed every last gook, but if we don't have our own people under control, what's the point? I'm talking about internal security, Stretch. Making sure there's a home front to come back to once all the overseas problems are taken care of. You don't get to ride in choppers or burn down whole villages, you don't get medals and citations, but they do make it worth your while.'' He pointed to the racks of weapons. A large American flag hung behind the counter.

''That's why I don't get it with you, Stretch. You were supposed to be smarter than me. You could have had all of this even better maybe. But you piddled it all away. They told me what kind of work you've been doing the last few years. Those are rent-a-cop jobs, Stretch. You could have been hunting down the honest-to-God enemies of society. You could have been keeping your eye on all sorts of scum. Doing real important work.''

He poked Marx in the chest with the muzzle of the automatic. "I'm disappointed in you. How come plain old Nelson R. Armstrong gets this far and you end up helping crazy people run loose? It doesn't make any sense.

"They waited years to call you up and what happens? You're a goddamned mess. You look like shit." He poked Marx again.

"If you were in combat, pal, and went over to the enemy, then we got our hands on you, it's a sure thing you'd get executed as a traitor. Right? Well, it's no different now, Stretch. This is war. You might not know it, but it's war just like in 'Nam, only this time we're going to win."

At the tail end of the war, Marx had been assigned work security at one of the big chemical plants where defoliants were being manufactured. There'd been some civil unrest there, protesters and a few true believers who'd handcuffed themselves to the gates. Not as much trouble as at the places where napalm was made, but enough. They blocked the front entrance for a while, and got front-page coverage in the newspapers. Marx had spent most of his time monitoring the closed-circuit TVs and getting photographs of all the people involved. It was an ordinary assignment. He'd often get shipped around to beef up security at plants where government work was being done. He remembered working with a fattish, pink-faced Spec 2 who might have been Armstrong.

"You have a shunt, don't you?" Marx said.

Armstrong nodded proudly, as though Marx had asked if he'd been decorated for courage in battle.

"We were assigned to that chemical plant together, weren't we? The one outside Buffalo."

"Damn straight. That's exactly what I'm talking about. It's war and that was one of the battles." He poked Marx harder, in the soft spot below his collarbone. "You were on the right side then."

They'd been exposed to something there, all of them. During the height of the protest, so they were told, an intruder had gotten into the plant and opened up a sealed area. All the men assigned to that detail had ended up in the hospital. Marx supposedly came down with pneumonia.

"That was the testing ground, Stretch. We were the elite.

The ones who tested out highest got the shunts. We were singled out. It was our trial by fire.

"We're the soldiers of tomorrow." It sounded as though he was reading a prepared speech. "Fighting for our country and what we know is right. The important battles are right here, not five thousand miles away. The enemy is among us, and if we don't keep fighting, they're going to win. The big battles are right here, down the street, on your doorstep."

He stopped. They both heard a low hum, like locusts singing in the trees. Armstrong shook himself, as if waking up.

"They're coming to get the boy about supper time. But apparently you're not in the plan anymore. You've been dropped right out of the program, Stretch."

He backed up a few steps. "All right, get up. I don't want to make a mess in here."

Armstrong led him down the aisles of guns and ammunition and out the back door. There was a barn a few hundred feet away, and just behind it was one of the huge steel towers. The path of the power lines cut across Armstrong's land. It might have been the hum from those lines that they'd heard. A few cows were grazing underneath the wires. They were all pointed the same direction, like needles on a compass.

The hum was louder outside. It came in steady surges. Armstrong led him down a dirt path away from the house, but stopped short of the barn. They listened. Now it seemed that the hum was behind them, coming from the house.

Marx looked back. On the side of the building was a screen door. Above it was a plywood sign that read, "DARLENE'S BEAUTY NOOK, NO APPOINTMENT NECESSARY."

Marx felt something probing at him, trying to gain entrance through his shunt. It appeared that Armstrong felt the same thing. He slapped the back of his neck, as if trying to kill a mosquito. He rubbed the muscles that extended from his shoulders.

From one direction came the huge, almost tidal pull of the power line's field. And from the other came a weaker but sharper current. They met inside Marx, dissonant and loud.

Almost as vivid as the actual pasture and house and sky before him, Marx saw the dark insides of the barn. He saw Armstrong press the pistol against his head, then his own brains and blood and bone shards sprayed on weathered boards. He saw Armstrong rolling him up in a sheet of canvas and carrying him far back into the pastures to a burial spot directly beneath one of the power lines.

Armstrong had talked about the two of them being like blood brothers. To link with Brian's mind he'd needed wires, direct physical connection. It didn't seem possible that he could be looking into Armstrong's mind, but there was no other explanation. He saw a filthy, ragged, bloody bum and realized that it was Armstrong's image of him.

They were both still waiting to be pushed one way or the other. Armstrong turned slowly toward the house, looking at the sagging screen door. Marx got a picture of what was inside, a rudimentary beauty shop. A makeshift chair, a few tables with brushes and curlers and combs. A few pictures cut out of magazines, hair styles that had been obsolete for years. A big mirror surrounded by bulbs. He saw Armstrong's wife with Brian. The boy was free, sitting with her, their arms around each other's shoulders. Brian's wire ran from the back of his head and into her. Marx could tell she was on the line, receiving Brian's cable feed.

Armstrong pulled himself free of the field and bolted toward the shop. The spell holding Marx broke too. Armstrong tore the screen door back and went inside. The humming ceased suddenly.

Marx went around the corner of the building. He heard Brian's voice inside his head, telling him keep going.

24

Darlene's husband came into the little beauty salon, aiming his gun right at Brian's face. "What the hell do you think you're doing in here?" His face was red and flecks of spittle flew off from his mouth when he yelled. "I asked you a question, woman. Answer me!" He wanted to come closer and yank Brian and Darlene apart, but he was afraid. And the more afraid he got, the more he yelled and waved the gun.

Once Brian had cut through the chain on his handcuffs to free himself, Darlene had led him into the beauty salon and taken off her wig to show him what was underneath. Scars and pockmarks covered her scalp. At the back of her head, directly behind her eyes, were a couple of rough slices in the skin, with ridges of scar tissue around them. It wasn't pretty, but Brian didn't mind much. She was being nice to him. She wanted to help him and then go through the wall with him into the Funk.

She'd pushed two chairs together so they could sit side by side. Her arms were around him and the buzzing electrol-

230

ysis gun was alive in her hand, throwing off a low-level field.

Then her husband had burst in and started yelling. He pointed to Brian's wrists. The chain had been burnt through. "What did you use? My welding torch? Goddamn it, I can't turn my back on you for a couple of minutes and you're messing around with this Nuts-boy." He jabbed at her but missed. "I thought I taught you a lesson last year after you went off with that shit you met at Louie's."

Darlene wouldn't let go of him. "You're making me mad, woman, awful mad. Once this is all over, you're going to regret you pulled this stunt. Regret it with your whole body."

She lifted the electrolysis gun and pointed it at him. A tiny spark popped from the needle, like a cinder thrown out by a fire. Her husband went on yelling, then backed away suddenly, aimed the gun just above their heads, and pulled the trigger. The blast broke bottles and one of the mirrors. The smell of hair-setting chemicals started to fill up the air.

"Now let go of him and get your ass over here."

The sound of Darlene's voice made him even madder. "You can't do a thing to him, Nelly. They want him alive and you'd be in big trouble if he wasn't when they got here."

"Well, they don't give two shits about you, woman," he said, grabbing her by the wrist and pulling her out of Brian's arms. He flung her against the wall and she lay there, keeping her face away from his. "Now get your ass in the living room while I take care of Nuts-boy." She didn't move. "Now! Every time I have to repeat myself, you're just making it worse."

Brian's wire hung from the back of his neck, the loose end in his lap. A faint bluish spark was flickering from one metal point to the other. Darlene's husband was looking at him, but he was too angry to see the light or know what it was.

"Don't call him Nuts-boy, Nelly. He's more a man than you ever hoped to be."

"I told you not to call me that in front of people," he said, kicking her in the side.

She huddled up like a baby trying to protect herself, but didn't stop talking. "He might look like a boy, Nelly, but twenty of you couldn't add up to one of him. He doesn't have to play with guns all the time to make up for being such a nothing.''

It seemed he was paralyzed, he was so angry. He wanted to kick her, punch her, and drag her outside. He wanted to put the gun in her mouth, all the way in, and pull the trigger. But he just stood there, trembling with rage.

''You're nothing, Nelly. Just a piece of trash they're going to throw away as soon as they're done with you.''

Finally he moved again, kicking her, and Brian could feel the blow, slamming hard against her stomach. ''I'll show you who's a man and who's a boy.'' He turned to Brian. ''Give me that wire.'' Brian could see already what he wanted to do with it. ''I said, give me the goddamned wire.'' He grabbed it from Brian, yanking it clean out of his shunt. For a moment Brian felt he was going to pass out, nerves raw and suddenly exposed to the air.

Darlene's husband grabbed her by the ankle and pulled her away from the wall. She tried to anchor herself by holding onto a table leg, but the whole thing moved and he got on top of her, pressing her flat to the floor with his knees. She squirmed and jabbed at him, but he hardly felt it, he was so full of red-hot hate. He sneered over at Brian, as if proud of himself, then spat on the two ends of the wire and jammed them into the slits in her neck. She was making horrible sounds, like a cat who's been hit by a car but isn't dead yet. She wriggled and fought, but he was too heavy for her.

''You talk all the time about satisfaction, woman. How I'm not man enough for you. Well, this is all you really need to be satisfied. This is it, the real thing.''

He took hold of his hair by the stiff crest on top and pulled. The whole thing came off. He'd been wearing a wig just like her. Underneath, he was just as bald as she was, but his scalp wasn't as scarred and marked. And instead of the rough slits in the back of his neck, He had two black pinpricks like Dr. Haak and Saul and Brian. He popped the rubber dots out quickly and slid in the wire leads.

Darlene's electrolysis gun was still plugged in and humming, building up a charge. He reached for it and pressed the hot tip against his chest, shooting in the load. It went through him and into her, hot, wild, and dirty. It was filling her up, pushing into every nerve cell.

Brian had seen plenty of others at the Red House getting ECT. This was far worse. The charge wouldn't stop. He kept jolting her, pressing her face against the floor, grunting and laughing.

Brian got whiffs of pain through the air. He tried to draw the pain out of her, absorb it into his body, but he was too far away and her husband was too wild.

The smell of scorched flesh was thick in the air. Brian lunged toward them, and before her husband could stop him, he'd pulled the wire out of Darlene and plugged it into himself. The cold fire erupted immediately. He felt the power running into him, flooding his system. This time it was like poison, gritty and foul and awful. He was locked with his enemy now, wired head to head and wrestling body against body.

He was plugged in and running at maximum. This time, though, it was different. He seemed to be in two places at once. He saw the rundown, cluttered little beauty shop and another place at the same time. When Darlene and the chair and the humming dimmed, he saw that he was in a place where the white and the black light churned together, like hot and cold currents mixing, spinning in a whirlpool.

In this other place he wasn't wrestling on a cold cement floor with a sweaty, red-faced man. It was combat and his enemy was just as eager to crush the life out of Brian. But this other body he fought against came apart in his hands. Fingers and skin tore loose. Brian punched hard against the torso and his hand went right through, ripping into cold, leaking guts. He choked the rubbery neck and the bones went soft in his grasp. Poison light streamed out of the eyes, and a breath like something long dead and rotten rushed out of the mouth.

From somewhere nearby came voices like the old people's in Ward 25 back at the Red House, cackling and laughing, though there was nothing funny. They were like dried-up husks of old bugs, the soft flesh inside long before sucked out by the air and the light. The air was full of acid vapors, belched out of holes he couldn't see. Everything there was ugly, broken, dying.

The eyeballs pulsed, croaking like swamp frogs. The fingers and intestines squirmed in the smoky dust. Patches of skin flapped like moths trying to fly after being crushed by a foot. The biggest part, a stomach or liver, was crawling away from him, leaving behind a wet, slimy trail like a slug.

And as the last oozing parts slipped out of his hands, Brian looked around and knew that he was inside his enemy. Somehow it had gotten larger, or he'd shrunk and had been swallowed up in this vast body.

Brian looked down at his hands. Light was streaming out of his fingertips. Red, smoking wounds pulsed in his palms. The steel loops of the handcuffs were still on him, golden now, not silver. They'd changed too, just as his body had been converted in passing into that place. The aura was in his fists. He heard it whining like a transformer with too heavy a load. The air was cooking, particles of white ash forming around his hands and falling like snow to the ground.

When he tried hard, he could almost see into the little room where Darlene and her husband lay. She was crying, stroking Brian's hair, thinking he was dead just like her husband. They were both motionless on the floor, tangled arm and leg like a knot of rope. Brian was looking through her husband's eyes, and the picture was dimming very quickly. The body itself was losing its heat, stiffening.

It took a great deal of work to squeeze himself up and see through the eyes. He hung on as long as he could. He tried to make the mouth work, to tell her that he was okay, but the muscles were hardening already. The jawbone was broken and the throat was filled with blood.

He gave up and slipped back downward. By then the place where he'd fought his enemy was darker and smaller. The air was thick, not like fog, but as though it was congealing. He took a few steps and the air pushed against him, pitchy and unyielding. He was pressing through the dark earth, through heavy rock and veins of ore. He knew as soon as he stopped, he'd be trapped there, alive but buried in death. He'd be stuck there like a fossil in the dead mass of his enemy.

So he did what had always worked in the past. "Owwww, I got the power! Ooo-eeee, let me have it!" The chant got him moving. It got stronger and more rhythmic and picked up a second voice, saying, "Chuka chuka chuka" like a railroad engine huffing, and then he heard the whistle blast and the howl of the rails, and he was cutting a tunnel through the black earth. He was Soul Train again, carrying his precious cargo of golden ore out of the mother lode. He picked up steam. The tracks were fully formed there, snaking up and around tight curves. The driver wheels slammed like drums. The fire in his boiler was building and out of his smokestack came a coil of pure black funk. The beam of the headlight cut into the darkness and the whistle blew again and he knew who'd given him the power to get out of there. It was Soul Brother Number One: grinning huge white teeth and skin black as slag. He was behind the wheel, pulling the whistle chain and shoveling pile after pile of coal into the flames with his bare hands.

He careened around a tight bend and things began popping out of the walls, screaming and laughing at him like in a fun house ride. Men in white coats flew down on wires and jabbed at him with needles. A bird with Dr. Haak's face glided alongside the train for a while, spitting sparks. He saw a circle of men dressed in black gowns sitting around a boiling pot. They were using long, glowing bones to stir the murky goo. Their faces were pinched and twisted. They all grinned at Brian as he went past, and shouted out filthy words. Chittering bats flew out of their mouths and clouds of tiny bugs surrounded their heads like living crowns.

The track veered upward and looped above this scene. Brian looked back as he spiraled above them and saw that mixed in with the black muck in the pot were floating lumps of gold. The men poked at the nuggets and scooped them out as they rose to the surface. And though they were glowing hot from the fire, the men popped them into their mouths like candy.

Then Brian had risen too high to see these men, spiraling tighter and tighter as he rose until he was a corkscrew boring into the soft, flaky soil, cutting his way toward the light. Somewhere above him, voices called. First and clearest was the God Father of Souls shouting, "Yassss, bring it on up." Then came a less familiar one but just as true. It wasn't speaking English. It was old and thin and shaky and was telling him secrets he needed to know. And last he heard a pair of voices, a man and woman, and they were saying they wanted him to come home and how much they missed him.

With that he put on a last surge of steam and found the soil turning to plasma and the plasma turning to smoky air and the smoke finally clearing away.

He was on the surface at last. He'd made it out of the body.

The ground there was scorched and blighted. He was walking on asphalt. It was split and weeds grew through the cracks. The tar went on as far as he could see, like a huge scar, holding down everything Brian had just traveled through. He began to see houses, small and regular. They had been nice once, brick faces with swing sets in the yard and little porches out front. The lawns had been green once. The trees had been alive. It was deserted now and forbidden. But still the two voices kept calling to him, "Welcome home, Brian." There was a light at the end of the street. The front door on a small brick house was open. The doorbell button glowed like a tiny red eye. He went into that house and was home.

Inside, the house was bare, just as vacant and broken and poisonous as all the other houses there. The carpets had been pulled up. On the walls were squares of a slightly different color where pictures had hung. All the furniture and books and decorations were gone. This was the house he'd lived in. He was home, but he didn't see who was calling to him.

He went down the hallway toward his bedroom. He opened the door and the voices ceased suddenly, as if sucked out through the chimney.

He saw a thing lying on the bare floor where his bed had been. It was disgusting to look at but impossible to take his eyes off of. It was a man, or had been a man a very long time ago. The limbs and the head were still there. But the bones seemed to have been softened or removed, its skin hanging like gray jelly. It had a mouth and two eyes and a few fingers that worked. The lips pulsed open and closed, gasping for air. The fingers twitched, as though trying to bring Brian closer. "Welcome home, my boy. I've been waiting a long time for this. A very long time." The voice sounded more inside him than through his ears. It was a sloppy, wet whisper. "You've passed all the tests. You're everything I hoped you'd be. It's all gone exactly according to the plan. And in thirty-six hours it'll all be over." The thing tried to smile. Greasy bubbles appeared in its nostrils. It seemed very happy. It nodded slightly, dismissing him, and Brian felt as though he was starting to dissolve, liquify, and run right into the floorboards. First his vision went, then his hearing and sense of touch. The smell lasted longest, a foul, chemical stench.

25

Marx carried enough firearms and ammunition to eradicate a small village. Before heading down the road and sticking out his thumb to catch a ride, he'd looted through Armstrong's store and picked out all the ordnance he thought he'd need. In one leather satchel he had a World War II-vintage Luger and two Italian assault rifles, broken down for easy carrying. And in the other bag he had a few hundred rounds of ammunition. He was no expert when it came to guns, but he knew how to aim and pull the trigger. That's all it was going to take.

Once Whitehead and Price had snagged him and pulled him away from Dr. Haak, once they'd gone inside and wrung him out like an old towel, he'd stopped caring whether he lived or died. That lack of caring had freed him. They had nothing to threaten him with and nothing to offer as a bribe. He had no reason not to kill them all. He wasn't even sure whom he was after, but once he found them, he'd know.

He had a slight regret that after arming himself, he hadn't gone into the house and shot Armstrong to pieces. And he felt bad for leaving the boy behind. But he just wanted the

whole thing to be over with. Armstrong wasn't worth killing. He could have been any of a hundred other wired-in,
well-armed patriots who'd been assigned to take care of him.
He wanted to see the man in charge. He was going to kill
the person who'd invaded his brain, dripped pain and poison
into him for years, and taken away the only two women he'd
ever wanted. He wasn't going to cut off a finger or a hand.
He wanted the whole head, severed clean.

He got a ride with a squarish, dark little man in a VW
bug. In the backseat was a German shepherd almost as big
as its owner. The driver went on at great length about problems he was having with his neighbors, and Marx grunted
"uh-huh" and "I know what you mean" in the appropriate
places. His mind, though, was far from the cramped, dog-
smelling car. He was imagining what it would be like to
pull the triggers, to see the hot blood and flecks of gray
matter spraying in the air.

"They play their damned music so loud. Sometimes I
can't get to sleep until two in the morning," the driver said.

Bullets roaring out like a stream of black fire. Flesh being
torn apart.

"I'd call the cops on them, but they got an uncle or
brother-in-law or somebody on the force and nothing ever
happens."

Marx looked up and saw a bend in the road. There were
no houses within sight, only a bent-backed old farm shed
and a billboard that had lost its message years before.

"And to top it off, they complain to me that my Dusty
barks too much. Can you believe such nerve?"

They were approaching the corner where Lenny had been
killed. Marx had only seen that curve once since she'd died.
The grass had still been torn up and the telephone pole yet
to be replaced. Now, fifteen years later, the evidence was
obliterated. There was no sign that anyone had been mur-
dered there.

The field where her car had come to rest had been fallow
for over a decade. The owner was waiting for suburban
sprawl to reach that far so that nice tract houses and con-
venience stores could be built there. And then a patch of
new asphalt would cover the spot where they'd dragged
Lenny out of the car and her blood had run into the ground.

"This is wrong," Marx said, feeling a surge of panic. "I thought you said you were going to Niagara Falls."

"No, Lewiston. I live in Lewiston."

"But I need to get to Niagara Falls."

"It's only about ten more miles. You can get another ride."

As the car went around the corner, Marx saw what he knew wasn't really there. His whole body wound in on itself, tensing for a crash. He heard the squeal of brakes and saw another car slamming into the one he was in, forcing it off the road. And behind the wheel was a smiling, pink-faced man with his hair in a military cut. It was Armstrong, fifteen years younger and made even more repulsive by the grin he was wearing. The crunch of metal against metal filled Marx's ears, then vanished suddenly, a dead silence rushing in to replace it.

"You know, sometimes I think it was fate that I got stuck next door to those bastards. Of all the people in the world, it had to be them."

Marx opened his eyes. The car was on a short expressway ramp, heading into traffic. They were riding along the crest of a ridge. Below them, a few miles away, was a small town that shaded into suburbs on three sides. Beyond that was a river, a deep notch in the green landscape.

They passed a sign pointing toward the bridge to Canada and one with a picture of a squat dome topped by a cross, saying, "3½ MILES TO THE FATIMA SHRINE."

The aftershocks were still echoing inside Marx, as though the car crash was being replayed inside him. He felt his head driven again and again through the windshield, a twist of bare metal jammed repeatedly into his spine. He saw two scenes at once: the corner where Lenny had been killed and the peaceful, almost sleepy town below. The driver was still droning on about the hard lot he had in life.

Marx sucked air into his lungs and he felt bladelike shards piercing him, his ribs tearing his flesh. He twisted in his seat, trying to escape, and it seemed the skin was peeling off his neck, like bark off a burning log. The scream of brakes and the groan of tearing metal kept sounding inside him, played as an endless loop.

The car came to a stoplight and Marx scrabbled franti-

cally for the door latch. Getting it open at last, he lunged
out of the car and tumbled into a weedy ditch. As the sounds
of traffic receded, the pain drained back into the sump it
had belched out of. The smell of burning flesh was blown
away by the wind. He squatted in the weeds for a while,
clutching his two bags to his chest. Realizing that he was
still armed, still able to do what he'd come to do, helped
clear away the last of the hallucination.

He peeked over the top of the ditch. His ride was long
gone. He thought of trying to thumb again, but he knew
what he must look like: covered with mud, his eyes wild
and unfocused. It occurred to him that he could unpack the
assault rifles and wade into traffic, firing randomly. He'd get
a ride that way. But then he'd never find the people he
needed to see. He'd end up in one more dead end, spending
days or weeks trying to get back on track. He had an important goal. He had places to go, things to do, people to
kill. They were waiting for him, probably a little klatch of
men with business suits and thinning hair. Perhaps some
would be in uniform, military people and doctors.

He tried brushing the mud off his legs and chest, but gave
up quickly and climbed out of the ditch. He hoisted himself
up by the bare metal shaft of a road sign. Using his two
bags to balance himself, he read, "WELCOME ALL ROTAR-
IANS. MEETING EVERY THIRD TUESDAY OF THE MONTH."
He repeated the address like a rote prayer and set out to find
the meeting. He was in luck. It was the third Tuesday of
June. Tomorrow would be the longest day of the year. It
was nearly eight o'clock. They'd all be waiting for him. He
wouldn't need to know the secret handshake or password.
He had two bags full of guns. That would be just as good.

Soon he came to a bland residential part of town. The
houses there were large and had plenty of room around
them. The grass was uniformly well trimmed and well wa-
tered. There were no sidewalks, though. He had to walk
along on the shoulder of the street, too close to traffic.

A carload of teenagers zoomed past and he heard their
shouts and jeers. They thought he was drunk. They didn't
get to see many derelicts in that part of town. They came
back for a second look, yelling insults, and slowed to come
up alongside him. He stuck his hand into one of the bags

and pulled out his Luger. Aiming it directly at the face of the driver, he said, "Can you kids tell me where the Rotary meets?"

They were terrified, like little children about to be spanked. He tilted the gun slightly and shot out the car's headlights. Then turning his back on them, seeing that they weren't going to be any use, he started walking again. They were gone quickly, tearing around and heading in the opposite direction.

It wasn't long before another car pulled up beside him. He took hold of the gun again, eased it out of the bag, and turned to face them. It was a mud-spattered red station wagon. Dr. Haak was behind the wheel. And the orderly from Mt. Kinnsvort, Ollie, was sitting next to her, bandaged and stiff like a mummy. Dr. Haak was smiling, as if glad to see a pistol aimed at her face.

26

Ollie was quite cooperative once Dr. Haak had burnt, bruised, and blown his nervous system. Even after giving him an injection of Thanadryl, though, and dumping a few buckets of ice on him, it still took quite awhile for him to regain consciousness. Not that there was that much consciousness left.

In one eye a number of blood vessels had burst. He seemed to have lost the power of speech. With his good eye he gazed up at her, not afraid anymore but not awed either.

She sprayed on some topical painkiller and set to work bandaging him. She enjoyed the process, wrapping yards of gauze and tape around him. By the time she was done, his entire torso was encased in white, porous armor, and he had a helmet of gauze on his head. She went too far perhaps, working until she ran out of bandaging material, but Ollie didn't seem to mind. By then he didn't mind anything.

He complied with her wishes, shuffling out to the car and waiting patiently there as she packed her belongings in the back. She put a small electrical device in Ollie's lap, pulled

the billed cap down over his head, and they were on the
road before the sun had come up.

The scanner was crude; she'd cobbled it together out of
the heaps of parts in her car. It wasn't very accurate, but
did give her a direction and a rough idea of the distance she
still needed to travel. It lay in Ollie's lap, beeping and humming, searching for a signal that would lead them to Saul.

Ollie held the antenna like a divining rod. The noise from
the scanner grew louder as they aligned themselves with the
field they needed to move inside. And after about twenty
miles, Dr. Haak noticed a distinct increase in pitch. They
were definitely getting closer.

But the signal came and went, blocked at times by the
hilly terrain or garbled by the output from a radio tower.
For a while they lost it completely, driving near a line of
power derricks. They doubled back, made a wider loop
around the fields, and found Saul's signal again, this time
stronger and more consistent.

They went through a fast-food drive-thru at supper time,
and Dr. Haak parked in the far corner of the lot, to feed
Ollie french fries and let him suck a watery milkshake
through a straw. All the while they sat there eating, the
beeping diminished. But once they were on the road again,
they started gaining ground, and by the time they'd crossed
the Niagara County line, the sound was strong and regular
again. She knew they'd all end up in that place—Brian, Ollie, Saul, Price and Whitehead. She'd known for years that
the whole thing would come together a few miles from the
falls. And so she was surprised that Saul was now north of
the city, apparently heading away. He might have been aiming for the bridge to Canada. He might have been drawn to
the big energy-research complex a few miles from Lewiston. Or he might just have been lost and wandering.

They came into the suburbs and began cruising the streets,
jogging back and forth as the signal swelled and ebbed.
Soon the scanner was locked on him, beeping loudly and
insistently, almost shaking itself out of Ollie's hands.

It took a moment to recognize Saul. She saw a man in a
filthy suit, shambling along the road, talking nonstop to
himself. He looked like a drunken derelict, carrying all he
owned in two small bags. The top of his head had been

shaved, and blackish scabs had formed like a crest on his scalp. She pulled up beside him.

He turned, aimed the pistol at her face, and smiled like one of her shakers back at the Red House. The smile had nothing to do with joy or pleasure. It was more like the curling back of lips on a cornered dog.

The scanner was squawking rhythmically, loud enough to hurt her ears. She grabbed the device from Ollie and ripped the batteries out of their compartment. This seemed to make Saul relax somewhat. Perhaps he'd felt the scanner hunting for him through the air, keeping its finger on him. His grimace-smile disappeared, but he didn't lower the gun.

She shut off the engine and got out, imagining all the suburbanites peering through their picture windows. Probably half a dozen of them had already called the police. She thought it might take quite a bit of coaxing to make him put away the gun and get into the car with her, but once he heard her voice, he was hers again, back under her wing as though he'd never left.

"It's me, Caroline. Aren't you glad to see me?"

She opened the back door, shoved a few bags and boxes to the side. "You remember Ollie, don't you?"

As soon as he handed her his gun and shut the door, she started the engine and got out of there, zigzagging from one side street to another. She reached the edge of town quickly, driving down a road that developers had just started staking out for new houses. When she thought they were sufficiently far from town, out among pastures and fallow fields again, she pulled over.

The haunted look was still on Saul's face. He was staring down at his hands, holding another gun now. He seemed afraid it would turn on him of its own accord and fire. "They can find me anywhere," he said. "They let me go for a few hours, but they'll be back again. I can feel them inside."

"Does it hurt?" she said.

He nodded. Just the mention of pain seemed to make it worse. His finger curled around the trigger. The other hand was clamped on the barrel, as though two halves of him were fighting for control. His right hand won, at least for the moment. He pressed the gun against his forehead. But he didn't pull the trigger. "They don't need us anymore. It's all over."

Her voice, though, made whatever was pulling on him weaker, less sure:

"Saul, listen to me. They can't make you do anything you don't want to do."

They heard police sirens coming toward them, but had yet to see the flashing lights. Pulling the gun gently out of Marx's hands, she laid it with the other one on the front seat. The sirens seemed to excite Ollie. He was moving his lips, hissing and wheezing, trying to form a word.

Dr. Haak set out again, driving a short distance before seeing a one-lane drive heading into an area of scrub and overgrown weeds. They went that way and came out onto another driveway, this one paved.

Looking back to make sure Marx was all right, she saw he was holding a third gun to his head. His right hand seemed to be winning again. "Saul! Listen to me, Saul. I think we can fix you up. If you can hold out a little longer. We need to—" She stopped in mid-sentence. They'd come out onto a small parking lot. A few corrugated metal sheds and service buildings were clustered there. None of them were lit. Beyond, she saw what looked like a huge, squat hemisphere, glowing pearly white. On top was a crownlike platform. It was hard to tell the scale of the dome, but it seemed to be as tall as the trees.

The light streamed upward, making a luminous haze around the dome. By then the sun was almost down, as though sped toward the horizon by this glowing, moonlike apparition. It seemed that shadows had lengthened suddenly, night coming on as soon as she'd seen the dome.

"Saul, listen to me. I think we can do something about the shunt." She got out and went around to his door. "I opened you up without too much trouble. Yours was one of the earliest ones. I think I can remove most of it, or at least shut it down. But we need to get you somewhere safe first. If you can just hold out a little while longer. Until we can get out of here safely."

He still was holding the gun to his head. It slipped easily out of his hand. He winced and shook as another wave of pain hit him from inside.

"I have to figure out where we are," she whispered. "I'll be back in a few minutes." A soft, quaking sound rose from his throat, like an animal in heat. He didn't want to be left alone. "All right, all right. Come on." She took him by the hand and they went into the woods, heading toward the glow. Ollie would be fine in the car. He was barely conscious, and unless he was told what to do, he sat perfectly still.

As they got closer, it became clear that the glowing dome was some sort of building. It was perhaps three stories high, a huge half-globe with metal shapes attached to the outside, representing continents. The building's skin was made of curved glass and plastic panels held together by metal strips like the lines of longitude and latitude on a globe. On top of the building was a platform that could have held a few dozen people. And rising from this platform was a large statue with outstretched arms.

She saw a trail nearby and followed it toward the dome. A short distance along it they came to a bronze statue of a woman in a long gown. She was standing on a block of granite with a plaque attached to the front. A tiny light glowed at the base of the stone. Dr. Haak came closer to read the inscription. "St. Lucy of the Divine Light. Among her works of self-denial and mortification is the act here depicted, for which she is most well known. Though a beautiful young lady with many men desirous to have her hand in marriage, Lucy was convinced that she should keep herself consecrated to her Lord. One of her suitors was so smitten by the beauty of her eyes that he could find no rest. Fearing that her eyes would cause the man to harbor sinful thoughts, Lucy tore them from her head." The statue showed a young woman holding out a shallow dish. Staring up from this dish were two eyeballs.

They went on, passing two other saints before reaching the main area. But Dr. Haak was afraid of leaving the cover of the wooded trail.

The building was lit from the inside, the solid metal lattice which held it together casting gridlike shadows on the trees nearby. And in front of it, stretched out over ten or twenty acres, was a complex network of hedges, paths, and fountains. Laid out in this parklike setting were a few hundred life-sized statues.

A flat-roofed building stood to one side of the domed church. A light burned by the front door, but it looked as though it was closed for the night. Next to the front door was a sign reading, "WELCOME VISITORS TO THE SHRINE OF OUR LADY OF FATIMA." Beyond the gift shop and the cafeteria was a large parking lot. There were only a few cars left there, and as they waited still in the shade of the trees, the last few employees left the building and headed for the lot. Finally a priest came out of the basilica, locked the doors, and went down a paved path toward a building Dr. Haak assumed was the rectory.

The attacks of pain were still hitting Marx. She had him sit in the dewy grass and positioned his hands on the trunk of a small tree to keep him from falling over. By then the sun was gone. And though it was the day before Midsummer's eve, the air was quite cool. Marx and Dr. Haak stayed there awhile, listening, but heard no voices from the direction of the rectory or sirens from far off.

"I think we'll be all right here for the night," she said. "I doubt they'd be searching around here; certainly not before morning." She helped him to his feet and led him back the way they'd come.

She made Ollie sit in the backseat. And though he obeyed, it was obvious he wasn't pleased. His breathing was like a broken organ, low and reedy. He sat stiffly with his hands in his lap, staring downward as though ashamed.

Dr. Haak slid into the front seat, bunched up a coat for a pillow, and worked her arm around Marx's shoulder. She wanted to comfort him, or at least give him something to cling to as the shock waves passed through him. He too was in great need of sleep, but he remained awake in her arms, waiting for the next and then the next jolt of pain. Crickets and peepers were out, making a wash of white noise. No traffic sounds reached them there. And though Ollie was behind her, glowering, and Marx was in her arms wrenched and wrung by the attacks, she felt asleep moving quickly in on her.

She woke suddenly, moving from deep dreamless sleep to complete wakefulness in an instant. She sat up straight,

trying to orient herself, remember where she was. Ollie was
still in the backseat. His eyes were wide open, staring dead
ahead. He'd been motionless for hours, gazing at the back
of her neck. It was still dark out. The moon, a day or two
shy of full, hung above the treetops. The light it cast was
almost orange, tainted somehow.

It took her a moment to see what was wrong, then realized that Saul was gone.

"Did you see him, Ollie? Which way did he go?"

It seemed that Ollie was smiling.

"This is important. Did you see him leave?"

He tilted his head forward slightly, a hint of a nod. She
pointed toward the trail she'd followed earlier and again
Ollie nodded. "How long ago? When did he leave?"

Ollie didn't respond. He stared forward, blank and im-
passive.

Dr. Haak ran toward the trail and was soon back at the
domed shrine basilica. The building itself was dark. She
tried the doors, yanking on the handles, then ran up the set
of stairs that curved around the dome, leading to the platform on top.

A huge crucifix stood like an antenna on top of the shrine,
pulling transmissions out of the air. The face was expres-
sionless, as if the spirit had already fled the tormented flesh.

Dr. Haak went to the guardrail at the edge of the platform
and looked out over the grounds. The statues of saints were
laid out precisely along three main avenues. There were
hundreds of them: gesturing forever, blessing forever, suf-
fering martyrdom or being shot through with ecstasy forever. The trees and shrubs were all neatly trimmed from
that vantage point looking like purely geometric shapes. The
flower beds were all perfect too, though in the orange-red
moonlight their colors were muted. A few miles away, on
the main route leading to Niagara Falls, a semi-tractor trailer
lumbered along. Even at that distance, she could hear it
changing gears as it made its way up the escarpment.

Once it was past, the shrine was silent. The night insects
had all ceased. The wind was dead. She imagined herself
staying on the platform until dawn, watching the sun rise
over the acres of grass and legions of saints, but she saw

movement suddenly on one of the farthest paths. It was Saul, staggering down a row of dark saints, a black bag in either hand.

She ran down the steps and headed for him. Once on ground level, though, his location was unclear. She slowed to a walk, the sound of her footsteps uncomfortably loud in her ears. She peered down one long corridor and thought she saw him sitting on a wrought-iron bench. Coming closer, she realized it was just a shrub trimmed low to the ground.

The statues all seemed familiar. She recognized some from the Red House. She passed St. Jerome, beating his heart with a stone. At his feet were his symbols, a skull and an owl. Beyond him stood St. Ambrose holding a beehive. The grounds became more like a maze as she hunted for Marx. At every corner it seemed she saw some sign of him, but going toward it, again and again she found herself alone and unsure of where she was.

It wasn't her eyes that finally led her to Marx, but her ears. She heard a low moaning and went toward it cautiously. After a few wrong turns, the sound was louder and she saw him sitting at the feet of a large statue. The two black bags were on the ground, open. Bright metal shone inside them. For a moment she thought he might pull out one of his guns and start firing, but by the time she reached him, she saw they were her bags and not his. He'd taken her surgical tools instead of his weapons. A scalpel hung from his fingers. It was coated with blood.

He looked up as she approached. His entire face was slick and red. His voice came weakly: "I couldn't stand it anymore. I had to do something."

She turned his head to the side and saw that he'd been trying to remove the shunt by himself. He'd cut and hacked the back of his head. Blood was everywhere, coating his shoulders and hands, spattered on the ground. Bright coils and black wormlike shapes were visible in his flesh. He'd cut a few of the connections, but apparently had known better than to just yank the whole apparatus out.

She dumped her bags on the concrete walkway, found a few gauze pads, and, pouring alcohol into the wound, began clearing away the blood and torn tissue. He barely winced as she worked on him. The pain must have been considerably less than that filling him from the inside.

Once she'd cleaned him off as best she could and snipped out a few of the tiny wires, she held his face in her hands and tried to get him to understand. "Saul, listen to me, Saul. I've got to take the rest of it out. Right now. You're going to die if I don't. I think I can get the main body of the shunt out, but I don't know about all the inner connections. You've sliced yourself up pretty badly. I'm not sure I'll be able to get everything back the way it should be."

Before Marx had even shown up at the Red House, she'd seen his schematics. The technology was considerably less sophisticated than Brian's shunt. It was possible that she could at least deactivate it. The actual connective cord to his nervous system was beyond removal. It would surely kill him to go after that. But the outer apparatus, stomas and chips and Olin coils, these she could probably remove. And if they were going after him and attacking through these, he might be free once they were cut out.

She shot him full of morphine and set to work. She'd heard in med school of battlefield surgery that seemed impossible, removing bullets and shrapnel with tools that would have been antiquated at the turn of the century. She knew that people had survived steak knife tracheotomies and appendectomies performed with barber tools and only whiskey for an anesthetic. It was obvious that Marx would be dead in a few hours if she didn't do something. It was possible that he'd already doomed himself. She'd never seen any hard evidence of it, but she'd heard rumors that some of the shunts were designed to let loose a final, fatal blast if their structural integrity was altered from the outside.

She laid Marx facedown on the sidewalk, jammed a flashlight into St. Blaise's two-pronged candlestick so that it shown on the back of Saul's neck, and got to work. Marx had already done most of the dangerous cutting. Dr. Haak found that her task consisted more of repair than removal. She got the stomas out clean, seared a few veins to stop the bleeding, and trimmed back the ragged tissue. She went in as far as she thought safe, following the main line. The whole operation seemed ridiculous, impossible. She might have done a better job putting him back together with electrical tape and wire nuts.

Eventually, though, she had him sewn back together. The flashlight was almost dead by then. Her hands were numb. Her eyes stung from squinting. Her hands and face and chest were covered with blood. Certainly without a great deal of cosmetic surgery, Marx's head was going to look like the surface of an old butcher's block, but it seemed he was going to live. She was hopeful that he was free at last.

It took her the better part of an hour to get him back to the car, holding his hands around her front and drag-carrying him. She knew it was foolish to do such major surgery on him and then lug him a half mile like a bag of trash. But she knew also that the state police would be there soon, and he was in no condition to resist if they did catch him. He'd end up in the county hospital under armed guard and then be shipped off to jail. She'd lost him once; she wasn't going to lose him again.

27

Ollie waited. He just needed to be patient. There was no way for him to get back at her directly now. He was too weak to fight her face to face. But soon enough they'd find the boy, and then Ollie could get his revenge.

He sat all night in the parking lot, listening to Marx moan and whine. Ollie waited for them to fall asleep. Instead, Marx had snuck out of the car and gone back where he'd been earlier. Then Dr. Haak had woken and gone after him, and a few hours later she dragged him back to the car like a deer she'd shot and wanted to tie to the fender. They drove on. It was June twenty-first, the longest day. Before the sun rose the next morning, it would all be over.

She must have known for months, even years, how it was all supposed to end, Ollie thought. She'd tested the patients, weeding the bad from the good. And had finally settled on Brian to be the little white lamb. At one time Ollie had been her favorite. Then Brian had appeared and Ollie was pushed back to second best. He couldn't go through the wall like Brian. He couldn't fire the discharge through the line. He couldn't even do the good-foot dance. So they'd thrown him away, like all the other also-rans.

Back when it hadn't been decided yet who would be the little lamb, when Ollie had still been in the running, he'd been an inmate at the Red House just like all the others. Then one day he'd been moved to a new room, and instead of receiving the treatments and pills, he was giving them out. He didn't know whether the other orderlies were former patients too, but it seemed unlikely. They treated him differently. They knew he was special, under Dr. Haak's wing.

He thought for sure once he'd been transferred and made an orderly that he was the chosen one. However, Brian showed up and his position began to change. He spent less time with Dr. Haak. He stopped getting tested altogether and was stuck handing out dinner trays and making sure that no one made noise after lights out. Time passed and it became harder to remember when he was locked up and not one of the jailers. Staff changed steadily, and after a while there was hardly anyone there who had known Ollie when he was a patient.

If it hadn't been for Brian, he would have been the number one, the little lamb that everyone was so worried about, asking a million questions, watching like he was some strange flower from far away waiting years and years to bloom.

And that day had finally come, but little Brian wasn't going to get a chance to strut his stuff. Ollie was going to make sure that if he wasn't the one in the spotlight, then no one would be.

They tried using the scanner machine, but that wouldn't work with Brian. Ollie could have told her that. A little piece of toy junk wasn't going to be enough to track down the boy. The field he was putting out wasn't something so ordinary that a piece of cheap hardware could pick it up. It took something better. And Ollie was that something.

After driving all morning, diddling with the dials on the scanner, cursing and coming close to tears, Dr. Haak finally threw it in a trash can at the hamburger place where they stopped for lunch. She checked Marx every once in a while to make sure he was all right. After a few hours his color had came back and he didn't seem so frail. Dr. Haak sat staring at her french fries: depressed, angry, and frustrated. She knew that today was going to be the big day, but she had no idea how to find the boy.

"The Power Authority," Ollie said. They were the first words he'd spoken since their time together at the motel. She was afraid of his voice, surprised that he could talk. That meant that there was more of him left than she'd assumed.

"Try the Power Authority, by the river." It didn't take a genius to know where Brian would be. It took someone like Ollie, a blood brother. He felt the same pull, the same huge waves flowing out from the generators. Maybe it was intuition or just common sense. Ollie was positive that the boy would be near the generators, like a tiny chip of iron drawn by the magnetic waves as huge and powerful as ocean tides. If Ollie could have lifted his feet off the ground and floated, he'd be there too, pulled directly to the gigantic cores.

It didn't take her long to agree. Time was moving by them quickly. It was already the middle of the afternoon. In a few hours the sun would be down and then it would be too late. She needed to find him before the last players were in position.

Ollie could feel it in the air. Something was happening not far away. As they sat there eating greasy french fries, things were moving, unseen, into alignment. Forces set into motion a year, ten years, ago were finally in place. They were waiting for Brian, the last piece.

There were even street signs pointing the way to the Power Authority. It was one of the tourist attractions. Dr. Haak followed the signs and parked in a lot with all the other station wagons and vans, travel trailers and cars packed with luggage. A family was sitting on the hood of their car, passing around a bottle of orange drink. The father was looking at a map, trying to find where he was in relation to the falls.

Dr. Haak looked back at Ollie, depending now on him for direction. They could go in with the others and take the guided tour, looking at the dioramas and displays. But Brian wasn't going to be there. He'd be at the heart of the complex, as close to the turbines as he could get.

Everywhere they looked huge power lines crowded the sky. Strange shapes of concrete and steel stuck out of the

roofs, painted bright orange. Ollie had no idea what these
structures did, nor did he care. That close, surrounded on
all sides by the power plant, Ollie was drunk, light-headed.
He felt he would drift into the air or unravel if he didn't
concentrate on staying there, body and mind. Brian was
nearby, that was for sure. He was trapped in the complex
like a moth trapped by a spotlight.

They followed the flower-bordered path toward the main
entrance. Dr. Haak looked over at Ollie, as if to say,
"You're absolutely sure?" and he nodded.

They left Marx in the car. He was still too weak to walk
very far. Dr. Haak checked his bandages, readjusted his
pillows, and after making sure no one was watching, she
gave him another shot to make him sleep. Ollie had on a
loose-fitting jacket that covered most of his bandages. And
Dr. Haak had bought him a fisherman's cap at one of the
gift shops. It came down low, hiding his wounds. He looked
like all the others going along that path. He could have been
Dr. Haak's husband. They could have been just one more
couple out seeing the sights.

Except that Ollie had one of her scalpels in his pocket to
use on Brian when he found him.

They passed through the main gate, took a pamphlet out
of the rack, and studied it for a while. Dr. Haak was getting
nervous. "Are you sure he's here?"

Ollie was sure. He pointed to the escalator, and they went
up two flights in a long line of tourists. At the top they
followed the signs to one of the Power Vista Observation
Decks. Behind the glass, laid out in front of them like a
town devoid of all inhabitants, was the main generating
plant. The machinery was huge, larger than good-sized
houses. Cables and insulating towers were everywhere above
the turbines and transformers. Finally Dr. Haak felt what
he'd been feeling all along. Ollie imagined that even people
without shunts would be aware of it too: the magnetic field
surging around them, rising out of the mechanical ghost
town below. Quite a distance down the viewing gallery, a
guide was droning on, explaining how the water from the
river was converted into electricity. Ollie wasn't listening,
he was feeling. Brian was down there. He was hiding somewhere below.

Even through the glass and with the people chattering around him, Ollie could hear the enormous humming that came from the plant. It was as though the floor itself was alive, discharging through his feet and into his nervous system.

The tour group came their way. Dr. Haak moved to let them pass, but Ollie stood his ground. Soon he was surrounded by the visitors. "There are actually seven different power-generating facilities here at Niagara Falls," the guide said. "This is the largest. If you'll look over here in this display area, you'll see some of the original turbine blades used in the Goat Island plant, the first ever." The guide pointed to a few huge iron blades. "These were preserved when the plant was relocated from Goat Island because they still bear the patent plates with the original patent numbers on them. And if you'll look closely, you'll see that the name Nikola Tesla is visible too. It is believed that these pieces were fabricated in Dr. Tesla's laboratory in New York City and shipped here by railroad."

Dr. Haak was alarmed upon hearing the name Tesla. She wormed her way into the crowd to get a better look at the corroded fins. A family with four children came up the escalator, and the noise of the toddlers drowned out the guide's voice. Dr. Haak was still peering at the display, as if trying to decode the numbers and symbols on the brass plates. For a moment she forgot about Ollie. He moved quickly with the tour group out of the gallery and, seeing a door marked, "AUTHORIZED PERSONNEL ONLY," ducked through it. As the door hissed shut, the sound of human voices faded. The hum of the plant grew louder. He thought he could almost hear Brian's voice underneath, a weak, babyish whine.

Ollie pulled the scalpel out of his pocket. He held it in front of himself, using it as an antenna to pick up Brian's frequency. Soon enough it would reach its mark. And then it would perform a little surgery on the boy. He'd make sure that Brian was no longer number one. He'd cut out the shunt, or at least tear out the wiring, and then Ollie would have to be the chosen one. Then they'd have no choice but to use Ollie as the little white lamb that night.

He went to the end of the corridor, through another door, and down an echoing metal stairway. A few more turns and he was on the ground floor, hunting among the huge generating machines. The sound was enormous there, but instead of causing him pain, it lifted his spirits even higher. He was close, very close. The boy was somewhere in the maze of turbines: motionless, stuck like a fly on flypaper.

How long Ollie wandered there, he didn't know. Twice he had to duck into a corner to avoid being spotted by the technicians. He crossed steel catwalks, descended, and went down a long concrete tunnel. He peeked into alcoves and alleyways, and at last found the boy.

It was a dark place. And cooler too. There were no levels in the plant like floors in a house, but Ollie was sure that he'd reached the lowest point there, far below the surface of the ground. On every side, huge shapes of concrete surrounded him. And from above he could feel the weight, millions of tons of water rushing through the turbine tunnels, magnets the size of houses turning on their dark, greasy gears. The boy was crouched on the floor. He looked like a monkey in the zoo, arms around his chest, head resting on his knees.

"Long time no see, Brian." Ollie laughed. The scalpel in his hand was vibrating. It wanted even more than Ollie to plunge into Brian's neck and cut out the shunt wires.

Brian looked up. He was shaking too, at the same frequency as the knife blade. Everything was vibrating together, even the air.

"I missed you, Brian. Things just haven't been the same since you took off. You were the life of the party." Ollie laughed again, but the sound was quickly swallowed up. He doubted Brian could even hear what he'd said.

"I guess this is the end of the line," he shouted. By then he was only a few paces away. He could have jumped forward right then and started hacking. Brian still hadn't moved. He'd made no attempt to defend himself. He must have known what Ollie had come to do. Brian's eyes were tiny black dots aimed at Ollie's hand. The scalpel was hot and getting hotter.

"Tonight's the big night. Everybody's coming into town for this," Ollie said. "You ought to be proud: all these important people coming to see you do your stuff." Ollie switched the knife to his other hand. "But guess what,

Brian? They're all in for a big surprise. You're not going to be the one they use tonight. It's going to be me. I was the first one, you know. It wouldn't be fair if they used somebody else.'' He shifted the scalpel again, using his shirt tail to insulate it. ''I could have messed you up a long time ago, only I didn't want to upset Dr. Haak. But she's not the big shot anymore. They threw her away. She went bad and now there's other people, more important people, in charge. This is the big time now.''

He looked down at the scalpel. The blade was glowing, a little sphere of light pulsing around the tip. Brian was staring directly at it, concentrating. He looked the way he used to in the cradle, wired in and heading straight for the wall.

''Cut it out, Brian. You're going to make it even worse for yourself.'' The blade was ringing, a high-pitched tone like a tuning fork. ''Stop it, right now. I'm not kidding around, Brian.'' Then the scalpel was too hot. He dropped it and Brian relaxed.

It shook for a moment, lying on the floor. Then it was still, and its light died.

''I'm the number one. I always was. That's the way it's got to be.'' Ollie reached down for the knife and held onto it, though the heat was intense, searing him. He jabbed at Brian, but before he could hit him and start cutting, something latched onto him from behind. He spun, trying to fight it off. It was gone in an instant, right through his shunt and inside him.

He thrashed, seizing now the way Brian had in the cradle. The knife was still in his hand, though, burning him now like a hot grill burning meat. But he wouldn't let go. He had to kill the boy; that was his job, his duty. And nothing— not any of the boy's tricks—would save him. Ollie lunged again, and again the pain shot into him exactly at the spot where he was aiming on Brian. ''I'm the number one,'' Ollie hissed. ''I was here first.'' He froze for a moment, hearing Brian's voice inside him, though the boy's lips were clamped shut. It was more of his secret gibberish, his magic words. Ollie's mouth moved and the nonsense poured out of him: Funky Butts, Bri-nor Components, Hit-me-hit me's, and a long, squealing Owwwww!

It was more than Ollie could stand, pushing his anger into the red zone. He'd been lied to, passed over, abandoned, his flesh had been burnt and was burning again, but to be made a puppet like that, forced to imitate the boy's babbling, was too much. He grabbed Brian by the long hair on the back of his head and lifted him off the floor, pressing the knife against his throat.

The knife wouldn't cut, though. Again Ollie felt the boy inside him, a fiery ghost ransacking his body. There was something else now too, called up by Brian with his babbling. Ollie could almost see the little man stooped over, nose like a bird beak, wearing a long, gownlike lab coat. And then a third presence appeared, as though chasing the little man wherever he went. Ollie heard voices arguing, but had no idea what they meant. He heard the names Tesla and Edison. He felt the two men—if in fact they were men—struggling just as he was struggling with Brian. He tried to press the knife into the boy's windpipe, but one of the invisible hands clamped around his wrist, holding it back. Another seemed to grab Brian, jerking him first toward Ollie and then away.

By then Ollie was like a drowning swimmer, waves of panic already over his head. He groped out and found the boy again. His nails raked down his arm, cutting four dark lines. "I was always the favorite. You were second best."

It seemed that his hands were on fire. Where his nails had slashed Brian's skin, the blood ran out like liquid flame. Smoke and steam choked the air. Inside, the two men were still fighting, one shouting in a strange language and the other cursing him and laughing wildly. For a moment he saw the one called Tesla completely englobed in shimmering light. It seemed that he actually saw him with his eyes, there in the generating station, staggering toward him. But also he saw him inside his mind. And the other one too, Edison with a great ape as his assistant, the shaggy hair burning and the eyes emitting rays of scarlet light. The ape was screaming, flailing his arms, leaving behind burning footprints.

Deep down, the boy was screaming too, and with each burst of sound Ollie felt another part of himself converted, transformed into energy. Fluids inside him were boiling, popping their vessels. Red darkness was oozing from the walls, bubbling up from the floor. The noise weighed more than all the mountains of water above him. For an instant the twin presences swelled up together: hacking, burning, shrieking at each other. And then they were gone. But by then it was too late for Ollie. The fire was everywhere now, running through his veins, his nerves, his marrow, the channels in his brain. Then the fire and blood turned quickly to blackness and Ollie saw nothing more.

28

The boy didn't resist as they lifted him to his feet. He held his arms out straight, as he was told, and let them slide the heavy canvas sleeves onto him. He didn't make a sound as they pulled the straps around behind and fastened the buckles.

He'd been severely drained by the confrontation with the orderly. His eyes were still open and he seemed to be able to hear, but all the fight had gone out of him. He watched Price and Whitehead emerge from the shadows of a huge cooling stack, as if he'd known all along they'd been watching.

Ollie was dead. He lay like a pile of half-incinerated trash. Luckily he was on his stomach. Price and Whitehead didn't want to see what the boy had done to his face. In some of the electrocution videotapes they'd seen, the prisoners' mouths had been seared into idiotic expressions: grinning, grimacing, sticking their tongues out like defiant children.

The two stepped aside as the security men rolled the body into a plastic sheet and zipped up the sides. They kept their eyes averted as they worked, apparently afraid to look directly at either Price or Whitehead. They were instructed to hold the body for a few days. An autopsy would be performed to see exactly what the boy had done to Ollie, but more important things needed to be taken care of first.

They led Brian away from that place, down a narrow hallway. With a few doors now between them and the generators, the humming was less oppressive. The boy relaxed as they got farther from the throb. And the odor of singed hair faded.

A pair of blank steel doors swung open for them, and they led the boy down another long passageway. There were no guards to check their passes and no signs warning unauthorized personnel to stay out. They passed dozens of unmarked doors, entryways barred with steel grates, and a few translucent panels. Spectral lights moved behind these frosted glass windows.

They walked and walked and at last came to a door marked with a simple emblem: a circle split by a lightning bolt. It was the *O* for Oberfurst, and the egg splitting, cracked by an electrical discharge. They went inside and closed the door carefully, making no noise.

The room was full of men, all dressed in similar conservative business suits. They might have been executives of any of a hundred different corporations. Though mostly in their fifties and sixties, a few had enough wrinkles and white hair to place them well beyond that age range.

There was at least one Nobel Laureate, a few generals in civilian clothes, chemists from bioengineering companies flung from New York to Los Angeles, one of the developers of synthetic endorphins, and the director of the United States Interutility Agency. And mixed in with these notables were men who Price and Whitehead didn't recognize, but assumed were operatives much like themselves, men who'd worked on other branches of the project, foot soldiers in this secret war. It was an impressive gathering, an auspicious moment, and the men all felt it. But underneath their self-satisfaction was a current of anxiety, even fear. They all looked toward the door. They stared raptly at the boy as Price and Whitehead presented him to the group.

Price cleared his throat. "Gentlemen, my partner and I would like to express our pleasure in being able to play a part, however small, in this event. We're both honored and wish to thank you all for entrusting us with the completion of this phase of the operation." He'd rehearsed the speech a hundred times before, in hotel rooms, in public lavatories, in the back of dark taxis.

The men acknowledged the speech, but they were far more interested in the boy than the two operatives who'd brought him there. From then on Price and Whitehead became more observers than participants. Their moment had come and was soon to be over. Though they continued to be the ones who guided Brian about and guarded him, their role had been played out. He belonged no longer to the two of them but to the entire council, to all the gray-haired men.

"He's all right?" one of bankers asked. "We heard there was some kind of a struggle."

"He's fine. Just a little drained," Whitehead said. "You would have been proud of him, gentlemen. He's everything that we were hoping for."

One of the doctors came forward and ran the boy quickly through a few tests. He nodded finally after peeling the last electrode patch off Brian's scalp. "Everything is just as it should be. He's almost ready."

A murmur ran through the group. They came forward, one at a time, and filed past Brian as though paying him their respects. Whitehead and Price brought up the rear, one on either side of the boy. The grayish fog had lifted from his eyes, but still Brian had said nothing. He knew where he was going now. He'd waited over ten years to return.

They took him to Love Canal.

As they went down Buffalo Avenue, they passed one huge chemical plant after another. All the major corporations were represented, plus a few whose names Whitehead and Price had never heard of. And prominent on their route, the largest and most forbidding, was Oberfurst Chemical. The tanks and towers of the refinery rose high in the blue-black sky like turrets above a medieval city. The towers which carried the high-tension lines were like the spires of a cathedral. The Oberfurst symbol was everywhere, a black rune carved into a red and gold background. As they went by this stretch of the avenue, the stench penetrated quickly through their clothes and into their skin. No on who went near that area went away untouched by Oberfurst's spoor.

The sun had already set. It was midsummer's eve and quickly the dark emanations had started to rise. The air was laden with greasy vapors and flecks of crystalline ash. It was a perfect summer night, a warm breeze blowing off the river, carrying invisible chemical traces.

Since Price and Whitehead had last been to Love Canal, a few changes had been made. They noticed another state police checkpoint and a few more signs warning visitors away. The domain surrounded by the chain-link fence had been expanded. A new pile of rubble stood where a small grocery store had been. They heard barking from far off, probably patrol dogs being used to make sure there was no one near the perimeter that night.

They approached the main gate and a pair of uniformed guards emerged to unlock it. The whole entourage passed through and the gate clanked shut behind them. They were perhaps forty strong by then, a few more having joined them on the way. They were on foot now, moving as a crowd. Few words were spoken as they penetrated deeper into the area where the blight had been the worst. All of the men felt the presence. They were quiet, somber, even reverent, believers on a pilgrimage to an important shrine.

They walked down the middle of the street. On either side were small, uniformly unlit houses. Windows were broken and boarded up. Gutters hung twisted from the eaves. And everywhere was the vapor, like nothing else in the world. It was caustic, irritating to the eyes and throat tissue and at the same time irresistible. They marched together, approaching the source.

Turning at 96th Street, they passed a school building. Brian jerked suddenly awake. He turned his head as they went past, drinking in the sight of the now desolate playing field, the swing set and teeter-totters long ago buried in high weeds and scrub.

A light glowed at the end of the street, in the picture window of a small brick house. They marched toward the light, all of them now sure of their destination.

It was the house where Brian had grown up and where his parents had died. Once past the school yard, Brian turned his attention toward the house. "I want to go home," he said softly.

Price patted him on the shoulder. "Soon, soon. We're almost there."

A wooden pole stood in front of the house, with a wrought-iron lantern on top. It wasn't lit. The glass panes had all been broken. The garage was only big enough to hold one car. The door was sagging off its hinges. The paint had fallen away in long curls. Where rose bushes had been were now dense thickets. The front door was open. Light throbbed from inside, and sound too, like breathing heard from miles away.

They'd come to the house where Brian had lived until he was nine years old. His bedroom window looked out on the backyard. There had been a square of sand in back, where he'd dug and played with his trucks. The sandbox was now the color of pitch. It was a dark, yawning sinkhole where bubbles burst occasionally, adding to the already foul stench. There had been a split-rail fence along the side yard. Even the numbers had been removed from the front doorway, though if inspected closely, their outlines could still be seen.

"Brian, there's somebody inside waiting for you. He needs your help. We all need your help."

"My mother and father." Brian's voice was wispy, barely audible.

"No, they don't live here anymore. But there is somebody who cares very much about you. Somebody who's been watching out for you all these years you've been away. He needs you. You'll help him, won't you?"

Scattered about the lawn, specks of light fluttered. It was the week when the fireflies were out, signaling to one another in the dusk. Brian watched the yellow-green pinpricks circle around each other. He seemed to remember them, or some event connected to them.

"This is very important, Brian. We're going to need your help. Are you willing to do that for us?"

He was still in the straitjacket. He was locked inside a compound with razor wire around the fence tops. There were probably a score of armed police patrolling the perimeter, and still Price and Whitehead were wheedling with him, talking as though he was a three-year-old who'd locked himself in the bathroom. "We're all going in now. Remember, you came here to help us. And if you do as we ask, there'll be a reward for you."

Price and Whitehead went to the front of the group and walked with Brian up the red brick steps. The rest of them followed in single file.

The breathing sound was louder and more powerful inside. It was far slower than a person would breathe, perhaps once or twice a minute. The light in the living room glowed and ebbed with the sound. It was a lone standing lamp, a corroded brass stand with no shade. It stood in the middle of the room, the only furnishing left. The carpets had all been torn up and carted off. The curtains and even some of the molding around the ceiling were gone. Some of the doors were missing, and squares of roughly cut cardboard had been fitted into the rear windows.

"This way," Price said, leading Brian to the cellar stairs.

The boy resisted, jerking free of Price's grasp. "Where are my parents? Why is everything different?"

"They don't live here anymore. Nobody does now. All their things had to be moved."

"Where are they?" Brian asked.

"They're gone. Don't think about them anymore. There's something more important for you here." They tightened their grasp on him, one on either side, and led him to the bottom of the steps.

There, erupting through the cinder block wall, was a seething blackish mound, a bolus like the one at Cornell. But this one was larger and more powerful. It was like a huge, nameless, malignant organ. The surface was slick, almost iridescent. Beside the visible light it emitted, ultraviolet and probably higher frequencies were being thrown off by its glistening black skin. Everything in the basement had a strange glow to it, as though infected with an extreme fever, burning to kill the disease. The smell too was intense, a distillation of the reek outside. It was foul and oppressive, quickly engulfing them.

And sitting beside the small mountain of throbbing darkness was Stefan Oberfurst. They knew it was him before he spoke. He was in a wheelchair, his arms strapped to the side handles, his head supported by two padded braces. A few wisps of colorless hair stuck to his parchmentlike scalp. His hands were tiny, like little knots of dead twigs. His eyes were open, but were both glazed whitish-gray. Though it appeared he was quite blind, he looked directly at Brian and said, "Bring the boy here."

His voice was barely audible, even amplified by the device he had strapped to his throat. "Now!"

Whitehead and Price went forward with their eyes averted, ushering Brian into the presence. They'd heard secondhand reports that Oberfurst was still alive, but it seemed impossible. They'd also heard rumors that he'd been cryogenically preserved, embalmed like a pharaoh. And once, back at Cornell, someone had hinted that Oberfurst's personality had been transferred to a electromechanical vault, his soul saved like pickled fruit in a silver canister.

In fact, the situation was much simpler. He was just a very old man who couldn't die.

Oberfurst couldn't even lift his arm to touch the boy. "Free him," the far-off voice said. Price quickly unbuckled the straps, and with his partner's help he got Brian out of the straitjacket.

By then all of the others had filed down the steps and were lined up around the perimeter of the basement, gazing reverently at the old man. He was what all of them would become if Brian failed that night. They'd all been exposed to the bolus at one time or another, most of them during an initiation ceremony. They were all just as damned as Stefan Oberfurst. Slowly their souls were being sucked away, swallowed, and absorbed by the huge, stinking lumps.

As far as they could tell, Price and Whitehead were the last men to be exposed. They probably had the most time before the symptoms began to set in. They were no less damned than Oberfurst, though. It might take decades, but they too would eventually shrivel, weaken, and collapse, yet still remain chained to their failed flesh.

The boy was more fascinated than afraid. He was looking straight into the gullet of a monster so large it could hardly be measured, and still he was unbowed. Stefan Oberfurst, for all his money and power and legendary status, might have been a freakish animal seen at the state fair.

"This was your house once. A long time ago," Oberfurst said.

Brian nodded.

"You were conceived in this house, boy. Do you know what that means?"

Oberfurst waited a moment and, getting no reply, went on, "The bolus was here long before your parents bought this house, before there even were houses here. I owned this land." All of the others were listening as if to an oracle. They were huddled together in the quaking darkness. Some moaned and sighed as Oberfurst spoke, responding to him like a spirit-filled congregation. "A man named William Love owned this place first. He dug part of a canal, thinking he would make a fortune connecting Lake Erie to Lake Ontario. But the whole enterprise fell apart. About the turn of the century. It was left abandoned. I bought the land. I knew I'd be needing it someday. We'd won the war. A.C. had beaten D.C. We were sitting on top of a gold mine. Tesla was dropping patents like they were cigar butts. I just stooped to pick up a few." With great effort he managed to lift two fingers and point in the direction of the bolus. "That was one of them. The most powerful source of energy to be discovered until fission. We were decades ahead of the Manhattan Project. A-bombs, atoms for peace, such a waste of time. We were running cables and selling power when people were still riding horses and using chamber pots." He began hacking, a thin, weak noise like a kitten coughing. He said the words "chamber pots" again. it seemed to amuse him. His hands quaked. A spasm ran through him and he clutched the padded armrests on his chair. "I planted the bolus here. It was my seed. And now it's going to blossom. It's going to bear fruit."

He started hacking again and a man in a white jacket came out of the weirdly colored shadows. It was Dr. Valentine. He looked like he'd aged ten years since they'd last seen him in the tunnels under Oberfurst House. He attended to the old man, making sure he didn't collapse completely. Oberfurst whispered something in his ear and then slumped back in the chair.

Dr. Valentine stepped away from the bolus and addressed the gathering: "Eleven years ago the first signs started to show. In this house. The event we'd been waiting for was finally on the horizon.'' He spoke like a priest addressing a body of the faithful. ''Ichor began to manifest here, penetrating the walls and collecting in the sump. We checked and rechecked. Then other signs began to appear in the neighborhood. The newspapers caught on and troublemakers started complaining. Soon it had gone all the way to the governor, and everyone knew about Love Canal. But that was part of our plan. That was the beginning of the end. Luckily, there is a dormancy stage after the first manifestations. The story blew over. The residents moved out and Love Canal was ours.'' He looked over at Brian. ''And our seed had been planted.

''Now Brian has reached the correct age, and the bolus is again at the most active stage. We've planned, we've waited, and now our time has come.''

The old man leaned slightly forward, hissing, ''Bring him closer.'' Price and Whitehead did as they were told. Only they and Dr. Valentine heard what he said to the boy. ''You've got to go through and open the door from the inside. Then we'll all be free. None of the rest will have to go through what I have. Dying, dying but never reaching death. Don't get me wrong, boy. I don't give a rat's ass about them. But people don't help you unless there's something in it for them. They're all in the same boat as me, just not as far along. They're all going to be like this eventually. That's why they're all so eager to help me today. If I can't get free, then no one can.'' He wriggled one hand, and Dr. Valentine unfastened the support strap. Oberfurst reached out, two talonlike fingers touching the boy's arm. ''I just want to die. That's all. And you can do it for me. Go through and open the door. That's all I want from you.''

Brian had been conceived, brought up, and watched over so that this moment could occur. He could do what no one else in the room could: die. And what made it seem even more unfair was that he could do it again and again. Whitehead and Price had been through the files countless times. They'd pored over reports and analyses, and every bit of the work had pointed to one conclusion: the boy could pass from one world to another. When he was deep in his seizures, he was medically and legally dead. And when he emerged from what he called the Ictus, he was alive again. Everyone in that basement believed wholeheartedly that Brian was the one to liberate them. The last holdout had been Dr. Haak. She'd have nothing to do with his talk of Funk and Ictus and joyrides and soul trains. She'd be an unbeliever to the end.

Dr. Valentine went into the shadows and came back shortly with a device that looked like a cross between a hospital gurney and an electric chair. It wasn't made of rough timbers like the one Edison had created and which had sat for decades in the death house at Sing Sing. But it did have arm clamps and restraints and a series of thick, heavily insulated cables connected to the electrodes. Instead of being hooked up to a transformer, though, the wires ran into the bolus. They penetrated the glistening black hides like spears piercing a reptile's skin. Clear liquid oozed from the wounds. The area around the points of entry were more swollen than the rest, throbbing like a fresh bruise.

Brian saw the chair and immediately began shaking. He certainly remembered the cradle back at the Red House. He remembered the hours he had spent strapped in, passing from one side to the other, a messenger between two worlds.

"He's seizing," Dr. Valentine said. "We need to get moving."

A pair of technicians took Price and Whitehead's places, preparing the hookup. The doctor tried to strap Brian into the chair, but he was shaking and twitching. His mouth opened and a hushed crackling sound came from inside. A veil of light had fallen over the boy's face. He clasped his hands together, squeezing, and when he pulled them apart, a stream of current flowed from one side to the other.

The bolus too was peaking, rising to a more excited state. The sides pulsed like the stomach of a beached whale. Wilder frequencies were streaming from it, making everything in the basement either a brilliant bone-white or absolute black. Price and Whitehead went forward to help with the boy, pinning his arms as the technicians prepared the chair. They felt the field radiating from the boy. First one, then the other, was sucked momentarily out of his body. For a tiny part of a second they were in a place like the basement, but totally transformed. The generals and chemists and bankers were all black-skinned, as if seen in negative. They were dancing or trying to dance. They thrashed as if in agony, consumed, controlled by an enormous heartbeat. They tore at themselves, ripping their clothes and hair. In this same fraction of a moment they saw Stefan Oberfurst now out of his wheelchair, shouting and shrieking, hopping up and down. It was impossible to tell if he was in great pain or transported by joy. He grabbed at his groin, screaming, "Say the word, boy. And it's all yours. Say it, say it. Say you'll open the door. And everything I have will be yours."

Then they were both quickly translated back to the stinking, overheated cellar. Sparks and little buds of fire erupted as Brian's skin touched the metal parts of the chair. Trails of light, like a woven crown, appeared around his head. And though the bolus and the boy were making the same inhuman noise, they could still hear Oberfurst whimpering underneath:

"I'll give you anything. Whatever you want. Money. Take it. You want money, take it all." It was like a prayer, the word *money* repeated reverently. The others, crouched by the wall, took up the chant.

By then Price and Whitehead were phasing from one place to another, flickering back and forth as if spinning in a revolving door. For an instant they saw the basement as they knew it really was: old man in wheelchair, boy with cables hanging off him, black mountain of toxic filth quaking as if about to explode. Then they got a flash of the other place, where no one could sit down, no one could help but dance like a maniac, where the thump of the bass was the throb of their blood. Where the squalling black voice told them again and again, "Let yourself go!"

29

Brian went through. Direct and nonstop. He tore the wet membrane and flew through the hole. Then he was inside the black thing. And so was the old man. He'd been there for years, long before Brian was born, before the houses were built on Love Canal. It was like a prison, worse than the Red House could ever be. It was like a tar baby, except the old man was hitting and kicking and biting from the inside.

Outside, back in the cellar, the old man's body was still in the wheelchair, barely alive. His skin was shiny like a maggot's. His eyes could see nothing. His breath whistled through his mouth full of black, stubby teeth. Someday, maybe even that day, the body would give up. The heart and lungs and liver would shut down. It might rot and turn to a puddle like a slug melted with salt, but still the old man's soul would be stuck. It wouldn't be able to get away.

Going through to the Other Side was different this time for Brian. Before, it had felt as though a hot rake of fire was tearing the meat off his bones and the bones away from his guts so that his soul could be free. But now it was easier, natural. He was positive and negative at the same time, flickering back and forth a hundred times a second. To get through he just needed to slow down the flickering. Splitting the gray into black and white.

"Brian, open the door. Let me out." The old man hissed instead of spoke. His tongue was long and black and divided at the end into two points. His eyes were pinpricks in his face. Two rays of light shone out through the holes. "Help me, Brian. If you get me out of here, I'll give you whatever you want."

The old man was lying on his stomach, wriggling toward him. His arms and legs were soft and spongy. He could barely hold his head up. "Just name it. If money can buy it, it's yours."

The walls were pulsed in and out. Little beads of clear fluid formed and ran down like sweat. As the walls sucked inward, the air pressed more tightly on Brian, hurting him through his ears. He turned and saw the place where he'd gone through. The rip had sealed itself already. Thick scar tissue had formed in the few seconds he'd spent inside the black thing.

"Just pick me up. Open the way again and carry me out. I'll give you whatever you want."

"Where are my parents?"

The old man shook, hearing this. Another eye hole opened in his forehead and black light streamed out.

"I want to see my parents."

"They're gone."

"Where did they go?"

The light pouring from the eye holes hit the wall, and like the beam of a projector, threw a picture there. Brian as a nine-year-old. His mother and father. He saw himself playing in the basement. His father staring at a crack in the wall. His mother coming down the steps. They were sick. They stood at the exact spot where the black thing now was and felt the poison filling them, overpowering them. Black ooze flowed around their feet. They were dying right there at the cinder block wall. A crack formed and zigzagged to the floor. His father was trying to cover the opening, keep the poison out of his house. Brian saw his parents fall, awful patches of red and brown blossoming on their skin. They were both looking at him, trying to speak. But the picture stayed silent. It started to fade.

A flapping sound came, like the end of film spinning around on its reel. It was the old man's tongue probing at him. He'd crawled closer while Brian watched those last pictures of his parents. "They're dead. They were in this house and it killed them. They couldn't stand the heat, so they got out of the kitchen." The old man was laughing or gagging, Brian couldn't tell which. The tongue had gotten longer, snaking toward Brian. The two pointy tips touched his leg and he felt what his parents must have felt, seeping in through the wall. It was bad, very bad. It hurt worse than any rod of correction or choke hold or isolation ward. It hurt right through his skin to his bones and nerves. And even deeper. Brian jerked his foot back. The old man kept coming at him. "If you don't get me out, then you'll have to stay here forever. Do you want that? Just you and me. Here, the two of us for all time." The tongue snagged around Brian's ankle, and he used that hold to pull himself forward. "Just open the way. Carry me out and then we'll be friends. Don't you want that? I can give you whatever you want."

He was crawling up Brian's leg, circling slowly. "Take me out of here. That's not so much to ask, is it?"

Brian was rooted to the spot, the crawling body and the probing tongue now wrapped a half-dozen times around him. "You can do it, boy. Just get me out of here. Open the way and carry me out."

A tremor ran through Brian, down the snaking body, into the floor, and out of the bolus. And as if in reply, a shock wave came back like an echo. An explosion of light followed, penetrating the skin of the bolus, making it into a shimmering curtain where it had been an opaque wall. Brian could see into the basement, where all the others were waiting for him: moaning, bowing, praying, weeping as if it were them and not the old man who'd gotten to the actual line between death and life but were forbidden from taking that last step over it.

The light filled the cellar: blazing hot and overpowering like X-rays cooking the men down to bare bone. They were skeletons now, clattering their bones and making wild, high noises as though they'd been caught naked doing something very wrong. A few of them still had a bit of their flesh and skin still on. One of the men was all bone except his hands, like a pair of padded gloves placed on two sticks. Another had one eyeball left in the dry white pits of his skull and a tuft of gray hair sticking up. Shreds of meat hung here and there off the bones, and on one of the men a few trails of ropy veins remained, like worms clinging to him to eat off the last traces of flesh. Close to the bolus were soft heaps of skin and meat, as if the men had unzipped themselves and sloughed off their bodies like old clothes. And hanging on the far wall, on a dozen pegs, were other suits of flesh, limp now and obscene-looking without the bones inside to fill them out.

Then Brian saw where the eruption of spectral light was coming from. Dr. Haak and Saul had come down the basement steps. The illumination was streaming from their hands, making the men scurry, squealing and trying to hide themselves like bugs when a big rock is lifted up and the dark places are exposed to sunlight. It was Dr. Haak and Saul, but seen through the wall of the bolus, they weren't the same. She was just as beautiful but no longer white. All the color had vanished from her flesh and her clothes. It was as though she was made of living ice, everything about her absolutely transparent. He could see all the organs inside her, heart and lungs pumping, veins and vessels, her brain and even the shunt in the back of her head throbbing with excitement. She moved with a slow, trancelike grace, the train of her almost invisible dress billowing around her as she waded into the skeleton men, firing the salvos of light from her hands.

Saul came behind her, and instead of being clear like the doctor, he was almost perfectly black, every inch of his skin charred like overcooked meat. Wisps of smoke blew off him, and where his feet touched the floor he left an ashen trail. As he joined in the fight, swinging his fists and stomping on the bonemen, a reddish glow throbbed from his chest. It grew in intensity, pulsing faster, as if making its way to the surface from some deep, hidden place. The redness was almost painful to Brian's eyes. The throbbing became synchronized with Brian's breathing, his heartbeat, and the waves of moaning from the skeletons. And like Dr. Haak, Saul soon turned to face the bolus. Then Brian saw the red light clearly. It was Saul's heart now on the surface of his chest, throwing off pulses of brilliant crimson light.

With every bone they broke, every skull Saul split with the hard, raw edge of his hand, the layer of ooze on the floor got deeper. The slime was the bonemen's lifeblood. The black filth that had filled the basement ten years before had flowed in their veins.

Brian had gotten himself free from the old man when Dr. Haak and Saul appeared. He pressed his face and hands against the bolus's rubbery membrane. They stretched the wall, but couldn't break through. Behind him the old man was slithering at him again, mouthing the same words, begging Brian not to leave him there. He cried, and his tears ran down as black ichor. His weeping went on and on, and it seemed that he was dissolving, his entire being turning to black slime and extruding through his tear ducts. He was lapping at Brian's feet. He blubbered and clung to him, and the oozy grip burnt like acid.

The doctor didn't seem to be able to see Brian. She couldn't hear him over the roaring of the X-ray light and the screaming of the skeleton men and her own siren war whoops. Saul fought on silently, his eyes, mouth, and nostrils all seared shut in a mask of burnt meat. Try as he might—calling her name, pounding his fists on the spongy walls, even pressing his mouth against the membrane and biting it—Brian couldn't get her to notice him.

Outside the bolus, the battle went on, and inside, the old man would not give up. He clung to Brian, begging and wheedling, though by then his mouth was little more than a ragged hole and his limbs were like gelatinous tendrils on a huge black amoeba.

30

rian heard sirens far away. He held onto the sound and climbed up from the darkness, using it like a rope. At the top he opened his eyes. He was lying on a bare wooden floor, his head in Dr. Haak's lap. She was stroking his hair, staring down into his face. She'd changed since the last time he'd seen her. Her hair was longer, uncombed and unbound. Her face was fuller, and her eyes had none of the faraway look he remembered from the Red House. She was there with him, all of her.

He tilted his head slightly to one side and saw Saul Marx standing by the window, looking out. He had a small machine gun in his arms and a pistol tucked under his belt in back. He too had changed, but it was harder to see how.

Dr. Haak said, "He's coming out of it," and Saul looked his way. He hadn't shaved in days. His clothes were torn and muddy. He had bandages on his head and neck and along the top of his shoulders.

It was still dark, but they weren't in the basement anymore. They weren't even in the same house. They were still in Love Canal, though. Brian could smell it, he could feel the pull.

"They're looking for us," Dr. Haak said. "They're not too happy about what we did to the old man."

Brian picked back through the darkness and saw again the fat, bloated shape. Then he saw the old man begging and cursing and threatening. Then everything began to collapse, shredding and blowing about like wet tissue paper. Brian had been shredded too. That was how he'd gotten away from the old man.

"It took us a while to catch up with you, but luckily there weren't that many places to look. I knew where your house was and we still had our security passes. They were a little suspicious at the gate, but they've seen a lot of awfully strange things going on here lately." Dr. Haak had a gun too. It was just like Saul's: bigger than a pistol, with a stubby barrel. The butt end wasn't wood. It was formed out of a piece of metal. The gun lay on the floor beside her.

Brian was still too weak to talk. He was still feeling the aftershocks. The old man had swallowed his legs and had been moving higher consuming Brian, when the whole thing blew apart. The tongue shriveled like a worm thrown onto hot coals. The arms and legs had turned to jelly and run back down to the floor. The hissing voice evaporated, still saying, "I'll give you anything."

It felt good to be in Dr. Haak's arms. He liked the sound of her voice and the brush of her breath on his forehead. She held him tightly, as if afraid to lose him again. "We went in the front door and downstairs and started shooting. They were too busy bowing and scraping in front of the bolus to put up much of a fight. By the time they'd woken up to what was going on, Saul had gotten the old man. There's not much left of him now. We grabbed you and ran. None of the others were armed. Those kinds never carry guns. They always have somebody else to do their dirty work."

Her lips ran across his forehead. They were soft and warm. Once she'd explained how he'd gotten there, she relaxed some. Smiling, she said, "How are you feeling?"

It seemed that he'd been swallowed whole, digested and squeezed out through a tiny opening.

"We've got to get going soon. Do you think you can stand up by yourself?"

Brian was pulled back from sleep by the sound of dogs barking.

"The sun will be up soon," Dr. Haak said. "We've got to get out of here."

Gunfire started up not far away. With her help Brian stood and went to the window. A few houses were on fire on the next street over. Smoke and a red glow were rising up through the trees.

Saul wasn't there anymore. He was the one out shooting and being shot at.

Dr. Haak held her machine gun with one hand. It didn't seem strange to see her with the weapon. It wasn't much different than the rod of correction. Both were made of shiny steel and black rubber. They were almost the same size.

She smiled and put her free hand on Brian's shoulder. "We'll be out of here soon. Then it'll just be the three of us. A happy family. No more running and hiding and being chased. We can go across the bridge to Canada. It's only a few miles away. They won't be able to get us there."

Saul came back in a little while through the back door. "They're going house to house. I think they've got the perimeter sealed off." He was swaying like a drunk. Dr. Haak left Brian and had Saul sit down on the floor. She took a hypodermic out of a small black case and quickly gave Saul an injection.

"He's in a lot of pain," she told Brian. "I have to give him this so he can keep going."

In a few minutes, Saul was able to talk again. "It looks like they've sent the local people away. I didn't see any state police or sheriffs. It's just Oberfurst security. And a few of the ones who were in the basement."

They left through the back door and cut across an overgrown backyard. Brian thought he remembered a swing set that they passed, though with all the people and their belongings gone, it was hard to tell one house from another. But there was no question, he remembered the fireflies. They'd been out blinking to each other the night the black slime had started to flow. He'd seen his parents fall, heard them whisper, "Get out, get out," and fled up the stairs.

Outside, he'd run as fast as he could away from the house, knowing that he'd never see his parents again. The fireflies had swarmed around him, surrounded him with a cloud of faint light, following him down the street.

That had been the first time into the Ictus, though he didn't know the name of it then. The fireflies had accompanied him, carried him to the Other Side. And there he met the first old man, the one called Tesla. He'd floated up out of the gloom and guided Brian to safety, then vanished, having said nothing. He appeared many more times to Brian, telling him where to hide, how to make a fort in the ground and keep away from the police, where to scrounge food, and, most important, given him a radio so that he could tune in to the funk and pick up the Godfather of Soul's frequency, keeping him always on the innermost groove. From then on Brian had his connection. He knew where he could turn when he needed help.

A muffled explosion came from the next block over. A moment later, they saw flames. Dr. Haak took Brian's hand and they crouched beside a red brick wall as Saul went to see what was happening. They heard more gunfire. And shouting. A dog barked crazily for a moment, then came a few shots and silence. Dr. Haak looked at her watch and then toward the rising sun. It had just peeked over the tops of the houses. The light was clear and colorless, like water. Dr. Haak and Brian stayed in their hiding place awhile longer, watching the shadows shrink and evaporate. Eventually she looked at her watch again and said, "It's getting late. We've got to get going."

They went through the side yard, then zigzagged between houses, trying to stay as far from the gunfire as they could. A siren started up, coming toward them.

"Where's Saul?" Brian asked. "Isn't he coming with us?"

She didn't answer. She was looking right and left, right and left, pulling Brian with one hand and pointing the gun in front of herself with the other.

A car cruised by on the next street. It had a red light on top and the Oberfurst symbol painted on the side. It paused a moment in the intersection, then moved on. Dr. Haak had dragged Brian into a ditch full of spiny weeds as the car came past. She waited until the motor sound was gone, then told him he could stand up.

Sneaking through the yards, hiding first behind a garage, then in an old metal shed full of newspapers, they got closer and closer to the fence. It looked as though no one else was around. The gunshots and bullhorn shouting were behind them now. Edging through a ruined flower garden now thick with gray-black moss and pricklers, they got a glimpse of the entrance gate. A patrol car was parked there, but it seemed that it was unoccupied.

"Where's Saul? We're not going without him, are we?"

Dr. Haak didn't answer.

"Did they get him?"

"I don't know. But we agreed to meet up later if we got separated. He knows the place. We'll just have to go on without him."

She held him by the arm, guiding him as though he were blind. They walked down the middle of the street, straddling the flecks of paint that had been a white line years before. The gate was open. Beyond it Brian saw more empty houses and deserted streets.

"Where did they all go?" Brian asked.

"They're hiding. They're waiting for us."

And even though Dr. Haak knew it was a trap, she walked straight for the gate. She had her machine gun aimed at the back of Brian's head. The muzzle was warm against his skin. It was just like back at the Red House. Only now she had a gun instead of the joy stick. Brian didn't understand, but he wasn't worried. He knew it was for his own good.

When they'd gotten almost to the gate, they heard a door open and turned to see Price and Whitehead coming at them down a red brick path. They too were holding guns. They too were aiming at Brian. A far-off explosion shook the street, then there were no more.

"If I can't have him," Dr. Haak yelled to the men. "Then nobody can."

They took their places directly to the west, blocking the way out. Dr. Haak stopped close enough that she didn't have to shout to be heard. The sun was at Brian's back. It grew hotter as they waited.

"I'm not kidding. Get out of my way. Right now. Or else the boy is dead." She pressed the gun harder against him.

"He's already died a hundred times," one of them said. "And he keeps coming back."

"He's not coming back if there's nothing left of his head." Her voice quaked. Her face was red and flushed, as though Brian had just shot his charge into her. "He's mine. Get out of the way or I'll blow his head off. I've got nothing to lose. Even if we did make a trade and you let me go, I might as well be dead without him. Either way, dead or alive, you're not going to take him from me again."

They heard a creaking sound and saw Dr. Valentine coming at them, pushing a wheelchair. He came up slowly and stopped a short distance away, taking the north position. Oberfurst was still in the chair, but there wasn't much of him left above the neck. Veins and split bones showed through the haphazard bandaging job. He was limp, broken, held in the chair with straps and web belts. But Brian could tell that there was still a little spark of soul left in the dead body. He hadn't been lying earlier. He was stuck. Brian hadn't opened the way for him, and now he was trapped forever in the ruins of his body.

Dr. Valentine was trembling. One eye twitched; the other was a narrow slit. He opened his mouth and snarled like an angry dog. Spittle flew from his mouth as he spoke: "Name your price. Anything. Just hand over the boy."

"I don't have a price," Dr. Haak said. "There's nothing you can give me that I want."

He snarled again, then reached into one of the wheelchair's side pockets and held up the joy stick. "We found it in your car," he said. Pressing the trigger, a loud crack flew off from the end. He waved it like a magic wand, trying to hypnotize Brian and Dr. Haak. "I won't let you turn me into this." He pointed to the old man. "I won't spend the next hundred years rotting into something like this." He jerked the wheelchair, furious at the old man. The head wobbled from side to side. A red bubble formed quickly, then popped, spitting flecks of blood on Dr. Valentine. He gestured with the joy stick again and pulled the trigger, hitting Oberfurst in the chest. He shook and a sound like a backed-up drain came from inside the body.

Brian's eyes were locked on the tip of the stick. As it discharged again, he was pulled slightly away from Dr. Haak. "I'm not joking," she said, holding on even tighter. "You're not taking him away from me again."

Dr. Valentine left the old man and came at them, waving the stick. Price and Whitehead separated and approached them from either side.

Brian heard the humming from the stick. He felt the pull of its field. He wanted to break free. He wanted all the guns and threats and arguing to be gone and the joy stick firing its payload directly into him.

Now they'd shifted positions; only the west was unoccupied. Brian was at the center, the hub of the compass. Price and Whitehead were far enough apart that Dr. Haak couldn't keep her eyes on both of them at the same time. And Dr. Valentine was straight ahead, throbbing like he was halfway into the Ictus. His tongue shot out, as if trying to catch flies. "Come here, Brian. Come here," he muttered. "I've got a present for you. A nice hot jolt from the stick. Wouldn't you like that?" He fired the rod, and as if a light switch had been flicked on and off, Brian got a glimpse inside the doctor: sweltering caves, ugly red light, moans and cries and a huge foul presence, brooding in the shadows.

Dr. Haak's grip was so tight that it hurt Brian's arm. Her mouth was almost touching his ear. "Don't leave me, Brian. Don't do it."

'Here boy, here boy. Don't you want this nice stick?"

Brian wanted to reach out. He felt the rod's field surrounding him, filling him. Dr. Haak felt it too, penetrating her through the shunt. She pressed the gun harder against his skull, her finger closing slowly, gently on the trigger.

Suddenly Dr. Valentine jumped forward, stabbing at them. A blast shot off from the end, and for a moment Brian could see nothing. Gunfire erupted. Bullets tore through the air over his head; they spattered on the asphalt nearby. Dr. Haak pulled Brian down to the ground, and when the glare had cleared, he saw Dr. Valentine's face close up: red, squinting, and furious. The two doctors were wrestling over the stick, trying to get control of the trigger. Blood flew off from Dr. Haak's hand. Her fingernails were dripping red. Dr. Valentine grunted and bit like an animal, his teeth clamped on her arm. A long string of machine-gun fire came and went. Price and Whitehead were running, spinning like dancers, firing into the nearby houses. Everything had finally come into proper alignment. Saul was still unseen, but he must have taken the western position. Price and Whitehead shot randomly, knocking out windows, tearing up the pavement. They knew Saul was somewhere close by, hidden. They were filled with panic, red, raw panic, out in the open and unprotected while Saul remained invisible.

Brian was buried under the thrashing bodies, feeling the stick discharge into him as the two doctors fought to control it. A knee dug hard into his back. Someone was shouting in his ear. Fingernails raked down his neck and he felt a stronger charge explode from the stick.

He smelled hair and clothing and flesh burning. Dr. Valentine's mouth was close to Brian's face. He tried to speak, but instead of words, only a choked rattle came out, and then a rush of black air, like a gas bubble rising to the surface of a swamp. Dr. Haak had one hand clamped on Brian's shoulder. A last tremor passed through her, and she squeezed tight, holding onto him to the end.

Then they were still, and it seemed that Brian was buried under a mountain of twisted, smoldering bodies.

He waited and soon heard Saul's voice, as if from very far away. The two bodies shifted slightly, and a hand was reaching down for him, pulling him upright. He got to his knees and then with Saul's help stood, as if emerging from a grave. Saul was tugging on Brian's sleeve, saying, "Come on, come on. We've got to get going."

Dr. Haak was dead. And Dr. Valentine too. They were tangled together on the pavement, their arms and legs and hands knotted. The smell of burnt meat came from the pile. They were joined together, seared as one by the electric discharge. She'd clamped her legs around his waist. One arm had him in a headlock. His hands were in her hair, clenched tight. She'd fused herself to Dr. Valentine, cooking the two of them into black, smoking slag so that Brian could escape.

She was free, but Dr. Valentine was still there, imprisoned in the charred remains of his body.

Price and Whitehead were dead too. They both lay on the

street, all blood and torn flesh. Saul had been hiding, waiting for the right time to strike.

As they went through the gate, Brian turned back for a last look. Oberfurst was still in his chair, held upright by the straps. Though he was totally motionless and his face was wound up in gauze like a mummy, Brian could tell there was still a flicker of life left in the body. The old man was stuck there, trying to get out. A loose end of gauze came free and flapped slightly. It might have been the old man's last feeble quiver. Or it might have been the wind.

Saul grabbed Brian's hand and set off running. They cut through the nearest yard, heading for 99th Street. Soon they were well beyond the fenced-in area. Approaching a neighborhood that seemed to be alive, Saul stopped to stuff his machine gun into a drain pipe. Brian heard a lawn mower running and a truck's horn. There was traffic up ahead. Dogs barking. People on the sidewalks.

Brian was a mess, and Saul was even worse. But he still had his wallet. They didn't have to wait long for a bus. They climbed in, put the coins into the slot, and went to the rear, where fewer people would notice them. A pair of old ladies got on at the next stop and stared. Saul stared back and they turned away.

31

At the main bus station they fit in better. The rest room was full of men in filthy, tattered clothes. Saul led Brian to a sink and helped him clean up as best he could. Then he washed out their shirts and showed Brian how to hold them up to the hand drier. He bought a razor from a vending machine and found a bar of soap stuck behind one of the faucets.

When they were done, they still looked shabby. They were cut and bruised and had no coats, but they could pass now without drawing too much attention.

They walked across the bridge to Canada, told the guard they were father and son going for the afternoon to see the sights, and headed up Clifton Hill. They passed the Believe it or Not Museum, the Palace of Wax, and the Niagara Falls Daredevil Gallery. At a little booth, Saul changed his money for Canadian, then they hiked up farther and found a small hotel.

As soon as Saul had locked the door, he rolled up his sleeve and gave himself another shot of the drug Dr. Haak had been using to keep him going. Flopping down on the bed, he was asleep in minutes. Brian turned on the air conditioner and sat directly in the cold stream of air. He liked the smell, the sound. And the faint electrical field it threw off.

Mixed in with the motor's hum, he heard voices singing him a lullaby. He stayed awake, though. He sat there listening for hours, watching over Saul as he slept.